FORGET ME NOT

FORGET ME NOT

Elizabeth Lowell

This title first published in Great Britain 1998 by
SEVERN HOUSE PUBLISHERS LTD of
9–15 High Street, Sutton, Surrey SM1 1DF.
This first hardcover edition published in the USA 1998 by
SEVERN HOUSE PUBLISHERS INC., of
595 Madison Avenue, New York, NY 10022,
by arrangement with Avon Books,
a division of The Hearst Corporation.

British Library Cataloguing in Publication Data
Lowell, Elizabeth
    Forget me not
    1. Love stories
    1. Title
    813.5'4 [F]

ISBN 0-7278-5347-3

6016 28019

Printed and bound in Great Britain by
MPG Books Ltd, Bodmin, Cornwall.

for my sister
Susan Mills
port in many storms

1

W HEN THE PHONE RANG, AL-
ana was almost relieved. Though it was before
dawn, she was wide awake. Since she had
come back from Broken Mountain, she had
slept very little, and never peacefully.

Kicking aside the tangled sheets, Alana
turned toward the phone. It was too early for
anyone she knew on the West Coast to be up
and about. That meant it was probably her
brother in Wyoming calling to see how she
was.

Calling to see if she remembered what had
happened on Broken Mountain.

"Hello," Alana said, keeping her voice
steady with an effort.

1

"Sis? Is that you?"

"Hi, Bob. How's Merry?"

"Counting the weeks until February," said Bob, laughing. "If she gets much bigger, we'll have to put her in a stall with the brood mares."

Alana smiled at the thought of petite, blond Merry tucked into one of the heated stalls Bob kept for his prize mares.

"Better not let Merry hear you say that," Alana warned.

"Hell, it was her idea." Bob paused, then said, "Sis?"

Alana's hand tightened on the phone. She had heard that tone before, little brother to big sister, a smile and affectionate wheedling.

He wanted something from her.

"When are you coming home?" Bob asked bluntly.

Alana's heart began to beat too fast. She didn't know how to tell her brother that she was frightened by the thought of returning to the ranch where Broken Mountain rose steeply, mantled in ice and darkness.

Before her last trip to Broken Mountain, Alana had loved the ranch, the mountains, the silence, the heights, and the clouds swirling overhead. She had loved the memories of Rafael Winter—Rafe reflected in every lake, every fragrant forest, sunsets and sunrises sweeping across the land like fire, the wind's keening harmonies echoing the music Rafe had made on his harmonica.

Alana had come to love the land even more

because she and Rafe had been part of it, lovers suspended between sky and mountains, more beautiful than either, timeless, burning with the sun.

But now those mountains terrified Alana.

Now the memories of Rafe were a brittle, cutting armor that she pulled around her like the colors of dawn, hoping to drive away the horror and darkness that crawled up out of the abyss of those six missing days.

"I don't—" Alana began.

Her brother interrupted before she could refuse.

"I've already talked to your agent," Bob said cheerfully. "He told me you've refused to accept any concerts and won't even look at the songs he sends to you."

"Yes, but— "

Bob kept talking.

"So don't tell me how busy you are," he said. "If you're writing songs again, you can write them just as well here. Better. You always did your best work here."

With a conscious effort, Alana loosened her grip on the phone. She had no more excuses, so she said nothing.

"Sis? I need you here."

"Bob, I don't think—" Alana began.

Then her voice broke.

"Don't say no," Bob said urgently. "You don't even know what I want yet."

And you don't know what I want, Alana thought rebelliously. You've never even asked if I want something.

The words went no further than Alana's thoughts, a silent cry of need. Yet even as the cry echoed in her mind, she recognized its unfairness.

What she needed, Bob couldn't provide. She needed warmth and reassurance, safety and a man's hard strength standing between her and the abyss, protecting her until she knew what had happened and could protect herself once more.

She needed love waiting instead of terror. She needed a dream to banish a nightmare.

She needed Rafael Winter.

But Rafe was just a dream. The nightmare was real.

With a deep breath, Alana gathered herself and set about living in her new world just as she always had lived. Alone, depending only on herself.

She had done this many times before, the deep breath and the determination to do the best she could with what she had, no matter how little that seemed to be when the nightmare descended like a storm.

"What do you want?" Alana asked softly.

"You know cash has always been a problem with the ranch," Bob said quickly. "Land poor, as they say. Well, Merry and I had this idea for a classy—and I mean *classy*—dude operation. High-country fishing safaris for people who can pay high prices."

Alana made a neutral sound.

"We had it all planned, all lined up, all our

ducks in a row," Bob said. "Our first two cus-
tomers are very exclusive travel agents. Their
clientele list reads like *Who's Who*. Everything
was going great for us, and then . . .'"

"And then?" Alana prompted.

"Merry got pregnant," Bob said simply. "I
mean, we're both happy, we've been trying for
two years, but . . .'"

"But what?"

"Dr. Gene says Merry can't go on the pack
trip."

"Is that a problem?"

"Hell, yes. She was going to be our cook and
entertainer and general soother, take the rough
edges off. You know what I mean, sis."

"Yes. I know."

It was the same role Alana had played in
the family since she was thirteen and her
mother died, leaving behind three boys, a devastated husband, and a daughter who had to
grow up very quickly. That was when Alana
had learned about reaching down into herself
for the smile and the touch and the comfort
that the people around her needed. She had
rebuilt the shattered family as best she could,
for she, too, needed the haven and the laughter and the warmth.

"It will really be more like time off than a
job," coaxed Bob.

Alana heard the coaxing, but it didn't move
her nearly as much as the disturbing thread of
urgency beneath the soft tone. .

"Riding and fishing and hiking in the high
country just like we used to do. You'll love it,

sis! I just know it. A real vacation for you."

Alana throttled the harsh laugh that was clawing at her throat.

Vacation, she thought, shuddering. In the mountains that nearly killed me. In the mountains that still come to me in nightmares.

Oh, God, that's some vacation my little brother has planned for me!

"Sis," Bob coaxed, "I wouldn't ask if I didn't really need you. I don't have anywhere else to turn. The pack trip is all set and the two dudes are here. Please?"

Unexpectedly, a vivid memory of Rafe came to Alana. . . . Late summer, a narrow trail going up Broken Mountain, a lame horse, and a saddle that weighed nearly as much as she did. She had been leading the horse, dragging the saddle, and watching the silent violence of clouds billowing toward a storm. At fifteen, she knew the dangers of being caught on an exposed ridge in a high-country cloudburst.

Without warning, lightning had come down so close to her that she smelled the stink of scorched rock. Thunder came like the end of the world. Her horse had screamed and reared, tearing the reins from her hand. Then the horse's lameness had been overridden by terror. The animal had bolted down the mountainside, leaving her alone.

She, too, had been terrified, her nostrils filled with the smell of lightning and her ears deafened by thunder. Then she had heard someone calling her name.

Rafe had come to her across the talus slope,

riding his plunging, scrambling horse with the strength and grace she had always admired. He had lifted her into the saddle in front of him and spurred his horse back down the slope while lightning arced around the mountain.

Sheltered in a thick growth of spruce, she had waited out the storm with Rafe, wearing his jacket and watching him with the eyes of a child-woman who was more woman and less child with every breath.

On Broken Mountain Alana had found first fear, then love, and finally horror.

She wondered if there was another balance to be discovered on Broken Mountain, opposites joined in harmony, freeing her from nightmare.

The possibility shimmered through Alana like dawn through night, transforming everything.

"Sis? Say something."

Alana was appalled to hear herself take a deep breath and say calmly, "Of course I'll help you."

She didn't hear Bob's whoop of victory, his assurances that he wouldn't tell any of the dudes that she was the famous singer Jilly, his gratitude that she was helping him out. She didn't hear anything but the echoes of her own terrifying decision to go back to Broken Mountain.

As though Bob sensed how fragile Alana's agreement was, he began speaking quickly.

"I've got you booked on the afternoon flight

to Salt Lake. From there, you're booked on a
little feeder flight into the airport here. Got a
pencil?"

Bemused, Alana stared at the phone. The
simple fact that Bob had thought to take care
of the details of her transportation was so unusual as to be overwhelming. It wasn't that
Bob was thoughtless; he was very considerate
of Merry, to the point that he was almost too
protective.

Alana, however, had always been taken for
granted in the manner that parents and older
siblings often are.

"Sis," Bob said patiently, "do you have a
pencil? He'll skin me if I louse this up."

"He?" asked Alana as she went through the
drawer in her bedside table looking for a pencil. "Who will skin you alive?"

There was a static-filled silence. Then Bob
laughed abruptly.

"The travel agent who made the arrange-
ments," he said. "Who else? Ready?"

"Hold your horses," Alana muttered.

She found a pencil, grabbed a credit card
receipt, turned it over, and wrote down the
flight numbers and times.

"But that's today!" she protested.

"Told you we needed you."

"That's not much warning, little brother."

"That's the whole idea," Bob muttered.

"What?"

"Nothing. Just be sure you're on that plane
or my butt is potato salad."

"Bob," Alana began.

"Thanks, sis," he said quickly, talking over her. "You won't regret it. If anyone can pull it off, he can."

"Huh?"

Alana felt as though she was missing half the conversation, and the most important half at that.

"He who?" she asked.

"*Damn,*" Bob said beneath his breath.

"The travel agent?" Alana guessed.

"Yeah, the travel agent. He's something else," said Bob dryly. "See you tonight, sis. 'Bye."

Before Alana could say good-bye, the line was dead.

She stood and stared at the receiver clenched in her hand. Silently she asked herself why she had agreed to do something that terrified her.

She was a fool to let warm memories of Rafe Winter lure her back to the icy source of nightmare. She didn't even know if Rafe was in Wyoming. In the past, Rafe's job had taken him all over the world. His time at the Winter ranch had been limited to a few weeks now and then.

It had been enough, though. Alana had learned to love Rafe and to accept his absences. She had learned to live for the day when he would come home and marry her and she would never cry for him at night again.

And then Rafe had died.

Or so the Pentagon had said.

The phone began to make whooping noises, telling Alana that the receiver had been off the hook too long. She hung up and stared at the phone.

It was deep red, like the flowers in the Spanish tile that covered the kitchen counters. Red, like the wildflowers that grew high on the mountain slopes.

Red. Like blood.

"Did I see Jack die on Broken Mountain?" Alana whispered. "Is that what my mind refuses to remember?"

With a shudder, she jerked away from the bright red telephone.

Rubbing her arms to chase away the chill that had been with her since Broken Mountain, Alana walked quickly to the closet. She pulled on jeans and an old cotton blouse. From habit, she buttoned the blouse completely, concealing the delicate gold chain that Rafe had given her years before.

As always, Alana's fingertip lingered on the tiny symbol of infinity that was part of the chain.

Love ever after, love without end.

A beautiful dream.

Reality was six days missing from her life and a nightmare whose end she was still trying to find.

Slowly Alana walked into the kitchen. With hands that wanted to tremble, she plugged in the coffeepot, scrambled two eggs, and buttered a piece of toast. She forced herself to eat and drink, to clean up after herself, to do all the things normal people did.

An untidy stack of papers on the kitchen counter caught Alana's eye. Unhappily she looked at them. She should read the song sheets her agent had sent over. New songs. Solo material for the sole survivor of the Jack 'n' Jilly duo.

Alana should read the music, but she wouldn't, for she no longer could sing.

That was the most bitter loss, the most unbearable pain. Before Broken Mountain, she had been able to draw songs around her like colors of love chasing away the gray of loneliness and the black of despair.

Alana had taken her love for a man she believed was dead and transformed that love into song. Singing had been her greatest pleasure, her reason for living after she was told that Rafe was dead.

Jack Reeves hadn't loved her, but she had always known that. Nor had Alana loved him. Theirs had been a business marriage, pure and simple. Jack loved fame and Jilly loved singing.

Now Jack was dead and Jilly could sing only in her dreams. And in her dreams it was Rafe's harmonica that accompanied her, not Jack's flawless tenor.

Awake, she had no music in her.

It wasn't stage fright. Even now, Alana wasn't afraid of being in front of people. Nor was she afraid of the savage doggerel that would be running through the fans' minds as they watched her.

Jack 'n' Jilly
Went up the hilly

To fetch a pail of vodka.
Jack fell down
And broke his crown,
And Jilly lost her mind.

Alana had listened to it all before, read it in print a hundred times, heard it whispered. She could face that.

But she couldn't face opening her lips and feeling her throat close with terrible finality, as though there were no more songs in her now and never would be again. Nothing but screams and the silence of death.

Uneasily Alana looked around, barely recognizing her surroundings. Even though she had lived in the Oregon apartment for three weeks, the place was neither comfortable nor familiar to her. It certainly wasn't as real to her as the nightmare about Broken Mountain.

But then, nothing was.

Abruptly Alana walked toward the wall of glass that opened onto a small patio. She stood near the glass, trying to shake off the residue of nightmare and death, fear and mistakes, and most of all a past that was beyond her ability to change.

Or even to understand.

"I'll remember what happened someday," Alana whispered. "Won't I?"

2

TAKING A RAGGED BREATH, Alana forced herself to look at the dawn that was etching the room in shades of rose and vermilion, gold and translucent pink. The September sun's radiant warmth was like a miracle after the endless hours of night.

Alana found herself staring at her reflection in the glass as she often had since Broken Mountain, searching for some outer sign of the six-day gap in her memory. Nothing showed on the outside. She looked the same as she had before she had gone up the mountain with the worst mistake of her life—her singing partner, Jack Reeves.

The singing hadn't been the mistake. The

marriage of convenience had. He had always pushed for more. She had always wished for less. He had wanted a reconciliation. She had wanted only an end to a marriage that never should have begun. So they had gone up Broken Mountain together.

Only one of them had come back.

No visible marks of the ordeal in the mountains remained on Alana's five-foot, five-inch body. Her ankle had healed. It ached only when it was cold. The bruises and welts and cuts were gone, leaving no scars. She no longer had to diet to fit into the slender image demanded by the public. Since Broken Mountain, her appetite was gone.

But it wasn't something that showed.

Alana leaned forward, staring intently at her nearly transparent reflection in the sliding glass door. Everything still looked the same. Long legs, strong from a childhood spent hiking and riding in Wyoming's high country. Breasts and waist and hips that were neither large nor small. Her skin was a golden brown. Nothing unusual. Nothing at all.

"Surely something must show on the outside," Alana told her reflection. "I can't just lose my singing partner and six days of my life and wonder about my sanity and not have any of it show."

Yet nothing did.

Though Alana's eyes were too dark, too large, too haunted, her mouth still looked as though it was curved around a secret inner smile. Her hair was still black and glossy, divided into two thick braids that fell to her waist.

Alana stared at her braids for a long moment, realizing for the first time that something about them made her ... uneasy.

She had never particularly liked having long hair, but she had accepted it as she had accepted the nickname Jilly, both necessary parts of the childlike image that audiences loved to love. The image went with her voice, clear and innocent, as supple and pure as a mountain stream. . . .

Water rushing down, cold, and darkness waiting, lined with rocks, ice and darkness closing around, clouds seething overhead, lightning lancing down, soundless thunder.

Fear.

It was too cold, no warmth anywhere, only fear hammering on her, leaving her weak.

She tried to run, but her feet weighed as much as the mountains and were as deeply rooted in the earth. Each step took an eternity. Try harder, move faster, or get caught.

She must run!

But she could not.

She was broken and bleeding, screaming down the night, running, stumbling, sprawling, and then lifted high, she was falling, she spun and screamed, falling. . . .

Alana's heart beat wildly, responding to the fragment of nightmare turning in her mind.

"Stop it!" she told herself fiercely, seeing the

reflection of her terror in dawn-tinted glass and sliding black shadows.

She took several deep breaths, bringing herself under control, telling herself that she had to stop treating her nightmare as though it was real. It wasn't.

The nightmare was simply a creation of her mind as it dealt with the horror of Jack's death in a mountain storm, and her own near death from exposure and the fall that had left her bruised and beaten.

That was what Dr. Gene had told Alana, and she had trusted his gravelly voice and gentle smile for as long as she could remember. He had said that her amnesia, while unusual, was not pathological. It was a survival reflex. When her mind felt she was strong enough to remember the details of her husband's death and her own suffering as she clawed her way down Broken Mountain, then she would remember.

And if she never remembered?

That, too, was all right, he had assured her. Alana was young. She was healthy. She could go out and make a new life for herself.

Alana's lips twisted bitterly as she remembered the conversation. It had been easy for Dr. Gene to say. He wasn't the one whose mind was turning six missing days into endless nightmares.

It wasn't that Alana missed her dead husband. She and Jack had been two very separate people bound together by the accident of perfect harmony. That was enough for a successful singing career. It wasn't enough for a successful marriage.

Yet sometimes Alana couldn't help feeling that maybe, just maybe, if she had done something different, Jack might have been different. If she had tried harder or not so hard. If she had been weaker or not quite as strong. If she had cared for Jack more or pitied him less . . .

Maybe it could have worked for the two of them.

But even as the thought came, Alana knew it was a lie. The only way she might have loved Jack was if she had never met Rafe Winter, never loved and lost him; Rafe, with his laughter and his passion and his gentle, knowing hands.

She had loved Rafe since she was fifteen, had been engaged to him when she was nineteen. And they had become lovers when she was twenty.

Rafael, dark hair and amber eyes glowing, watching her change as he touched her. Her fingers had looked so slender against the male planes of his face, the sliding sinew and muscle of his arms. His strength always surprised her, as did his quickness, but she had never been afraid with him. Rafe could hold her, could surround her softness with his power, and she felt no fear, only a consuming need to be closer still, to be held tighter, to give herself to him and to take him in return.

With Rafe there had only been beauty.

Then, four years ago, the Pentagon had told Alana that Rafael Winter had died. They had told her nothing more than that. Not where her fiancé had died. Not how. Certainly not why. Just the simple fact of his death.

It was a fact that had destroyed Alana. Never again would the lyric beauty of Rafe's harmonica call to her across the western night. Never again would her voice blend with that of the silver instrument that sang so superbly in Rafe's hands. She had sung with Rafe for pleasure and had known no greater beauty except making love with him, bodies and minds sharing an elemental harmony that surpassed everything, even song.

Alana had been empty after Rafe's death. She had cared for nothing. Even life. When the minutes and hours without Rafe had piled up one by one, dragging her down into darkness, she had turned instinctively to a singing career as her only salvation, her only way to hold on to the love she had lost.

Singing meant Jack Reeves, the man she had sung with in all the little cafés and fairs and roadhouses, the man for whom singing was a business rather than a pleasure. Jack had measured Alana's vulnerability, her desperation, and then he had calmly told her that there would be no more duets unless she married him and left the high plains for the high life in the city.

Alana had resisted marriage, wanting no man but the one who was dead.

Then the hours without Rafe had heaped into the hundreds, a thousand, fifteen hundred . . . and she had agreed to become Jack's wife

because she must do something or go insane.
Rafe was dead. There was nothing left but the
singing career that Jack had badgered Alana
for even while Rafe was alive.

So Alana had left the high plains and mountains of Wyoming, hoping that in another part
of the world she wouldn't hear Rafe in every
summer silence, sense him in every moonrise,
feel his heat in the warmth of the sun.

She had married Jack, but it was a marriage
in name only. With Jack Reeves there had been
nothing but an emptiness Alana had tried to
fill with songs.

Then, a year ago, she had been told that Rafael Winter was alive.

Rafe wasn't the one who told her. Rafe had
never called her, never written, never in any
way contacted the woman he once had said he
loved.

Now it was Jack who was dead, killed four
weeks ago by the wild country he had de-
spised. Alana had been with Jack on Broken
Mountain when he died. She didn't remember
it. Those six days were a blank wall.

Behind that wall, fear seethed and rippled,
trying to break free.

Alana closed her eyes, unable to face their
dark reflection in the glass door. Rafe was
dead and then not dead. Jack was dead now
and forever.

Her love for Rafe, undying.

With a small sound, Alana closed her eyes,
shutting out her reflection.

"Enough of that," she told herself sharply.

"Stop living in the past. Stop tearing yourself up over things you can't change."

She opened her eyes, confronting herself in yet another reflection, another window dawn hadn't yet made transparent. She looked like a mountain deer caught in the instant of stillness that precedes wild flight. Long brown limbs and brown eyes that were very dark, very wide, wild.

A black braid slid over Alana's shoulder and swung against the glass as she leaned forward. She brought the other braid forward over her shoulder, too. It was a gesture that had become automatic; when her braids hung down her back she pulled them forward.

That way if she had to run suddenly, the braids wouldn't fly out behind her, twin black ropes, perfect handles for something to grab and hold her and *lift her up, trapped, weightless, falling, she was falling—*

Alana choked off the scream clawing at her throat as she retreated to the kitchen. Her reflection looked back at her from the window over the kitchen sink.

Without looking away from her reflection, Alana groped in a nearby drawer. Her fingers closed around the handle of a long carving knife. The honed blade glittered as she pulled it out of the drawer.

She lifted the knife until the blunt side of the blade rested against her neck just below her chin. Calmly, deliberately, she began slicing through her left braid. The severed hair fell soundlessly to the floor. With no hesitation, she went to work on the right braid.

When Alana was finished she shook her head, making her hair fly. The loose, natural curls that had been imprisoned beneath the weight of the braids were suddenly set free. Wisps of hair curved around her face, framing it in soft, shiny black. Her brown eyes glowed darkly, haunted by dreams.

Abruptly Alana realized what she had done. She stared at the long black braids on the floor, the steel knife in her hand, the reflection in the window that no longer looked like Jilly.

The knife dropped to the floor with a metallic clatter.

Alana stared at herself and wondered if she had finally gone crazy.

She ran from the kitchen to the bedroom. There she pulled her few things out of drawers and off hangers, packing haphazardly. It didn't matter. Most of her clothes were still in L.A. or at the ranch, left there in anticipation of weeks spent with her brother and Merry.

Alana had been too frightened to go back to the ranch and pack after she had fled from the hospital. She had simply run to Portland, a city she had never lived in, hoping to leave the nightmare behind her.

It hadn't worked.

As Alana packed, she kept looking at the bedroom telephone. She wanted to call Bob, say that she had changed her mind, and then hang up before he could object.

Yet each time she reached for the phone, she

thought of Rafael Winter, a dream to balance her nightmare. She used memories of Rafe like a talisman to draw the terror from her six missing days.

The greatest pleasure and the greatest horror in Alana's life had both taken place on Broken Mountain. Perhaps they would simply cancel each other, leaving her free to go on with her life. Neutral, balanced.

No memories of the man she had loved, or of the husband she had not. No memories of the lover who had died and then come back, or of the husband who had died and would never come back.

Rafe, who came to her in dreams.

Jack, who came to her in nightmares.

When Alana finally picked up the phone, it was to call a nearby beauty salon and make an appointment to have her hair styled. The utterly normal activity reassured her.

By the time Alana got on the airplane, she felt more calm. Tonight she would be home. If nightmares stalked her, it would be down the familiar corridors of her childhood home rather than the strange hallways of a rented apartment.

She held to that thought as she switched planes in Salt Lake City and settled in for the flight to Wyoming. When the flight attendant offered her a newspaper, she took it automatically. As she flipped through the pages, a headline in the entertainment section caught her eye: *Jack 'n' Jilly's Last Song.*

Though Alana's stomach tightened just at

the headline, she knew she would read the article. She had read everything written about Jack's death, even the most sleazy imaginings of the yellow press. She would read this article too, because she could not help herself.

It had been a month since Jack's death. A month since the gap in Alana's memory had appeared. She kept hoping that someone, somewhere, would know more about Jack's death than she did, that a word or a phrase in an article would trigger something in her mind and the six days would spill through, freeing her from nightmare.

Or sending her into a more terrifying one.

There was always that possibility lurking in the twisting shadows of Alana's mind. Dr. Gene had suggested that there could be horrors Alana didn't imagine, *even in her nightmares.*

Amnesia could be looked at in many ways. Gift of a kind God. Survival reflex. Fountainhead of horror. All of them and none of them. But fear was always there, pooled in shadows, waiting for night.

Maybe Dr. Gene was right. Maybe she would be better off not remembering.

Impatiently Alana shoved the unwelcome thought away. Nothing could be worse than not trusting her own mind, her own courage, her own sanity.

Since her mother had died, Alana had always been the strong one, the one who saw what had to be done and did it. Then Rafe had died and Alana had been destroyed.

Music was her only solace after Rafe died.

With music she wove glowing dreams of warmth, of his laughter, and of a love that could only be sung, not spoken.

With song, Alana had survived even Rafe's death.

She could do whatever she had to. She had proved that in the past. Somehow, she would prove it again. She would survive.

Somehow.

Alana shook out the paper, folded it carefully, and began to read.

The first part of the story was a review of the Jack 'n' Jilly album that had just been released. The rest of the article was a simple recital of the facts of Jack's death.

A month ago, Jack and Jilly Reeves had gone on a pack trip in the Wyoming backcountry. An early winter storm had caught them. They had tried to get out, but only Jilly had made it. Jack had been killed in a fall. Somehow Jilly had managed to hobble down the mountain on a badly wrenched ankle until she had reached a fishing cabin and radioed for help.

Even so, she had nearly died of exposure. The experience had been so traumatic that she had no memory of the time she spent crawling down the mountain.

Hysterical amnesia, brought on by husband's accidental death, said the doctor. Apparently Sheriff Mitchell had agreed, for the autopsy listed the cause of Jack's death as a broken neck sustained in a fall.

Accidental.

Nothing new. Nothing unexpected. Nothing

to fill the horrifying gap six days had left in
Alana's mind. Yet still she reread the article,
searching for the key to her amnesia.

She didn't find it. She was neither surprised
nor disappointed.

As the plane slid into its landing pattern,
Alana sat up and nervously ran her fingers
through her hair. Her head felt strange, light,
no longer anchored by dense black braids. The
stylist had transformed the remnants of her
knife-cut hair into a gently curling cap that
softened but didn't wholly conceal the taut
lines of Alana's face. The result was arresting—glossy midnight silk framing an intelligent face that was haunted by loss and
nightmare.

The small commercial plane touched down
with a slight jerk. A few eager trout fishermen
got off before Alana, trading stories of the past
and bets for the first and biggest fish of the
future.

Reluctantly she stood up and walked slowly
down the narrow aisle. By the time she descended the metal stair, her baggage had already been unloaded and placed neatly beside
the bottom step. She picked up her light suitcase
and turned toward the small building that was
the only sign of habitation for miles around.

Behind her the aircraft began retreating. It
moved to the head of the runway, revved
hard, and accelerated, gathering speed
quickly, preparing itself for a leap into the brilliant high-plains sky.

Alana reached the building as the plane's engines gave a full-throated cry. She set down her bag and turned in time to see the aircraft's wheels lift. It climbed steeply, a powerful silver bird flying free. She listened until the engines were no more than a fading echo and the plane only a molten silver dot flying between the ragged grandeur of the Wind River and Green River mountain ranges.

For a moment, Alana closed her eyes. Her head tilted toward the sky, catching the surprising warmth of Wyoming's September sun. The wind was rich with scents of earth and sagebrush. Not the stunted, brittle sagebrush of the southwestern desert but the thick lavender-gray high-country sage, bushes as high as her head, higher, slender shapes weaving patterns against the empty sky.

A clean wind swept down from the granite heights, carrying sweetness and the promise of blue-green rivers curling lazily between rocky banks, of evergreens standing tall and fragrant against the summer moon, of coyotes calling from the ridge lines in harmonies older than man.

Home.

Alana breathed deeply, torn between pleasure and fear. She heard footsteps approaching across the cement. She spun around, her heart beating heavily. Since Broken Mountain, she was terrified if anything approached her unseen.

A man was walking toward Alana. The sun was at his back, reducing him to a black silhouette.

As he walked closer, he seemed to condense into three dimensions. He was about seven inches taller than she was. He had the easy stride of someone who spent as much time hiking as he did on horseback. His jeans were faded. His boots showed the scuff marks peculiar to riding. His shirt was the same pale blue as the sky.

Hair that was a thick, rich brown showed beneath the rim of his black Stetson. His eyes were the color of whiskey. His lips were a firm curve beneath a silky bar of mustache.

With a small sound, Alana closed her eyes. Her heart beat wildly, but it sent weakness rather than strength coursing through her. She was going crazy, hallucinating.

Storm and cold and terror, falling—

"Alana," he said.

His voice was gentle, deep, reaching out to her like an immaterial caress.

"Rafael?" She breathed raggedly, afraid to open her eyes, torn between hope and nightmare. "Oh, Rafe, is it really you?"

3

Rafe took Alana's arm, supporting her. Only then did she realize that she had been swaying as she stood. His warmth and strength went through her like a shock wave. For an instant she sagged against him.

Then she realized that she was being touched, *held*, and she wrenched away. Since Broken Mountain she was terrified of being touched.

"It's really me, Alana," said Rafe, watching her intently.

"Rafael—" Alana's voice broke as emotions overwhelmed her.

She extended her fingers as though she

would touch him, but did not. With an effort that left her aching, she fought down the tangle of emotions that was closing her throat. She was being torn apart by conflicting imperatives.

Run to him. Run from his male presence.

Be held by him. Fight not to be held by a man.

Love him. Feel nothing at all because the only safety lay in numbness.

Remember how it felt to be loved. Forget, forget everything, amnesia spreading outward like a black balm.

"Why are you here?" Alana asked in a ragged voice.

"I've come to take you home."

Inexplicably the words all but destroyed Alana.

With a small sound, she closed her eyes and struggled to control herself. Coming here had been a mistake. She had wanted a dream of love to balance a nightmare of terror. Yet Rafe was real, not a dream.

And so was terror.

Alana clung to the shreds of her control, wondering what had happened during those six missing days that had left a black legacy of fear. And most of all, she wondered if the nightmare would ever end, freeing her, letting her laugh and sing again ... or if she would simply give up and let the black balm of amnesia claim all of her mind. All of *her*.

Rafe watched Alana, his eyes intent. When

he spoke, his voice was casual, soothing, utterly normal.

"We'd better get going," he said. "I'd like to beat the thundershower back to the ranch."

He bent to take Alana's suitcase from her nerveless fingers. With the easy movements of a mountain cat, he straightened and walked toward a Jeep parked a few hundred feet away.

Alana watched, her hand resting on the high neck of her burgundy silk blouse. She took a deep breath, still feeling the warmth of Rafe's hand on her arm as he had supported her. Just that. Support. Help. There was nothing to fear in that.

Was there?

Motionless, her heart beating rapidly, her dark eyes wide, Alana watched Rafe turn back toward her. The slanting, late-afternoon sun highlighted the strong bones of his face and made his amber eyes glow. As he turned, his shirt stretched across his shoulders, emphasizing the strength and masculine grace of him His jeans fit the muscular outline of his legs like a faded blue shadow, moving as he moved.

Alana closed her eyes, but she could still see Rafe. He was burned into her awareness with a thoroughness that would have shocked her if she had any room left for new emotions. But she didn't.

She was still caught up in the moment when he had turned back to her, light brown eyes burning, mouth curved in a gentle male smile.

That was Rafe. Male. Totally. She had forgotten, even in her dreams.

Rafe hesitated as though he wanted to come back to Alana, to stand close to her again. But he didn't move. He simply watched her with whiskey-colored eyes that were both gentle and intent, consuming her softly, like a song.

"It's all right, Alana." Rafe's voice was as gentle as his smile. "I've come to take you home."

The words echoed and reechoed in Alana's mind, sending sensations sleeting through her. Cold and wind and snow, fear and screams clawing at her throat. Pain and terror and then . . .

It's all right, wildflower. I've come to take you home.

She had heard words like those before, and something more, other words, incredible words, dream and nightmare intertwined.

Without knowing it, Alana whimpered and swayed visibly, caught between hope and terror, dream and nightmare.

"What?" Alana demanded breathlessly, her heart beating faster, her voice urgent. "What did you say?"

Rafe watched Alana with a sudden intensity that was almost tangible.

"I said, 'I've come to take you home.' "

He waited, but Alana simply watched him with wide, very dark eyes. His expression shifted, gentle again.

"Bob threatened to have my hide for a saddle blanket if I didn't get home before Merry fell asleep. And," added Rafe with a smile, "since she falls asleep between coffee and dessert, we'd better hurry."

Alana watched Rafe with eyes that were dazed and more than a little wild.

"That wasn't what you said before." Alana's voice was as tight as the hand clutching her throat. Her eyes were blind, unfocused.

"Before?" asked Rafe, his voice intent, hard, his topaz eyes suddenly blazing like gems. "Before what, Alana?"

It was dark, so dark, black ice around her, a glacier grinding her down until she screamed and tried to run, but she couldn't run because she was frozen and it was so cold.

Alana shuddered and swayed, her face utterly pale, drained of life by the savage nightmare that came to her more and more often, stalking her even in the day, stealing what little sanity and peace remained.

Instantly Rafe came to her, supporting her, his hands warm and strong. Even as she turned toward his warmth, fear exploded in her. She wrenched away with all her strength.

Then she realized that it hadn't been necessary. Rafe hadn't tried to hold her. She was reacting to something that hadn't happened.

"I—" Alana watched Rafe with wild, dark eyes. "I don't—I'm—"

She held out her hands helplessly, wondering how to explain to Rafe that she was drawn to him yet terrified of being touched, and that above all she thought she was losing her mind.

"You're tired," Rafe said easily, as though Alana's actions were as normal as the slanting afternoon light. "It was a long flight. Come on. Bob and Merry are waiting for you like kids waiting for Christmas morning."

Rafe turned back to the suitcase, picked it up, and walked toward the Jeep. Before he arrived, a man got out of a Blazer and approached Rafe.

As Alana walked closer, she recognized Dr. Gene. He smiled and held out his arms to her. She hesitated, fighting against being held, even by the man who had delivered her, who had attended to all of her childhood ills, and who had cried in frustration at her mother's deathbed. Dr. Gene was as much a member of her family as her father or her brothers.

With an effort of will that made her tremble, Alana submitted to Dr. Gene's brief hug. Over her head, the doctor looked a question at Rafe, who answered with a tiny negative movement of his head.

"Well, it's good to have you back, " said Dr. Gene. "No limp, now. You look as pretty as ever, trout."

"And you lie very badly," said Alana.

But she smiled briefly at hearing the pet name from her childhood. Even so, she stepped back from the doctor's hug. Her haste was almost rude, but she couldn't help herself. That was the worst part of the nightmare, not being able to help herself.

"The only thing that was ever pretty about me was my voice," Alana said.

"No pain?" persisted the doctor. "How's your appetite?"

"No pain," she said evenly, ignoring the question about her appetite. "I don't even use the elastic bandage anymore."

And then Alana waited in fear for the doctor to ask her about her memory. She didn't want to talk about it in front of Rafe.

She didn't want to talk about her memory at all.

"You cut your hair," said Dr. Gene.

Alana raised her hand nervously, feeling the short, silky tendrils that were all that remained of her waist-length braids.

"Yes." And then, because the doctor seemed to expect something more, she added, "Today. I cut it today."

"Why?" asked Dr. Gene.

The doctor's voice was as gentle as the question was blunt.

"I . . ." Alana stopped. "I was . . . I wanted to."

"Yes, but why?" he asked.

The doctor's blue eyes were very pale, very watchful beneath the shock of gray hair and weathered forehead.

"The braids made me . . . uneasy," said Alana.

Her voice was tight, her eyes vague, frightened.

"Uneasy? How?" asked Dr. Gene.

"They kept . . . tangling in things." Alana

made a sudden motion with her hands, as though she were warding off something. "I . . ."

Her throat closed and she could say nothing more.

"Alana's tired," Rafe said, his voice quiet and very certain. "I'm going to take her home. Now. Excuse us, Dr. Gene."

Rafe and Dr. Gene exchanged a long look. Then the doctor sighed.

"All right," Dr. Gene said, his voice sharp with frustration. "Tell Bob I'm trying to get some time off to go fishing."

"Good. The Broken Mountain camp always has a cabin for you."

"Even now?"

"Especially now," said Rafe sardonically. "We may disagree on means, but our goal is identical."

Alana looked from one man to the other. "Goal?"

"Just a little fishing expedition in the high country," Rafe said, turning to her. "The good doctor prefers to drown worms. I, on the other hand, prefer to devise my own lures."

Dr. Gene smiled briefly. "Bet I catch more trout than you, Winter."

"I'm only after one trout. A very special one."

Alana wondered about the currents of emotion running between the two men, then decided she was being overly sensitive. Since Broken Mountain, she jumped at sighs and shadows and saw conspiracy and pursuit where there was nothing behind her but night and silence.

Dr. Gene turned to Alana. "If you need anything, trout, I'll come running."

"Thanks."

"I mean it, now," he added.

"I know," she said softly.

He nodded, got back in his Blazer, and drove off with a backward wave.

Rafe handed Alana into the Jeep truck and climbed in himself. She watched him covertly the whole time, matching memories with reality.

The Rafe Alana saw was older, much more controlled than in her memories. When he wasn't smiling, his face was hard, almost frightening in its planes and angles. Yet he still moved with the easy strength that had always fascinated her. His voice was still gentle, and his hands were . . . beautiful. It was an odd way to describe anything as strong and quick and callused as a man's hands, yet she could think of no better word.

Not all masculine hands affected Alana like that. Sometimes she saw hands and terror sleeted through her.

"We're lucky today," said Rafe as he guided the Jeep expertly over the rough field that passed as the parking lot.

"Lucky?" said Alana, hearing the thin thread of panic in her voice and hating it.

"No rain so far. It rained a lot the last few days."

Alana tried to conceal the shudder that went

through her at the thought of lightning and thunder, mountains and slippery black ice.

"Yes," she said in a low voice. "I'm glad there isn't a storm."

"You used to love storms," said Rafe quietly.

Alana went very still, remembering one wild September afternoon when a storm had caught her and Rafe while they were out riding. They had arrived at the fishing cabins, soaked and breathless. He had peeled her wet jacket off her, then her blouse, and his hands had trembled when he touched her.

Closing her eyes, Alana tried to forget. The thought of being touched like that by Rafe made her weak with desire—and all but crazy with fear, dream and nightmare tangled together in a way she could neither explain nor understand.

But if Rafe remembered the September storm when he had undressed and caressed Alana until there was only fire and the hushed urgency of their breathing, his memories didn't show in his face or in his words.

"We had a good frost above five thousand feet last week," continued Rafe. "The aspen leaves turned. Now they look like pieces of sunlight dancing in the wind."

He looked quickly at Alana, seeing the lines of inner conflict on her face.

"You still like aspen, don't you?" Rafe asked.

Alana nodded her head, afraid to trust her voice. Mountain aspen, with its white bark and quivering, silver-backed leaves, was her favorite tree. In fall, aspens turned a yellow as pure as . . . *sunlight dancing in the wind.*

A sideways glance told her that Rafe was watching her with intent, whiskey-colored eyes.

"I still like aspen," said Alana.

She tried to keep her voice normal, grateful for the safe topic. The present, not the past. The past was more than she could handle. The future was unthinkable. Just one day at a time. One hour. A minute. She could handle anything, one minute at a time.

"Even in winter," Alana added, her voice little more than a whisper, "when the branches are black and the trunks are like ghosts in the snow."

Rafe accelerated down the narrow, two-lane blacktop road. He glanced for a moment at the magnificent granite spine of the Wind River Mountains, rising on his left.

"Be a while before there's real snow in the high country," he said. "The frost put down the insects, though. Then it turned warm again. Trout ought to be hungry as hell. That means good fishing for our dudes—guests," he corrected immediately, smiling to himself. "Nobody likes being called a dude."

"*Our* dudes?" asked Alana slowly, watching Rafe with eyes so brown they were almost black.

Sunlight slanted through the windshield, intensifying the tan on Rafe's face and the richness of his dark brown mustache, making his eyes almost gold. His teeth showed in a sudden gleam of humor, but his expression said the joke was on him. He answered her question with another question.

"Didn't Bob mention me?"

"No," said Alana, her voice ragged. "You were a complete surprise."

Rafe's expression changed.

For an instant Alana thought she saw pain, but it came and went so quickly that she decided she had been wrong. She was being too sensitive again. Overreacting. Yet she still wanted to touch Rafe, to erase the instant when she sensed that she had hurt him and didn't even know how.

The thought of touching Rafe didn't frighten Alana. Not like being touched did. For an instant she wondered why, but all that came to her was . . . nothing. Blank.

Like those six missing days.

"Looks like we'll have to do it the hard way," Rafe said softly.

His voice was an odd mixture of resignation and some much stronger emotion in his voice, something close to anger.

Before Alana could speak, Rafe did.

"Bob and I are partners."

"Partners in what?" Alana asked.

"The dude—*guest* ranch. The cottages and fishing water are on Lazy W land. My land. The horses and supplies belong to Bob. He's the wrangler, I'm the fishing guide, and you're the cook. When Dr. Gene shows up," added

Rafe with a crooked smile, "he'll be the chief worm dunker."

Stunned, Alana could think of nothing to say. She would be going up Broken Mountain with Rafael Winter. Dream and nightmare running together, pouring over her, drowning her in freezing water.

She sat without moving, letting the sunlight and the landscape blur around her, trying to gather her fragmenting thoughts.

No wonder Bob didn't say anything to me about Rafael Winter, Alana thought unhappily. If I'd known that Bob had a partner, I might have let the partner bail Bob out of the mess.

Especially if I knew that the partner was Rafael Winter.

It was all Alana could do to handle the recent past, amnesia and accident and death. Bob should have known that she couldn't handle a present that included Rafe.

A year ago Bob had told her that Rafe was still alive. Then Bob had taken her letter to Rafe's ranch. Bob had come back with the letter unopened, *Deceased* written across the envelope's face—written in Rafe's distinctive hand.

Bob had seen Alana's pain and anger, then her despair. And now he was asking her to go up Broken Mountain with Rafael Winter, to confront the past love and loss all over again. And the present nightmare.

Alana shuddered and tried to think of nothing at all.

"Alana," began Rafe.

Somehow she was certain that he was going to talk about the past, about dying but not quite, about surviving but not wholly, about her and Jack and an envelope with a "dead" man's handwriting across its face, tearing her apart.

She wasn't strong enough for that. Not for the past. Not for anything but this minute. Now.

"Bob and Tom Sawyer have a lot in common," Alana said quickly, her voice as strained as it was determined. "Don't go near either of them if a fence needs painting. Unless you like painting fences, of course."

Rafe hesitated, visibly reluctant to give up whatever he had wanted to say. But Alana's taut, pale face and haunted eyes persuaded him.

"Yes," Rafe said slowly. "Bob could charm the needles off a pine tree."

Relieved, Alana sat back in the seat again.

"The only thing that ever got even with Bob was the hen he poured jam on and then dumped in the middle of eight half-grown hounds," Alana said. "That hen pecked Bob's hands until she was too tired to lift her head."

Rafe's laughter was as rich as the slanting sunlight pouring over the land. Alana turned toward him involuntarily, drawn by his humor and strength, by the laugh that had haunted her dreams as thoroughly as the scent of evergreens haunted the high country.

"So that's how Bob got those scars on his

hands," Rafe said, still chuckling. "He told me it was chicken pox."

Alana's lips curved into a full smile, the first in a long time. "So it was, after a fashion."

She glanced up at Rafe through her thick black lashes and caught the amber flash of his eyes as he looked away from her to the road. For an instant her heart stopped, then beat more quickly. He had been watching her.

She wondered if he was comparing the past and present as she had. And remembering.

"How did Bob talk you into painting his fence?" Alana asked quickly, wanting to hear Rafe talk, his voice deep and smooth and confident, like his laughter.

"Easy. I'm a sucker for fishing. I spend a lot of my time in the high country chasing trout. Might as well make it pay."

"Land poor," murmured Alana. "Rancher's lament."

"I have it better than Bob," Rafe said, shrugging. "I'm not buying out two brothers."

Alana thought of Dave and Sam, her other brothers. Sam worked for a large corporation with branches around the world. Dave was a computer programmer in Texas. Neither brother had any intention of coming back to the ranch for anything other than occasional visits. Of the four Burdette children, only she and Bob had loved the ranching life.

Nor had Jack Reeves loved the ranching life he had been born into. He couldn't leave Wyoming fast enough. He had hungered for city streets and applauding crowds.

"Jack hated Wyoming."

Startled, Alana heard the words echoing in the Jeep and realized she had spoken aloud.

"He's dead," she added.

"I know."

Alana stared at Rafe.

"How—" she began.

Then she realized that of course Rafe knew. Bob must have told him. They were partners. But how much had Bob told Rafe? Did he know about her amnesia? Did he know about the nightmares that lapped over into day, triggered by a word or a smell or the quality of the light? Did he know she was afraid she was going crazy?

Did Rafe know that she clung to her memories and dreams of him as though they were a lifeline able to pull her beyond the reach of whatever terror stalked her?

As though Rafe sensed Alana's unease, he added quietly, "It was good of you to help Bob. It can't be easy for you so soon after your ... husband's ... death."

At the word *husband* Rafe's mouth turned down sourly, telling Alana that her marriage was not a subject that brought Rafe any pleasure.

But then, Rafe had never liked Jack. Even before Rafe had "died," Jack had always been urging Alana to pack up and leave Wyoming, to build a career where artificial lights drowned out the cascading stars of the western sky.

"Did Bob tell you how Jack died?" asked

Alana, her voice tight, her hands clenched in her lap.

"No."

Rafe's voice was hard and very certain.

Alana let out a long breath. Apparently Bob had told Rafe only the bare minimum: Jack had died recently. Nothing about the amnesia or the nightmares.

She was glad Bob had told Rafe something. It would explain anything odd she might do. Jack was dead. Recently. She was a widow.

And when she slept, she was a frightened child.

The Jeep jolted off the pavement onto a gravel road. The miles unwound easily, silently, through a land of gently rolling sagebrush and a distant river that was pale silver against the land. Nothing moved but the Jeep and jackrabbits flushed by the sound of the car.

There was neither fence nor sign to mark the beginning of the Broken Mountain Ranch. Like many western ranchers, Alana's grandfather, father, and brother had left the range open wherever possible. They fenced in the best of their breeding stock and let the beef cattle range freely.

Alana searched the land for signs of Broken Mountain steers grazing the high plains.

"Has Bob brought the cattle out of the high country yet?" asked Alana.

"Most of them. He's leaving them in the middle elevations until late September. Later if he can."

"Good."

The longer the cattle stayed in the high and middle elevations, the less money Bob would have to spend on winter feed. Every year was a gamble. If a rancher left his cattle too long in the high country, winter storms could close in, locking the cattle into certain starvation. But if the rancher brought his cattle down too soon, the cost of buying hay to carry them through winter could mean bankruptcy.

"Grass looks thick," Alana said.

She wanted to keep to the neutral conversational territory of ranching, afraid that if the silence went on too long, Rafe might bring up the recent past and Jack's death. Or, even worse, the far past. Rafe's death and resurrection, a bureaucratic error that had cost Alana ... everything.

"I'll bet Indian Seep is still flowing," she said. "The hay crop must have been good."

Rafe nodded.

Alana's dark eyes cataloged every feature of the land—the texture of the soil in road cuts, the presence or absence of water in the ravines, the smoky lavender sheen of living growth on the snarled sagebrush, the signs of wildlife, all the indicators that told an educated eye whether the land was being used or abused, husbanded or squandered.

And in between, when Alana thought Rafe wouldn't notice, she watched his profile, the sensuous sheen of his hair and lips, the male lines of his nose and jaw. Rafe was too powerful and too hard to be called handsome. He was compelling—a man made for mountains, a man of strength and endurance, mystery and silence, and sudden laughter like a river curling lazily beneath the sun.

"Am I so different from your memories?" asked Rafe quietly.

Alana drew in her breath sharply.

"No," she said. "But there are times when I can't tell my memories of you from my dreams. Seeing you again, close enough to touch, *alive*..."

Alana looked away, unable to meet Rafe's eyes, regretting her honesty and at the same time knowing she had no choice. She had enough trouble sorting out truth from nightmare. She didn't have the energy to keep track of lies, too.

When the truck rounded the shoulder of a small ridge, Alana leaned forward intently, staring into the condensing twilight. A long, narrow valley opened up before her. A few evergreens grew in the long, low ridges where the land began to lift to the sky. The ridges soon became foothills and then finally pinnacles clothed in ice and distance.

But it wasn't the savage splendor of the peaks that held Alana's attention. She had eyes only for the valley. It was empty of cattle.

Alana sat back with an audible sigh of relief.

"Good for you, little brother," she murmured.

"Bob's a good rancher," said Rafe quietly. "There's not one inch of overgrazed land on Broken Mountain's range."

"I know. I was just afraid that—" Alana's hands moved, describing vague fears. "The beef market has been so bad and the price of feed is so high now and Bob has to pay Sam and Dave. I was afraid Bob would gamble on the land being able to carry more cattle than it should."

Rafe glanced sideways at Alana with the lightning intensity that she remembered from her dreams.

"Since when do people on the West Coast notice feed prices and the carrying capacity of Wyoming ranch land?" he asked.

"They don't. I do." Alana made a wry face. "People in cities think beef grows between Styrofoam and plastic wrap, like mushrooms in the cracks of a log."

Rafe laughed again, softly.

Alana watched him, feeling the pull of his laughter. Above his pale collar, sleek neck muscles moved.

She felt again the moment of warmth at the airport, the resilience of his muscles beneath her fingers before she had snatched back her arm. He was strong. It showed in his movements, in his laughter, in the clean male lines of his face. He was strong and she was not.

Distantly Alana knew she should be terrified of that difference in their bodies. Yet when Rafe laughed, it was all she could do to keep herself from crawling over and huddling next to him as though he were a fire burning in the midst of a freezing storm.

The thought of being close to Rafe both fascinated and frightened Alana. The fascination she understood; Rafe was the only man she had ever loved. She had no reason to fear him.

Yet she did.

Rafe was a man, and she was terrified of men.

The fear baffled Alana. At no time in her life, not even during the most vicious arguments with Jack, had she ever been afraid.

Am I afraid of Rafe simply because he's strong? Alana asked herself silently.

She turned the thought over in her mind, testing it as she had tested so many things in the weeks since she had awakened in the hospital, six days and a singing partner lost.

It can't be something as simple as physical strength that frightens me, Alana decided. Jack was six foot five, very thick in the shoulders and neck and legs. He never used his strength, though, or even seemed to notice it. He did only what was needed to get by, and not one bit more.

Jack had been born with a clear tenor voice that he had accepted as casually as his size, and he disliked working with his voice almost as much as he had disliked physical labor.

Alana had been the one who had insisted on rehearsing each song again and again, searching for just the right combination of phrasing and harmony that would bring out the levels of meaning in the lyrics. Jack had tolerated her "fanaticism" with the same easygoing indifference that he had tolerated crummy motels and being on the road three hundred and fifty-two nights a year.

Then Jack 'n' Jilly had become successful.

After that, Jack would rehearse a new country or folk song only as long as it took him to learn the words and melody. Anything beyond that was Jilly's problem.

A year ago Alana had left Jack and come to Broken Mountain Ranch to think about her life and her sad sham of a marriage. When word of their separation had leaked to the press, record and concert ticket sales had plummeted. Their agent had called Alana and quietly, cynically, suggested that she continue to present a happily married front to the world. Fame was transient. Obscurity was forever.

That same afternoon, Bob had come back from a trip to the high country babbling about seeing Rafe Winter. Alana had written the letter to Rafe, seen Rafe's rejection condensed into a single harsh word: *Deceased.*

She had wept until she felt nothing at all . . . and then she had gone back to L.A. to appear as half of Country's Perfect Couple.

Until six weeks ago, when Alana had told Jack that the sham was over. Country's Perfect Couple was an act she couldn't handle anymore. He had pleaded with her to think again, to take a trip with him to the high country she loved, and there they would work out something.

"Did you miss the ranch?" Rafe asked quietly.

Alana heard the question as though from a great distance, calling her out of a past that was another kind of nightmare waiting to drag her down. She reached for the question, pulling it eagerly around her.

"I missed the ranch more than . . . more than I knew."

And she had. It had been like having her eyes put out. She had hungered for the green and silver shimmer of aspens, but saw only dusty palm trees. She had searched for the primal blue of alpine lakes set among the chiseled spires of mountains older than man, but found only concrete freeways and the metallic flash of cars. She had always looked for the intense green silences of the wilderness forest, but discovered only tame squares of grass laid down amid hot stucco houses.

All that had saved Alana was singing. Working with a song. Tasting it, feeling it, seeing it grow and change as it became part of her and she of it.

Jack had never understood that. He had loved only the applause and worked just hard enough to get it. Alana loved the singing and would work to exhaustion until she and the song were one.

"If you missed the ranch that much, why did you leave after Jack died?"

Alana realized that she had heard the question before. Rafe had asked it at least twice and she hadn't answered, lost in her own thoughts.

"Jack died there," she whispered. "On Broken Mountain."

She looked to the right, where the Green

River Mountains lifted seamed granite faces toward the evening sky. High-flying clouds burned silver above the peaks, and over all arched an immense indigo bowl, twilight changing into night.

"You must have unhappy memories," said Rafe quietly.

"Yes, I suppose I must."

Alana heard her own words, heard their ambiguity, heard the fear tight in her voice. She looked up and saw that Rafe had been watching her.

But he turned away and said nothing, asked no more questions.

He simply drove her closer and closer to the ramparts of snow and ice where Jack had died and Jilly had lost her mind.

4

IT WAS DARK BY THE TIME RAFE turned onto the fork of the road that led to the Broken Mountain ranch house. An autumn moon was up, huge and flat and ghostly, balanced on the edge of the world. Clouds raced and seethed, veiled in moonlight and mystery, veiling the moon in turn.

The mountains were invisible, yet Alana could sense them rising black and massive in front of her. They comforted and frightened her at the same time as childhood memories and recent fear set her on an emotional seesaw that made her dizzy.

Alana knew she had been at the ranch just four weeks ago.

She knew she and Jack had ridden into the high country.

She knew Jack was dead.

She knew—*but she didn't.*

Alana had awakened in the hospital, bruised and cut, ice-burned and aching. And frightened. Every shadow, every sound, had sent her heart racing.

It had taken a huge effort of will to allow Dr. Gene to examine her. He had tried to explain the inexplicable in ordinary words, telling Alana that her fear was normal, the overreaction of someone who had never known physical danger, much less death. In time, her mind and body would adjust to the presence of danger, the nearness of death in everyday life. Then she would be calm again. Until then, Dr. Gene could prescribe something to help her.

Alana had refused the tranquilizers. She had seen too many musicians dependent on drugs. For her, chemical solutions were no solution at all.

But it had been tempting, especially at first.

The presence of Dr. Gene had unnerved Alana to the point of tears. Even Bob, her favorite brother, had seen Alana withdraw from any kind of physical touch, any gesture of affection he made. Bob had been hurt and very worried about her, his brown eyes clouded with conflicting feelings.

Then, on the third morning after Alana had awakened, she had quietly walked out of the hospital, boarded a plane, and flown to Port-

land, a place where she had never lived. She
hadn't waited for Sheriff Mitchell to come
back down off the mountain with Jack's body.
She hadn't stopped to think, to consider, to
reason. She had simply run from the black gap
in her mind.

Portland was big enough for Alana to lose
herself in, but not big enough to remind her of
L.A. and her life with Jack. There were mountains in Portland, but only in the distance.

Yet fear had run with Alana anyway.
Though she had never before been afraid of
flying, or heights, there had been a horrible
moment of terror as the plane had left the
ground.

*Earth falling away and her body twisting,
weightless, she was falling, falling, black rushing
up to meet her and when it did she would be torn
from life like an aspen leaf from its stem, spinning
away helplessly over the void—*

"It's all right, Alana. You're safe. It's all
right. I've come to take you home."

Vaguely Alana realized that Rafe had
parked the Jeep at the side of the road. She
heard Rafe's soothing murmur, sensed the
warmth of his hand over her clenched fingers,
the gentle pressure of his other hand stroking
her hair. She felt the shudders wracking her
body, the ache of teeth clenched against a futile scream.

Rafe continued speaking quietly, repeating
his words. They warmed Alana, words as un-

demanding as sunlight, driving away the darkness that gripped her.

Suddenly she turned her head, pressing her cheek against the hard strength of Rafe's hand. But when he would have drawn her closer, she moved away with a jerk.

"I—" Alana stopped abruptly and drew a deep breath. "I'm sorry. Something—" Her hands moved jerkily. "Sometimes I—since Jack—"

Alana closed her eyes. She couldn't make Rafe understand what she herself had no words to describe.

"Seeing death is always hard," said Rafe quietly. "The more sheltered you've been, the harder it is."

Rafe's hand stroked Alana's hair, his touch as gentle as his words, as his presence, as his warmth.

After a few moments Alana let out a long sigh, feeling the tentacles of terror loosen, slide away, the nightmare withdrawing. She turned her head and looked at Rafe with eyes that were no longer black with fear.

"Thank you," she said simply.

Rafe's only answer was a light caress across Alana's cheek as his hand withdrew from her hair.

He started the Jeep again and pulled back onto the narrow gravel road that led to the Burdette family house. Beneath the truck, the country began to roll subtly, gathering itself for the sudden leap into mountain heights.

The ranch house was on the last piece of

land that could be described as high plains.
Behind the ranch buildings, the country rose
endlessly, becoming ranks of black peaks
wearing brilliant crowns of stars.

Gradually, squares of yellow light condensed out of the blackness as the ranch house
competed with and finally outshone the
brightness of the stars. Dark fences paralleled
the road, defining corrals and pastures where
brood mares grazed and champion bulls
moved with ponderous grace. A paved loop
of road curved in front of the house before
veering off toward the barns.

As Rafe braked to a stop by the walkway,
the front door of the house opened, sending a
thick rectangle of gold light into the yard like
a soundless cry of welcome. Three quicksilver
dogs bounded off the porch, barking and bay-
ing and dancing as though the dewy grass
were made of icicles too sharp to stand on.

Rafe climbed out of the truck and waded
into the hounds with good-natured curses,
pummeling them gently until they had
worked off the first exuberance of their greet-
ing. Then they stood and watched him with
bright eyes, nudging his hands with cold
noses until each silky ear had been scratched
at least once. In the moonlight the hounds'
coats shone like liquid silver, rippling and
changing with each movement of their muscular bodies.

Alana slid out of the Jeep with a smile on
her lips and the hounds' welcoming song
echoing in her ears. She stood quietly, watch-

ing the dogs greet Rafe, feeling the cool breeze
tug at her hair.

One of the hounds lifted its head sharply,
scenting Alana. It gave an eager whine and
scrambled toward her. Automatically Alana
bent over to greet the animal, rubbing its ears
and thumping lightly on its muscular barrel,
enjoying the warm rasp of a tongue over her
hands.

"You're a beauty," Alana said, admiring the
dog's lithe lines and strength.

The dog nosed her hand, then the pocket of
her black slacks, then her hand again.

"What do you want?" asked Alana, her
voice carrying clearly in the quiet air.

"Vamp wants the crackers you spoiled her
with the last time you were here," called Bob
as he stepped out onto the porch, laughter and
resignation competing in his voice.

Alana looked up blankly.

"Crackers?" she repeated.

She looked down at the dog. The dog
watched her, dancing from foot to foot, obviously waiting for something.

"Crackers," said Bob, holding one out to
Alana as he walked toward her. "I figured that
you'd forgotten—er, I mean I figured that you
wouldn't have any crackers on you, so I
brought one."

"Vamp?" asked Alana.

She took the cracker and looked at the pale
square as though she'd never seen one before.
She held it out.

The hound took the tidbit with the delicate mouth of a well-trained bird dog.

"Vampire," Bob said, gesturing to the dog at Alana's feet. "You know, for all the sharp teeth she had as a pup."

The look on Alana's face made it clear that she didn't know the story behind the dog's name. Yet it was equally clear that Bob had told her the story before.

"*Hell*," said Bob under his breath.

Then he hugged Alana and spoke so softly that only she could hear.

"Sorry, sis. It's hard for me to keep track of all the things you've forgotten."

Alana stiffened for an instant as her brother's arms held her. Then she forced herself to relax. She knew she must get over her irrational fear of human contact. The source of fear was only in her nightmares, a creation of her mind that had nothing to do with here, now, reality. Withdrawing would hurt Bob badly, just as she had hurt him at the hospital.

She returned the hug a little fiercely, holding on too tightly, releasing her brother too quickly. Bob gave her a troubled look but said nothing.

Until he saw her hair.

"What in God's name did you do to your hair?" Bob yelped.

"I cut it."

Alana shook her head, making moonlight run like ghostly fingers through the loose black curves of her hair.

"Why?" asked Bob.

"It seemed like a good idea at the time."

"But you've always had long hair."

His voice was surprisingly plaintive for a man who was just over six-and-a-half feet tall and nearly twenty-three years old.

"Things change, little brother," Alana said tightly.

"Not you, sis," Bob said, confidence in every word. "You're like the mountains. You never change."

Alana stood without moving, not knowing what to say. In that moment, she realized for the first time how much like a mother she was to Bob, how fixed in his mind as a port for every storm. Somehow she had given a continuity of love and caring to him that she had never found for herself after their mother died. And Rafe, who had died and then not died. But he had come back too late.

Like now. Too late, Alana thought. How can I tell Bob that there are no ports anymore, only storms?

"You're forgetting something, Bob," said Rafe, his voice easy yet somehow commanding.

"What? Oh. Yeah. Damn. I told you, Winter, I'm no—"

"Sisters are women, too," Rafe said, cutting across whatever Bob had been about to say. "Some sisters are even beautiful women."

Rafe's amber eyes flashed as he looked briefly at Alana. His smile reflected the light pouring out of the ranch house.

Bob cocked his head and looked at Alana as though she were a stranger.

"A matter of taste, I suppose," Bob said, deadpan. "She looks like a stray fence post to me. Didn't they have any food in Portland?"

Quietly Rafe looked from the graceful curve of Alana's neck to the feminine swell of breasts, the small waist, the firm curve of hips, the legs long and graceful.

"Burdette," Rafe said, "you're as blind as a stone rolling down a mountain."

Alana flushed under Rafe's frankly approving glance. Yet she was smiling, too. She was used to being told she had a beautiful voice. As for the rest, she had never felt especially attractive.

Except when she had been with Rafe and he had looked at her the way he was looking at her right now, smiling.

"I guess Rafe told *you*, baby brother," Alana said, glad that the words came out light, teasing. She smiled at Rafe. "I'll bet you ride a white horse and rescue maidens in distress, too."

Rafe's face changed, intent, watching Alana as though he was willing her to do . . . something.

The look passed so quickly that Alana thought she had imagined it.

"Wrong, sis," said Bob triumphantly, yanking her suitcase out of the back of the Jeep. "The horse Rafe rides is as spotted as his past."

Alana looked from Bob to Rafe, wondering what her brother meant.

What had Rafe done in the years before, and after, he was declared dead in Central America?

"Bob, you need a bridle for that tongue of yours," said Rafe.

His smile was narrow, his voice flat.

Bob winced. "Stepped in it again. Sorry. I'm not very good at forgetting. Or"—he looked apologetically at Alana again—"remembering, either."

She sighed. "You couldn't even keep secrets at Christmastime, could you?"

"Nope," Bob agreed cheerfully. "Not a one. In one ear and out the mouth."

Rafe made a sound that was halfway between disgust and amusement.

"There are times when I can't believe you're Sam's brother," Rafe said dryly.

Alana looked quickly at Rafe. Something in his voice told her that Rafe had seen Sam more recently than the times when Sam had hero-worshipped the older Rafe from afar.

"Have you seen Sam? I mean, lately?" Alana asked Rafe.

When Bob would have spoken, Rafe gave him a quelling look.

"We met in Central America," Rafe said, "when Sam was drilling a few dry holes. I haven't seen him in a while, though."

Alana's lips turned down.

"Neither have I," she said. "It's been years.

I was in Florida doing a concert the last time he came to the States."

"My brother the spook," said Bob. "Now you see him, now you don't."

"What?" asked Alana.

"Oops," said Bob.

What Rafe said was mercifully blurred by Merry's voice calling out threats to the husband who had let her sleep through Alana's homecoming.

"Honey," Bob said, dropping Alana's suitcase and racing toward the steps, "be careful!"

The dogs ran after Bob, yipping and yapping with excitement. Alana couldn't help laughing as Bob swept Merry off her tiny feet and carried her across the grass, swearing at the dogs every step of the way. Merry was laughing too, her face buried against Bob's neck as she squealed and ducked away from the long-tongued, leaping hounds.

Rafe put his fists on his hips and shook his head, smiling. He turned to Alana and held out his hand.

"Welcome to Broken Mountain Dude Ranch," he said wryly. "Peace and quiet await you. Somewhere. It says so in the fine print in the brochure."

"I'll hold you to that," murmured Alana.

Smiling, she rested her hand lightly on Rafe's, feeling the heat and texture of his palm as his fingers curled around hers. The touch sent both pleasure and fear coursing through her.

The instant before Alana would have withdrawn, Rafe released her hand and picked up her luggage. She went ahead quickly, opening the screen door for Rafe and for Bob, who was still carrying a giggling Merry.

The dogs stopped short at the threshold and begged silently, their amber wolf eyes pale and hopeful.

Alana looked toward Bob.

"No," he said firmly. "No weimaraners allowed."

"Not even Vamp?" Alana asked coaxingly.

"Sis," Bob said in an exasperated tone, "I told you the last time that I don't want to take a chance of Merry tripping over—"

Bob stopped abruptly, remembering too late that Alana had no memory of her last trip to the ranch.

"Sorry," said Alana tightly, closing the door. "I forgot."

"So did I. Again. *Damn.*"

Bob ran his fingers through his thick black hair in a gesture both sister and brother had learned from their father.

"Oh, Alana," Merry said softly, her pretty face stricken as she looked at her sister-in-law. "Bob didn't mean to hurt you."

"I know."

Alana closed her eyes and unclenched her hands.

"Where do you want the suitcase?" asked Rafe into the silence.

His voice was matter-of-fact, as though he hadn't sensed the undercurrents of emotion swirling through Alana. She knew better. With every instant she and Rafe spent together, Alana became more certain that he was intensely aware of everything about her.

"Alana is sleeping in the upstairs bedroom on the east corner," said Merry, wriggling in Bob's arms. "Put me down, you big moose. There's nothing wrong with my feet."

"Never mind," said Rafe. "I know where the room is. Don't climb any more stairs than you have to."

"Not you, too!" Merry rolled her blue eyes and pulled on her long blond hair in mock despair. "Why me, Lord? Why am I stuck with men who think pregnancy is an exotic kind of broken leg?"

Rafe smiled crookedly as he watched the tiny woman's halfhearted struggle in Bob's thick arms.

"Enjoy it, Merry," Rafe said. "Come diaper time, Bob will develop an exotic kind of broken arm."

"Slander," muttered Bob to Merry, nuzzling her cheek. "Don't believe a word of it."

"Believe it," said Alana. "Every time there were grubby chores to be done, Bob evaporated."

"Hey, not fair," he said, a wounded look on his face.

"Not fair or not true?" Alana asked wryly.

"I grew up after that carnivorous hen ate half my hands."

"Chicken pox," called Rafe just before he disappeared down the hall at the top of the stairway. "Remember?"

Bob groaned. "He's worse than Sam when it comes to keeping track of life's little lies. Mind like a steel trap. No fun at all."

Privately Alana thought it would be wonderful to have a mind that forgot nothing, held everything. If she knew about those six days, her nightmares would be gone.

Or maybe they would just move in and take over her days, too.

Maybe Dr. Gene was right. Maybe she wasn't ready to accept what had happened, at least not all of it, every little horrifying detail.

Height and ice and falling . . .

"You look tired, sis," said Bob.

He set Merry on her feet with exaggerated care and watched lovingly as she yawned, waved good night, and went back to the downstairs bedroom. He turned back to Alana.

"Want to go right to bed?" he asked.

Bob waited, but there was no answer.

"Sis?"

With a start, Alana came out of her thoughts. Her hand was against her neck, as though holding back a scream.

"Sis? What is it? Are you remembering?"

Alana forced herself not to flinch when Bob's big hand came down on her shoulder.

"No," she said, hearing the harshness of her voice but unable to make it softer. "I'm trying, but I'm not remembering anything."

"Where does your memory stop?" asked Bob hesitantly.

"California. I was packing to come here."

"Where does it begin again?"

"When I woke up in the hospital."

"Six days."

"Nice counting, baby brother," Alana said sardonically. Then, "I'm sorry. It's just . . . not easy. I don't know why I forgot, and I'm . . . afraid."

Bob patted Alana's shoulder clumsily, not knowing how to comfort the older sister who had always been the one to comfort him.

"I love you, sis."

Tears burned behind Alana's eyes. She looked up into the face that was as familiar to her as her own. Familiar, yet different. Bob was a man now, but in her memories he was so often a boy.

"Thanks," she whispered. "I love you, too."

Bob smiled almost shyly and squeezed Alana's shoulder. A frown passed over his face as he felt her slight body beneath his big hand.

"You're nearly as small as Merry," said Bob, surprise clear in his voice.

Alana almost laughed. "I'm three inches taller."

Bob dismissed the inches with a wave of his hand.

"That's not what I meant," he said. "I've always thought of you as . . . bigger. You know. Physically."

"And I've always thought of you as smaller. Guess we both have some new thinking to do."

"Yeah, guess so." Bob ran his thick fingers through his hair. "I've been thinking a lot

since Merry got pregnant. It's kind of scary."
Then he grinned. "It's kind of fantastic, too."

Alana smiled despite her trembling lips.

"You'll be a good father, Bob. Just like
you're a good rancher."

Bob's eyes widened slightly, showing clear
brown depths.

"You mean that, sis? About being a good
rancher, too?"

"You've been good to the land. It shows.
Rafe thinks so, too," she added.

Bob smiled with pleasure. "High marks
from both of you, huh? That means a lot to
me. I know how much you love the ranch.
And Rafe, well, he's a hard son of a bitch, but
he's working miracles with the Lazy W. It had
really gone to hell by the time his father had
that last stroke."

"How long has Rafe lived at the Lazy W?"

Bob looked uncomfortable, obviously remembering the time Alana had come for a
visit and he had told her that Rafael Winter
was alive.

"Bob?" Alana pressed.

"A couple of years," he admitted.

"All that time?" asked Alana.

Before, when she had known Rafe, loved
him, been engaged to him, his work had taken
him on long trips to unexpected places.

"He used to travel a lot," she added.

"Yeah. About four years ago he was . . . uh,
he had some kind of accident in some godfor-
saken place. And then his father died. Rafe has
stayed on the Lazy W the whole time since

then. Guess he's here for good. Unless something goes to hell overseas or Sam gets in trouble again and needs Rafe to pull his tail out of
a crack."

"Sam? In trouble? How? And what could
Rafe do about it?"

Bob laughed wryly. "Sis, Rafe would—"

"Bring Sam a toothbrush," said Rafe from
the stairway.

Alana looked up. Rafe was leaning against
the wall, his hands in his pockets, his shirt
tightly across bunched shoulder muscles. For
all his casual pose, she sensed that Rafe was
angry about something.

Bob breathed a curse and an apology.

"I warned you, Rafe," Bob said. "I'm no
damn good at—"

"Burdette." Rafe's voice cracked with authority. "Shut up. If you can't do that, talk
about the weather."

There was a charged silence for a moment.
Alana looked from Bob to Rafe and back
again. Although her brother had five inches
and fifty pounds on Rafe, Rafe didn't seem the
least bit intimidated by the prospect of a
brawl.

"Storm coming on," said Bob finally.
"Should be thunder in the high country by
midnight, rain down here before dawn. It's
supposed to clear up at sunrise, though. Part
of a cold front that's moving across the Rock-
ies. Now, if you ask me, I think we should
roust those sleeping dudes upstairs and leave

for your lodge at dawn or as soon afterward as it stops raining."

"That," said Rafe distinctly, "is one hell of an idea. Do you suppose you can keep your feet out of your mouth long enough to sit a horse all the way to Five Lakes Lodge?"

"Didn't you know I'm a trick rider?" said Bob, his smile wide and forgiving.

"Who had chicken pox," retorted Rafe, but he was smiling, too.

"Now you got it," said Bob approvingly. "Keep that good thought until morning. And I'll practice biting my damned tongue. But only for a while."

"I'll hold you to it."

"Yeah. It goes both ways, Winter. Don't forget. I sure as hell won't. Goodnight."

Beneath the humor in Bob's voice there was something much harder.

Alana heard it, and she wondered if Rafe heard it, too.

And then she wondered why Bob, who was normally easygoing to a fault, was leaning on Rafael Winter.

5

RAFE SHOOK HIS HEAD AND said something harsh under his breath as Bob vanished. But Rafe was smiling when he turned to Alana.

"How did you hold your own?" he asked. "Sam and Bob together. My God. And Dave, too. Boggles the mind."

"What did Bob mean about your 'spotted past'?" asked Alana.

"Terrible work record," Rafe said laconically. "Moved around a lot. Remember?"

"And about Sam being in trouble?"

"He's not in trouble now."

"But he was?" persisted Alana.

"Everyone gets in trouble now and again."

Alana made an exasperated sound. "Am I permitted to ask about the dudes?"

Rafe's glance narrowed.

"Sure," he said. "Ask away."

"But will I get any answers?"

"Now I remember how you held your own with your brothers," Rafe said, smiling. "Stubborn."

"I prefer to think of it as determined."

"Good thing, determination."

Alana looked at Rafe's carefully bland expression, at the intelligence and humor that gave depth to his whiskey eyes, at the clean line of his lips beneath his mustache.

What she saw made her forget her unanswered questions. Rafe had taken off his hat, revealing the rich depths of color and texture in his hair. It was a very dark brown, with surprising gleams of gold, clean and thick and lustrous. No shadow of beard lay beneath his skin, which meant that he must have shaved before he picked her up at the airport.

The open collar of Rafe's shirt revealed hair darker than his mustache, more curly. Her glance went back to his forehead, where the rich brown hair had been combed back by his fingers.

Is it a memory or a dream, Alana asked herself silently, or did Rafe's hair once feel like winter mink between my fingers?

"What are you thinking?" he asked.

Rafe's voice was casual, as though he were asking the time.

Reflexively Alana responded to the offhand

tone, answering before she realized what he
had asked or what her answer would reveal.

"Your hair," she said, "like winter
mink . . . ?"

"Want to find out?"

"What?"

"If my hair feels like mink."

Rafe spoke as though it were a perfectly normal thing for Alana to do.

"Don't worry," he added softly. "I won't
touch you at all. I know you don't want to be
touched."

Rafe's voice was low, murmurous, as soothing as it had been in the Jeep when nightmare
had overtaken Alana without warning.

"Go ahead and touch me," he said. "I promise I won't do anything but stand here. You're
safe with me, Alana. Always. I'm the man who
came to take you home."

Alana looked at the amber eyes and gentle
smile while Rafe's voice surrounded her, caressing her. His hands were still in his pockets,
his body was still relaxed. His posture told
Alana that he understood and accepted her
fear of being touched, held. Restrained.

"How did you know?" Alana asked, her
voice trembling.

"That you didn't want to be touched?"

"Yes."

"Every time I touch you, you freeze. That's
as good as words for me. Better."

Alana was caught by the emotion she
sensed coiling beneath Rafe's surface calm.

He sent back my letter unopened, Alana

thought tensely. But did he dream of me, too? Is my coldness cutting him, making him bleed as I bled when my letter came back unopened?

Remembered grief ripped through Alana, shaking her.

That's in the past, she told herself harshly. I'm living in the present. Today, Rafe has shown me only kindness. And now I'm hurting him.

Alana wanted to hold on to Rafe, comforting both of them, but the thought of being held in return made her body tense to fight or flee.

"It isn't anything personal," she said in a strained voice.

"Are you sure it isn't something I've done?"

Alana looked at Rafe. His eyes were as clear as a high-country stream. Glints of gold and topaz mixed with the predominant amber color, radiating outward from the black pupil. He was watching her with strange intensity.

"I'm sure," she said, sighing, relaxing. "Very sure."

"Then what is it?" Rafe asked gently.

"I—I don't know. Since Jack died, I just don't like people touching me."

"Do you like touching people?"

"I—"

Alana stopped, a puzzled expression bringing her black brows together.

"I hadn't thought about it that way," she admitted.

Rafe waited, watching her.

And Alana watched Rafe, absorbing his silence and his restraint, the pulse beating

slowly in his neck, the slide and coil of muscles across his chest as he breathed in the even
rhythms of relaxation, waiting for her.

Slowly Alana's hand came up. He bent
down to make it easier for her to touch him.
Her fingers brushed over his hair lightly, hesitated, then quickly retreated.

"Well?" Rafe asked as he straightened, smiling. "Is someone going to skin me for a fancy
coat?"

Alana laughed a little breathlessly.

"I'm not sure," she admitted. "It was so
quick."

"Try again," he offered casually.

Alana climbed the stairs until she was on
the same step as Rafe. This time her hand lingered as she allowed his hair to sift over the
sensitive skin between her fingers. With a
smile that was both shy and remembering, she
lifted her hand.

"Better," Rafe said. "But you should take
lessons from a professional furrier."

She made a questioning sound.

"Professionals rub the pelt with their palms
and fingertips," said Rafe.

His glance moved from Alana's mouth to
her glossy black hair.

"And they tease the fur with their breath,"
he said, "hold its softness to their lips, smell
it, taste it, then gently slide the fur over their
most sensitive skin."

Alana's breath caught. A shiver of pleasure
spread through her at the thought of being
touched so gently . . . by Rafael Winter.

"Do they really?" she asked.

"I don't know," Rafe admitted, his voice a teasing kind of velvet as he smiled down at her. "But that's what I'd do to you if you were a fur and I were a furrier."

Though Rafe hadn't moved any closer, Alana felt surrounded by him, by sensual possibilities that sent warmth showering through her.

Suddenly, vividly, memories from the times they had made love went through Alana's body like liquid lightning. She had spent so long trying to forget, yet the memories were as hot and fresh as though newly made.

Or perhaps her memories of Rafe's exquisite touch were merely hunger and dream entangled so thoroughly that truth was lost. Another kind of amnesia, more gentle, but just as filled with pitfalls in the present.

Yet Alana had just touched Rafe, and he had felt better than in her memories.

Rafe smiled as though he knew exactly what Alana was feeling. Before she could retreat, he pushed away from the wall and passed her on the narrow stairway without touching her. When he spoke his voice was no longer teasing, husky, intimate.

"Get some sleep," Rafe advised. "Bob and I weren't kidding about leaving at dawn. If you need anything, I'm in the room next to yours. Don't worry about making noise. The dudes are still on Virginia time. Sleeping like babes all in a row."

She stared at Rafe as he walked toward the living room.

"And Alana..."

Rafe turned back toward her, his face half in light, half in shadow, his eyes the radiant gold of sunset rain.

"Yes?" she asked.

"Don't be afraid. Whatever happens, I'm here."

Rafe vanished into the living room before Alana could answer.

Slowly she walked upstairs to her room, hoping at every moment to hear Rafe's footsteps behind her.

Only silence followed Alana to her bedroom.

The exhaustion of sleepless nights combined with the familiar background sounds of the ranch to send Alana into a deep sleep. She slept undisturbed until clouds gathered and thickened, stitched together by lightning and torn apart by thunder.

Then she began to sleep restlessly, her head moving from side to side, her limbs shifting unpredictably, her throat clenching over unspoken words.

Riding next to Jack, arguing.

He's angry and the clouds are angry and the mountains loom over me like thunder.

Spruce and fir and aspens bent double by the cruel wind. Wind tearing off leaves, spinning them like bright coins into the black void, and the horses are gone.

Screaming but no one can hear, I'm a single bright leaf spinning endlessly down and down and—

Cold, sweating, Alana woke up, her heart hammering against her ribs, her breath ragged. She looked at the bedside clock. Three-forty. Too soon to get up, even if they were leaving at dawn.

Lightning bleached the room, leaving intense darkness behind, trailing an avalanche of thunder.

Suddenly Alana felt trapped.

She leaped out of bed, yanked open the door, and ran into the hallway. She raced down the stairs and out onto the front porch. Incandescent lightning skidded over the land, separated by split seconds of darkness that were almost dizzying.

Frightened, disoriented, a broken scream tearing at her throat, Alana turned back to the front door.

A man came out, walking toward her.

At first Alana thought it was Rafe; then she realized that the man was too tall. But it wasn't Bob. The walk was different.

Lightning came again, outlining the man, revealing his pale hair, long sideburns, blunt nose, narrow mouth, and eyes so blue they were almost black.

Jack.

Past and present, nightmare and reality fused into a seamless horror. Helpless, terrified, shaken by thunder and her own screaming, Alana scrambled backward, hands flailing frantically,

running, scrambling, falling, and everywhere ice and lightning, thunder and darkness and screaming.
Falling.
I'm falling . . . !

This time Alana could hear the screams tearing apart her throat. But it wasn't Jack's name she screamed as she spun toward the void.

It was Rafe's.

The front door burst open and slammed back against the wall. Abruptly Jack disappeared between one stroke of lightning and the next.

Shaking, holding on to herself, Alana told herself that Jack was a product of her imagination, a waking nightmare from which she would soon be freed.

Then she saw Jack laid out on the porch, Rafe astride him, Rafe's forearm like an iron bar across Jack's throat.

Panic exploded inside Alana, shards of ice slashing through her, paralyzing her. Jack was so much bigger than Rafe, as big as Bob, bigger, and Jack could be so cruel in his strength.

Then her paralysis melted, sliding away into darkness and lightning as Alana realized that' Rafe was in control. It was Jack who was down and was going to stay that way until Rafe decided to let him up again.

Bob ran out onto the front porch, flashlight in one hand and shotgun in the other. He saw Rafe and the man beneath him.

"What in the hell—?" began Bob.

Then he saw Alana backed up against the porch railing, terror in every line of her face, her hands clenched around her throat.

"Sis? Oh, God!"

Bob started for her, holding out his arms.

Alana screamed.

Rafe came to his feet in a single powerful lunge. He stood between brother and sister.

"Don't touch her," Rafe said flatly.

"But—" began Bob.

Lightning flared again. Bob saw Rafe's face, hard and utterly savage. Without another word, Bob backed up.

Rafe turned with the same fluid power that he had used to come up off the porch floor. As he looked at Alana, his eyes burned with rage and regret. He ached to gather her in his arms, to hold her, to feel her melt and flow along his body as she accepted his embrace.

And he knew that was a dream, and she lived in nightmare. Broken Mountain was destroying their future as surely as his "death" once had.

"It's all right, wildflower," Rafe said quietly. "I won't let anyone touch you. Not even me."

Numbly Alana nodded, hearing the word *wildflower* echo and reecho in her mind, a name from the deep past, before Rafe had died and been reborn, killing her without knowing it.

Wildflower.

A name out of dreams.

A name out of nightmares.

"Bob," Rafe said without turning around, "pick up Stan and get the hell out of Alana's sight. *Now.*"

Bob had no desire to argue with the whiplike voice, the poised fighting stance, the muscles visibly coiled across Rafe's naked back, ready to unleash violence. Silently Bob bent over, levered the man called Stan to his feet, and dragged him into the living room.

The screen door banged shut behind them like a small crack of thunder.

Distant lightning came, revealing Rafe's face, harshness and yearning combined.

Alana blinked, half expecting Rafe to vanish.

He stayed before her, outlined by forked lightning, a man both lean and powerful, wearing only jeans, and regret was a dark veil across his features.

Instinctively Alana swayed toward him, needing the very comfort that her mind wouldn't let her take.

Rafe stood without moving, looking at her slender body shaken by shudders of cold and fear, his own private nightmare come true. He would have put his arms around her, but he knew that she would only scream again, tearing both of them apart.

In the end, Rafe could not help holding out his hand to Alana. It was a gesture that asked nothing, offered everything.

"Hold on to me, wildflower," he said softly. "If you want to."

With a small sound, Alana took Rafe's hand between her own. She held on to him with bruising intensity. He didn't object. Nor did he so much as curl his fingers around hers. She took a shuddering breath, then another, fighting to control herself.

"I thought—" Alana's voice broke.

She bent over, pressing her forehead to the back of Rafe's hand. He was as warm as life itself, flowing into her, giving her peace. She swallowed and spoke without lifting her head.

"I thought he was J-Jack."

Rafe's left hand hovered over Alana's bent head, as though he would stroke her hair. Then his hand dropped to his side and remained there, clenched in a fist.

He was afraid to touch her, to frighten her and rend the fragile fabric of trust being woven between them.

"Stan is one of the dudes," Rafe said quietly, but emotions turned just beneath the smooth surface of his voice, testing his control. "Stan is big, like Jack was. And blond."

Alana shuddered and said nothing.

"If I had known that the first time you saw Stan it would be in the lightning and darkness, a storm, like Broken Mountain—" Rafe didn't finish. "I'm sorry, wildflower. For so many things."

But the last words were said so softly that Alana wasn't sure she had heard them at all. For a moment longer she clung to Rafe's hand, drawing strength and warmth from him, the nightmare draining away, fading like thunder into the distance.

Slowly Alana's head came up. She drew more deep breaths, sending oxygen through a body that had been starved for it, paralyzed by fear to the point that she had forgotten to breathe. Gradually the shuddering left her body, only to return as shivers of cold rather than fear.

For the first time she realized that she was wearing only a thin silk nightshirt, which the icy rain had plastered across her body. The vivid orange cloth was nearly black where water had touched it, as dark as her eyes looking up at Rafe.

Alana shivered again, and for an instant Rafe held his warm hand against her cheek. A single fingertip traced the black wing of her eyebrow with such exquisite gentleness that she forgot to be afraid. Tears stood in her eyes, magnifying them. Tears flowed down silently, tears as warm as Rafe's hand.

With dreamlike slowness, Alana turned her face until her lips rested against his palm. When she spoke, her breath was another caress flowing over his skin.

"Thank you for understanding," Alana whispered.

Rafe's body tensed visibly as he fought his impulse to hold Alana, to turn her lips up to his own, to taste again the warmth of her, to feel her respond. He knew that if he reached for her she would retreat, terrified.

And that knowledge was a knife turning inside him.

Slowly Alana released Rafe's hand. For a moment he held his palm against her cheek, then he withdrew.

"I feel like such a fool," said Alana, closing her eyes. "What must that poor man think of me?"

"Stan thinks he was a real horse's ass to come barging outside after you in a storm, scaring you half to death," said Rafe, his voice like a whip once more. "He's lucky I didn't take him apart."

Alana made a sound of protest.

"It was my fault, not his," she said. "I'll have to apologize."

"Like hell. Stan will apologize to you, in good light, when you can see him clearly. *And then he will stay away from you.*"

Rafe's words were clear and hard, like glacier ice. Alana realized that he was furious, but not with her. He was enraged with Stan, because Stan had frightened her.

Then she realized that Rafe was also furious with himself, because he hadn't prevented her from being frightened.

"It wasn't your fault," whispered Alana.

"The hell it wasn't."

Then, before she could respond, Rafe was talking again.

"You're shivering. Are you ready to go back inside?"

Alana hesitated. The thought of seeing the man who looked so much like Jack disturbed her deeply. But she had no choice. She refused to spend the rest of her life at the mercy of her own fears.

She clenched her hands at her sides, took a deep breath, and lifted her chin.

"Yes, I'm ready," Alana said.

"You don't have to." Rafe's voice was gentle despite his tightly leashed anger. "I'll go in and tell Bob you'd rather not meet Stan right now."

"No. I've got to stop being so damned . . . fragile."

"You've been through too much, too recently. You've been through more than anyone should have to bear. Don't be so hard on yourself. Ease up. Give yourself a chance to heal."

Alana shook her head.

She wasn't healing. The nightmare was getting worse, taking over more and more of her waking hours.

"Life goes on, Rafe. The biggest cliché, and the one with the most truth. I have to go on, too. I have to leave those six days behind me. *I have to.*"

For an instant Rafe closed his eyes, unable to bear either Alana's pain or her courage.

"Just like a wildflower," he whispered. "Delicate and tough, growing in the most difficult places."

He opened his eyes and held his hand out to her.

"Will you let me help you?" Rafe asked.

After a moment's hesitation, Alana put her hand in Rafe's. The warmth of his skin was like fire, telling her how cold her own body was.

"Thank you," Rafe said simply.

Then he opened the door and led Alana back into the living room, where her nightmare waited.

6

BOB AND STAN WERE SITTING in the living room, talking about storms and high-country trout. Both men looked up, then away, clearly not wanting to intrude if Alana needed privacy.

Rafe plucked a flannel shirt off a coatrack standing near the door, draped the colorful plaid folds over Alana, and turned toward the two men.

Instantly Stan stood up.

Alana took a quick breath and stepped backward until she came up hard against Rafe's chest. Over Alana's head, Rafe smiled coldly at the blond, muscular giant who was every bit as tall as Bob.

"Alana Reeves, meet Stan Wilson," said Rafe. "Stan, you'll understand if Alana doesn't want to shake hands. You have an unnerving resemblance to her recently deceased husband."

For a long moment, Rafe and Stan measured each other.

Stan nodded, a brief incline of his head that was almost an apology. Then his head moved slightly as he looked toward Alana.

At the sight of Stan's cobalt-blue eyes, Alana made a small sound. Like Jack. Just like Jack. Only the solid warmth of Rafe at her back kept her from falling into nightmare again.

"I'm sorry, Mrs. Reeves," Stan said. "I sure didn't mean to frighten you like that."

Relief uncurled deep inside Alana. The voice was different, entirely different, deeper, permeated by the subtle rhythms of the Southwest.

"Please call me Alana," she said. "And I'm sorry for—"

"You have nothing to apologize for," said Rafe, cutting across Alana's words. "Now that Stan is aware of the situation, I'm sure he won't take you by surprise again."

Rafe's voice was smooth and polished, steel hard, having no soft surfaces that might admit argument. His eyes were narrowed, watching Stan with the intensity of a cougar stalking deer.

Again, Stan hesitated before responding. Again, Stan nodded slightly, though his expression was as hard as Rafe's.

Alana looked from one man to the other and then to Bob, whom she feared would be worried about the fate of his dreams for a dude ranch. If Stan Wilson had an awful vacation at the Broken Mountain Dude Ranch, he would hardly recommend the place to his wealthy clients.

Yet Bob didn't look upset. He looked more like a man making bets with himself, and winning.

When Bob realized that Alana was watching him, he smiled at her.

"Some homecoming, sis," Bob said, shaking his head.

"Yes," she whispered. "Some homecoming."

Yawning, Bob looked at the wristwatch he always wore.

"Well, there's not much point in me going back to sleep," Bob said, stretching. "I'll start working on the pack string. Stan, you said you wanted to watch a real cowboy at work. Still game?"

The faint challenge in Bob's voice brought a smile to Stan's face.

Quickly Alana looked away. The smile was like an echo of Jack, charming and boyish. Stan was a very handsome man . . . and Alana's skin crawled every time she looked at him.

It wasn't rational or fair to Stan, but it wasn't something she could control, either.

"I'll be glad to help you," drawled Stan, "seeing as how you're such a puny thing."

Bob looked startled, then laughed out loud. He clapped Stan on the shoulder and led him toward the kitchen. Bob's voice drifted back as the two huge men left the room.

"Merry left some coffee warming. We'll need it. And I've got a jacket that I think will fit you, seeing as how you're such a puny thing, too."

Listening, Alana realized that her brother liked Stan. That was different from before, from Jack. Bob hadn't liked Jack at all. None of the Burdettes had.

Alana heard Stan's laughter trailing back into the living room, laughter as charming as his smile. Yet, unlike the smile, Stan's laughter didn't remind Alana of Jack. Jack had rarely laughed, and never at himself.

Even so, she was glad that Stan was out of sight. It was unnerving to catch a glimpse of him out of the corner of her eye, blond shades of Jack stalking behind her. She let out a long sigh as the kitchen door slammed, telling her that the two men were on the way to the barn.

"Okay?" asked Rafe, feeling the deep breath Alana had taken and let out, for her back was still pressed against his chest.

Alana nodded. "He—he's nice, isn't he?"

Rafe grunted, a sound that told her nothing.

"Bob likes him," said Alana.

"They're a lot alike," Rafe said dryly. "Muscle and impulse in equal amounts and places."

"Between their ears?" suggested Alana.

"Sometimes." Rafe sighed. "Just sometimes."

Alana shifted her weight slightly. The movement reminded her that she was standing very close to Rafe, all but leaning on him. The contact didn't bother her. He wasn't touching her. She was touching him.

The difference was both subtle and infinitely reassuring. The warmth of Rafe's bare chest radiated through the flannel shirt and her damp silk nightshirt, a warmth as natural as the embers glowing in the living room hearth.

For an instant Alana wanted to turn and wrap herself in his warmth, chasing away the chill that had come the day they'd told her that Rafe was dead.

She shivered again, but not from cold.

"You should try to sleep a little more," Rafe said. "You're still on West Coast time."

He was so close to Alana that she felt the vibration of his chest as he spoke, the subtle movement of his muscles as he bent slightly toward her, and the brush of his breath over her ear. She closed her eyes, savoring a tactile intimacy that demanded nothing from her.

"I feel safer here with you," she said simply.

Alana felt Rafe's quick, subdued breath and realized what she had said. She tensed, knowing that if Rafe accepted her unintended invitation and put his arms around her, she had only herself to blame.

The worst of it was that part of her very much wanted his arms around her.

And part of her panicked at the thought of being held.

Suddenly Alana wondered if Jack had been

holding her when they fell, if that was why she froze at a man's touch.

Does my mind equate the act of being embraced with falling and terror and death? Alana asked herself silently.

She stiffened, listening intently, hoping to hear an inner voice say *yes* or *no*, hoping to tear the veil of amnesia and look upon just a few minutes of those six missing days.

The only answer, if answer it was, came in the sudden coldness of her skin, nausea turning in her stomach, her heart beating quickly, erratically.

"What's wrong?" asked Rafe, sensing the change in Alana. Then, sadly, "Does being close to me frighten you?"

"No, it's not that. I was thinking of Jack."

Behind Alana, Rafe's expression changed, tightening in anger and defeat. But his voice was neutral when he spoke.

"Did you love him?"

Alana closed her eyes.

"No," she said flatly. "I didn't love him."

"Then why did you marry him so fast? Not even two months after—"

Abruptly Rafe stopped speaking.

"They told me you were dead," Alana said, her voice ragged. "Music was all that was left to me. And that meant Jack, a voice to make angels weep."

"I'm sorry," said Rafe, stepping backward. "I had no right to ask."

Rafe's voice was neutral, distant, and Alana's back felt cold without his warmth. She spun around, suddenly angry, remembering the letter that had come back, Rafe's own handwriting telling her that he didn't want to say anything to her, not even good-bye.

"That's correct," Alana said tightly. "You have no right. You didn't even open my letter."

"You were another man's woman."

Rafe's voice was as opaque as his eyes, his mouth a thin line of remembered anger beneath his dark mustache.

"I never belonged to Jack. Not like that."

"You were his wife. Didn't that mean anything to you?"

"Yes," Alana said harshly. *"It meant you were dead!"*

Tears spilled suddenly down her cheeks. She spun away, wanting only to be alone, not to be torn between a past she couldn't change and a present that was trying to destroy her.

"Alana, please don't turn away."

Rafe's voice was gentle, coaxing, making subtle music out of her name. She knew without turning around that he was holding his hand out to her, asking her for something she could not give.

Trust. Caring. Warmth. Passion. Love. All the things she needed but no longer believed in. Not really.

Those things had been taken away from her once too often. She had survived her mother's death. She had survived her lover's death. She had survived her husband's death.

Now Alana was trying to survive a different

kind of death, a shattering loss of belief in her own strength, her own mind, her music. Now she was trying not to ask herself if it was worth it, any of it, if there was no end to fear and loss and death.

"I'm sorry, wildflower. I shouldn't have brought up the past. It's too soon. You're too close to what happened on Broken Mountain."

Rafe walked to Alana, not stopping until he felt the cool, rough flannel he had draped around her shoulders rubbing against his chest. She sensed his arm moving and held her breath, anticipating his touch, not knowing whether she would run or scream or stand quietly.

It was agony not to know, not to be able to trust anything, most of all herself.

"No," Alana said hoarsely, stepping away. "I can't take any more. Leave me alone, Rafe."

"Is it the letter? Is that what you can't forgive me for?" Rafe asked sadly.

"No. It's worse than the letter, although that was bad enough, losing you a second time . . ."

Alana's voice died.

"If not the letter, what?" Rafe said softly, urgently. "What have I done? *What are your memories?*"

At first Alana thought she wasn't going to tell him. Then words rushed out of her in a bittersweet torrent.

"After you, I couldn't bear another man's touch. God, how Jack hated you! You ruined me for any other man."

Rafe's face changed, all anger and urgency gone, only hunger remaining. He reached for Alana and could not help protesting when she flinched away.

"Alana. Don't. Please."

She turned and looked at Rafe with eyes that were wild and dark, shadows as deep as despair.

"Jack got even with me, though," Alana whispered. "Somehow he ruined me for any man at all. Even you!"

Alana turned and fled up the stairs, not stopping even when Rafe called out her name in a voice hoarse with emotion, a cry out of her dreams and nightmares.

She locked the bedroom door behind her and stared out the window until dawn came, bringing color and life to the black land. She watched the world change, born anew out of the empty night.

Just as the last star faded, she heard Bob's voice.

"Sis? You awake?"

Alana realized she was shivering, her skin icy, roughened by gooseflesh. Every muscle ached with the tension that hadn't left her since Broken Mountain. Now she faced another day like all the other days.

But not quite. This day would bring the exquisite torture of being close to the only man she had ever loved. So close and yet so very, very far away.

Dream and nightmare and nothing in between, no safety, no port in the unending, violent storm.

"Alana?"

"Yes," she said tiredly. "I'm awake."

"Don't sound so happy about it," teased Bob.

Alana tugged the flannel shirt more firmly around her, opened the door, and pulled her mouth into the semblance of a smile.

"Morning, little brother," she said, grateful that her voice sounded better than she felt. "Is it time for me to cook breakfast?"

"Nope. Merry's doing the honors this morning. I just came up to get your gear."

Alana gestured toward the small duffel bag on the bed.

"Have at it," she said.

"That's all?"

"This is a pack trip, right? I don't think the trees will care how I'm dressed," Alana said, shrugging.

"Er, right."

Bob gave his sister a sidelong glance, then asked softly, "Are you sure you're up to this?"

"What does that have to do with it?" asked Alana sardonically. "Ready or not, here life comes."

She smiled to take the sting out of her words, but she could tell from Bob's look that she hadn't been very convincing.

"It's okay, Bob. Not to worry. I'm doing fine. Just fine."

He hesitated, then nodded. "Like Dr. Gene says, Burdettes are survivors. And you're the toughest Burdette of all, sis. You taught the rest of us how to survive after Mom died."

Alana blinked back sudden tears.

"Would you mind very much if I hugged you?" she asked.

Bob looked startled, then pleased. Remembering Rafe's blunt instructions, Bob kept his arms at his sides while Alana gave him a hard hug.

"You're stronger than you feel," said Bob, patting her slender shoulder.

Alana laughed strangely and shook her head.

"I hope so, baby brother. I hope so."

"Are you—are you remembering anything now that you're home?" asked Bob in a rush. Then, "Damn, there I go! Rafe will nail my dumb hide to the barn if he finds out."

Alana stiffened at Rafe's name.

"What happens between me and my brother is none of Rafe's business."

Bob laughed. "Don't you believe it, sis. That is one determined man. Makes a pack mule look positively wishy-washy."

She looked narrowly at her brother.

"You don't resent Rafe, though, do you?" Alana asked.

Surprised, Bob stared down at Alana. His dark eyes, so like her own, narrowed as he measured the emotion on her face.

"Rafe is quite a man. I don't resent learning from him. Granted," said Bob with a smile, "he's a jealous son of a bitch. I thought he was going to fieldstrip Stan and feed him to the coyotes."

Alana blinked, seeing the previous night through Bob's eyes, a totally different view.

"Jealous?" she asked.

Bob snapped his fingers and waved his hands in front of her face.

"Wake up, sis. Stan wouldn't have minded, er, soothing you. And Rafe has made it pretty plain that..."

Shrugging, Bob shut up, his caution for once getting the better of his tongue.

"Rafe cares about you," Bob said, "and Stan is bigger, stronger, and better looking than Rafe. No surprise that Rafe's jealous."

"Stan's bigger," agreed Alana, "but it was Stan who ended up flat on his back. And there's more to looks than blond hair, bulging muscles, and a big smile. A lot more."

Bob grinned. "Does that mean you've forgiven Rafe for not opening your letter?"

Alana's face changed, darkness and grief clear on her features. Bob swore.

"Goddamnit, sis. I'm sorry. I'll never learn when to keep my big mouth shut."

"Sure you will," said Rafe from the doorway, "even if I have to pound the lessons into your thick skull one by one with a twenty-pound sledgehammer."

Alana spun around and saw Rafe lounging against the door frame, his rich brown hair alive with sunlight, his mouth hard and yet oddly sensual, his face expressionless except for the whiskey eyes burning with suppressed emotion.

Distantly she wondered how Bob could think that Stan was better looking than the utterly male Rafe.

And then Alana wondered how much of the conversation Rafe had overheard.

"Morning, Rafe," said Bob with a cheerful grin.

He turned and grabbed Alana's duffel off the bed, ignoring both of them.

Rafe simply looked at Alana. The flannel shirt she still wore was in shades of russet and orange and chocolate brown. The long tails came nearly to her knees, and the sleeve cuffs lapped over her fingertips, making her look very small, very fragile. Only in her face and in her movements did her strength show, a woman's strength made of grace and endurance.

A wildflower with pale cheeks and haunted eyes, watching him.

The sound of Bob unzipping Alana's duffel bag seemed very loud in the silence. He rummaged for a few seconds, muttered under his breath, and went to the closet where she had left her clothes after the last disastrous visit.

Bob ran a critical eye over the contents of the closet, then began pulling bright blouses and slacks off hangers. He hesitated between a scarlet dress and a floor-length indigo wraparound that was shot through with metallic gold threads.

"Which one of these travels best?" asked

Bob, looking over his shoulder at Alana.

With a start, Alana pulled her attention away from Rafe. She saw Bob in front of her closet, his arms overflowing with color and silk. In his large hands, the clothes looked exquisitely feminine, as intimate as French lingerie.

"What are you doing?" asked Alana.

"Packing for my big sister," Bob said patiently. "As cute as you look in Rafe's flannel shirt, that wasn't what I had in mind when I told the dudes we dressed for dinner. This is a classy operation, remember?"

Alana looked down at the big flannel shirt folded around her like a warm blanket.

Rafe's shirt.

The thought disturbed Alana. She had assumed that the shirt belonged to Bob.

"Sis? Anybody home?"

"Oh. Um, the dark blue one packs best."

Bob began folding the wraparound with more determination than expertise.

Alana started to object, then shrugged. Whatever Bob did to the silk could be steamed out at the other end. But when he went back to the closet for more clothes, and then more, she finally protested.

"How long are we staying on Broken Mountain?" she asked.

"As long as it takes," Bob said laconically, folding bright clothes.

"As long as what takes?"

"Finding out what—"

Abruptly Rafe's voice cut across Bob's.

"As long as it takes to convince the dudes that Broken Mountain is a good place to send clients. Right, Burdette?"

Bob gritted his teeth.

"Right," he said, folding clothes industriously. "I'm counting on your cooking to win them over, sis."

"But—" began Alana.

"But nothing," Bob said suddenly.

His dark eyes looked at Alana with a combination of affection and maturity that was new to him.

"You signed on for the duration, sis. Get used to the idea. No running out this time, no matter what happens. We'll come after you if you do. Right, Rafe?"

"Right," said Rafe, looking narrowly at Bob. "You're learning, Burdette."

"And not a sledgehammer in sight," pointed out Bob, smiling widely.

Rafe glanced at Alana and saw her baffled look.

"Better get dressed," Rafe said as he went back into the hallway. "Breakfast is getting cold."

Bob zipped up Alana's bag and left her standing in the room with a bemused look on her face.

"Hurry up, sis. Like Dad always used to say, 'You can't keep the mountain waiting.' "

The phrase from her childhood gave Alana a dizzying sense of déjà vu. She remembered her first pack trip up Broken Mountain. She had been only nine and wild with pride that her father was taking her on a fishing expedition, just the two of them together. It had been a wonderful time, full of campfires and long conversations while stars moved in slow motion overhead like a silent, glittering symphony.

It hadn't been like that the last time, when she and Jack had gone up the mountain.

Six days gone.

Six blank days poisoning past memories, poisoning each day, poisoning her; Broken Mountain looming over her with inhuman patience, waiting, waiting.

For what? Alana asked silently. For me to die, too?

You can't keep the mountain waiting.

With a shudder Alana turned away from her thoughts, dressed quickly, and went downstairs. The thought of food didn't appeal to her. She avoided the dining room, where she heard laughter and strange voices, Stan's and the woman whom Alana hadn't officially met. She didn't feel up to meeting Janice Simpson right now, either.

Quietly Alana let herself out the front door, then circled around to the barn where the pack mules waited patiently.

There were five horses lined up at the hitching posts. One horse was a magnificent Appaloosa stallion. Two were good-looking bays, their brown hides glossy in the sun. Of the two remaining horses, one was as black as midnight and one was a big, dapple-gray gelding.

Alana went to the black mare and stood for a moment, letting the velvet muzzle *whuff* over

her, drinking her scent. When the mare returned to a relaxed posture, accepting Alana's
presence, she ran her hand down the animal's
muscular legs and picked up each hoof, check-
ing for stones or loose nails in the shoes.

"Well, Sid," Alana said as she straightened
up from the last hoof, "are you ready for that
long climb and that rotten talus slope at the
end?"

Sid snorted.

Alana checked the cinch and stirrup length,
talking softly all the while, not hearing Rafe
approach behind her.

"Good-looking mare," said Rafe, his voice
neutral.

Alana checked the bridle, then stepped back
to admire the horse.

"Sid's a beauty, all right, but the best thing
about her is the way she moves," Alana said.
"She just flattens out those mountain trails."

"Sid?" Rafe asked, his voice tight.

"Short for Obsidian," explained Alana, returning to the bridle. "You know, that shiny
black volcanic glass."

"Yes, I know," he said softly. "You say she
has a good trail gait?"

"Yes," Alana said absently, her attention
more on loosening the strap beneath the bit
than on the conversation. "Riding her is like
riding a smooth black wind. A real joy. Not a
mean hair on her shiny hide."

"She didn't mind the talus?" continued Rafe
in a voice that was restrained, tight with emotion.

"No. The gray didn't like it much, though," said Alana, rearranging the mare's forelock so it wouldn't be pulled by the leather straps.

"The gray?" Rafe asked.

"Jack's horse," she said casually, gesturing toward the big dapple-gray gelding. "It—"

Alana blinked. Suddenly her hands began to shake. She spun and faced Rafe.

"It balked," she said urgently. "The gray balked. And then Jack—Jack—"

She closed her eyes, willing the memories to come. All that came was the thunder of her own heartbeat. She made an anguished sound.

"It's gone!" Alana cried. "I can't remember anything!"

"You remembered something," said Rafe, his whiskey eyes intent. "That's a start."

"Jack's horse balked. Six seconds out of six days." Alana's hands clenched until her fingernails dug deeply into her palms. "Six lousy seconds!"

"That's not all you remembered."

"What do you mean?"

"Sid. You walked out here today and picked her out of a row of horses without any hesitation at all."

"Of course. I've always ridden—" Alana stopped, a startled look on her face. "I can't remember the first time I rode Sid."

"Bob bought her two months ago. He hadn't named her by the time you and Jack came up. You named her, Alana.

"And then you rode her up Broken Mountain."

7

THE FIRST HALF OF THE eight-hour ride to the fishing cabins on the Winter ranch wasn't strenuous. The trail wound through evergreens and along a small, boulder-strewn river that drained a series of lakes higher up the mountain. The air was vibrant with light and fragrance.

The horses' hooves made a soothing, subtly syncopated beat that permeated Alana's subconscious, setting up tiny earthquakes of remembrance beneath amnesia's opaque mantle.

Little things.

Simple things.

Sunlight fanning through a pine branch, stilettos of gold and quivering green needles.

The ring of a horse's steel-shod hoof against stone. The liquid crystal of a brook sliding through shadows. The creak of a saddle beneath a man's shifting weight.

The pale flash of blond hair just off her shoulder when Jack's gray horse crowded against Sid's side.

No, not Jack's horse, Alana corrected instantly. Stan's horse. Jack is dead and the sky over Broken Mountain is clear. No clouds, no thunder, no ice storm poised to flay my unprotected skin and make walking a treacherous joke.

There was sunlight now, hot and pouring, blazing over her, warming her all the way to her bones. She was hot, not cold. Her hands were flexible, not numb and useless. Her throat wasn't a raw sore from too many screams.

It was just rigid with the effort of not screaming now.

Deliberately Alana swallowed and unclenched her hands from the reins. She wiped her forehead, beaded with cold sweat despite the heat of the day.

She didn't notice Bob's concerned looks or the grim line of Rafe's mouth. When Rafe called for an early lunch, she thought nothing of it, other than that she would have a few minutes of relief, a few minutes longer before she had to face Broken Mountain's savage heights.

Alana dismounted and automatically loosened the cinch. She was a little stiff from the ride, but it wasn't anything that a bit of walking wouldn't cure.

Janice, however, wasn't as resilient. She groaned loudly and leaned against her patient horse. Rafe came up and offered his arm. Janice took it and walked a few painful steps. Alana watched the woman's chestnut hair gleam in the sun and heard Janice's feminine, rueful laughter joined by the deep, male sound of Rafe's own amusement.

Slowly the two of them walked back down the line of horses on the opposite side of the trail, coming closer to Alana, who was all but invisible as she leaned on Sid.

Envy turned in Alana as she watched Janice with Rafe. To be able to accept touch so casually. To laugh. To feel Rafe's strength and warmth so close and not be afraid. To remember everything.

Did Janice know how lucky she was? And did she have to cling so closely to Rafe that her breasts pressed against his arm?

Alana closed her eyes and choked off her uncharitable thoughts. Obviously Janice wasn't at all accustomed to riding. Her legs must feel like cooked spaghetti. Yet she hadn't complained once in the four hours since they had left the ranch.

Bob had demanded a brisk pace, wanting to reach Five Lakes Lodge on Broken Mountain before the late-afternoon thundershowers materialized. The hard ride hadn't been easy on the two dudes, who weren't accustomed either to riding or to the increasingly thin air as the trail climbed toward timberline.

But no one had objected to the pace. Not even Stan, who had good reason to be feeling irritable.

Stan, who had been first screamed at and then attacked with no warning, laid out flat, choking beneath Rafe's hard arm.

Blood rose in Alana's cheeks as she remembered last night's fiasco. She put her face against the smooth leather of the saddle, cooling her hot skin.

Stan came up on the other side of Janice and took her arm, supporting her. She smiled up at him in rueful thanks. The smile was vivid, inviting, a perfect foil for Janice's clear blue eyes. Stan smiled back with obvious male appreciation.

"I'll leave you in Stan's capable hands," said Rafe, withdrawing. "But don't go too far. We have to be back on the trail within half an hour."

The big blond man looked at the meadow just beyond the trees, where several trails snaked off in various directions.

"Which trail?" asked Stan.

"That one."

Rafe pointed toward the rugged shoulder of Broken Mountain, looming at the end of the meadow.

Janice groaned and rolled her eyes.

"Only for you, Rafe Winter," she muttered, "would I get on that damned horse again and ride up that god-awful trail."

Alana lifted her head and looked over Sid's
back with sudden, intense curiosity. Janice's
words, her ease with Rafe, everything about
the two of them together added up to people
who had known each other longer than a few
hours. Stan, too, seemed familiar with Rafe,
more like an old friend than a new client for
Broken Mountain Dude Ranch.

As Janice and Stan hobbled off down the
trail, Rafe smiled after them with a combination of affection and amusement. Alana
watched both the smile and the man, and she
wondered how well Rafe knew Stan and Janice.

Especially Janice.

As though Rafe sensed Alana's scrutiny, he
looked up and saw the black of her hair blending perfectly with Sid's shiny hide. Other than
her eyes and hair, Alana was hidden behind
the horse's bulk.

"You know them," Alana said when she
saw the whiskey eyes watching her. Her voice
sounded accusing.

Rafe waited for a long moment, then
shrugged.

"I used to travel a lot. The two of them were
my favorite agents." He smiled swiftly,
amused by a private joke. "We've done a lot
of business together, one way or another."

"She's very attractive."

There was a question mark in Alana's eyes,
if not in her voice.

Rafe glanced in the direction of Janice, now
well down the trail, leaning on Stan.

"Yes, I suppose she is," said Rafe, his voice indifferent. Then he turned suddenly, pinning Alana with amber eyes. "So is Stan."

"Not to me."

"Because he reminds you of Jack?"

Alana thought of lying, then decided it was too much trouble. It was hard enough to keep dream separate from nightmare. If she started lying to herself and to Rafe, it would become impossible to separate the threads of reality from the snarl of amnesia and unreality.

"Stan isn't attractive to me because he isn't you."

Rafe's nostrils flared with the sudden intake of his breath. Before he could speak, Alana did, her voice both haunted and unflinching.

"But it doesn't matter that you're attractive to me and other men aren't," she said, her voice low, "because it's too late."

"No."

Rafe said nothing more. He didn't have to. Every line of his strong body rejected what she said.

Slowly Alana shook her head, making sunlight slide and burn in her black hair.

"I can't handle any more, Rafe," she said, a thread of desperation in her voice. "I can't handle you and the past and today, what was and what wasn't, what is and what isn't. Just getting through the days is hard enough, and the nights . . ."

Alana took a sharp breath, fighting to control herself. It was harder each hour, each minute, for her mind was screaming at her that with every moment, every foot up the trail to Broken Mountain, she came closer to death.

Her death.

It was irrational. She knew it. But knowing didn't stop the fear.

"Seeing you and then remembering the days before and knowing that it will never again ..." said Alana in a rush.

Her breath came out raggedly, almost a sob. She closed her dark eyes, not wanting to reveal the hunger and fear and helplessness seething inside her.

"I just can't!" Alana said.

"No," countered Rafe, his voice both soft and certain. "I lost you once. I won't lose you again. Unless you don't want me?"

Alana made a sound that was halfway between a laugh and a sob.

"I've never wanted anyone else, for all the good that does either one of us," she said. "It wasn't enough in the past, was it? And it isn't enough now. *Even you can't touch me.*"

"It's been hardly a month," Rafe said reasonably. "Give yourself time to heal."

"I'm starting to hate myself," she said.

Alana's voice was husky with the effort it took to speak rationally about the panic that was turning her strength to water and then draining even that away.

"I'm a coward," she whispered. "Hiding behind amnesia."

"That's not true!"

Alana looked longingly at Rafe, an unattainable dream.

"Yes, it is," she said. "I shouldn't have come back. I'm getting worse, not better."

Rafe's face showed an instant of pain that made Alana catch her breath.

"Was it better for you in Portland?" he asked, his voice quiet, almost without inflection.

Slowly Alana shook her head.

"No. When I slept the nightmares came, more each time, and worse. I'd wake up and fight myself. Hate myself. That's why I'm here. I thought . . ."

Rafe waited, but when Alana didn't say any more, he asked, "What did you think?"

She took a deep, shuddering breath, then another.

"I thought there was something here for me, something that would help me to be strong again. Something that would . . ."

Alana's voice broke but she went on, forcing herself to tell Rafe what she had told no one else.

"Something that would let me sing again," she whispered.

Rafe wondered if he had heard correctly. Her voice was so soft, so frayed.

"What do you mean?" asked Rafe.

"I haven't sung since Broken Mountain. I can't. Every time I try, my throat just closes."

Alana looked at Rafe desperately, wondering if he knew how much singing meant to her.

"Singing was all I had left after you died," she said. "And now I can't sing. Not one note.

Nothing. You're alive now, and I can't bear to be touched. *And I can't sing.*"

Rafe's eyes closed. He remembered the sliding, supple beauty of Alana's voice soaring with his harmonica's swirling notes, Alana's face radiant with music and love as she sang to him.

He wanted to reassure her, protect her, love her, give her back song and laughter, all that the past had taken from her and from him. Yet everything he did brought Alana more pain, more fear.

She could not sing.

He could not hold her.

Rafe swore softly, viciously. When his eyes opened they were clear and hard, and pain was a darkness pooling in their depths.

"I'll take you back down the mountain, Alana. And then I'll leave you alone if that's what you want. I can't bear hurting you like this."

"Rafe," she said, catching her breath, touching his cheek with fingers that trembled. "None of this is your fault."

"All of it is," he said harshly. "I leaned on Bob to get you back here. Now you're here and everything I do hurts you."

"That isn't true," said Alana.

She couldn't bear knowing that she had hurt Rafe. She had never wanted that, even in the worst times after her letter had come back unopened.

"Isn't it?" Rafe asked.

He looked at her with narrow amber eyes.

His anger at himself showed in his lips, sensual curves flattened into a hard line.

"No, it isn't true," she whispered.

But words weren't enough to convince Rafe. Alana could see his disbelief in his grim expression. If she could have sung her emotions to him, he would have believed her, but she couldn't sing.

Hesitantly she lifted her hand to Rafe's face, the face that had smiled and laughed and loved her in her memories, in her dreams. He had always been a song inside her, even in the worst of times.

Especially then, when nightmare and ice avalanched around her, smothering her. He had given her so much, reality and dream and hope. Surely she could give something of that back to him now, when his eyes were dark with pain and anger at himself.

Alana's fingertips pushed beneath the brim of Rafe's Stetson until it tipped back on his head and slid unnoticed to the ground. Fingers spread wide, she eased into the rich warmth of his hair.

"You do feel like winter mink, Rafael," she murmured, giving his name its liquid Spanish pronunciation, making a love song out of the three syllables. "Rafael . . . Rafael. You feel better than in my dreams of you. And my dreams of you are good. They are what kept me sane since Broken Mountain."

Alana felt the fine trembling that went through Rafe, the outrush of his breath that was her name. For an instant she was afraid he would touch her, breaking the spell.

Instead, he moved his head slowly, rubbing against her hand like a big cat. He closed his eyes and concentrated on the feel of her fingers sliding deeply through his hair.

His sensual intensity sent a new kind of weakness through Alana, fire licking down her fingers and radiating through her body, fire deep inside her, burning.

Rafe's dense brown lashes shifted as he looked at Alana, holding her focused in the hungry amber depths of his eyes.

"I've dreamed of you," he said. "Of this."

Alana said nothing, for she could not. Her fingers tightened in his hair, searching deeply, as though she would find something in his thick male pelt that she had lost and all but given up hope of ever finding again.

Even when the sound of Janice and Stan walking back up the row of horses reminded Alana that she and Rafe weren't alone, even then she couldn't bring herself to withdraw from the rich sensation of his hair sliding between her fingers.

Bob's voice cut through Alana's trance.

"Twenty minutes to trail time, everyone," he called from the front of the line of pack mules. "If you haven't eaten lunch, you'll regret it."

Slowly, reluctantly, Alana released the silk and warmth of Rafe's hair. Just before her hand dropped to her side again, her fingertips paused to smooth the crisp hairs of his mustache, a caress as light as sunshine.

He moved his head slowly, sliding his lips over the sensitive pads of her fingers. When her hand no longer touched him, he bent swiftly, retrieved his hat, and settled it into place with an easy tug.

"Bob's right about food," Rafe said, his voice husky and warm. "You didn't have breakfast."

Alana shook her head, though it hadn't been a question.

"I forgot to pack lunch," she admitted.

"Merry packed enough for twenty in my saddlebag." Then, smiling, Rafe added in a coaxing voice, "Share it with me, Alana. Even wildflowers have to eat something."

Beneath his teasing was real concern. Alana was thinner than he had ever seen her. Too thin, too finely drawn, like an animal that had been hunted too long.

"Roast beef, apples, homemade bread, chocolate chip cookies . . ." he murmured.

Alana's mouth watered. She licked her lips with unconscious hunger.

"Sold," she said breathlessly.

She and Rafe ate in the shifting shade of a windblown pine. They sat side by side, almost touching, sharing his canteen. The mint-flavored tea Merry had made for Rafe tasted extraordinary in the clean mountain air.

Alana ate hungrily, enjoying food for the first time in weeks. Rafe watched her, smiling. This, too, had been part of his dreams. Alana and the mountains and him.

When everything else in his life had reeked

of death and betrayal, he had dreamed of her.

"Saddle up," called Bob.

Alana stopped, her hand halfway into the paper bag of cookies. Rafe scooped up the bag and handed it to her.

"Take them," he said, smiling.

"Are you sure? I don't want you to be hungry just because I was too stupid to remember my own lunch."

"There's another bag of cookies in there," Rafe assured her, gesturing to the saddlebags draped across his leg. "Apples, too."

He dug into the supple leather pouch and pulled out two apples.

"Here," he said. "One for you and one for Sid."

Rafe stood and pulled Alana to her feet with one hand, releasing her before she had time to be afraid.

"I'd better help Janice," he said. "She's going to be sore."

Alana winced slightly, flexing her legs.

"She's not the only one," Alana muttered. "Although, considering that it's been more than a year since I rode this hard, I'm not very sore at all."

Then Alana heard the echo of her own words. Her face changed, tension coming back to her in a rush.

"That's not true, is it?" she said, her voice raw. "It hasn't been a year. It's been less than a month. Why can't I remember?"

"Alana," said Rafe urgently.

He bent over her, so close that he could see

the pulse beating in her throat, smell the minty sweetness of her breath. Close but not touching her, afraid to hold her and bring back nightmares in place of dreams.

"Alana, don't. Clawing at yourself won't help you heal."

She drew several long, ragged breaths. Her eyes opened again, very dark but not as wild. She nodded almost curtly, then turned and went back to her horse, clutching a bag of cookies in one hand and two forgotten apples in the other.

The rest of the ride became a waking nightmare for Alana. It began with the first of the five Paternoster lakes, so named because they were strung out like beads on a rosary, shining circles of blue water joined by silver cascades.

The first, lowest lake was at six thousand feet and the highest was just above eight thousand. Pines grew down to the shores of the lower lakes, making dark green exclamation points against the silver-gray boulders that embraced the transparent water. The first lake was beautiful, reflecting the sky in endless shades of blue, serene and quiet.

And after one look, Alana felt fear rise and begin to prowl the corridors of her mind. She heard thunder belling from a cloudless sky, saw violent lightning in every golden shaft of sunshine, heard Jack's voice where nothing but ravens spoke from high overhead.

Gradually, without realizing it, Alana's hands tightened on the reins until Sid fretted, tossing her sleek black head. After a time, Alana's nervousness was reflected in Sid's actions. A line of foam grew around the steel bit. The horse's long, easy stride became a mincing walk. Streaks of sweat radiated from Sid's flanks despite the coolness of the air.

The pressure of Alana's hands on the bit increased by subtle increments until finally Sid stopped. But even then the pressure didn't decrease.

Sid shook her head repeatedly, seeking freedom from the bit.

"Alana."

Rafe's voice was soft and undemanding, despite the harshness of his expression as he watched Alana's blank, unfocused eyes. He leaned over and pulled forward slowly on the reins, easing them out of her rigid fingers. Gradually the thin leather strips slid free, ending the relentless pressure of the bit.

"It's all right, wildflower," murmured Rafe. "I've come to take you home."

Alana blinked and looked around with eyes that were still caught between nightmare and reality.

"Rafael . . . ?"

"I'm here."

Alana sighed and flexed hands that were cramped from the tension of hanging onto reins as though they were a rope pulling her up out of a nightmare. She started to speak, couldn't, and swallowed. The second time she tried, her throat no longer closed around her dead husband's name.

"Jack and I rode this way."

Beneath the shadow of the hat brim, Rafe's narrowed eyes looked like brilliant lines of topaz. He knew that the trail they were on was only one of three trails that led to Five Lakes Lodge. If Alana recognized this particular trail, she must be remembering at least parts of the six lost days.

"You're sure," said Rafe, no question in his voice.

She nodded stiffly. "The first storm began here."

"The first?"

"There were several, I think. Or was it just one long storm?"

She frowned intently, reaching for memories that vanished even as she touched them.

"I don't remember!" Then, more calmly, Alana said, "I don't remember."

She closed her eyes, hiding the shadows that haunted her.

When Alana finally opened her eyes again, she was living only in the present. Rafe and the two horses were waiting patiently. No one else was in sight.

"Where is everyone?" she asked.

"Over the next ridge. I told them we'd catch up later, if you felt well enough."

Distantly Alana wondered what the two dudes thought of her. A woman with strange moods. Hysterical.

Crazy.

The word kept ringing in Alana's mind, an interior thunder drowning out the rational words she kept trying to think of, to cling to.

"Am I crazy?" Alana wondered aloud, not realizing she had spoken. "Or does it matter? If sanity is terror, is there peace in madness? Or is there only greater terror?"

Abruptly Alana shuddered.

"You aren't crazy," Rafe said, his voice gentle and angry and sad. "Do you hear me, Alana? You aren't crazy. You've been beaten and terrified. You've seen your husband killed and you damn near died yourself. And then you were out of your head with shock and exposure. You've hardly eaten at all and slept even less since Broken Mountain."

Wide-eyed, Alana watched Rafe, feeling his words sink into her like sunlight.

"You aren't crazy," he said. "You're just at the end of your physical resources, driven right up to the edge of hallucination in order to keep reality at bay until you decide there's no choice but to face it."

Alana listened, heard the certainty of Rafe's voice, heard the state of her mind and body described so precisely in his deep tones.

"How did you know?" she asked achingly.

"It happens to people when they're pushed too hard, too long."

Slowly Alana shook her head. "Not to strong people. Like you. I used to think I was strong."

Rafe laughed. It was a harsh sound, almost cruel.

"Anyone can be broken, Alana. Anyone. I know. I saw it happen in Central America time and time again."

"Rafe," she whispered.

"They said that I died. For a long time I believed them. It was like dying, only worse. There was no end to it. And then it happened again here."

Alana searched Rafe's eyes and found emotions she had never seen in him before. Violence and hatred and a rage so deep it went all the way to his soul.

"What . . . what happened in Central America?" asked Alana.

Rafe's expression changed, becoming remote, shutting down, shutting her out. The muscles in his jaw flexed and he spoke slowly, with a reluctance that told Alana more than his words.

"I've never told anyone. But I'll tell you. On Broken Mountain, I'll tell you. Unless . . ." Rafe looked at her swiftly, concerned again. "Unless you want to turn back. I'll take you back, Alana. If that's what you want. Is that what you want?"

"I want to trust myself again, to trust my mind and my memory and my emotions," she said in a rush. "I want to be *me* again. And I want . . ."

Rafe waited, an expression of restraint and longing drawing his face into taut planes and angular shadows.

"What do you want?" he asked softly.

"You," Alana said simply. "I was never more myself than when I was with you."

But even as she spoke, she was shaking her

head, not believing that what she wanted was possible.

Rafe held out his hand, palm up, not touching Alana but asking that she touch him. She put her palm lightly on his.

"I'm yours, wildflower," said Rafe. "I have been since I saw you on that exposed trail with a lame horse and lightning all around. You were brave then. You're even more brave now."

"I don't feel brave."

"You came back to Broken Mountain. You're honest with yourself, and with me. If that isn't courage, I don't know what is."

Rafe's voice was deep and sure, conviction reflected in every syllable and in the amber clarity of his eyes as he watched her, approving of her.

With fingers that shook slightly, Alana brushed away the tears that starred her eyelashes. Teardrops gleamed on her fingertips as she almost smiled at him.

"Thank you," she said.

"For telling the truth?" Rafe smiled sadly. "I have a lot more truths for you. But not now."

"What do you mean?"

"My truths wouldn't help you now. And that's what I want. To help you, and me. We'll heal each other and then the past will stay where it belongs. In the past. Memories, not nightmares."

Rafe held out his other hand, palm up.

Alana put her hand in his, felt the strong

pulse in his wrist beneath her touch, saw the glitter of tears transferred from her fingertips to his smooth, tanned skin. Unerringly, he found the pulse point of her wrists and rested lightly against it, savoring the strong flow of her life beneath his fingertips.

"Are you ready for the mountain?" asked Rafe softly.

Slowly Alana withdrew her palms, letting his touch caress her from wrists to fingertips.

"I'm ready," she whispered.

8

FOR THE REST OF THE TRIP, Rafe and Alana rode side by side when the trail permitted. When it didn't, Alana rode first. When pieces of the nightmare condensed around her, she looked over her shoulder to reassure herself that it was Rafe rather than Jack who followed her.

The fragments of nightmare and memory came unexpectedly, out of sequence, torment- ing Alana because she couldn't be sure whether it was true memory or false night- mare that stalked her. When she heard Jack's voice raised in anger, she didn't know if it came from the far past or the recent past, or if the words were a creation of her own mind trying to fill in the six missing days.

Sometimes there was no doubt. The sound of wind through the aspens, the shiver of yellow leaves, the song sticking in her throat . . .

Those were real. Those she had heard before, seen before, felt before, and remembered only now. She and Jack had rested by the second lake, there, down by the glacier-polished boulder. They had drunk coffee from their individual canteens and watched trout fingerlings rise in the turquoise shallows.

Then the wind had come again, moving like a melancholy hand over the lake, stirring reflections into chaos, bringing the scent of the heights and storms boiling down.

Jack had watched the clouds seething around the lonely ridges. He had smiled. And he had said . . .

What had he said? Alana asked herself. Something about the land. Something. . . . Yes, that was it: *I always knew this country was good for something. I just never knew what.*

And then he had laughed.

Shivering, Alana drew an imaginary jacket around her shoulders. Sid stumbled slightly, jarring her into the present.

Alana loosened the reins, giving the horse more freedom. She looked over her shoulder. Rafe was there, riding the big Appaloosa stallion, his hat pulled low against the restless wind. She sensed his quick regard, his concern for her. She waved slightly, reassuring him that she was all right.

Other fragments of memory returned, hoofbeats following, wind twisting and booming between ridges, ice-tipped rain. An argument . . .

She and Jack had argued over something. The storm. And the fishing camp. She had wanted to stay at the Five Lakes Lodge until the storm passed. Jack had refused, even though the fishing camp's five buildings were deserted and looked as though they had been empty for years.

In the end Jack had won, but only because Alana couldn't bear to see the site of her greatest happiness standing blank-eyed and empty, cabin doors ajar and porches heaped with dead needles and random debris.

Everywhere she turned, she had seen shadows of Rafe. Every breath she drew had reminded her of the first time Rafe had made love to her, in the loft of the main cabin with a storm coming down, surrounding them. But she hadn't been afraid then. She had been an aspen shivering, and Rafe the mountain wind caressing her.

Sid snorted and shied as she came around the shoulder of an old landslide. Again, Alana was jarred out of the past. Bob was waiting there, riding the big bay mare that was his favorite.

"Everything okay?" asked Bob.

His dark glance roamed his sister's face, looking for and finding signs of strain.

"Yes," Alana said tightly.

"You don't look it," he said, blunt as only a brother can be.

"I'm remembering a few things. Little things."

"That's great!"

"Is it?" she countered quickly. Then, "Sorry. Of course it is."

"Have you told Rafe about remembering?"

Before Alana could answer, Bob was talking again, words rushing out in excitement and triumph.

"He was right!" Bob said, delight in every word. "He said you'd remember once you were here and knew it was safe. And neither doctor would let him go to Portland because—"

"*Burdette.*"

Rafe's whiplash voice stopped Bob's tumbling words.

Bob looked startled, then stricken. "Oh, God, I really stepped in it this time. Damn my big mouth anyway."

Rafe gave Bob a narrow glance that spoke volumes on the subject of loose lips and secrets.

Alana looked from Rafe to Bob, questions in her eyes, questions Rafe knew he would have to answer, questions whose answers she wasn't ready to hear. So he chose his truths and half-truths carefully.

"I told you I leaned on a few people to get you here," said Rafe.

Uncertainly, Alana nodded.

"When Merry couldn't be chief cook and tour guide, I thought of you," Rafe said. "It would be a perfect opportunity to get you back home, where you belonged."

Then Rafe looked toward Bob and spoke in a soft, cold voice. "Isn't that how you remember it, Burdette?"

"Rafe leaned like hell," Bob agreed, looking relieved. "Sis, you aren't mad, are you? I mean, about coming home? We just want what's right for you."

Alana sighed, caught as always by her affection for the brother who rarely had an unspoken thought.

"No, baby brother, I'm not mad. Maybe," she added, smiling crookedly, "I'm not even crazy."

Bob drew in his breath sharply. "Alana, what in hell gave you the idea that you were crazy?"

"What would you call it when someone runs scared from six missing days?"

"I'd call it shock," Rafe cut in smoothly. "Survival reflex. In a word, sanity."

He looked from Alana to Bob.

"Let's get to the camp," Rafe said. "That storm won't hold off forever."

There was an urgency in his voice that allowed no argument. He didn't want Alana to be caught in the open in a storm. Not now. She was off balance, easily startled, too tired. Too fragile.

She needed rest now, not a resurgence of nightmare and violence. It was enough that she had begun to remember. More than enough. He didn't want the past to rise up and rend the delicate fabric of trust binding her to him.

He didn't want her to remember too much, too soon. If she did, then he would lose her again. Only this time there would be no hope. She would be lost to him irrevocably, forever.

Don't remember all of it, wildflower, Rafe prayed silently. Not yet. Give us time to love again.

"Move it, Burdette," Rafe said aloud. "The storm won't wait much longer."

At Rafe's curt signal, Bob set a fast pace to the cabins. Rafe hoped that riding hard would keep Alana's mind in the present rather than in the nightmare he saw too often in her eyes.

Even after they reached the cabins, Rafe watched Alana without seeming to while she prepared supper. He saw no signs that the storm building outside the cabin was bothering her.

After dinner, Bob and Stan went to Janice's cabin for a round of poker and conversation. Alana didn't go. She spent as little time as possible near Stan.

Rafe, too, turned down the offer of cards. His excuse was the flies that needed to be tied for tomorrow's fishing. But he doubted Bob was fooled. He was certain Stan wasn't fooled. The cynical gleam in the big man's eyes said he knew Rafe wanted to be alone with Alana.

As Alana finished setting the table for tomorrow's breakfast, Rafe came back from turning off the generator for the night. He shrugged out of a yellow slicker that sparkled with rain. So far, the evening storm consisted mainly of fat drops randomly sprayed and distant mutters of thunder stalking elusive lightning.

Alana adjusted the wick on the kitchen light until it burned with a clear, steady glow. Rafe hung his slicker on a hook by the back door.

"Hope the dudes don't mind kerosene lamps," said Alana.

"So long as they can see the cards, they'll do just fine. Besides, it will nudge them into bed at a decent hour. Trout rise early. If you want to catch them, you'd better rise early, too."

Eyes the color of whiskey measured the signs of fatigue on Alana's face.

"You should think about going to bed," Rafe said.

"It's hardly even dark," she protested, despite the tiredness welling up in her.

She didn't want to be alone. Not yet. Not with lightning and thunder loose among the peaks.

"It won't be completely dark until nearly ten," Rafe said reasonably. "That's too late for you, if you're going to get up at five to cook breakfast. Tell you what, I'll do breakfast tomorrow. You sleep in."

"No," said Alana quickly. "You look like you haven't been sleeping too well, either. Besides, I came here to cook and that's what I'm going to do. If I get too tired, I'll take a nap tomorrow afternoon."

Rafe looked as though he was going to protest. Then he let out a long breath.

"Will the light bother you if I work down here for a while?" he asked.

Alana looked at the loft bedroom that was simply a partial second story. One "wall" of the room was a polished railing that prevented anyone from wandering out of bed and taking a fall to the living room floor. Curtains could be drawn across the opening of the loft, but that cut off the welcome currents of warmth rising from the hearth. Even though it was only the first week of September, the nights at sixty-three hundred feet crackled with the promise of winter.

"You won't bother me," said Alana. "I always sleep with the light on now."

Again, Rafe paused. Again, he said nothing, merely looked at Alana with eyes that saw everything, accepted everything, even her fear. Knowing that he didn't withdraw from or judge her gave Alana a small measure of acceptance of her own irrational feelings.

"Go to sleep, Alana. If you need anything, I'll be in the downstairs bedroom. So will Bob, unless he plays cards all night like a young fool." As Rafe turned toward the dining room, he added, "There's plenty of hot water for a bath."

The thought of a tub full of steaming water made Alana close her eyes and all but groan with pleasure.

"A hot bath. Damn. That's my idea of roughing it," she said emphatically.

Smiling, Rafe turned back to Alana. He leaned against the door between the living room and dining room.

"From what Dad told me, Mother and Grandmother felt the same way," Rafe said.

"How about you?"

"I'm not all that upset at having hot water," Rafe drawled. "Only thing that bothers me is that damn noisy generator. As for the rest, this is home for me. It took me a lot of years and pain to realize it, but it was worth it."

Slowly Rafe looked around the lodge, enjoying the vivid Indian blankets and brass camp lamps, the suede furniture and a fireplace big enough to stand in. Luxury and simplicity combined. The generator provided electricity for the refrigerator, the water pump, and the lights. The kitchen stove, which also heated water for the cabin, burned wood.

All that was lacking was telephone service. His father had taken care of that by adding a shortwave radio and a repeater on the nearby ridge. By tradition, though, the radio was reserved for emergencies.

Alana watched Rafe quietly, sensing his pleasure in his surroundings, a pleasure she shared. She had loved the Lazy W's lodge and cabins from the first time she saw them, when she and Rafe had raced a storm and lost. They had been drenched and laughing when they arrived.

They would have been cold, too, but the bright currents of passion that raced through them made a mockery of cold. He had started a fire in the hearth to dry their clothes. Then he had led her up to the loft and taught her about other kinds of fire, and the beauty that a man and a woman in love can bring to each other.

Alana blinked, coming back to the present, bringing with her part of the past's shimmering warmth. She saw Rafe watching her with hungry whiskey eyes, as though he knew what she had been thinking.

Or perhaps it was simply that Rafe, too, was remembering a storm and a loft and the woman he loved burning in his arms.

"I laid out your things in the bathroom," Rafe said.

"Thank you," Alana said, her voice almost husky.

Rafe nodded and turned away, leaving her alone.

The bath relaxed Alana, taking the soreness from her body and the tightness from her mind. When she pulled on the long, soft cotton nightgown and went up to the loft bedroom, Rafe was nowhere in sight.

The hearth fire was blazing hotly, ensuring that she wouldn't be chilled by the trip from the bathroom to bed. The bed itself had also been warmed. The metal warmer was still hot to the touch, the coals from the fireplace still glowing when she opened the lid. The covers had been turned down, inviting her to slide in and sleep deeply.

"Rafael," Alana said softly, though she

knew he couldn't hear. "Oh, Rafe, why does it have to be too late for us?"

There was no answer, unless the bed itself was an answer, a bridge between past and present, a promise of warmth and safety.

With a sigh, Alana discarded her robe and slid underneath the covers, pulling them up to her chin as she snuggled into the haven Rafe had so carefully prepared for her. Sleep came quickly.

So did dreams.

As the storm outside the cabin strengthened, dreams twisted into nightmares called by thunder and wind screaming from the ridge lines. A lake condensed around Alana . . . *a landscape subtly blurred, like water pushed by the wind. A glacier-polished boulder stood crookedly, laughing.*

Jack was laughing and the sound was colder than the wind.

Rain swirled, laughing, showing clear ice teeth, stirring water and rocks and trees until another lake condensed. Small, perfect, utterly real but for the shadows of terror flowing out of the trees.

Jack's arms reaching for her, his words telling her of desire and his eyes telling her of death. Jack holding her despite her struggles and then pain came, pain and terror and her screams tearing apart her world.

Alana woke with her heart pounding and her skin clammy. She was breathing in short, shallow bursts. She had recognized the third lake in her nightmare, but not the other lake, the beautiful lake surrounded by horror.

Jack, too, was new, unrecognizable, desire and death inextricably mixed. A raw nightmare, a horrible compound of today's memories and . . . what?

Truth? Imagination? Both? Neither? Alana asked herself frantically. Jack wanted me, yes, but only as the other half of Jack 'n' Jilly. He didn't want me as a woman.

And if he had, it wouldn't have mattered. I didn't want him. I never wanted any man but the one I loved and couldn't have. Rafael Winter. Jack didn't like it, but he finally accepted it—after I told him I would leave him if he ever touched me again.

Is that what we argued about on Broken Mountain?

Shivering, Alana wrapped her arms around her body and let reality condense around her once more. It was so long ago, all of it, on the far side of a six-day gap in her mind that might as well be eternity.

So far away and so futile. Jack was dead and she was not, not quite. She couldn't sing, she couldn't be touched, she couldn't love. But she was alive.

And so was Rafael Winter.

Lightning burst silently into the room, bleaching everything into shades of gray and a white so pure her eyes winced from it. Thunder came, but only slowly, telling of a storm retreating down the mountainside.

Taking a deep breath, Alana lay back once

more, trying to sleep. Even as her head
touched the pillow, she knew that it would be
futile. Her body was too loaded with adrena-
line and the aftermath of nightmare to go back
to sleep right away.

She got up, barely feeling the chill. Her deep
green nightgown settled around her ankles.
The soft T-shirt material clung and flared as
she walked to the edge of the loft. The tiny
silver buttons that went from her collarbones
to her thighs sparkled like raindrops in the
muted light from the living room.

Below Alana, engrossed in the multicolored
materials spread before him on a table, Rafe
worked quietly. His back was to her, so she
couldn't see precisely what he was doing.

Alana hesitated long enough to be startled
by another burst of lightning. Then she went
quickly down the stairs. The battery-powered
clock over the mantel told her it was just after
eleven.

Though Alana would have sworn that she'd
made no noise, Rafe knew she was there.

"Take the chair that's closest to the fire,"
Rafe said without looking up from the small
vise in front of him.

Alana pulled out a chair and sat, careful not
to come between Rafe and the light radiating
from the kerosene lantern. He was focused on
a tiny hook held in a small vise. Silently, delicately, he tied an iridescent bit of feather to
the hook's shank using gossamer thread.

In the warm light Rafe's eyes were almost
gold, his lashes and hair nearly black. Horn-

rimmed half glasses sat partway down his nose, magnifying the work in front of him. Deft, tapered fingers handled special tweezers and dots of glue no bigger than the tip of a needle. He wound the thread once more around the shank of the hook, made a half hitch, tugged gently, and cut the thread.

"There are two schools of thought about fly-fishing," said Rafe as he picked up a delicate shaft of iridescent black feather. "One school is that you attract a trout by presenting it with something it's never seen before, something flashy but not frightening. Like this."

Rafe opened a small metal box. Inside were neat rows of flies, their sharp hooks buried in the wool fleece that lined the box. The fly that Rafe selected was nearly as long as his thumb. The colors were bright, a whimsical combination of blue, yellow, and rose that culminated in graceful silver streamers reminiscent of lacy wings.

"Now, Bob swears by this Lively Lady," Rafe said, neatly replacing the fly in its box. "And I admit to using it a time or two when the fishing was so bad I'd tried everything but a DuPont spinner."

"What's a DuPont spinner?"

"Dynamite," Rafe said dryly. "The Lively Lady is outrageous, but it's more sporting than shock waves."

"Does it work?" asked Alana, watching the play of light over the hair on the back of Rafe's hand.

"Only for Bob." Rafe smiled crookedly.

"The times I used it, you could hear the fish snickering all up and down the canyon."

Alana smiled and almost forgot to jump when lightning flicked again, washing the room with shards of white light. Rafe's deep, calm voice smoothed off the jagged edges of the night for her.

"What's the other kind of fly-fishing?" she asked.

"The kind that imitates natural conditions so exactly that the trout can't tell the difference," said Rafe.

His voice was casual yet reassuring, as though he sensed the fear that had driven Alana out of bed and downstairs to the table where he worked. He set aside the fly he had just tied and picked up a hook that already had been wound with mink-brown thread.

"Usually at this time of year, all you have left are larger, darker flying insects," Rafe said. "Most of the smaller bugs have all been killed off in the same frost that turned the aspens pure gold. I'm a little short on autumn flies, so I decided to do a few tonight."

As Rafe talked, his fingers searched delicately among the boxes. There were feathers and tiny, shimmering drifts of fur, as well as nylon and tinsel and Mylar threads of various thicknesses. It was as though he searched with his touch as well as his eyes, savoring the subtle differences in texture with skilled, sensitive fingertips.

There was no sense of hurry or frustration in Rafe's actions. If the thread he chose was stubborn or slippery, refusing to wrap neatly around the hook's shank, he didn't show any impatience. He simply smoothed everything into place and began again, his fingers sure, his expression calm, his mouth relaxed.

With eyes darker than the night, Alana watched Rafe's every movement. He had rolled up the sleeves of his navy-blue flannel shirt past his elbows. Dark hair shimmered and burned with gold highlights as his arms moved. Muscles tightened and relaxed, making light slide over his skin with each supple movement of his body. Beneath the skin, veins showed like dark velvet, inviting her fingers to trace the branching network of life.

"It's important to match environments precisely if you hope to lure a trout out of the depths of a lake or a river," said Rafe, tying a tiny bit of deep red feather to the body of the hook.

"Why?" Alana asked softly.

"It's so quiet down where they hide, safe and deepest blue. But being safe isn't enough for living things. They need more. They need to touch the sun. At least," Rafe added, smiling, "the special ones do."

Alana watched Rafe's face, her eyes wide and intent, feeling his words slide past the fear in her, sinking down into her core, promising her something for which she had no words, only a song that couldn't be sung.

"So my job is to tempt a special trout out of those safe, sterile depths," said Rafe. "To do that, I have to know what's happening around

the fish. If dun-colored mayflies are flying,
then a black gnat will be ignored by my special trout, no matter how beautifully the fly is
tied or presented."

Deftly he added a radiant filament of black
to the shank of the hook.

"You see," Rafe added softly, "my special
trout is neither stupid nor foolish. It's unique
and strong and wary. Yet it's hungry for the
sun."

Tiny shafts of color shimmered as Rafe
worked, feathers as fragile as they were beautiful. He handled them so gently that not a
single filament was crushed or broken.

When he had taken whatever tiny contribution he needed for the fly he was making,
his fingers smoothed the remaining feather,
making each iridescent shaft into a graceful
arch once more. Tufts of color curled and
clung to his fingertips as though thanking him
for understanding their delicacy and beauty.

Alana closed her eyes and let memories rise,
welcoming them the way a flower welcomes
sunlight. Rafe had touched her like that the
first time, his strength balanced with his understanding of her innocence.

And she had responded, sighing and curling
around him, clinging to his fingertips while
his lips feathered across her breasts until she
sang a love song that was his name. He had
called to her in return, the exquisite beauty of
his hands caressing her until she knew nothing but him, felt nothing but ecstasy shivering
through her as she sang his name.

Then he had come to her like gentle lightning, moving deeply until she learned what it was to die and be reborn in the arms of the man she loved.

To be touched like that again, exquisitely . . .

Alana shivered deep inside herself, a tiny ripple that was reflected in the subtle color high in her cheeks.

Glancing up, Rafe saw the faint flush and rapid pulse beating just above the soft emerald neckline of Alana's nightgown. For an instant his fingers tightened and the color of his eyes became a smoky amber fire.

Then he forced himself to concentrate again on his work, knowing it wasn't time yet. He must be patient or he would frighten her back into the bleak safety of withdrawal from memory, from life.

From him.

Alana's brief, ragged breath sounded like fire flickering inside the glass cage of the kerosene lamp. She opened her eyes and watched Rafe, wanting to touch him, to savor the textures of his hair and skin as delicately as he was savoring the materials with which he tied flies.

Yet if she did, he would touch her in return and she would be afraid. Then she would despise herself for her fears.

"Dad never used flies," said Alana, her voice husky as she searched for a safe topic. "Worms or metal lures only. Spinning rods. That's what I was raised with."

"A lot of people prefer them," Rafe said.

His voice was calm, neutral, demanding nothing of her.

"But you don't?"

Rafe smiled slightly as he tied another tiny piece of feather onto the mink-brown body of the fly.

"I prefer the special fish, the shy and elusive one hiding deep in the secret places known only to trout," he said. "To tempt that trout out of the depths and into the sunlight will require all my skill and patience and respect."

He turned a feather, letting light wash over it from various angles, admiring the play of color.

"But wouldn't it be easier to fish down deep rather than to try and lure the trout to the surface?" asked Alana, watching Rafe intently.

"Easier, yes. But easy things have so little value."

Rafe looked up at Alana over the dark rims of his glasses. His eyes were gold, as hot as the flame burning in the lantern.

"The trout should want the fisherman," he said. "Otherwise it's a simple exercise in meat hunting. I want to create a lure so perfect that only a very special trout will rise to it."

"And die," Alana said, her voice almost harsh.

"No," Rafe said very softly. "My hooks have no barbs."

Alana's eyes widened. She looked at the hooks set out on the table, flies finished and half finished and barely begun. Each hook was

a clean, uncluttered curve, not a single barb
to tear at the flesh. She looked back up into
Rafe's amber eyes and felt the breath stop in
her throat.

"Would you like to learn how to fly-fish?"
he asked.

While he waited for an answer, he turned a
golden pheasant feather in the lamplight, making color run in iridescent waves over the
shaft.

"I'd be all thumbs," said Alana.

Rafe laughed softly and shook his head.
"Not you."

She held out her hands as though to convince him of her awkwardness. Slowly he ran
the feather from her wrists to her palms to her
fingertips, stroking her with the delicacy of a
sigh, seeing her response in the slight tremor
of her fingertips.

"Your hands are just right," Rafe said.
"Graceful and long and very, very sensitive."

Alana's breath came in raggedly as she saw
Rafe's expression. She knew that he was remembering being touched by her, the sensual
contrast of her hands against the male contours of his body, the heat and pleasure she
had brought to him.

"You'll enjoy it," continued Rafe softly. "I
promise you."

"I—yes," Alana said quickly, before she
could change her mind and be afraid again.
"After breakfast?"

"After breakfast."

Rafe turned his attention to the hook in his

vise. He released the hook and carefully buried the sharp tip in the fleece-lined box.

"Can you sleep now," he asked, "or would you like me to sit next to your bed for a while?"

Then he looked up, catching and holding Alana's glance with his own.

"I wouldn't touch you unless you asked me to," Rafe said. "And I don't expect you to ask."

"I know," Alana said, her voice low.

And she did. She trusted him.

The realization sent a quiver of light through the dark pool that fear and amnesia had made in the depths of her mind.

"Would you mind staying with me?" she whispered. "For just a few minutes? I know it's childish—"

"Then we're both children," said Rafe easily, cutting across her words, "because I'd rather sit with you than be alone."

Alana brushed his mustache with her fingertips.

"Thank you," she breathed.

The touch was so light, it was almost more imagined than real. Yet she felt it all the way to her knees.

And so did he. His eyes were tawny, reflecting the dance of flame from the lamp.

"My pleasure," Rafe said.

Then he looked away from Alana, not wanting her to see his hunger.

"Go upstairs before you get cold," Rafe said. "I'll clean up here."

"Can I help?"

"No. It will just take a minute."

Alana hesitated, then turned away as Rafe began deftly sorting materials and stacking small boxes onto a tray.

But as soon as she no longer watched him, Rafe looked up, ignoring the brilliant materials at his fingertips. Motionless, entirely focused on Alana, he watched as she climbed up the narrow stairs to the loft.

The glossy black of her hair caught and held the lamplight like stars reflected in a wind-ruffled midnight lake. The green of her nightgown clung and shifted, revealing and then concealing the womanly curves beneath. Her bare feet looked small, graceful, oddly vulnerable beneath the swirling folds of cloth.

Silently, savagely, Rafe cursed Jack Reeves.

9

$\mathcal{A}$LANA OPENED THE CAST-
iron stove door, using a pot holder that had
been crocheted by Rafe's grandmother. Inside
the belly of the stove, a neat pattern of wood
burned brightly, sending vivid orange flames
licking at the thick iron griddle above.

"So far, so good," Alana muttered.

She closed the door, adjusted the vent,
dipped her fingers into a saucer of water, and
flicked drops on the griddle. Water hissed and
danced whitely across the griddle's searing
black surface.

"Perfect."

The kitchen was washed in the golden
warmth of a kerosene lamp, for it was at least

147

half an hour until dawn. The smell of bacon and coffee permeated the lodge and spread through the crisp air to the other cabins, prodding everyone out of bed.

From just outside the kitchen door came the clean, sharp sound of Rafe splitting wood for the stove. It was a strangely peaceful sound, a promise of warmth and a reminder that Rafe wasn't far away.

The rhythm of a song began to sift through Alana's mind, working its way down to her throat. She hummed almost silently, not knowing what she did. It was only the barest thread of sound, more a hope of song than song itself.

Alana picked up the pitcher of pancake batter and poured creamy circles onto the griddle. When the bubbles burst and batter didn't run in to fill the hollows, she flipped each pancake neatly. Soon she had several stacks warming at the back of the stove next to the thick slices of bacon she had already cooked and set aside.

As she poured more batter onto the griddle, she sensed someone walking up behind her.

"I don't need any more wood yet, Rafe," Alana said, setting aside the pitcher as she turned around. "Not until I—*oh!*"

It was Stan, not Rafe, who had come up behind Alana. Reflexively she took a step backward, forgetting about the hot stove.

"Watch out!" said Stan, reaching toward her automatically, trying to prevent her from being burned.

Alana flinched away, bringing the back of her hand into contact with the cast-iron stove. She made a sound of pain and twisted aside, evading Stan's touch at the cost of burning herself again. Again, he reached for her, trying to help.

"Don't touch her."

Rafe's voice was so cold, so savage, that Alana almost didn't recognize it.

Stan did, though. He stepped back instantly. When his blue eyes assessed the fear on Alana's face, he stepped back even more, giving her all the room she needed.

"What in hell do you think you're doing?" demanded Rafe.

His voice was flat and low, promising violence. The stove wood he had carried inside fell into the wood box with a crash that was startling in the charged silence.

Though Rafe hadn't made a move toward Stan, the blond man backed up all the way to the door between the dining room and the kitchen before he spoke.

"Sorry," muttered Stan. "Bob and I thought Alana might need help with . . . whatever."

"Bob and you? Christ," snarled Rafe. "That's an idiots' duet if ever there was one."

Stan flushed. "Now look here, Winter."

"Go tell Bob that if Alana needs the kind of *help* that you had in mind, I'll be the first one to suggest it. Got that?"

Stan's mouth flattened, but he nodded his head curtly, accepting Rafe's command.

"That was your free one," Rafe said grimly. "Do you read me?"

Again, Stan nodded curtly.

Rafe turned his back on Stan and went to Alana. He held out his hand.

"Let me see your burn," Rafe said softly.

The change in his voice was almost shocking. Warm, gentle, reassuring, it seemed impossible that the words came from the same man who had flayed Stan to the bone with a few razor phrases.

"It's all right, wildflower," murmured Rafe. "I won't hurt you."

With a long, shuddering release of breath, Alana held out her burned hand to Rafe.

He looked at the two red bars where her skin had touched the stove and felt rage like raw lightning scoring his gut. Turning on his heel, he went to the refrigerator and pulled out a handful of ice. He dampened a kitchen towel, wrapped the ice, and held it out to Alana.

"Put this over the burns," he said gently. "It will take away the pain."

Numbly Alana did as Rafe said. Within seconds the pain from the seared flesh was gone.

"Thank you," she said, sighing. Then, "It seems that I'm always thanking you."

He took the spatula from Alana and scraped off the pancakes that had begun to burn.

"Funny," Rafe muttered, "it seems that I'm always hurting you."

"It wasn't your fault. It wasn't Stan's, either. It was my own foolishness," said Alana.

151

"Bullshit," Rafe said in a clipped voice.

He scraped charred batter off the griddle with short, vicious strokes.

"You wouldn't be here if it wasn't for me," he said, "and neither would Stan."

Alana was too surprised to say anything.

With a disgusted sound, Rafe threw the spatula onto the counter and turned to Alana. His eyes were nearly black with the violence of his emotions.

"Forgive me?" he asked simply.

"There's nothing to forgive."

"I wish to Christ that was true."

Abruptly Rafe turned back to the stove and began greasing the griddle.

"I'll finish cooking breakfast," he said.

"But—"

"Sit down and keep those burns covered. They aren't bad, but they'll hurt unless you leave the ice on for a while."

Alana sat on the kitchen stool and watched Rafe covertly. He cooked as he did everything, with clean motions, nothing wasted, everything smooth and sure. The stacks of pancakes grew.

By the time everyone was seated in the dining room, there were enough pancakes to feed twice as many people as were around the table. At least it seemed like that, until everyone began to eat. The altitude and crisp air combined to double everyone's appetite.

Even Alana ate enough to make her groan. At Rafe's pointed suggestion, Bob did the dishes. Stan insisted on helping, as did Janice.

Rafe set out fishing gear while Alana packed lunches.

There were still a few stars out when Rafe led the two dudes to a stretch of fishing water and gave advice on the most effective lures and techniques to use in the extraordinarily clear water.

When Bob turned to follow Rafe and Alana back up the trail, Rafe gave him a long look.

"I promised to teach Alana how to fly-fish," Rafe said. "For that, she definitely doesn't need an audience."

"I won't laugh," said Bob, his lips quirked around a smile. "Much."

"You won't laugh at all," Rafe said smoothly, "because you're not going to be around."

Bob looked quickly at Alana, but she shook her head. He shrugged and accepted the fact that he wasn't going fishing with his older sister.

"Oh, well," Bob said. "I promised Stan I'd show him how to use the Lively Lady. Bet we catch more than you do."

"You'd better," retorted Alana. "Rafe uses barbless hooks. If we're going to eat trout, it's up to you, baby brother."

"Barbless?" asked Bob, giving Rafe a swift look. "Since when?"

"Since I was old enough to shave."

"Hell of a way to fish," Bob said, turning away. "A man could starve."

"Fishing is more than a way to feed your rumbling gut," pointed out Rafe.

"Depends on how hungry you are, doesn't it?" retorted Bob over his shoulder as he walked down the trail.

"Or what you're hungry for," added Rafe softly.

He turned to Alana.

"Ready?" he asked.

"Um..."

"I've got a spot picked out by the lake. Lots of room and nothing to tangle your line on the back stroke."

"You're assuming that I'll get enough line out to tangle," Alana said, smiling wryly.

Rafe's soft laughter mixed perfectly with the sound of the stream flowing along the trail.

Though the sun hadn't yet cleared the ridges, predawn light sent a cool radiance over the land, illuminating the path and making boulders look as though they had been wrapped in silver velvet. In the deep pools where water didn't seethe over rocks, trout rose, leaving behind expanding, luminous rings.

Silently, letting the serenity of the land and the moment seep into Alana, Rafe led her to a narrow finger of glacier-polished granite that almost divided the lake into two unequal parts. As she stepped out onto the rock shelf, Rafe touched Alana's shoulder and pointed across the lake.

A doe and two half-grown fawns moved gracefully to the water. While the fawns drank, the doe stood guard. Beyond them the granite face of Broken Mountain flushed pink beneath the gentle onslaught of dawn. The sky was utterly clear, a magic crystal bell ready to ring with exquisite music at the first touch of sunlight.

The doe and fawns retreated, breaking the spell. Alana let out her breath in a long sigh.

Rafe watched her for an instant longer, then began assembling his fishing rod.

"Have you ever used a fly rod before?" he asked.

"No."

Alana watched intently as the long, flexible rod took shape before her eyes.

"I've always wondered how a fly rod works," she admitted. "With spinning rods, the weight of the lure is used to pull line off the reel. But there's no weight worth mentioning in a fly."

"With fly rods, the weight of the line itself is what counts," Rafe said. "The leader and the lure barely weigh anything. They can't. Otherwise they land with a plop and a splash and scare away any fish worth catching."

Using a smooth, complicated knot, he tied a nearly weightless fly onto the thin, transparent leader. Then he pulled a length of thick fly line off the reel, showing her the line's weight.

"Handled correctly, the fly line will carry the fly and set it down on the water as lightly as if the fly really had wings," Rafe said. "The point is to mimic reality as perfectly as possible. The leader is transparent and long enough that the fish doesn't associate the heavy fly line lying on the surface with the tasty insect floating fifteen feet away."

Alana looked at the opaque, thick fly line.

"If you say so," she said dubiously.

"See that fish rising at about two o'clock?" asked Rafe.

She looked beyond Rafe's hand to an expanding ring. It was at least fifty feet out in the lake.

"Yes, I see it."

"Watch."

With his right hand, Rafe held the butt of the fly rod near the point where the reel was clamped on. With his left hand, he stripped line off the reel. As he did so, his right hand began to move the rod forward and back in a smooth, powerful arc.

Kinetic energy traveled up the rod's supple length, bending it with easy, whiplike motions, pulling line from the reel up through the guides. With each coordinated movement of Rafe's arm, line leaped out from the tip of the rod, more line and then more, until it described fluid curves across the luminous sky.

Silently, smoothly, powerfully, Rafe balanced the forces of line and rod, strength and timing, gravity and flight, until an impossibly long curve of line hung suspended between sky and water. Then he allowed the curve to uncurl in front of him, becoming a straight line with the fly at its tip.

Gently, gently, the fly settled onto the water precisely in the center of the expanding ring left by the feeding trout. Not so much as a ripple disturbed the surface from the fly's descent. It was as though the fly had condensed out of air to float on the dawn-tinted mirror of the lake.

And then there was a silver swirl and water boiling as the trout rose to the fly.

The rod tip lashed down at the same instant that Rafe began pulling line in through the guides with his left hand. The supple rod danced and shivered as the trout tail-walked across the dawn like a flashing silver exclamation point.

Line slid through Rafe's fingers, drawn by the trout's power. But slowly, gently, the line returned, drawn by his sensitive fingers, until finally the trout swam in short curves just off the granite shelf, tethered to Rafe by an invisibly fine length of leader.

Just as the first rays of sunlight poured over the lake, the trout leaped again. Colors ran down its sleek side, forming the iridescent rainbow that gave the fish its name.

In reverent silence, Rafe and Alana admired the beauty swimming at their feet. It would have been a simple matter for Rafe to unhook the net at his belt, guide the fish into the green mesh, and lift it from the water. Instead, Rafe gave an expert flick of his wrist that removed the hook from the cartilage lining the trout's mouth.

There was a moment of startled stillness, then water swirled as the trout flashed away.

"See how easy it is?" murmured Rafe, watching Alana with eyes as luminous as dawn. "It's your turn now."

* * *

For what seemed like the hundredth time, Alana stripped line from the fat reel, positioned her hand to feed line from reel to rod, lifted her right arm, and began the forward and backward motion that was supposed to send line shooting up through the guides on the rod.

As she stroked the rod forward and back, line inched up through the guides and started to form the lovely, fluid curve that was the signature of fly-fishing.

And then the curve collapsed into an ungainly pile of line on the rock shelf behind Alana.

"I waited too long on the forward stroke, didn't I?" Alana muttered. "All the energy that was supposed to hold up the line went *fffft*."

"But you got out nearly twice as much line," pointed out Rafe, his voice and smile encouraging her.

"And before that, I broke three hooks on the rock, hooked myself on the back stroke, hooked you on the back stroke, lashed the water to a froth on the forward stroke, tied ruinous knots in your beautiful leader, and in general did everything but strangle myself on the fly line."

Alana shook her head, torn between frustration and rueful laughter. Rafe had been incredibly patient. No matter how many times the line or the leader snarled hopelessly, he had neither laughed at her nor gotten angry. He had been gentle, reassuring, and encouraging. He had praised her and told funny stories about the monumental tangles he used to make when he was learning how to fly-fish.

"Alana," said Rafe softly, capturing her attention. "You're doing better than I did the first time I had eight feet of limber rod and fifty feet of fly line in my hands."

She grimaced. "I don't believe it. I feel so damn clumsy."

"You aren't. You're as graceful as that doe."

"Outrageous flattery," she said, smiling, "will get more knots tied in your line."

Alana positioned the rod again. "Here goes nothing."

Not quite nothing. A rather impressive snarl came next. Rafe untangled it with the same patience he had displayed for the last hour.

As he turned the rod over to Alana once more, he hesitated.

"If it wouldn't bother you," Rafe said quietly, "I could stand behind you, hold on to your wrist, and let you get the feeling of the timing. And that's all it is. Timing. There's no real strength involved. Fly-fishing is a matter of finesse, not biceps."

Alana nibbled on her lower lip as she eyed the deceptively simple appearance of fly rod and reel.

"All right," she said. "Let's give your way a try. Mine sure hasn't done much."

Rafe stepped into position behind Alana. Less than an inch separated them, for he had to be able to reach around her to guide the rod. He stood for several moments without touch-

ing her, letting her get used to his presence
very close behind her.

"Okay so far?" he asked casually.

"Yes. . . . Just knowing that you understand
how I feel makes it easier," Alana admitted in
a low voice.

She took a deep breath. The mixed scents of
high-country air and sunshine and Rafe swept
over her. His warmth was a tingling sensation
from her shoulders to her knees. She felt his
breath stir against the nape of her neck, sensed
the subtle movements of his chest as he
breathed, the slight catch of his flannel shirt
against hers.

"Ready?" asked Rafe.

Alana nodded, afraid to trust her voice. The
breathlessness she felt had little to do with her
fear of being touched.

"Take up the rod," he said.

She lifted the fly rod into position.

"I'm going to put my hand around your
wrist and the rod at the same time," said Rafe.
"Okay?"

She took a deep breath. "Okay."

He reached around Alana until his hand
covered hers and wrapped around the rod.

The contrast of his tanned skin against her
hand was arresting. It reminded Rafe of just
how smooth Alana's skin was, how pale
where the sun had never touched it, how incredibly soft when she had welcomed his most
intimate caresses.

For an instant Rafe closed his eyes and
thought of nothing at all.

"All right so far?" he asked.

His voice was too husky, but there was nothing he could do about that any more than he could wholly control the growing ache and swelling of his desire.

"Yes."

Alana's breath drew out the word until it was almost a sigh. The warmth and strength of Rafe's fingers curling around her hand fascinated her. She wanted to bend her head and brush her lips over his fingers. Just the thought of feeling his skin beneath her mouth made liquid fire twist through her.

Rafe took a quiet breath and hoped that Alana had no idea of how her closeness threatened his carefully imposed self-control.

"Now, remember," he said. "The rod is only supposed to move in the arc between ten and two on our imaginary clock. That's where the greatest power and balance are. You go above or below that and you'll get in trouble. Ready?"

Alana nodded.

Rafe guided her arm and the rod through the short arc between ten and two, counting softly as he did.

"*One*, two, three, four. Now *forward*, two, three, four. And *back*, two, three, four."

Smoothly, easily, the rhythm flowed from Rafe to Alana and then to the rod. She felt the energy curl up the length of the rod, pulling line through the guides, bending the rod tip at the end of the arc. Then came the soft hiss of line shooting up and back over her shoulder just before the rod came forward smoothly, en-

ergy pouring up its length on the forward
stroke, fly line shooting out magically, Rafe's
voice murmuring, counting, energy and line
pulsing along the rod.

Alana felt the rhythm take her until she
forgot everything but Rafe's voice and his
warmth and the line suspended in curving
beauty above the silver lake.

And still the rhythm continued, unvarying,
serene and yet exciting, line pulsing out like a
soundless song shimmering, lyrics sung in silence and written in liquid arcs curving across
the dawn.

"Now," murmured Rafe, bringing the rod
forward and stopping it precisely at ten
o'clock. "Let it go."

Line hissed out in a long, ecstatic surge.
Gracefully, delicately, the fly line, leader, and
fly became a part of the lake. Not so much as
a ripple marred the perfect surface of the water at the joining.

Alana let out a long breath, enthralled by
the beauty of the line uncurling, the sweeping
blend of energy and rhythm, the timeless con-
summation of line and lure and silver water.

"That was . . . incredible," she said softly.
"Thank you, Rafe."

"What for?"

"For your patience. For teaching and sharing this with me."

Rafe felt the shifting surface of Alana's body
against his as she sighed. He wanted to close
his arms around her, enfolding her. He

wanted to feel her flow along his body as she
fitted herself against him.

At the very least, he wanted to be able to
trace the velvet edge of her hairline with the
tip of his tongue, inhaling the sunlight and
womanly scent of her, testing the resilience of
her flesh with gentle pressures of his teeth.

Ruthlessly Rafe suppressed the hunger that
pulsed through him, tightening his body with
each heartbeat, drawing it upon a rack of passion.

"You're a joy to teach," Rafe said in a quiet
voice. "You should take it easy for a while,
though. You're using muscles you didn't
know you had. Why don't we just sit in the
sun and be lazy? There's a patch of grass and
wildflowers farther up the lake."

"Sounds wonderful," said Alana.

As she spoke, she stretched the muscles in
her shoulders by twisting them from side to
side. She didn't hear the subtle intake of Rafe's
breath as she accidentally rubbed against him
when she straightened again.

"But aren't you supposed to be helping the
dudes, too?" Alana asked.

"They know one end of a fishing rod from
the other."

Rafe took the fly rod from Alana, removed
the hook, and wound in the line. He began
breaking the rod into its component parts with
quick movements of his hands, working with
an economy and expertise born of long famil-
iarity.

Alana watched Rafe's skilled fingers and the

flex of tendons beneath the rolled-up sleeves of his navy flannel shirt.

"The dudes aren't what I expected," she said.

Rafe looked up suddenly. His whiskey glance pinned her.

"What do you mean?" he asked quietly.

The intensity of his voice belied the softness of his tone.

"Stan's looks, for one thing," Alana said, shrugging. "I'm having a hard time getting used to seeing Jack's ghost. Poor Stan. He must think I'm more than a little unwrapped."

"He'll survive," said Rafe unsympathetically.

"I know. It's just a bit awkward." Alana sighed. "He and Janice have been such easy guests. They don't complain. They don't expect to be waited on. They're funny and smart and surprisingly fit."

Rafe made a neutral sound.

"Not many people could have ridden the trail to Broken Mountain one day and popped out of bed the next morning ready to slay dragons—or even trout," Alana said dryly.

Rafe shrugged.

"And no matter how strange I act," Alana said, "the two of them take it in stride. Even Stan, when I literally ran screaming from him, acted as though it was his fault, not mine."

Rafe said something savage under his breath.

Abruptly Alana laughed. "I guess the dudes are as unusual as the dude ranch."

"Luck of the draw," he said tersely.

With quick motions Rafe slipped the rod into its carrying case.

"The fact that these good sports are your friends has more to do with it than luck," retorted Alana.

Rafe's eyes narrowed into topaz lines. "What are you hinting at?"

"I know what you're doing, Rafe."

"And what is that?" he asked softly.

"You're helping Bob get started."

Rafe said nothing.

"You know how much he needs cash to buy out Sam and Dave," Alana persisted, "and you know Bob doesn't want to destroy the land to make a quick cash killing. So you beat the bushes for friends who could help Bob launch a dude ranch."

Rafe grunted.

"Don't worry," added Alana quickly, resting her hand for an instant on Rafe's arm, "I won't say anything to Bob. I just wanted you to know that I appreciate what you're doing for him. He's got four left feet and he keeps them in his mouth most of the time, but he's a good man and I love him."

With a long, soundless sigh, Rafe let out the breath he had been holding. He smiled ruefully at Alana as he packed away the last of the fishing gear.

But Rafe said nothing about Bob, neither confirming nor denying her conclusions.

In companionable silence, Alana and Rafe walked along the margin of the lake, skirting

boulders and gnarled spruces. Spring and summer had come late to the high country this year.
Wildflowers still bloomed in the sheltered
places, making windows of color against the
pale outcroppings of granite. Delicate, tenacious, radiant with life, drifts of wildflowers
softened the harsh edges of rock and stark
blue sky.

At the head of the third lake, a broad cascade seethed over slick rocks into the shallows. The cascade drained the second, higher
lake in the chain. That lake was invisible behind the rocky shoulder of Broken Mountain.

The cascade itself was a pale, shining ribbon
of white that descended the granite slope in a
breathtaking series of leaps. The sun was more
than halfway to noon, pouring transparent
warmth and light over the bowl where the
third lake lay.

Rafe stopped in a small hollow that was a
hundred feet from the cascade. Evergreens so
dark they were almost black formed a natural
windbreak. Topaz aspens burned in the sunlight and quivered at the least movement of
air, as though the trees were alive and
breathing with tiny, swift breaths.

Rafe pulled a waterproof tarp from his pack.
Silver on one side, deepest indigo on the other,
the tarp could gather or scatter heat, which-
ever was required. He put the dark, heat-
absorbent side up, knowing that the ground
was cool despite the sun. Spread out, the tarp
made an inviting surface for two people to eat
or sleep on comfortably.

"Hungry?" asked Rafe, lifting Alana's pack off her shoulders.

Alana was about to say no when her stomach growled its own answer.

With an almost soundless chuckle, Rafe went to his backpack. Quickly he pulled out a snack of apples, hard-boiled eggs, and chocolate raisins.

Alana's stomach made insistent noises. She looked chagrined.

"It's the air," said Rafe reassuringly, concealing a smile.

"If I do everything my stomach tells me to, I won't be able to fit into my clothes," she grumbled.

"Then buy new ones," he suggested, uncapping a canteen full of cold tea. "Ten more pounds would look good on you."

"You think so?" she asked dubiously.

"I know so."

"My costume designer is always telling me to lose more weight."

"Your costume designer is as full of crap as a Christmas goose."

Rafe divided the food between Alana and himself.

She smiled blissfully. "In that case, I'll have another handful of chocolate raisins."

"What about me?" asked Rafe, his voice plaintive and his eyes brilliant with amusement.

"You," she said with a sideways glance, "can have my hard-boiled egg."

Rafe laughed aloud and pushed his pile of

chocolate raisins over to Alana's side of the tarp. He left her egg in place. But when Alana reached for the new pile of sweets, he covered it swiftly.

"Nope," he said, smiling at her. "Not until you eat the egg and the apple."

"Slave driver."

"Count on it," said Rafe.

He bit into his own apple with a hearty crunching sound.

They ate slowly, enjoying flavors heightened by clean air and healthy appetites. When she had eaten the last chocolate raisin, Alana sighed and stretched luxuriously. The exuberant splash of the cascade formed a soothing layer of sound between her and the rest of the world. Nothing penetrated but Rafe's occasional low-voiced comments about fly-fishing and ranching, and the silky feel of high-country sunshine.

"Why don't you take a nap?" he suggested finally.

Alana caught herself in mid-yawn. "There's something sinful about taking a nap before noon."

"In that case, let's hear it for sin." Rafe smiled crookedly. "Go ahead, wildflower. You didn't get enough sleep last night, or a lot of nights before that."

He unbuttoned his flannel shirt, revealing a dark blue T-shirt beneath. With a few quick motions, he shaped the thick flannel shirt into a pillow.

"Here," Rafe said to Alana. "Use this. I don't need it."

Alana tried to object but couldn't get any words past the sudden dryness in her mouth.

Even in her dreams, Rafe had not looked so overwhelmingly male. The T-shirt defined rather than concealed the slide and coil of muscles. With every movement Rafe made, every breath he took, his tanned skin stretched over a body whose latent power both shocked and fascinated her.

Suddenly Alana wanted to touch Rafe, to trace every ridge and swell of flesh, to know again the compelling male textures of his body.

She closed her eyes but still she saw Rafe, sunlight sliding over his skin, sunlight caressing him, sunlight burning in his eyes and her blood.

"Alana?" Rafe's voice was sharp with concern.

"You're right," Alana said in a shaky voice. "I haven't been getting enough sleep."

Rafe watched as she stretched out on the tarp, her cheek against the shirt he had rolled up for her. He would rather she had used his lap as a pillow, but was afraid if he suggested it, the relaxed line of her lips would tighten with tension and fear.

Yet for a moment, when Alana had looked at him as though she had never seen him before, Rafe had hoped . . .

"Better?" he asked, watching Alana's body relax into deep, even breathing.

"Yes."

"Then sleep, wildflower. I'm here."

Alana sighed and felt herself spiraling down into a sleep where no nightmares waited.

10

WHEN ALANA WOKE UP, the sun was on the other side of noon. She rolled over sleepily and realized that she was alone.

"Rafe?"

No one answered.

She sat up and looked around. Through the screen of evergreens and aspens she saw Rafe outlined against blue water. He had found another rock shelf leading out into the lake. He was standing at the end of the granite finger. The fly rod was in his hands. Line was curling exquisitely across the sky.

For a few moments Alana watched, captured by the grace of the man and the moment when line drifted soundlessly down to lie upon still water.

Except Alana couldn't actually see the line touch the surface of the lake, because trees blocked her view.

She stood up and started toward the shoreline, then realized that once Rafe saw her, he would probably stop fishing and start teaching her once again. She wasn't ready for that. She felt too relaxed, too at peace—and too lazy— to attempt anything that required concentration.

What she really wanted to do was to sit quietly, watching Rafe and the lyric sweep of line against the high-country sky.

Alana looked back down the lakeshore to where she and Rafe had been earlier. She saw no place to sit and watch him that wouldn't immediately bring her into Rafe's view.

She looked left to the cascade dancing whitely down rocks turned black by water. Rafe was facing away from the cascade, looking down the lake toward the cabins. The position gave him a hundred feet in front of the fly rod and an equal amount in back without anything to obstruct the motion of the line.

And he was using every bit of that two hundred feet.

On tiptoe, Alana peered through the wind-twisted branches of a fir, holding her breath as the curve of the fly line grew and grew, expanding silently, magically. Rafe's left arm worked in perfect counterpoint to his right as he stripped line off the reel, almost throwing fly line up through the guides as his right arm pumped smoothly, sending energy coursing through the rod.

"How are you doing that?" muttered Alana, knowing Rafe couldn't hear her. "You aren't a magician, are you?"

She stepped farther to her left, but she still couldn't see exactly what Rafe was doing to make the line lengthen so effortlessly. With a small, exasperated sound, she worked her way along the increasingly rugged shoreline, trying to find a spot that would allow her to watch Rafe without being seen.

Alana leaped from stone to stone, avoiding the small boggy spots where coarse grass and tiny flowers grew, until she found herself confronted by the barrier of the cascade. She turned around and looked back at Rafe, who was about sixty yards away from her by now.

Unfortunately, she still couldn't see what he was doing with his hands. Nor could she go any farther forward without coming up against the cascade. She could either go back, or she could go up the boulder-tumbled slope.

With a muttered word, Alana looked at the jumble of stone rising on either side of the frothing water. She wouldn't have to go very far up the cascade to get the view she wanted. Just far enough to allow her to look over Rafe's shoulder, as it were. If she didn't get too close to the water, the climb wouldn't be too hard. Besides, she had been raised hiking and scrambling along mountain rivers and up steep slopes.

Alana turned and began climbing over the lichen-studded boulders. Twenty feet away, the cascade churned and boiled, making both mist and a cool rushing thunder. She avoided the slippery rocks, seeking the dry ones.

Within a few minutes she was breathless, gaining two feet in height for every foot forward. She persisted anyway, scrambling and balancing precariously, until she stood on a ledge of granite that was barely eighteen inches deep.

She stopped because there was no other choice. In front of her rose a slick outcropping of rock six feet high, and not a handhold in sight.

"Well, this had better be far enough."

When Alana turned to look, it felt like the earth was dropping away beneath her feet. Unexpected, overwhelming, a fear of heights froze her in place.

Twenty feet away, the cascade frothed down the steep mountainside, water seething and racing, white and thunder, and wind whipping drops of water across her face like icy rain. Thunder and ice and the world falling away, leaving her *helpless, spinning, darkness reaching up for her.*

Alana clung to the rough face of the granite and closed her eyes, struggling to separate nightmare and memory and reality.

The feeling of falling didn't stop. The boom of water over rock became remembered thunder. Drifting spray became ice-tipped winds and her screams were lightning as memory and nightmare and reality became one.

Cold.

God, it was cold, cold all the way to the center of the earth. Jack with anger twisting his face. Jack cursing her, grabbing her, hitting her, and the storm breaking, trees bending and snapping like glass beneath the wind.

Like her. She wasn't strong enough. She would break and the pieces would be scattered over the cold rocks.

Running.

Scrambling.

Breath like a knife in her side. Throat on fire with screams and the storm chasing her, catching her, yanking her backward while rocks like fists hit her, bruising her, and she screamed, clawing and fighting.

But she was swept up, lifted high, helpless, nothing beneath her feet, and she was falling

   screaming

and Rafe was calling her name.

You're safe, wildflower. I've come to take you home.

Distantly Alana realized that she had heard the words before, over and over, Rafe's voice reaching out to her, peeling away layers of nightmare until only reality remained.

"You're safe, wildflower. I've come to take you home."

Shaking like an aspen in a storm, Alana clung to the rock face. She sensed Rafe behind her, heard his voice, felt the warmth of his body along her back, Rafe standing between her and the drop-off at the end of the rocky ledge.

"R-Rafe," Alana said shakily.

It was the only word she could say.

"I'm here, wildflower. You're safe," he murmured, his words and the tone of his voice soothing her. "You're safe."

Alana let out a breath that was more a sob.

"Rafe? I'm so s-scared."

She couldn't see the darkness of his eyes or his savage expression so at odds with the reassurance of his voice.

"I know," Rafe said. "You had a bad time up along the lakes, even if you don't remember it. Or," softly, "did you remember?"

Alana shook her head.

"Then why are you frightened?" he coaxed. "Is it because I'm close to you? Are you afraid of me?"

She shook her head again. "No."

Though weak, her voice was positive. It wasn't Rafe she feared.

For an instant, Rafe closed his eyes. A strange mixture of emotions crossed his face. Then his eyes opened. Relief eased the tightness of his mouth and brought light to his eyes again.

"What is it, then?" he asked. "Can you tell me?"

"Height," said Alana in a trembling voice. "I'm afraid of heights now and I never was before, not until Jack fell and I guess I fell, too."

The words tumbled over each other like water in the cascade. She made a ragged sound.

"Rafe, I felt so good when I woke up a few minutes ago. All morning I hadn't thought about Jack or Broken Mountain or the missing days. I hadn't thought about anything since breakfast but fly-fishing and sunshine and you being so patient and gentle with me."

"I'm glad you enjoyed the morning," Rafe said, his voice low and husky. "I know that I haven't enjoyed anything so much in years."

"Do you mean that? Even though I ruined your line and scared every fish away?"

Rafe's lips brushed against Alana's shoulder in a caress so light she didn't feel it.

"I'll buy a hundred miles of leader," he said, "and let you tie knots in every inch of it."

Alana let out her breath in a rush, then took another breath. She almost felt brave enough to open her eyes.

Almost.

"Don't make any rash promises," she said shakily, trying to make a joke even though her voice wouldn't cooperate. "I'll hold you to every one of them."

"Wildflower," whispered Rafe, brushing his cheek against her glossy hair, "brave and beautiful. I'd carry away Broken Mountain stone by stone if that would let you come to me again with a smile on your lips."

The words were a warmth unfolding in the center of Alana's icy fear. As fear melted away, some of her strength returned.

She opened her eyes. The rough granite textures of rock were only inches from her face. On either side of her shoulders, close but not touching her, were Rafe's arms. His hands were flattened on the rock as he stood behind her, his legs braced, his feet wide apart on the narrow ledge, his body between her and any danger of falling.

Slowly Alana put one of her hands over his. The warmth of him was almost shocking.

"But I'm not brave," she said, her voice tight with anger at herself.

Rafe's laughter was as harsh as it was unexpected.

"Bravery isn't a square jaw and a thick head," he said. "Bravery is standing toe-to-toe with fear every minute of every hour, never knowing if you're going to get through this second, and afraid the next second might be one too many."

Alana's breath stopped. It was as though Rafe were in her mind, reading her thoughts, putting into words what she had only sensed without understanding.

"And the worst of it is that you're strong," Rafe said, "so you survive when others would have broken and gone free, crazy free, but you survive day after day no matter how bad it gets. And it gets very bad, doesn't it?"

Alana nodded, unable to speak.

So Rafe spoke for her, and for himself.

"Some of those days are endless," he said,

"and the nights . . . the nights are . . . unspeakable."

Alana's grip on Rafe's hand was so tight that her nails left marks on his skin.

"How did you know?" she whispered.

"I've been there, Alana. Like you, I've served my time in hell."

She whispered Rafe's name as tears slid from her eyelashes down her cheeks, crying for him and for herself.

His lips brushed her neck very lightly. She wouldn't have felt it if she hadn't been so sensitized to him, his emotions, his physical presence, Rafe like a fire burning between her and the freezing blackness that came to her in nightmares.

Alana bent her head until her lips touched the back of Rafe's hand. She kissed him gently, not withdrawing even when his hand turned over and cradled her cheek in his palm.

Slowly Rafe leaned down, unable to resist the lure of Alana's tears. He murmured her name as his lips touched her eyelashes, catching the silver drops. He expected her to stiffen at the caress, at the knowledge that she was trapped between his strength and the granite face of the mountain.

She turned her cheek to his lips, leaning lightly against him, her eyes luminous with emotion. He kissed the corner of her mouth, delicately stealing the tears that gathered there, until finally there were no more tears.

"Are you ready to climb down now?" Rafe asked softly.

Alana took a ragged breath, then looked beneath Rafe's arm to the rocks tumbling away to the lake.

Everything spun for an instant. She closed her eyes and hung on to him, hard.

Rafe saw the color leave Alana's face even before he felt her nails digging into his arms and the shaking of her legs against his. Quickly he leaned inward, bracing Alana against the rock with his body so that she wouldn't fall if her legs gave way.

"Don't be afraid," said Rafe softly, urgently. "I'm not going to hold you or hurt you in any way."

There was an instant of stiffness before Alana sighed and nodded her head, unable to speak.

When Alana accepted his presence, his reassurance, relief came in a wave that for an instant left Rafe almost as weak as she was.

And with relief came hunger for Alana, the hunger that had haunted Rafe ever since he had come back to find the woman he loved married to another man . . . desire and rage burning Rafe like acid every time he saw a picture of Alana with Jack, Country's Perfect Couple, happiness condensed into two smiling faces on millions of album covers.

Ruthlessly Rafe suppressed both desire and the corrosive memories of rage. He ignored the sweet warmth of Alana's body pressed along his as he braced her against the cold granite.

"I'll support you until you aren't dizzy," he

said, his voice even, calm. "Tell me when you can stand again."

Eyes closed, Alana savored the sound of Rafe's deep voice, his warmth and reassurance, and his patience. If he didn't condemn her for being foolish, for being afraid, she wouldn't condemn herself, either.

"Alana?" asked Rafe, unable to see her face. Concern made his voice almost harsh.

"It's all right," Alana said.

And as she spoke, she realized that it really was all right. When she stopped being disgusted with herself, when she stopped being afraid of fear, she was able to react more rationally.

Rafe's strength and closeness made Alana feel as she should, protected rather than threatened. She sighed and felt the shaking in her legs diminish.

"You didn't frighten me, Rafael. I looked down the mountain, that's all."

He let out his breath with an explosive sigh.

"That wasn't a very bright thing to do, sweetheart."

Alana's mouth formed a smile that was gone as swiftly as it had come.

"I figured that out real fast," she said. "Now maybe you can figure out how I'm going to climb off this damned ledge with my eyes closed."

"Gracefully, smoothly, and quickly," murmured Rafe, brushing Alana's neck with his lips, not caring if she felt the caress, "like you do everything else."

"Including tie knots in your leader," retorted Alana.

Her voice was almost steady, but her eyes were still tightly closed.

"Most especially tying knots in my leader," he answered, laughing softly against her hair. "Ready?"

"To tie knots? I was born ready for that, obviously. No practice needed. Perfect tangle on the first try."

Then Alana took a deep breath.

"Rafe," she said softly, "I really don't want to open my eyes."

"How else can you admire the gorgeous tangles you make?"

"Braille," she said succinctly.

"Okay. Braille it is." Rafe hesitated. "For that to work, I'll have to be very close to you, Alana. Sometimes I'll have to take your foot and place it, or hold you, or even lift you."

"*No.*"

Then she spoke quickly, desperately, wanting to be sure Rafe understood how important it was.

"Don't lift me, Rafe. *Please.* That's my worst nightmare, my body being lifted high and then falling and falling and Jack— Oh, God," she said, horrified. "Jack. He fell. He fell into the darkness and rocks, and the water was like thunder everywhere and he died and—"

Alana's throat closed around screams and her eyes opened dark and wild, dilated with terror and memories that faded in and out like a nightmare.

Rafe ached to hold her, but he was nearly
certain it would trigger the terror he sensed
seething beneath her words, waiting to claim
her.

"Hush, wildflower," Rafe murmured. "I
won't lift you. You're safe with me."

Slowly Alana's eyes focused on the strong
hands braced on either side of her. She made
a despairing sound.

"Rafe, each time I come closer to remembering but never close enough. And each time
I'm so afraid. Does it ever end?"

"It will end," Rafe said, his voice a curious
mixture of reassurance and shared pain. "It
will end. And you'll survive. Like the wildflowers survive ice and darkness, sure of the
summer to come."

His lips brushed her nape.

"You're strong, Alana. So strong. I know
you don't believe that now, but you are. If you
didn't go under before, you won't go under
now. Believe me. I know. I've been there, too.
Remember?"

Alana put her forehead against Rafe's hand
and fought to control her breathing. After a
few minutes, she succeeded.

Only then did Rafe say quietly, "We're going to climb down, now. You'll have to help
me, Alana."

"H-How?"

"You'll have to trust me," he said simply.
"If you don't, you'll panic and then I'll have
to knock you out and carry you down. I don't
want to do that, Alana, even though I could

do it and never leave a bruise on your body.
Your mind, though . . ."

Alana shuddered, not noticing how intently
Rafe was watching her.

"Being knocked out and carried down the
mountain would be your worst nightmare
come true, wouldn't it?" Rafe asked softly.

The words went through Alana's mind like
a shock wave. Was that her nightmare? Being
knocked out and carried?

Slowly, hardly even realizing it, Alana
shook her head.

"No, that's not my nightmare. My nightmare is being lifted and then thrown, something throwing me away and then I'm falling,
falling forever, ice and darkness and death."

Rafe's voice was calm, but his eyes were
burning with the rage that came to him every
time he thought of Alana hurt, frightened,
screaming his name.

But none of his emotions showed in his
voice.

"Then you won't panic if I have to hold
you?" he asked matter-of-factly.

"I don't know," said Alana starkly. "I guess
we'll just have to find out the hard way, won't
we?"

"Yes, I guess we will."

When Alana felt Rafe move away, felt the
cool wind on her back where his warmth had
been, she wanted to cry out in protest. For a
moment she simply stood, eyes closed, hands
pressed against cold stone.

"About one foot below and slightly to your left is a flat stone," Rafe said.

He watched while Alana crouched slightly and felt around with the toe of her walking shoe, trying to find the surface he had described.

"Another inch down," he said. "That's it. Good."

Legs braced, arms outstretched but not touching her, Rafe followed Alana's progress.

"Now your right foot," he said. "Straight down, more, just another few inches. There. Feel it?"

Alana's answer was a drawn-out sound of relief when she felt the rock take her weight. She thought of opening her eyes again, but she didn't trust herself not to freeze.

Rafe described the next step, then the next, his hands always hovering just above Alana without touching her. He talked constantly, encouraging her.

Slowly Alana backed down the steepest part of the slope.

"Now, use your left foot," Rafe said. "This is a tricky one. There are two rocks close together. You want the one on the left. No, not that one, the—*Alana*."

The rock turned beneath her foot, throwing her off balance. Rafe grabbed her and held her in a hard grip, but only for an instant. Carefully he put her back on her feet.

Other than a choked cry when the stone first slid out from beneath her foot, Alana had made no protest, even when Rafe's hands closed around her arms. Yet she was very pale, and her hands shook noticeably as she searched for support among the tall boulders. Shudders rippled through her body.

Rafe sensed that Alana had fallen into nightmare again. Gently he turned her until she was facing him. He kept his hands on her shoulders, more to give her contact with the world than to support her.

"Alana, open your eyes. Look at me, not at the lake or the rocks. Just at me."

Slowly Alana's black eyelashes parted.

Rafe was only inches from her, his amber eyes narrowed and intent. His mustache was a deep, rich brown shot through with metallic highlights of bronze and gold. The pulse in his neck beat strongly, hinting at the heat and life beneath his tanned skin.

"It's daylight, not night," Rafe said softly. "It's warm, not icy. Jack is dead. You're alive and safe with me."

Mutely Alana nodded. Then she sighed and leaned against him.

Rafe wanted very much to put his arms around her, to hold her against his body and rock her until both of them felt only the other, knew only the other, comfort replacing fear.

But, like Alana, Rafe was afraid if he held her, there would be only fear and no comfort at all.

"I'm sorry you were frightened," murmured Rafe, smoothing his cheek against her hair.

"I was—but I wasn't. Not really." Alana took another long breath. "I knew after I called your name that you wouldn't let me fall."

And Rafe knew that Alana hadn't called his name. Not *this* time.

If she thought she had, she was still caught between the past and the present, a hostage to fear. Yet she had trusted him not to let her fall.

That, at least, hadn't changed.

After a few moments, Alana straightened and stood on her own.

"Let's finish it," she said, her voice flat.

"Aren't you going to close your eyes?"

"I don't think so. It's not as steep here, is it?"

"No. If you're going to take a look, though, do it now, when I'm close enough to catch you if you get dizzy."

Alana's mouth relaxed into a tiny smile. "I can't see through you, Rafe."

He turned partially, just enough to give her a brief view of the tumbled slope behind him. As he turned, he watched her face, ready to grab her if vertigo struck again.

Other than a flattening of her mouth, Alana showed no reaction. Even so, Rafe stayed very close for the first few steps. She glanced at him and tried to smile.

"I'm all right now," she said.

Rafe nodded, but he remained within reach of her. Together they worked their way down the last of the slope. When there was only lake in front of them, they stopped.

With a sense of triumph, Alana turned and looked back. She shook her head as she realized that the slope, which had seemed so steep and deadly from above, didn't look like much at all from the bottom.

"Fear always looks like that from the other side," Rafe said quietly.

Alana looked from the mountainside to the man beside her. Rafe's understanding of what she had been through, and his acceptance of her fear, untied knots deep inside her as surely as he had untied the snarls of fly line she had created. She put her palm against his cheek, savoring his warmth and the masculine texture of his skin.

"Rafael," she murmured, making music of his name. "You make me believe that someday I may even sing again."

Rafe turned his head until he could kiss the slender palm that rested against his cheek. He whispered Alana's name against her hand and smiled as her fingers curled up to caress his lips. Slowly Alana's other hand crept up to Rafe's head, hungry for his warmth and the smooth thickness of his hair between her fingers.

Moving as slowly as Alana did, Rafe tilted his head down until his lips could slant across hers. The kiss was so gentle that it was impossible to tell the exact instant when it began.

Alana neither hesitated nor pulled back when she felt Rafe's mouth caress hers. Instead, she whispered his name again and again, lost in the sensations that came as his lips brushed slowly against hers. His mouth moved from side to side with gentle pressures that made her fingers tighten in his hair, pulling his head closer in silent demand.

The tip of Rafe's tongue slid lightly over

Alana's lower lip, then traced the curves of her mouth until she sighed and her fingers kneaded down his neck to his shoulders, seeking the long, powerful muscles of his back. Her mouth softened, fitting itself to his.

When Alana's tongue touched first his lips, then his teeth, Rafe made a sound deep in his chest. His hands clenched at his sides as he fought not to give in to his hunger to hold her, to feel her body soften and flow over his as surely as her mouth had.

Hesitantly Rafe touched the warmth and sweetness of her tongue with his own. Even then she didn't retreat. The kiss deepened until the sound of his own blood beating inside his veins drowned out the cascade's rushing thunder.

Rafe heard Alana call his name with hunger and need, a sound out of his dreams. As gently as a sigh, his fingers dared to touch her face, the smooth curve of her neck, the slenderness and feminine strength of her arms. When she showed no fear, he rubbed his palms lightly from her shoulders to her hands and back again.

She murmured and moved closer to him, letting his heat radiate through her. He shifted his stance, fitting her against him, touching her very gently with his hands while the sweet heaviness of desire swelled between them.

Alana forgot the past, forgot the nightmare, forgot everything but the taste of Rafe and the rough velvet of his tongue sliding over hers. Fire shimmered through her, called by his hunger and her own, fire melting her until she sagged against him, giving herself to his strength.

Rafe's arms circled Alana, holding her as she held him, molding her against the heat and hunger of his body. She responded with a movement that brought her even closer, standing on tiptoe, trying to become a part of him.

And then she moved sinuously, caressingly, stroking his body with her own.

With a ragged sound, Rafe let his arms close around Alana. As his arms tightened, they tilted Alana's hips against his thighs. The movement lifted her just enough that for an instant her toes lost contact with the ground.

In that instant, Alana went from passion to panic.

11

Even as Alana tried to wrench free of his embrace, Rafe realized what had happened. Cursing himself, he released her completely.

"I'm sorry."

They both spoke quickly, as one, identical words and emotions.

"It's not your fault."

Again their words tangled, each hurrying to reassure the other.

When Alana would have spoken again, Rafe gently put his fingers across her mouth.

"No," he said in a husky voice. "It's not your fault. I should have known better than to hold you. I thought I could trust myself. But

I'd forgotten how sweet and wild you are. Even in my deepest dreams, I'd forgotten."

Alana's black lashes closed. She tilted her face down so that Rafe couldn't see her expression until she was more certain of her self-control. When she looked at him again, there was no fear in the dark clarity of her eyes, only apology and the luminous residue of passion.

"Did you really dream of me, Rafael?" Alana asked, music and emotion making her voice as beautiful as her eyes.

"Yes," he said quietly. "It was all that kept me sane in hell."

Alana's breath caught at the honesty and pain in Rafe's voice. Her eyes searched his expression.

"What happened?" she asked.

Rafe hesitated. "It's not a pretty story. I'm not sure it's something you want to know."

"If you can stand to tell me, I can stand to hear it."

When Rafe still hesitated, Alana took his hand and started back along the lakeshore, leading him with a gentle pressure of her fingers.

"Never mind," she said. "We'll eat lunch and then we'll lie in the sun and count aspen leaves. Remember?"

The darkness left Rafe's eyes. His lips curved into an off-center smile.

"I remember," he said. "The first one who blinks has to start all over again."

"After paying a forfeit."

"Of course," Rafe said in a husky voice. "I remember that part very well."

A sideways look into his brilliant whiskey eyes told Alana that Rafe indeed hadn't forgotten. Her fingers tightened in his as he brought her hand up to his lips. He rubbed his mustache teasingly over her sensitive fingertips. Then he nibbled on the soft pad of flesh at the base of her thumb.

"What's that for?" asked Alana breathlessly.

"I blinked," admitted Rafe. "Didn't you see me?"

"No. I must have blinked, too."

"That's one you owe me."

"But we haven't started counting aspen leaves yet," Alana pointed out.

"Well, if you're going to get all technical on me, I guess I won't start keeping score until after lunch."

Smiling, Alana led Rafe to the hollow where they had left their backpacks. While he retrieved the fishing gear he had abandoned when he heard her scream, Alana set out a lunch of sandwiches and fruit.

They ate slowly, letting the sun and silence dissolve away the last residue of fear and nightmare. When Rafe was finished, he stretched out on his back with his hands linked behind his head.

After a few moments he said lazily, "Twenty-three."

"What?"

"I counted twenty-three aspen leaves before I blinked."

"You can't even see any aspens from where you are."

"Sure I can," Rafe said, his voice deep. "Just off over your shoulder."

Alana turned and looked. Sure enough, a golden crown of aspen leaves rose above a thick screen of dark evergreen needles.

"You blinked," Rafe said. "How many?"

"Eleven."

"That's two you owe me."

Saying nothing more, Rafe resumed staring over her shoulder.

"Aren't you ever going to blink?" asked Alana finally.

"Nope." Then, "Damn. Got me. Thirty-seven."

Alana shifted until she could look at the aspen without twisting around. She counted swiftly, then groaned when she blinked.

"It's coming back to me now," she said. "I used to lose this game all the time."

Rafe smiled. "Yeah. I remember that best of all. That's three you owe me."

He settled into counting again.

After a long pause he said, "It's coming back to me now. The trick is not to stare too hard—and be sure the wind isn't in your face. Then—damn. Forty."

Alana got as far as thirty-five before she blinked. She groaned again.

"That's four," Rafe said.

"Aren't you worried about collecting?" Alana asked, for he had made no move to kiss her.

Rafe's glance shifted.

"Are you?" he countered in a soft voice, watching her.

Alana's breath shortened, then sighed out.

"I don't know," she admitted, remembering both the pleasure and the panic she had felt by the lakeshore.

"Then I'll wait until you know," he said simply.

Alana propped herself on her elbow and rolled over to face Rafe. He ignored her, counting quickly, aspen leaves reflected in his amber eyes.

She looked at the grace and strength of him as he lay at ease, legs crossed at the ankles, jeans snug over his muscular thighs and lean hips. The dark blue T-shirt had pulled free of his pants, revealing a narrow band of skin the color of dark honey. A line of hair so deeply brown that it was almost black showed above the low-riding jeans. Where the shirt still covered him, it fit like a shadow, smooth, sliding, moving when he did, a cotton so soft that it had felt better than velvet against her palms when she had touched him by the lake.

"Seven thousand six hundred and ninety-two," Rafe said.

"What?"

"Seven thousand six hundred and ninety-two."

"You can't have counted that many leaves without blinking," she protested.

Rafe smiled. For the last few minutes, he had been watching Alana rather than aspen leaves, but she hadn't noticed because she had been watching every part of him except his eyes.

And her smile told him that she very much approved of what she saw.

"Would you believe two thousand?" Rafe asked innocently.

Alana shook her head so hard that the motion sent her silky cap of hair flying.

"Two hundred?" asked Rafe.

"Nope."

"Fifty?"

"Well . . ."

"Sold," Rafe said smoothly. "That's five you owe me."

"But I haven't had my turn yet."

"Think it will do any good?"

Alana sighed and stared very hard at an aspen, but all she saw was the image of Rafe burned into her mind, into her very soul. She blinked to drive away his image, then groaned when she realized that single blink had cost her the contest.

"Fifteen," she said in disgust.

Rafe smiled and turned his attention back to aspen leaves quivering in the breeze. When Alana's fingers touched his cheek, his counting paused, then resumed. When her hand slid up the arm that was pillowing his head, his counting slowed. When her fingertip traced the supple veins showing beneath his skin, her touch sliding slowly up and down the sensitive inner side of his arm, Rafe stopped counting altogether.

"You're cheating, wildflower," he said in a husky voice.

"I finally remembered."

"What did you remember?"

"How I used to win this game."

"Funny," he said, "I remember us both winning. Every time."

"I wish—" Alana's voice broke. "I wish that it could be like that again. I wish you had never gone away that last time."

She took a ragged breath and then asked the question that she had asked herself a thousand times since she had learned that Rafe was alive.

"What happened, Rafe? What did I do to deserve your silence?"

He didn't answer for so long that Alana was afraid he would refuse to answer at all.

"Do you mean the letter I returned to you?" he asked finally.

"Yes, but even before that. Why did you let me believe you were dead? Other people knew you were alive, but not me. I didn't find out until a year ago."

"I thought you were happily married."

Alana searched Rafe's expression with eyes that were too dark, remembering too much of pain and not enough of happiness.

"How could you believe that?" she asked. "I loved you. I thought you loved me."

"I did."

"Then how could you believe I loved Jack?"

Rafe's lips flattened into a grim line. "It happens all the time to soldiers. The Dear John syndrome. One man goes off to war and another man stays to comfort the girl who was left behind."

"It wasn't like that," whispered Alana. "I married Jack because singing was all I had left after they told me you were dead. It was a business marriage."

"Alana—"

"He never touched me," she said, talking over Rafe. "I wouldn't let him. I couldn't bear to be touched by any man but you."

Rafe closed his eyes. When they opened again, they were hard, focused on the past, a past that had nearly destroyed him.

"I didn't know," he said. "All I knew was that six weeks after I 'died,' the woman who once said she loved me became half of Country's Perfect Couple. Everywhere I turned I saw Jack 'n' Jilly, America's favorite lovers, singing songs to each other, love songs that were beautiful enough to make Broken Mountain weep."

"Rafael . . ." Alana's voice frayed.

"Let me finish," Rafe said tightly. "I may never talk about it again. God knows I'd just as soon forget it, every second of it."

"The way I did?" she asked, her voice flat, all music gone. "That wouldn't make it better. Believe me, Rafe. Forgetting the way I did just makes it worse in the long run. I can't imagine anything more awful than my nightmares."

Rafe closed his eyes and let out a long, harsh breath.

"I know," he said. "I learned the hard way

that forgetting or ignoring doesn't make anything go away. So I'm going to tell you something that's buried in filing cabinets in the
Pentagon and in the minds of the very few
men who survived. Something that never happened at all, officially."

Alana said nothing, afraid to move, straining to hear Rafe's low voice.

"I told you I was in the army," he said.
"Well, I was, but in a very special branch of
it. I was trained in counterinsurgency, with
special attention to rural areas." He smiled
grimly. "Really rural. God, but I learned to
hate jungles."

After the silence had stretched for several
moments, Alana touched Rafe's arm with gentle fingers.

"What happened?" she asked, her voice
soft.

"Four years ago, I'd just about decided that
I'd rather fight lost causes with my thick-
skulled father in Wyoming than fight lost
causes in the jungles of Central America. I
owed the army some more time, though."

Alana waited, remembering. When Rafe had
asked her to marry him, he had also told her
that they would be separated a lot of the time
for two more years. Then he would quit the
army and come back and marry her.

"Just before I left Wyoming the last time,
some of our men were taken prisoner along
with a native guerrilla leader," Rafe said.
"There was no chance of getting our men back
through regular diplomatic means, because

the men weren't officially there in the first place. The records had them posted to Chile or West Germany or Indochina, anywhere but Central America."

Motionless, Alana listened.

"We couldn't just write off the men," Rafe said, "even though word was that nobody survived prison there for long. And we needed that guerrilla leader. My group was asked to volunteer for a rescue attempt."

Alana's eyes closed, knowing what was coming next.

"You volunteered," she said, her voice barely a thread of sound.

"I knew the men who had been caught. One of them was a very good friend. Besides," Rafe said matter-of-factly, "I was good at what I did. With me leading the raid, it had a better chance of succeeding."

She took a deep breath and nodded. For the first time, some of the agony she had gone through four years ago began to make sense.

"I understand," she said quietly.

"Do you?" Rafe asked.

He looked directly at Alana for the first time since he had begun to speak of the past.

"Do you really understand why I left you?" he asked. "Why I *volunteered* to leave you?"

"You couldn't have lived with yourself if you had stayed safe and the other men had died," Alana said simply, stroking the hard line of Rafe's jaw with a gentle fingertip. "That's the kind of man you are. You'd never buy your own comfort with another person's life."

Rafe kissed the finger that had moved to caress his mustache.

"Most women wouldn't understand."

"Most women never know a man like you."

"Don't kid yourself," Rafe said harshly. "I'm no hero. I scream just as loud as the next guy when the rubber-hose brigade goes to work."

Alana's eyes widened darkly as the meaning of Rafe's words sank in. She touched his face with gentle fingers, smoothing away the lines of rage that had come when he remembered the past.

"You're a man of honor, Rafael. That's all anyone can ask."

For long moments Rafe said nothing, responding to her with neither look nor words. Then he let out his breath.

"I'm glad you think so, Alana. There were times I didn't think much of myself. Men died. I was their leader. I was responsible for their lives."

"They were soldiers. Volunteers. Like you."

"And I led them right into hell."

Alana's fingers smoothed the grim lines bracketing Rafe's mouth.

"Was there another way you could have done it?" she asked softly.

"No." His voice was bitter. "That's how I knew I'd led them into hell. The road there is paved with the best intentions. The better the intentions, the deeper you go.

"And all the way down you know that there was nothing you could have done differently, that if you were put in the same position again you'd do the same thing again, the honorable thing . . . and you'd take the same good people down with you.

"And that," he said savagely, "is my definition of hell on earth."

Words crowded Alana's throat, all but choking her. She spoke none of them, sensing that the only words that could help Rafe right now were his own. She caressed him gently, her fingers smoothing his skin in undemanding touches that told him she was there, listening, sharing his pain as much as she could.

"I've thought about that mission a lot," Rafe said after a time. "But I've never said anything to anyone since I was debriefed."

"You couldn't."

"It wasn't so much the security regulations that kept me quiet. I just never found anyone who I thought would understand what it was like to be scared every second of every day, to be scared and fight not to show it, to face each dawn knowing that it probably wouldn't be better than yesterday and often it would be worse."

Alana touched Rafe's wrist, felt the life beating beneath his supple skin.

"Not many people know what it is like to serve an indeterminate sentence in hell," Rafe said. "Waiting and listening to the screams while the damned are tortured, waiting and listening and knowing that soon you would be screaming, too."

Alana made a stifled sound and turned very pale. Yet after a brief hesitation, her hand never stopped touching Rafe, giving him what comfort she could while he relived a nightmare she could barely imagine, but could understand all too well.

The man she loved had been imprisoned and tortured until he screamed.

Whatever memories I have hidden in my nightmares, Alana told herself silently, Rafe's must be worse, memory and nightmare alike. Yet he survived. He is here, strong despite the cruel violence of the past, patient with me despite my weakness, gentle with me despite the brutality that he has known.

As Rafe continued talking, low-voiced and intense, Alana took his hand and pressed it against her cheek, as though simple touch could take the agony and bitterness from his past. And her own.

"I went into the jungle alone," he said, "about three days ahead of the others. They needed someone to get inside the prison for a fast recon so we'd know how many of the men were alive and able to walk on their own. It was too dangerous a job to ask anyone to volunteer for."

Rafe stared past Alana, his eyes unfocused, remembering. Yet even then his fingers moved lightly against Alana's cheek, telling her that her presence helped him as much as anything could.

"I got into the prison without any problem," Rafe said. "Wire fences and a few perimeter guards. They were counting on the jungle and the prison's reputation as a hellhole to keep people away."

Rafe's fingers tensed on Alana's cheek.

"It was a hellhole, all right," he said. "What I saw there made me want to execute every guard, every government officer, everyone I could get my hands on. And then I wanted to burn that prison with a fire so hot it would melt through to the center of the earth."

Rafe closed his eyes, afraid that if they were open, Alana would see what he saw. Men chained and tortured, maimed and slowly murdered for no better reason than the entertainment of guards who were too brutal to be called men and too inventive in their savagery to be called animals. Grinning devils ruling over a green hell.

"I got the information and I got out," Rafe said. "The next day I led my men back in."

His eyes opened. They were clear and hard as topaz, the eyes of a stranger.

"As soon as we pulled out the men we came for, I went back to that prison. Three of my men came with me, against my orders. They were the three who had seen the wing where prisoners were tortured. The four of us freed every prisoner and then we blew that building straight back to the hell that had spawned it."

Alana held Rafe's hand against her lips, trying to comfort him and herself, rocking slowly.

"One of the men who came back with me

was injured. The other two carried him to the rendezvous while I stayed behind to cover the retreat.

"Some of the guards survived the blast. I held them off until my gun jammed. They caught me, shot me, and left me for dead in the clearing. The helicopter got away, though. I heard it lift off just after I was shot."

Alana made a low sound.

"I survived. I don't remember much about it. Some of the peasants hid me, did what they could for my wounds. Then the government soldiers came back. I was too weak to escape."

Alana bit her lips against the useless protests aching in her throat.

Rafe kept talking quietly, relentlessly, getting rid of the savage memories from the past.

"They took me to another prison just like the one I'd blown to hell. I knew there was no hope of rescue. My men had seen me shot. They would assume I was dead. Besides, you don't risk twenty men to save one, unless that one is damned important. I wasn't."

Wanting to speak, afraid to stop the flow of Rafe's words, Alana murmured softly against his palm and tried not to cry aloud. Her hands smoothed his arm and shoulder again and again, as though to convince herself that he really was alive and she was with him, touching him.

"I spent a long time in that prison," Rafe said. "I don't know why I didn't die. A lot of men did and were happy to."

Then Rafe turned and looked at Alana.

"That's not quite true," he said. "I know why I survived. I had something to live for. You. I dreamed of you, of playing the harmonica while you sang, of touching you, making love to you, hearing you laugh, feeling and seeing your love for me in every touch, every smile."

"Rafael," she whispered, and could say no more.

"The dreams kept me sane. Knowing that you were waiting for me, loving me as much as I loved you, gave me the strength to escape and to live like an animal in the jungle until I crossed into a country where I wouldn't be shot on sight."

Alana bent over to kiss Rafe, no longer caring if he saw her tears.

"And then," Rafe said, his voice flat, "I came home to find that the woman I'd loved enough to live for didn't love me enough to wait for me."

"That's not true!" Alana said, her voice a low cry of pain.

"I know. Now. I didn't know then. All I knew was what the papers told me. Jack 'n' Jilly. Perfect marriage. Perfect love. No one told me any different."

"No one knew," Alana said raggedly. "Not even my family. Jack and I worked very hard to keep the truth of our marriage a secret."

"You succeeded."

Rafe looked at Alana for a long moment, seeing his pain and unhappiness reflected in her dark eyes and pale face. He touched her lips with his fingertip, loosening the tight line of her mouth.

"I left the army as soon as my time was up," Rafe said. "My father was dead by then. I came back to the ranch as bitter a man as has ever watched the sun rise over Broken Mountain. Until a year ago, I ran the ranch through my lawyers and lived out of the Broken Mountain fishing camp. Alone."

Alana closed her eyes against the tears she couldn't control.

"If only I had known you were alive . . ." she whispered.

"But I wasn't sure that I was alive," Rafe said. "Not really. Most of my time was still spent in hell. No one on this side of the mountain even knew that I hadn't died. Except Sam, and he wouldn't tell anyone."

"Sam?" Alana asked, startled.

"He took some training in Panama. Different outfit. Civilian, not military. We worked together once, just before I left the army. He's a good man, if a bit hardheaded. And that's all I have to say on the subject of Sam Burdette."

Alana started to object, then realized that it would do no good. Rafe might share his own secrets with her, but her brother's secrets were not Rafe's to share. She looked at Rafe with eyes that understood, eyes as dark as midnight, as dark as her nightmares.

"When did you decide to tell people that you were alive?" she asked.

"I didn't. It just happened."

Rafe shook his head slowly, remembering his rage and bitterness at life and the woman who had married another man just six weeks after her fiancé had been declared dead.

"I ran into Bob one day in the high country," Rafe said. "He was fishing that crazy fly he favors. And he went straight down the mountain to you."

Without realizing it, Alana's fingers tightened on Rafe's arm as she remembered the moment that Bob had burst into the house talking about Rafe Winter, a man come back from the dead—and looking like it. Hard and bitter, eyes as cold as a February dawn.

Rafe. *Alive.*

And Alana was married to a man she didn't love.

"A day later," Rafe said, watching her, "Bob brought me a letter. I recognized your handwriting on the envelope. I looked at it for a long, long time."

"Why didn't you—" she began.

"I knew I couldn't open my own Dear John letter," Rafe interrupted savagely. "I couldn't force myself to read the words describing your perfect marriage, perfect career, perfect man, perfect lover. I couldn't read the death of my dream written in your own hand, the dream that had kept me alive when most of me hurt so much that death looked like heaven itself."

Alana shook her head. Tears fell from her tightly closed eyes. With a ragged sound, she put her head on Rafe's chest and held him until her arms ached. She couldn't bear the thought of Rafe being tortured, dreaming of her, surviving because he loved her.

And then coming home to find her married.

"What was in the letter?" Rafe asked.

His voice was so soft that it barely penetrated the sound of Alana's tears.

"The truth," Alana said hoarsely. "I was going to leave Jack. When I was free, I was going to write to you again, if you wanted me to."

"But you didn't leave Jack."

"No." She drew a ragged breath. "When I lost you a second time, I thought nothing mattered. I went back to Jack."

Rafe's eyelids flinched. It was the only sign he gave of the pain within him at the thought that he had sent her back to Jack Reeves.

"But when I knew you were alive," Alana said, "I couldn't stay with Jack. Not even to save our singing career. So we lived separately, but very discreetly."

Slowly she shook her head, remembering the past.

"Separation wasn't enough," she whispered. "You didn't want me, hadn't even cared for me enough to tell me you were alive, but I had to be free of the sham marriage. I had lived with lies for too long. When you were dead, the lies hadn't mattered to me. Nothing had mattered except singing.

"That's how I survived, Rafe. I sang to the memory of the man I loved, not to Jack. Never to him."

"And then," Rafe said bitterly, "I wrote

your death sentence on an envelope and sent it back to you."

"What?"

Rafe swore savagely.

Alana trembled, not knowing why he was so angry with himself.

"What did you mean?" asked Alana, her voice shaking as she looked at Rafe's narrowed eyes. "Why was that envelope my death sentence?"

"It sent you back to Jack Reeves."

"What—"

"The answer is in your nightmares," Rafe said, cutting off Alana's question.

Her eyes searched Rafe's, looking for answers but seeing only herself reflected in the clear amber.

"How do you know?" she asked.

"That, too, is in your nightmares."

Rafe's hands came up to frame Alana's face.

"There's something else in those lost days, wildflower," he murmured, kissing her lips gently. "There's the moment you saw me, knew me, turned to me."

He kissed her again, more deeply.

"Rafe—"

"No," he said softly. "I've told you more than the good doctor wanted me to. But I thought it might help you to know that something other than horror is buried with those six missing days."

12

FOR A LONG TIME THERE WAS only silence and the rushing sound of the distant cascade.

Rafe's expression told Alana that questioning him would be futile. He had the same closed look that he had worn when he talked about leading his men into hell.

But it angered her that Rafe knew something about her six lost days and wouldn't tell her.

"Why?" Alana asked finally, her voice harsh. "Why won't you help me?"

"You didn't know Jack was dead. People told you he was. How much help was that?"

Alana searched Rafe's topaz eyes.

"But—" she began.

"But nothing," he interrupted in a flat voice. "Did knowing Jack was dead help you remember anything?"

Alana clenched her hands.

"No," she said.

"Did waking up in that hospital beaten and bloody tell you how you got hurt?"

Silence. Then, tightly, "No."

"Did reading about Jack's death in every newspaper help?"

"How did you know?" she whispered.

"In some ways you're a lot like me," Rafe said simply.

"But if you'd tell me what you know, it would help me sort out reality from nightmare."

"The doctors don't think so. They're afraid I might tell you something you don't want to know."

"What?"

"I might tell you that your nightmares are pieces of the truth."

Rock and ice and wind, something lifting her, throwing her out into the darkness
falling
she was falling and rocks waited below, waited to break her, hatred breaking her.

Alana made a small sound and went pale. She wrapped her arms around herself as she felt the cold of nightmares congeal inside her, fear and truth freezing her. She closed her eyes as though it would shut out the fragments of nightmare.

Then she wondered if it was memory that she was shutting out, reality chasing her through her nightmares, truth saying to her, *remember me.*

Rafe reached for Alana, wanting to gather her into his arms and comfort her.

When his hands touched her, she gasped and flinched away.

Rafe withdrew instantly, but the cost of controlling himself made muscles stand out rigidly along his jaw. He looked at Alana's pale skin and black lashes, her mouth shaped for smiling but drawn by fear into a thin line, the pulse beating too quickly in her throat.

With a soundless curse, Rafe closed his eyes. The doctors were right. Telling her wouldn't help.

Even worse, it could hurt her.

At first Rafe had been afraid that Alana would remember too soon, before he had a chance to win her love again. Now he was afraid that she wouldn't remember soon enough, that she would lose faith in herself and then tear herself apart.

Yet Rafe couldn't bring back Alana's memory for her, no matter how much he wanted to. The bitterness of that knowledge made the brackets around his mouth deeper, harder.

"If telling you everything I know about those six days would stop you from freezing when I touch you, I'd shout the truth from the top of Broken Mountain," Rafe said, his voice rough with suppressed emotion.

Alana said nothing.

"My God, don't you know that I'd do anything to have you in my arms again?" Rafe whispered. "I want you so badly. I want to hold you, comfort you, love you . . . *and I can't.* All I can do is hurt you again and again."

Rafe's hands became fists. With a quick movement, he rolled over until his back was turned toward Alana.

"It's like Central America all over again," he said harshly, "only it's worse because this time it's you I'm leading into hell, knowing with every step that there's no other way, knowing and hating myself just the same."

His laugh was a short, savage sound.

"Christ," Rafe said harshly, "I don't blame you for shrinking away every time I touch you."

The raw emotion in Rafe's voice called Alana out of the depths of the nightmare as nothing else could have. She knew what it was like to feel snarled and helpless, hating yourself, feeling as though everything you did made the tangle worse, not better.

The thought of Rafe feeling that way because of her made Alana ache with tears she couldn't shed. In just the past day, Rafe had given so much to her, laughter and protection, patience and companionship, subtle passion, and, above all, acceptance.

She might rail at herself for being weak, she

might be angry and disgusted with herself . . . but Rafe was not.

When she was close to hating herself, he had told her about strength and weakness and survival, torture and the breaking point every human being has. He had told her about his own time in hell, and in doing so he had coaxed her out of the depths of her own self-disgust.

Rafe had given her hope when all she had was nightmare.

And for that she flinched when he touched her.

"Rafael," murmured Alana, touching his arm.

He made no response.

She shifted her position until she was on her knees. She leaned over Rafe, stroking him from the thick silk of his hair down to the corded tension of his neck. She repeated his name again and again, a slow litany that was nearly a song.

Her hand moved down, trying to loosen the rigid muscles of his shoulders and back. The dark cotton of his T-shirt felt like warm velvet to her. Her fingers kneaded the hard flesh beneath. He felt so good to her, heat and smoothness and strength.

With a sigh, Alana bent over until she could put her lips just below the dark brown of his hairline. Rafe's neck was warm and firm, tanned skin stretched tautly over tendons, tempting her tongue to taste and trace each subtle change in texture.

She kissed him lightly, lingeringly, before

she gave in to temptation and touched his skin with the tip of her tongue. He tasted of salt and heat and man, slightly rough where his beard began and amazingly smooth on the back of his neck.

Delicately Alana's teeth closed on Rafe's neck, testing the resilience of the muscle beneath. He moved his head and shoulders slowly, increasing the pressure of her teeth on his flesh, making her hand slide over the muscles of his back.

Rafe tasted good, felt good. Alana wanted to touch and savor more of him. Her fingers dug into the bunched muscles beneath her hand as her teeth tested the male power of his shoulders.

Rafe arched against her touch like a hungry cat.

The honesty of his response made an equal hunger sweep through Alana, a hunger that only Rafe had ever called from her. She wanted to lie down next to him, to fit her body along his, to feel his passion surround her as she surrounded him.

Yet even as fire licked through her, melting her, Alana knew that if Rafe's arms closed around her, she would freeze. And in freezing, she would hurt him cruelly. Then she would hate herself all over again.

"Oh, Rafe," she said, her voice breaking on his name, "what are we going to do?"

"What we're doing right now feels wonderful."

"But I'm afraid I'll freeze."

Alana's words trembled with fear and the beginning of anger at herself.

"Does touching me frighten you?" Rafe asked.

Alana made an odd sound that could have been laughter.

"Touching you is like singing, Rafael. Only better."

She heard his breath come in sharply and felt the fine tremor that went through his body.

"Then touch me as much as you want," he said simply.

"That isn't fair to you."

Rafe's back shifted beneath Alana's hand, urging her to explore him, telling her more clearly than words that he wanted to be touched by her.

"Remember when you were nineteen?" he asked.

Alana's hand hesitated, then slid up Rafe's back to his hair. Eagerly her fingers sought the warmth of him beneath the thick pelt.

"Yes," she whispered. "I remember."

"You didn't object then."

"I didn't know what I was doing to you. Not really. Virgins can be very cruel."

"Did I complain?" asked Rafe, laughter and memories curling just beneath his words.

"No," she said softly.

"Did I ask for more than you wanted to give?"

"No. Never, Rafael."

"I never will."

With a smooth motion, Rafe rolled onto his back and looked at her with eyes that were clear amber, brilliant with emotion and desire.

"Do you believe me?" he asked.

"Yes."

"Then touch me."

"Even though I can't . . ." Alana's voice faltered.

"Yes," said Rafe swiftly, almost fiercely. "However much or little you want. Everything. Anything. I've dreamed of you for so long. Touch me, wildflower."

Hesitantly Alana's hands came up to frame Rafe's face. Her lips brushed across his while her fingers again sought the silky brown depths of his hair. With a sigh, her breath mingled with his and she knew again the heat and textures of his mouth. She made a throaty sound of pleasure as his taste spread across her tongue.

Forgotten sensations stirred, awakening. The kiss deepened into a timeless sensual joining as they gave themselves to each other, knowing only one another.

Finally, Alana lifted her mouth and looked at Rafe with eyes that remembered passion.

"The first time you kissed me like that," whispered Alana, "I thought I would faint. I think I could faint now. You take the world out from under me."

"Are you frightened?" Rafe asked quietly, watching Alana with smoky amber eyes.

She smiled slowly and shook her head.

"With you, there's no danger of falling,"

Alana said. "With you, I'm as weightless as heat balanced on fire."

She bent her head and kissed Rafe again, savoring every instant, every changing pressure of tongue on tongue, the heat and pleasure of his mouth joined with hers.

Her hands slid from his hair, caressing him with each tiny movement of her fingers. One hand curved around his neck just beneath his ear, her palm fitting perfectly against the slide and play of muscle as he moved his mouth across hers. Her other hand slid down his arm, only to return as her fingers sought the warmth of his skin beneath the short sleeve of his T-shirt.

She stroked Rafe, murmuring her pleasure as she felt him flex against her touch. Her hand slid higher until her palm rubbed his shoulder under the soft T-shirt. Catlike, Rafe arched into her caress, telling her how much he liked having her hand on his bare skin.

When Alana's mouth left his and she began to nibble on his mustache and his neck and finally, delicately, his ear, Rafe made a deep sound in his throat. She responded by tracing the outline of his ear with her mouth, then caressing him with slow, probing touches of her tongue that made his breath quicken.

"I remember how I shivered the first time you did that to me," whispered Alana, her breath warm against Rafe. "Do you remember?"

"Yes," he said huskily. "You had goose bumps all the way up and down your arms."

"Like you, now."

"Like me, now."

Alana's tongue touched Rafe's neck just as her teeth closed on his skin. Rafe moved his head, urging her to touch more deeply, to bite harder. Her teeth pressed into his flesh and she felt the male power in the tendon sliding beneath her mouth.

He had caressed her like that when the storm had chased them to the Broken Mountain cabin. His bite had been just short of pain and had brought a pleasure that had left her weak.

With a small sound, Alana caressed Rafe's neck down to his shoulder until her teeth closed on the T-shirt. Her hands kneaded down his chest to the warm band of skin where his shirt had pulled free of his jeans.

When her fingers touched his naked skin, Rafe's breath came in sharply. His weight shifted as his arms moved.

Alana waited, frozen, anticipating his embrace.

"It's all right," Rafe said softly. "See? No hands."

And it was true. Rafe had moved, but only to put his hands behind his head, fingers tightly laced against the nearly overwhelming temptation to touch Alana as she was touching him.

Alana smiled and relaxed against Rafe's side.

"Does that mean I can still touch you?" she asked.

He smiled just enough to show the tip of his tongue between the serrations of his teeth.

"What do you think?" he asked in a deep voice.

Alana's approving glance went from the rich pelt of Rafe's hair down the hard, masculine length of him.

"I think," said Alana, "that it's a miracle I kept my hands off you until I was twenty."

"And here I thought I was the one who deserved a medal."

"That's probably true," Alana admitted, her eyes brilliant with memories of a storm and a cabin loft. "I didn't know what I was missing. You did."

"Not really," Rafe said softly. "You were unique, sweet and wild, as generous as summer. You gave yourself to me so completely that you made me realize that I'd never made love to a woman until you. Not completely. And I've never made love since. Not completely."

"Rafael," Alana said softly, pleasure and pain and regret in a single word.

"I'm not asking you for anything," he said. "I know you're not ready to give yourself again. That doesn't mean I've forgotten how it was between us once—and how it will be again.

"But not now, this instant," Rafe added, regret and certainty evenly balanced in his deep voice. "I don't expect that now. It's enough that you're touching me, that you're here with me, that you're alive."

Alana felt the heat of Rafe's skin beneath her fingers, the tempting, silky line of hair curling down below his navel, and the sharp, involuntary movement of his body as her fingers slid beneath the soft T-shirt. She traced the long muscles of his torso from his waist to his ribs.

Eyes closed, smiling, Alana let her hands savor Rafe's strength and stillness and the changing, compelling textures of his body beneath her palm. Her fingers searched among the crisp hairs on his chest, alive to the feel of him, the silk and the hardness and the heat of him.

And Rafe watched her, wanting her.

Without stopping to think, Alana tugged at his T-shirt, impatient with even the soft cotton restricting the freedom of her touch. She had the T-shirt bunched up beneath his arms before she realized what she was doing.

"I'm sorry," Alana said raggedly, her eyes still closed. "I wasn't thinking."

"I was."

Rafe's voice was deep, caressing.

"What were you thinking?" she whispered. "That I'm a tease?"

"Open your eyes and I'll tell you."

His voice was gentle, coaxing, an intangible caress that made Alana shiver.

Her eyes opened slowly. She saw her hands against Rafe's chest, his nearly black hair curling up over her slender fingers. Her hands flexed sensuously, pressing her nails against his skin.

"What are you thinking?" she asked, watching his eyes as her nails bit gently into his flesh with tiny, sensual rhythms.

"I was thinking of the first time we made love. When I unbuttoned my shirt, you looked at me as though you'd never seen a man before, but I knew damn well that you lived with three brothers. And now," added Rafe softly, "you're looking at me like that again."

"Am I?" asked Alana, her voice barely a breath of sound.

"Do you want to take off my shirt?" Rafe asked, his eyes watching her with hungry intensity.

"Yes."

Alana bent to brush her lips across Rafe's mouth, loving the feel of him, firm and sweet, answering his heat with her own. She felt his lips smile beneath her caress; then his tongue moved teasingly over her mouth until she smiled in return.

"Then what are you waiting for?" asked Rafe. "Take off my shirt."

As he spoke, he unlocked his hands and stretched his arms above his head.

Alana's hands moved up Rafe's body, pushing the soft folds of T-shirt over his chest, his head, his arms, until the shirt fell aside, forgotten. Her breath came in, then went out in a long sigh as she ran her hands freely from Rafe's fingertips to his waist. His breath sounded more like a groan as he laced his hands behind his head once more.

For an instant, Alana hesitated. Then Rafe's

body twisted sinuously beneath her hands, asking to be touched. She whispered his name as she bent down and kissed him, hungry for the feel of his tongue against hers. Her palms rubbed slowly over his chest, stroking him, enjoying him. When her nails scraped gently over his nipples, she felt him shiver. Her fingertips circled him caressingly, then tugged at the small, hard nubs. His tongue moved sensually in her mouth, stealing her breath until she was dizzy.

With a ragged sound, Alana shifted her position and sought the powerful contours of Rafe's shoulders, tasting and biting and kissing him until her mouth slid down and found the hard male nipples her fingers had teased. Her teeth closed lightly over him. She felt the tension in him, felt his body flexing, felt the powerful muscles of his arms harden beneath her palms.

Memories raced through her, burning her.

"Funny," Alana murmured, rubbing her cheek over Rafe's chest, "I never thought of you as really strong, until the storm and the cabin loft."

Rafe smiled, though his fingers were so tightly laced around each other that his hands ached.

"Thought I was a weakling, did you?" he said, his voice soft but almost rough, hungry and laughing at the same time.

"Weakling?"

Alana laughed against Rafe's ribs before she turned her head and began caressing the long muscles of his torso with slow movements of her cheek and hand.

"No," she said. "But Dad was six foot five, and my brothers were all over six feet tall when they were twelve. Bob was six foot six and weighed two hundred and twenty pounds when he was fourteen."

"Whatever attracted you to a shrimp like me?" asked Rafe.

The question ended in a groan when the hard tip of Alana's tongue teased his navel.

"First it was your eyes," she said, her voice blurred as she caressed the taut skin of Rafe's stomach. "Like a cougar, clear amber and more than a little untamed."

"And that made you want to tame me?"

"No. It made me want to be wild with you."

Rafe's hands clenched until the fingers went numb. He tried to speak, but Alana's fingers had gone from his waist down to the hard muscles of his thighs. He could think of nothing except her touch and the fierce ache of hunger swelling so close to her hand.

"But I didn't know it then," continued Alana, kneading the long muscles that flexed and shifted beneath her fingers, "not in so many words. I just knew I got a funny, quivering feeling deep inside whenever you looked at me in a certain way."

"What way?"

Rafe fought to keep his voice even despite the waves of hunger that hammered through his blood. His fingers twisted against each other until bone ground over bone.

"The way you looked at me when you took off my wet blouse and hung it by the fire," Alana said.

Her breath was a warm flow across the naked skin above Rafe's waist.

"The way you looked at me when you peeled off that soaking, lacy bra," she whispered. "And then you touched me until I couldn't stand by myself. Do you remember?"

"God, yes." Rafe closed his eyes, remembering. "You were barefoot. Your jeans were black with rain and outlined you perfectly, those beautiful legs and hips. . . . Did you know that my hands were shaking when I took off your blouse?"

"Yes," she whispered, her fingers clenching for an instant on Rafe's leg. "I was trembling, too."

"You were cold."

"Was I?" she asked.

Her voice was almost breathless as she caressed Rafe's navel again, biting him gently.

"I burned when you touched me," Alana whispered. "Your hands were so warm on my skin."

"I didn't mean to undress you, not at first. But once I started, I couldn't stop. You were so beautiful, wearing only firelight. I couldn't stop looking at you, touching you."

"I didn't want you to stop. I felt like the most exquisite woman ever born when you looked at me, when you kissed me, touched me. And your body fascinated me."

Alana traced the line of skin just above

Rafe's jeans with her tongue. Her hand smoothed his thigh, enjoying the feel of his strength, remembering.

"When I finally touched you," she said, "every bit of you tightened until each muscle on your body stood out. You felt like warm steel. You feel like that now."

"*Alana.*"

The word was involuntary, a response torn from his control when he felt her hand settling over him.

"I found out how strong you were then," Alana whispered. "You lifted me high, then let me slide slowly, slowly down your body. So strong, yet so gentle. The eyes of a mountain cat and the hands of a poet."

Alana's mouth caressed Rafe's skin as her fingers unfastened his jeans, seeking him beneath layers of cloth, finding him. Her breath came out raggedly.

"And the rest of you so very male," Alana said huskily.

She rubbed her cheek across Rafe's stomach, then she turned her mouth to his skin and kissed him quickly, fiercely.

"Alana," Rafe said, his voice hoarse as he moved reflexively, sensually against her hand. "I can't take much more of this."

"Then don't," she said simply.

She traced the rigid muscles of his arm with one hand, feeling the mist of passion and restraint that covered his body.

"You've given me so much," she said. "Let me give you something in return. It's not as much as either of us wants, but it's all I have right now."

Rafe closed his eyes for a moment, knowing if he looked at Alana, he wouldn't be able to keep his fingers locked behind his head.

Her hand moved again in a devastating, sensual glide of flesh over flesh. Fire thickened in Rafe's veins, fire pooling heavily beneath Alana's hand until he could only twist against the sweet agony of her touch. He groaned aloud, his breath hissing between clenched teeth.

"Oh, God . . . don't," he said hoarsely.

"Rafael," said Alana. "I can't give myself to you now, but you can give yourself to me. Please, give yourself to me. Let me know that I've been able to bring you some pleasure. I need to know that."

Her voice was husky and urgent as she rubbed her cheek against his hot chest.

Rafe's eyes opened, an amber hot enough to burn.

"Look at me," he said.

Alana lifted her head. He saw the silent plea in her dark eyes, saw the fire and fierce pleasure when he moved against her hand, and he knew that she had been utterly honest with him.

Slowly he unlocked his fingers, but he moved only one hand, and then only to hold it out to her. When her lips pressed against his palm, his hand shifted, gently bringing her mouth up to his. What began as a simple brush of lips deepened with each heartbeat until it became a kiss of shattering hunger and sensuality.

And then he gave himself to her as freely and generously as she had given herself to him four years ago, in a cabin warmed by firelight and love.

13

ALANA PULLED THE BUB-bling, spicy apple pie out of the oven, using oversize pot holders that felt as soft to her touch as Rafe's T-shirt had. She smiled to herself as she set the second pie on the wooden counter to cool, feeling more at peace than she had in a long time. Notes of music kept gliding through her mind, chased by lyrics that hadn't yet condensed into songs.

"What is that marvelous smell?" asked Janice from the doorway.

"Pie," said Alana, turning and smiling over her shoulder at the tall, slender woman.

"A miracle," Janice said.

Alana smiled. "Actually, it's just dried apples, sugar, and spices."

"In this wilderness, on that stove, those pies are a miracle," said Janice firmly. She looked at Alana with blue eyes that missed nothing. "Anything I can do to help?"

"I've got everything under control, but thanks anyway."

Janice smiled. "Must be a wonderful feeling."

"What?"

"Having everything under control."

Alana looked startled for an instant. Then she nodded slowly.

It was true. Since she had awakened in the hospital, she had felt as though her life was out of her control, as though she was a victim instead of a person. Fear had eroded her self-respect and confidence.

But today she had been able to talk and laugh with Rafe. Today she had taken the first steps toward overcoming her fear of heights. Today she had realized that Rafe respected and cared for her despite her amnesia and irrational fears.

Rafe had accepted her as she was, imperfect, and then he had given himself to her instead of demanding that she give herself to him.

"Yes," Alana said quietly. "It's an incredibly good feeling."

Janice's eyes narrowed in an instant of intelligent scrutiny that Alana didn't notice.

"I'm glad," said Janice, unmistakable satisfaction in her voice.

Alana looked up quickly, seeing for the first time the compassion in the other woman.

"Rafe told you about my husband, didn't he?" Alana asked.

Janice hesitated while her shrewd blue eyes measured the emotions apparent on Alana's face.

"Don't be angry with him," Janice said finally. "Rafe just wanted to be sure that Stan and I wouldn't accidentally hurt you."

Frowning, Alana wiped her hands on the enormous white apron that she wore.

"It's not fair to ask you to walk on eggs so I won't be upset," Alana said. "This trip is for your pleasure, not mine."

Janice smiled. "Don't worry. We're having a ball."

Alana looked at her with skeptical dark eyes.

"Uh-huh," Alana muttered. "Sure you are—when I'm not screaming at Stan or stealing your fishing guide."

"Stan's a big boy," said Janice dryly. "And as for Rafe, he showed us the water and we caught our limit. Besides, he cleans the trout for us and you whip up hot apple pies. What more could we ask?"

Laughing and shaking her head, Alana gave in.

"You two are very special dudes," Alana said. "If other clients are half as easy to be around, Bob will think he's died and gone to heaven. Most dudes can't find their way downhill without directions and a hard push."

From the next room came the sound of cupboard doors being opened and closed briskly.

"Hey, sis," called Bob from the dining room, "where did I put the dishes last night after I washed them?"

Janice and Alana exchanged a look and burst out laughing. Bob stuck his head in the kitchen.

"What's so funny?" he asked.

"You wouldn't understand," said Alana. "But that's all right. I love you anyway."

She stood on tiptoe and kissed Bob's cheek quickly.

He looked surprised, then very pleased. He started to hug Alana in return, then stopped, remembering. He patted her shoulder with unexpected gentleness and put his blunt index finger on the tip of her nose.

"You look better, sis. Rafe was right. You needed to be home."

Then Bob shook his head and smiled, giving Alana a somewhat baffled look. He still wasn't used to seeing his sister as a contemporary rather than as a substitute mother.

"What?" Alana asked.

"How did you get to be so small, anyway?" Bob said in a rueful voice.

"You grew up."

He smiled. "Yeah, guess so. Why don't you go get dressed? I'll whip up the potatoes and get everything on the table."

Alana blinked, startled by the offer. Then she blinked again, several times, fighting back sudden tears. Bob was being as protective of her as he was of Merry.

"Thanks," Alana said, her voice husky. "I'd like that."

She showered quickly, then climbed into the loft wrapped in Bob's oversize terry cloth robe, which she had found hanging from a peg in the downstairs bathroom. She stood in front of the closet and tried to choose from the array of clothes that Bob had packed for her.

After an unusual amount of time, she decided on a pair of heavy silk slacks that were a rich chocolate color. The blouse she chose was long sleeved and the color of fire, its sensuous texture and folds in stark contrast to its businesslike cut.

Automatically Alana began to button up the blouse so the chain she always wore was concealed. Then she stopped, realizing that she no longer had to hide Rafe's engagement gift. It no longer mattered if people asked her about the unusual design of the necklace.

Jack was dead.

She no longer had to conceal the fact that half of Country's Perfect Couple wore another man's gift in the vulnerable hollow of her throat.

Alana smoothed the collar open. The elegant symbol of infinity shifted and gleamed with each movement of her head. She touched the symbol with her fingertip and felt another tiny bit of peace settling inside her, another step on the way to rebuilding her strength.

For the first time since she had awakened in

the hospital, she began to believe that she not only would survive, but would be able to love again.

Even if her nightmares were true.

"Alana?" Rafe's voice came from the bottom of the steep stairway. "Are you ready?"

"Almost," she whispered, too softly for Rafe to hear. "Almost."

She hurried downstairs, truly hungry for food for the first time since the six missing days. High-country air had a magical effect on her appetite.

It was the same for everyone else. Even after a dinner of trout, potatoes, green beans, and biscuits, everyone found room for a piece of pie.

Rafe sliced and served the warm apple pie to the accompaniment of good-natured complaints as to which person was or wasn't getting the biggest piece. Bob and Stan swapped pieces with each other several times before Rafe gave in and put the last piece of pie between them.

Smiling, Rafe watched Alana as she ate the last bite of the generous slice of pie he had cut for her. When she threw back her head and sighed that she was too full to move, he saw the gleam of gold in the hollow of her throat.

With a callused fingertip, he traced the length of the chain and its elegant symbol.

"You still wear this," he said softly.

"I've never taken it off since you gave it to me."

Rafe's eyes were tawny in the late-afternoon

light that was streaming through the window, tawny and very intent.

"Not even after I sent back your letter?" he asked, searching her eyes.

"Never. It was all I had left of you."

The back of Rafe's finger caressed Alana's throat.

"I wish we were alone," he whispered. "I would like very much to kiss you. Many times. Many places. Would you like that, wildflower?"

A suggestion of color bloomed beneath Alana's skin. She smiled and smoothed her cheek against Rafe's finger.

"Yes," she murmured. "I'd like that."

Then Alana looked across the table and saw Stan watching her closely, his eyes so blue they were almost black, his fair hair shimmering in a shaft of sunlight that came through the cabin window and fell across his thick shoulders. Quickly she looked away, still unable to accept Stan's unnerving physical resemblance to Jack Reeves.

When Stan asked Rafe about a particular kind of dry fly, Alana turned to Janice and asked the first question that came to mind.

"Somehow you aren't what I'd expect a travel agent to be. How did you choose that career?"

There was a sudden silence, then a determined resumption of the casual conversation taking place around the women.

Alana looked at Rafe suddenly, wondering if she had done something wrong.

Rafe ignored her, apparently caught up in his talk with Stan.

"I'm sorry," Alana said to Janice. "Did I ask the wrong question?"

Janice's smile had a wry twist as she glanced sideways at Rafe.

"I'd say you asked just the right one," Janice said.

Rafe looked up sharply but said nothing.

"I used to be a psychiatrist," Janice explained. "After ten years, I burned out. So many problems. So few solutions."

Her voice was light but her eyes were narrowed against memories that still had the power to hurt her.

Alana thought of what had happened to Rafe, to her, to Jack. *So many problems. So few solutions.*

"So I became a special kind of travel agent," Janice said. "I match people with the kind of vacation that will do the most for them."

"Solutions," said Alana.

"Yes."

Alana wanted to ask more. Suddenly she was very curious about Janice's past, about the pressures that had driven her to change careers.

And about Rafe, who had known Janice before.

"Would you like to hear about what happened?" asked Janice.

"If you don't mind," Alana said.

Janice and Rafe exchanged a quick look. He

raised his dark eyebrows slightly, then shrugged.

Janice turned back to Alana.

"I used to work for the government, like Rafe," said Janice.

Though she spoke quietly, at her first words Stan and Rafe's conversation died.

Stan gave Janice a hard look, then looked questioningly at Rafe. Rafe ignored him. Stan seemed about to speak when a gesture from Rafe cut him off.

"Men and women who work under impossible conditions," Janice said calmly, "often have trouble living with themselves. If something goes wrong and people die, or if nothing goes wrong and people die anyway, the person in charge has to live with it."

Alana looked at Rafe. His eyes were hooded, unreadable.

"The key words are *in charge*," Janice said. "These are intelligent people who care about the world. They are the actors, not the audience. They are in control of themselves and of life."

Janice smiled wryly and took a sip of her coffee.

"At least," she added softly, "they *think* they're in control. Then it all goes from sugar to shit and they're left wondering what hit them. My job was to explain that it was reality that ran over them and left them flat."

Stan made a sound halfway between protest and laughter. When Janice looked at him, he

winked. The smile she gave him was both gentle and sensual.

Alana sensed the nearly intangible currents
of affection and respect that flowed between
the two people.

"People come in all kinds," Janice said,
turning back to Alana, "but the ones I dealt
with usually fell into three categories. The first
was people who couldn't cope with an unpre-
dictable, unforgiving reality and simply fell
apart."

Alana looked down at the bit of pie left on
her plate and wondered if she was one of the
ones who couldn't cope.

"In the second category were the people
who survived by stuffing down their feelings
of inadequacy, bewilderment, and fear. These
people did exactly what they had been trained
to do and they did it magnificently."

Alana looked at Rafe. He was watching her.
For an instant he put his fingertip on the
golden symbol she wore around her neck.

"The third category," Janice said, "was
made up of people who had so little imagination or such great faith in 'going by the
book' that they had the same untouchable serenity that religion gives to some people."

"It must be nice," Alana said.

"I wouldn't know," Rafe answered.

Janice picked up her coffee cup, sighed, and
put it down again without tasting the dark
brew.

"People in the first category, the ones who
couldn't cope, didn't last long as operatives,"

Janice said bluntly. "The third type, the ones who went by the book, did very poorly in the fluid world of fieldwork. We tended to put them in office positions as soon as they were discovered."

"And the second category?" Alana asked Janice, but it was Rafe whom she watched.

"Those in the second category did most of the work," Janice said. "They were the survivors, the people who got the job done no matter what it cost them."

The brackets around Rafe's mouth deepened.

"Unfortunately," Janice said, glancing quickly at Rafe, "sooner or later the survivors paid a high psychic price when they were confronted by the randomness of reality and the fact that Superman exists only in cartoons."

Alana touched the corner of Rafe's mouth as lightly as he had touched her necklace. He turned and brushed a kiss over her fingertip.

"Real men bleed and make mistakes," Janice said softly. "If, once the crisis is past, the survivors can't deal with their feelings of weakness, can't accept that all any person can do is his or her best . . . well, then they begin to hate themselves. If they can't accept the fact that they can be afraid, be hurt, even be broken and *still* be damned fine, brave, effective human beings, then they tear themselves apart."

Alana's hand trembled. Rafe caught it between his own, kissed her palm, and released her.

"My job was to help the survivors accept their own limitations, their humanity. I was supposed to help them accept themselves." Janice stared out over the table, seeing something from the past. "Because if they couldn't accept their humanity, I lost them. I—lost—them."

Janice's hand clenched into a fist, softly pounding the table with each word.

Impulsively Alana put her hand over the other woman's.

"It wasn't your fault," Alana said quickly. "You couldn't open up their hearts and make them believe in their own worth. All you could do was care, and you did."

Janice looked at Alana for a long moment. Then Janice's lips shaped a sad smile.

"But when you love them, and you lose them," Janice said, "it hurts like hell. After awhile there was one too many, and I quit."

Alana looked quickly at Rafe, wondering if he had been the "one too many" for Janice.

"You did all anyone could," Rafe said quietly, "and that was a lot more than most."

"So did you." Janice's blue eyes measured Rafe. "Did you think that was enough?"

"No," he said, meeting her eyes without flinching, "but I'm learning to live with it. Finally."

Janice looked at Rafe for a long moment, then smiled gently.

"Good for you, Rafe Winter," she said. "Very good. It was a near thing, wasn't it?" Janice turned and looked at Alana.

"The strongest ones," Janice said quietly, "have the hardest time. They go the longest before they come up against human limitations. And then they blame themselves. They reach a state where they are, in effect, at war with themselves. Some survive even that. A lot don't."

Alana looked at Rafe with dark, haunted eyes. The thought of how close she had come to losing him forever was like a knife turning in her soul.

"For the strong ones," Janice said, "it's a case of the sooner they accept their own limitations, the better. There are very few ways to win a war with yourself, and a whole lot of ugly ways to lose."

There was silence. Then Janice set down her coffee cup and said briskly, "Enough of my past. Who's going to catch the biggest fish tonight?"

"I am," Bob and Stan said at the same moment.

The two big men looked at each other, grinned, and began placing bets on the outcome.

Rafe and Janice exchanged knowing glances and shook their heads.

After Bob and the guests left, Alana stood and began to clear the table. Rafe immediately took the plates out of her hands.

"You look too elegant to handle dirty dishes," he said. "Come sit in the kitchen and talk to me."

Alana looked at Rafe in disbelief. He was

wearing black wool slacks and a tailored black
shirt made of a wool so fine it felt like silk.
The supple fabric fit him like a shadow, outlining the power of his arms and shoulders.

"You look too elegant, too," Alana said.

She touched the black fabric where it pulled
lightly across Rafe's chest. The warmth of him
radiated through the shirt to her hand, making
her want to rub her palm against him, to curl
up next to him like a cat by a fire. And then
she wanted simply to hold him, to comfort
him, to take away whatever hurt she could
from his past.

Alana had no doubt that Rafe was one of
the very strong ones whom Janice had talked
about, the ones who had the hardest time accepting their own limitations.

"What are you thinking?" Rafe asked, his
voice deep, velvety.

"That you're one of the strong ones."

"So are you."

The thought startled Alana. She didn't feel
strong. She felt weak, useless, foolish, hiding
from herself and reality behind a wall of amnesia and irrational fears.

Before she could protest, Rafe spoke, his
voice quick and sure.

"You are strong, Alana. You were only a
child, yet you held your family together after
your mother died. When you thought I was
dead, you saw your best chance of emotional
survival in a singing career, and you took it.

"And when another crisis came, you fought

for life. You fought as bravely and fiercely as anyone ever has."

"Then why am I afraid?" whispered Alana.

"Because it wasn't enough," Rafe said grimly. "You came flat up against the fact that Wonder Woman, like Superman, doesn't exist in the real world."

"I didn't think that I was Wonder Woman."

"Didn't you? Who was the strongest Burdette, the one everyone came to when dreams and favorite puppies died? Your dad? No way. It was years before he was worth a damn after your mother's death. As for Jack—"

Alana's mouth turned down in a sad, bitter smile.

"Jack was a user," Rafe said, his voice clipped. "If it hadn't been for your discipline, your intelligence, your sheer ability to take apart a song and put it back together in a new, vivid way, Jack would have been just another beer hall tenor."

"He had a fine voice."

"Only with you, Alana. He knew it better than you did. He used you to make the world more comfortable for himself. And he acted as though using you was his God-given right."

Alana closed her eyes, hearing her own unwanted thoughts coming from Rafe's lips.

"I used him, too," she whispered. "I used him to survive after they told me you were dead."

"Were you the one who demanded marriage?"

Alana shook her head. "I just wanted to sing."

"That's what Bob said. He remembered Jack hounding you and then finally telling you that if you wouldn't marry him, he wouldn't sing with you."

"Yes," Alana whispered, her voice shaking.

"Jack knew exactly what he wanted, and he knew how to get it. When it came to his own comforts, he was as selfish as any man I've ever known."

"But he didn't want me, not as a wife, not as a woman."

Rafe laughed harshly.

"Wrong, Alana. You didn't want *him*. He could have your singing talent, but he couldn't have you. Easy street was more important to Jack than sex, so he accepted your conditions."

"I didn't want him to want me," Alana said.

Her voice was strained, her eyes tightly closed, memories and nightmares turning. She shivered despite the warmth of the cabin, for she was feeling again the cold afternoon before the storm, hearing fragments of words, *Jack cursing, reaching for her.*

"I think—" Alana's voice broke, then came back so harshly that it sounded like a stranger's. "I think Jack wanted me on Broken Mountain. I think we fought about it."

From the front porch came the sound of Stan's laughter as he and Bob shouldered each other to see who would be first through the door.

Alana swayed alarmingly. Her eyes opened, black with memories and nightmare combined.

"No," she whispered. "Oh, God, *no*."

14

ALANA DIDN'T HEAR THE clatter of plates as Rafe put them on the table and stood close to her, not touching her, prepared to catch her if she fainted.

Rafe was afraid she was going to do just that. Her skin was as pale and translucent as fine china. Her pupils were dilated to the point that only a small rim of brown remained.

"Jack was laughing," Alana whispered.

Rafe's eyelids flinched. He bit back the words he wanted to say, the futile cry that she shouldn't remember. Not yet. Reality was brutal.

And Alana looked so fragile.

"The lake was ice cold and Jack was laughing at me," she said. "All my clothes, my sleeping bag, me—soaked and so cold. He said I could sleep in his sleeping bag. For a price. He said he'd be glad to warm me up."

Rafe's breath came in swiftly.

Alana didn't notice. She heard nothing but the past that haunted her.

"At first, I didn't believe him," she said numbly. "Then I tried to ride out. He grabbed my braids and yanked me out of the saddle and kicked Sid until she bolted down the trail. He—he hit me. I couldn't get away. He wrapped my braids around his hand, holding me, and he hit me again and again."

Rafe's expression changed, pulled by hatred into savage lines of rage, the face of a man who had once gone through a jungle hell like an avenging angel.

Alana didn't see. Her wide eyes were blinded by the past that she had hidden from herself, but not well enough.

Not quite.

"Then Stan tied me and dumped me on a rock ledge by the lake," Alana said. "He said we wouldn't go down the mountain until I changed my mind. 'When we come down off this damned mountain, you're going to heel for me like a bird dog.' And then he laughed and laughed."

Rafe reached for Alana with hands that trembled, rage and love and helplessness combined.

He couldn't touch her.

"But Jack didn't want me," Alana said in a

raw voice. "He just wanted to—to break me.
I think he must have hated me."

Alana's eyes closed slowly. She made an
odd sound and covered her mouth with her
hand.

"It was so cold. The lake and the rock and
the night. Cold."

The words were muffled, but Rafe heard
them, felt them like blows.

Helpless.

In the silence of his mind, Rafe cursed the
fact that Jack Reeves had died quickly, pain-
lessly, a hundred feet of darkness and then the
deadly impact of granite.

Alana drew a deep, shuddering breath.
When her eyes opened, they were focused on
the present. She ran shaking fingers through
her hair. Short hair. Hair that couldn't be used
as a weapon against her, chaining her.

"That's why I cut off my braids," Alana
said, relief and pain mixed in her voice. "I'm
not crazy after all."

"No." Rafe's voice was soft and yet harsh
with the effort of holding his emotions in
check. "You're not crazy."

"Are you sure?" she asked, trying to smile.
"Because I have a really crazy thing to ask
you."

"Anything. Anything at all."

"Run your fingers through my hair. Take
away the feel of Jack's hands."

Rafe brought his hands up to Alana's head,
ready to retreat at the first sign of returning

fear. Gently he eased his fingers through her soft, short hair.

Slowly closing her eyes, Alana concentrated on the sensation of Rafe's strong fingers moving through her hair. She tilted her head against his palms, increasing the pressure of his caresses.

Chills of pleasure chased through her.

"More," she murmured.

Rafe's fingers slid deeper into the midnight silk of Alana's hair, rubbing lightly over her scalp, caressing her.

"Yes," she sighed.

Alana moved against his hands, increasing the contact, deepening the intimacy, until the heat of Rafe's hands surrounded her, taking away memories, warming her.

When Alana opened her eyes, Rafe's face was very close. His concentration on the intimate moment was as great as hers. So was his pleasure. By quarter inches he lowered his mouth to hers, waiting for the least sign of the fear that might come when she realized she was caught between his hands and his lips.

Alana's answer was a smile and a sigh as her lips parted, welcoming Rafe. He kissed her very gently, not wanting to frighten her. Her arms stole around his waist, held him.

"You feel so good," Alana whispered against Rafe's lips. "So warm, so alive. And you want me. Not to break, but to cherish."

She kissed him slowly, savoring the heat of him, shaping herself to him, absorbing him like a flower absorbing sunlight.

"So warm," she murmured.

Rafe felt Alana's breasts press against him as her arms tightened around him. Hunger swept through him, a fierce surge of fire.

"Very warm," he agreed, smiling, nibbling on the corner of her mouth.

One of Rafe's hands slid from Alana's hair to her shoulder, then to her ribs. Instead of retreating, she moved closer. Her scent and sweetness made the breath stop in Rafe's throat.

Slowly he moved his hand away from the soft temptation of Alana's breast. With light touches he ran his right hand over her back, enjoying the resilience of her body. His left hand rubbed through her hair, then stroked her neck.

Finally, slowly, he moved his left hand to her back until he held her loosely in his arms.

"I'm not frightening you, am I?" Rafe asked huskily.

Alana shook her head and burrowed closer to him.

"I love your warmth, Rafael. When I'm close to you like this, I can't even imagine ever being cold again."

The front door slammed open.

"Hey, sis, where did I put the—oops, sorry!"

Rafe glanced up over Alana's black cap of hair.

Stan, who had followed Bob inside, gave Rafe a long, enigmatic look.

"Lose something?" asked Rafe mildly, keeping his arms around Alana.

"My net," admitted Bob. "I had it when I came in for dinner, but I can't find it."

"Last time I saw your net," Rafe said, "it was leaning against the back door of the lodge."

"Thanks."

Bob walked quickly around the dining room table and out the back door. When he realized Stan wasn't following, Bob called back over his shoulder to the other man.

"Come on, Stan. Don't you know a losing cause when you see one?"

The instant Alana realized that Bob wasn't alone, she stiffened and turned to face the living room.

Stan was walking toward her.

Quickly Alana spun around, holding on to Rafe's arms as though he were all that stood between her and a long, deadly fall.

"Stan," Rafe said.

Rafe's voice was quiet, yet commanding.

Stan paused, waiting.

"The trout are rising," Rafe said. "Why don't you try that dark moth I tied for you? *The one we both agreed on.*"

"You sure it will get the job done?" Stan asked sardonically. "You have to be real careful with trout. If they get away, they're even harder to lure the next time."

"What I've made matches the environment almost perfectly," Rafe said, choosing each

word with care. "That, and patience, will get
the job done. Ask Janice."

Stan paused, then nodded.

"I'll do that, Winter. I'll do just that."

Without another word, Stan brushed past
Rafe and Alana. In a few seconds, the back
door banged shut.

"Two bulls in a china shop," Rafe muttered,
resting his cheek against Alana's hair.

Alana shifted in Rafe's embrace. Immediately he loosened his arms. She moved closer,
kissed him, and stepped back.

"I'm going to change clothes and then do
the dishes," she said. "You should get into
fishing clothes and help Stan win his bet with
Bob."

"I'd rather stay here. With you."

"I'm all right, Rafe. Really. Stan startled me.
He looks so damn much like Jack."

"Are you afraid that Stan is going to pick
you up and throw you in the lake?" asked
Rafe, his voice easy, casual.

Alana stood very still for an instant before
she slowly shook her head.

"No. I don't think . . ."

Her voice died and her eyes were very dark.
She said nothing more.

"What is it?" asked Rafe softly, coaxingly.

"I don't think that was the worst of it," she
said starkly.

"Alana," he whispered.

She stepped away from Rafe.

"I need to think," Alana said, "but when
you're near, all I can think about is how good

you feel, how patient you are with me, how much I want to reach back four years and touch love again. Touch *you*."

She took a breath and let it out slowly. "I'll catch up with you at sunset, when it's too dark to fish."

"That's two hours from now," protested Rafe. "You won't even know where Stan and I will be."

"Sound carries in this country. And Stan has the kind of voice that carries, period. I'll find you."

"We'll be fishing just below the cascade," Rafe said. "If you don't show up before sunset, I'm going to stuff Stan into his own net and come looking for you." Then, softly, he said, "I wanted to fish with you tonight."

"Oh, no," Alana said, shaking her head. "I can hear your fly line whimpering for mercy right now."

Rafe's smile flashed, softening the hard lines of his face.

"But," Alana added, running her fingertips across his mustache, "I'd love to watch you fish. You please me, Rafael Winter. You please me all the way to my soul."

Then Alana turned and slipped from Rafe's arms. Hungrily he watched her walk across the living room to the loft stairs. His skin tingled where she had touched him, her scent was still sweet in his nostrils, and he wanted her so much that he hurt.

Abruptly Rafe turned away and went to the downstairs bedroom. With quick motions he changed into his fishing clothes. Then he let himself out of the cabin quietly, knowing if he saw Alana again, he wouldn't leave her.

Alana changed into jeans and a sweater and had the kitchen cleaned long before sunset. Her mind was working as swiftly as her hands. She reviewed what she remembered about the six missing days, and what she didn't.

She remembered parts of the ride up the trail with Jack. Then the first night . . .

Was it the first night when Jack and I fought? Alana asked herself silently.

Frowning, she stacked wood in the stove for the morning fire.

Three days in the hospital, of which she remembered only one. That left three days unaccounted for.

No, two.

We must have spent one day traveling to Wyoming and one night at the ranch house, Alana thought. So it must have been the first night on Broken Mountain, up by the lake, when Jack threw me and my clothes and my sleeping bag into the lake.

Alana's body tightened as she remembered what had followed. Jack had slapped her all but senseless when she had tried to run from him. That was the night she had spent curled over herself on a piece of granite, shivering.

That's why I'm so cold in my nightmares, Alana realized. Memory and nightmare combined.

She let out a long breath, feeling better

about herself. Not all of her fears were irrational.

But then, why does the sound of a storm terrify me? Alana asked herself.

The wind hadn't been blowing that night. It hadn't been storming. No lightning. No ground-shaking thunder. Alana was certain of it. If that night had been the ice-tipped storm of her nightmare, she would have died of exposure before morning.

Yet wind and thunder and ice were a vivid, terrifying part of Alana's nightmares.

"The storm must have come the second night on Broken Mountain," Alana whispered, needing more than the cabin's silence to comfort her. "The night I fell."

The night Jack died.

"Why did Jack untie me? Did I give in, go to him?"

The sound of her own questions made Alana shudder. She wasn't certain she wanted to know if she had traded her self-respect for a dry sleeping bag and cold sex with Jack. Prostitution, in a word.

Alana waited, listening to her own silences, sensing her body's response to her thoughts.

Nothing changed. No nightmare closing around. No fear. No sense of connection with hidden reality.

"All right," Alana said tightly. "It's probably not that. Did Jack get too drunk to be patient? Did he untie me, rape me, beat me?"

Once more, Alana waited, forgetting to breathe, anticipating the return of nightmare as her waking thoughts closed in on the truth.

Once more, nothing came.

When Alana remembered Jack hitting her, her stomach turned over and her breath came shallowly.

When she thought of submitting to him, there was . . . nothing. When she thought of being raped, there was . . . nothing. No fear, no desire to scream, no sickness rising in her throat, no chill, no hammering heart or cold sweat. None of the physiological signals that had warned her in the past when she was approaching the truth.

If the truth could even be approached.

Abruptly Alana pulled off her apron and went to find Rafe, unable to bear any more questions, any more answers, any more fear and silence.

The path to the lake was overgrown, clearly showing the bruised grass that marked the passage of at least two people. Alana walked quickly, barely noticing the crimson cloud streamers stretched across the sky. Nor did she see the deep amethyst mountain slopes crowned by luminous ramparts of stone, nor the fragrant shadows flowing out of the forest around her.

The path approached the lake at an angle in order to avoid an area that was a bog in the early summer and an uneven, rough meadow in the fall. Winding through the trees, yielding only occasional glimpses of the water, the path kept to the forest until the last possible moment.

Alana heard Rafe and Stan before she could see them. At least, she heard Stan, his voice pitched to carry above the exuberant thunder of the cascade. She could only assume he was talking to Rafe.

Then Stan's voice came clearly and Alana was certain. He was talking to Rafe.

"No, you listen to me for a change, Captain Winter, *sir*," Stan said sardonically. "I've got a nasty mind for situations like this. I was trained to have a nasty mind."

There was a pause, but whatever Rafe replied was lost in the sound of the cascade. Alana hesitated, then continued toward the lake, screened by spruce and aspen.

"Try this scenario on for size," Stan said. "There's a woman you've wanted for years. Another man's woman. It grinds on you real hard. So the woman you want and the man you hate come up here for a little camping trip."

Alana froze in place, suddenly cold.

She didn't want to hear any more, but she couldn't move.

"You wait around, see your chance, and chuck good old Jack over the nearest cliff," continued Stan. "Then you go to collect the spoils."

"... half-assed pop psychol..." Rafe's voice wove in and out of the cascade's throaty rumble.

Stan's voice was as clear as thunder.

"But she's not used to that kind of violence," Stan said. "She runs away. She spends a night in the open, cold and exposed. And then she just shuts it all out, forgets."

"... leave the thinking to people with ..."

"Her amnesia leaves you with a real problem," Stan said, ignoring the interruption. "If she remembers, it doesn't matter whose friend the sheriff is. Your ass is in a sling."

Alana took a ragged breath and continued down the trail. She stumbled like a sleepwalker, using her hands to push herself away from the rough trunks of the trees that seemed to grow perversely in front of her feet, as though to hold her back.

"... crock of ..." Rafe's voice faded in and out of the cascade's thunder.

"I'm not finished," cut in Stan, his voice very clear, carrying like a brass bell across the evening. "You can save yourself by marrying her. She won't go telling tales on her own husband."

"Jesus, you've been reading too many tabloids."

"Maybe. From what Bob tells me, good old Jack wasn't much of a loss to this world, so it's not like Alana is going to spend a year mourning the son of a bitch. Besides, it's plain enough that she likes you."

"You noticed," Rafe said sarcastically.

"You've got a little problem, though. If she remembers before you marry her, you're up shit creek without a paddle."

"Then why am I helping ..."

Alana leaned forward, straining to hear all of Rafe's words. She couldn't. Unlike Stan,

Rafe's voice became softer, not louder with anger.

Rafe was furious.

"Are you really helping her to remember?" retorted Stan. "Then why in hell won't you let me off the leash?"

". . . Janice."

"Janice would do a marine crawl through hot coals for you, Winter, and you damn well know it!"

"I'd . . . same for . . ."

Alana left the trees behind and began walking over the rocks and logs that were between her and the lake. Each step brought her closer to the men.

Closer to their words.

"And I'm supposed to just shut up and go along with the program," shot back Stan.

"Hell of an idea, hotshot!"

"Maybe, and maybe not. That's a damned good woman you're hunting, Winter. I'm not real sure she wants to be caught. I think she should remember first. That's the only way her choice will have any meaning. That's the best chance she has of surviving."

"Is that what Janice thinks?" Rafe asked.

Alana was less than fifty feet away, close enough to hear Rafe clearly. He and Stan were facing one another. If the men noticed her slow progress toward them, they made no sign.

"I'm not sure Janice is able to think straight where you're involved," said Stan.

Alana stopped, held by the stark pain in Stan's voice.

"There's nothing between me and Janice," Rafe said. "There never was."

Stan hesitated, then made an odd gesture, turning his hands palms up as though to accept or hold something.

"I'd like to believe that. I really would."

"Believe it," Rafe said.

"Hell, it doesn't matter right now. It wouldn't matter at all, except that I don't want Alana trapped because Janice allowed emotion to louse up her judgment."

"She hasn't."

"If it all goes to hell," Stan said, "I don't want Janice blaming herself. She's been through enough of that on your account. But that doesn't matter, either. Not up here. It's just like the bad old days. All that matters is the mission."

"Then quit screwing it up."

"You've got two more days," Stan said flatly. "If your way doesn't work by then, I'll try mine."

When Rafe spoke, the suppressed violence in his voice curled and cracked like a whip, making Stan flinch.

"If you do anything that hurts Alana," Rafe said, "you'll go back down Broken Mountain the same way Jack Reeves did—in a green plastic bag. Do you read me, corporal?"

"I'm not a corporal anymore. And you're not a captain."

Stan turned slightly.

For a moment Alana thought he had spotted her, for she was directly in his line of sight.

Suddenly Stan made a swift feint toward Rafe. At the first hint of movement, Rafe swiftly assumed a fighting stance. Legs slightly bent, hands held slightly apart at chest level, he waited for Stan to move again.

"You're as fast as ever," Stan said, something close to admiration in his voice.

Stan moved again very quickly, his big hands reaching for the other man. Rafe stepped into the attack, pivoted smoothly, and let Stan slide by, not touching him except for the hand that closed around Stan's wrist.

With fluid grace, Rafe twisted Stan's arm and brought it up behind his back, applying pressure until Stan was on his knees. Stan's blond hair shimmered palely in the twilight as Rafe bent down, his face a mask of cold rage.

"No!"

Rafe's head snapped around at Alana's scream. When he saw the frightened, hunted look on her face, he released Stan and started toward her.

"Alana!" Rafe said.

Alana spun away from him and ran back into the forest.

Rafe started after her, then realized that chasing her would only increase her fear. With a soundless snarl, he turned on Stan, who had made no move to get to his feet.

"You knew she was there, didn't you?" Rafe demanded.

Stan nodded and smiled grimly.

"I saw her out of the corner of my eye," he agreed. "That's why I jumped you. Think it reminded her of something, old buddy?"

"Get up."

Rafe's voice was soft and deadly.

"So you can take me apart?" Stan asked, smiling oddly. "No way, Winter. I've seen what you can do when you're mad. I think I'll just sit out this dance."

"And I think," Rafe said, spacing each word carefully, showing how much his control cost, "that if you don't get out of my sight, I'll take you apart anyway."

15

WIND FLEXED AND FLOWED around the lodge, bringing with it the sound of laughter. After the laughter came words without meaning, wind, more laughter.

Alana rolled over in bed, tangling in the covers for the tenth time and wishing that everyone would enjoy the poker game with a little less enthusiasm.

She wondered if Rafe was with the happy card players. Then she remembered his fury at Stan. She doubted that Rafe was in the last cabin, laughing and drawing cards.

Stan's accusations turned and prowled inside Alana's mind like the wind. She wanted to reject them out of hand, completely, yet they kept finding weaknesses in her resolve, cracks in her wall of refusal, little doubts clinging like tentacles.

From the moment Alana saw Rafe at the airport, she had been certain that he still loved her. It wasn't a thoughtful conclusion; it was instinct, pure and simple and very, very deep. Yet assuming that Rafe loved her was groundless, even ridiculous.

He had believed she was happily married six weeks after his "death" had been reported. A year ago he had returned her letter unopened. Before yesterday, nothing had happened to make him believe any differently.

Before yesterday, Rafe must have hated her.

Then why did he pressure Bob to get me home? Alana asked silently. Why has Rafe been so very gentle, so understanding, from the moment he met me at the airport?

No answer came but that of the wind blowing over mountains and forest and cabin alike.

Did something happen on Broken Mountain? Alana wondered. Something that I can't remember, something that made Rafe believe my marriage to Jack was a desperate sham from the beginning?

The wind curled and shook the cabin like a powerful, transparent cat.

A chill condensed in Alana. She pulled the covers closer and rolled over again, seeking the comfort that had never come to her since Broken Mountain.

Yet no matter where she turned, she kept

hearing Stan's voice, Stan's accusations.

They horrified her.

Is the truth that brutal? Alana cried silently. Did Rafe pursue me to save himself?

Was Jack's death less than accidental?

Is that why Rafe refused to tell me what happened on Broken Mountain?

Waves of coldness swept over Alana, roughening her skin. She lay very still, curled around herself, shivering despite the blankets heaped on top of her.

Alana knew that Rafe was capable of deadly violence. He had been trained for it, was skilled in it, had lived with it for most of his adult life. But she couldn't believe that he was capable of such sly deception, that he would coolly plan to murder Jack and then seduce and marry her in order to ensure her silence.

That didn't sound like the Rafe she had known, the Rafe she had loved.

The Rafe she still loved.

If Stan had accused Jack of such vicious lies, Alana would have been sickened—*but she would have believed.*

Jack had been a totally selfish man. Jack had been capable of smiling lies and chilling cruelties, whatever it took to bend the world to his comfort.

Jack had been capable of cold-blooded murder.

Alana's stomach moved uneasily. Cold sweat broke out over her body. Suddenly she couldn't bear the clammy sheets and slack, heavy blankets any longer. She needed the

lively warmth and flickering companionship
of a fire.

She sat up in bed and groped for her house-
coat. All she found was the thick robe she had
borrowed from the downstairs bathroom. Impatiently she pulled on the indigo robe, letting
the sleeves trail down over her knuckles. The
hem was long enough to brush the tops of her
toes.

Groping along the wall, Alana worked her
way down the inky darkness of the stairway.
The living room was empty, without light. The
fireplace ashes were as cold and pale as the
moon.

Rafe hadn't been in the lodge at all tonight.
He hadn't seen or spoken to Alana since she
had run from him through the forest. After her
irrational panic had passed, she had waited for
Rafe by the trail.

He hadn't come.

Finally, when the moon had risen in pale
brilliance over Broken Mountain, Alana had
given up and gone inside, shivering with cold
and loneliness.

She struck a wooden match on the fireplace
stone. Using its flickering light, she peered
into the wood box. There was a handful of kindling and a few small chunks of stove wood.
Not enough to warm the hearth, much less
her.

With a dispirited curse, Alana let the top of
the wood box fall back into place. She turned
to go back to bed, then froze.

A subtle sound drifted through the cabin, a

distant keening that floated on the shifting mountain wind.

The strange, bittersweet music held Alana motionless, aching to hear more. She held her breath, listening with an intensity that made her tremble.

Music curled around her lightly, tantalizing her at a threshold just below memory, music curving across the night like a fly line, lengthening in grace and beauty with each surge of energy, each magic, rhythmic pulse.

Blindly Alana felt her way through the lodge to the front door, lured by the elusive music. She opened the door, shut it silently behind her, and held her breath, listening and looking.

There was laughter tumbled by wind, bright squares of light glowing from the cabin at the end of the row. Silhouettes dark against one curtained window, wordless movements of hands and arms, more laughter.

But no music.

It wasn't somebody's transistor radio or tape player that had slid through Alana's defenses, calling to her in a language older and more potent than words.

Yet there was nowhere else the music could be coming from. Of the three cabins that stretched out east of the lodge, only one was glowing with light, only one was brimming with laughter when people won or lost small bets. The two other cabins were empty, as black as night itself. Blacker, for the cabins had neither moon nor stars to light their interior darkness.

The wind stirred, blowing across the back of Alana's neck, teasing her ears with half-remembered, half-imagined music. Slowly she turned, facing west.

The fourth cabin was several hundred feet away, wrapped in forest and darkness, not really part of the fishing camp. No light gleamed from the cabin in welcome, no laughter swirled, no sense of brimming life came to her.

And then the music called to Alana, an irresistible lure drawing her closer with each note.

She stood and listened for a moment more, her heart beating hard, her blood rushing so quickly that it overwhelmed the mixed murmur of music and wind.

Without stopping to think, she stepped off the porch onto the overgrown path to the fourth cabin. Pine needles and sharp stones smarted against her bare feet, but she noticed them only at a distance. The small hurts meant nothing, for she had recognized the source of the music.

Rafe.

Rafe and his harmonica, mournful chords lamenting love and loss.

It was Alana's own song curling toward her across the night, drifting down on the seamless black surface of her despair, music shimmering with emotion. Once she had sung this song with Rafe. Once they had looked into

each other's eyes and shared sad songs of
death and broken dreams.

And they had smiled, certain of the power
and endurance of their own love.

> *I heard a lark this morning*
> *Singing in the field.*
> *I heard a lark this morning*
> *Singing wild.*
>
> *I didn't know*
> *You had gone away.*
> *I didn't know*
> *Love had gone to yesterday.*
>
> *I heard a lark this morning*
> *Singing wild.*
> *I heard a lark this morning*
> *Singing free.*
>
> *Maybe tomorrow I'll know.*
> *Maybe tomorrow you'll tell me*
> *Why the lark sang.*
> *And maybe yesterday*
> *Never came.*
>
> *I heard a lark this morning*
> *Singing in the field.*
> *I heard a lark this morning*
> *Singing free.*
> *It did not sing for me.*

The music Alana had once picked out on her
guitar now came back to her in haunting

chords sung by Rafe's harmonica. The words she had written ached in her throat and burned behind her eyes.

Thick terry cloth folds wrapped around her legs, slowing her. She picked up the hem of the robe and began to run toward the cabin, not feeling the rough path or the tears running down her face, drawn by her music.

By Rafe.

The cabin stood alone in a small clearing. There was no flicker of candlelight, no yellow shine of kerosene lamps, nothing but moonlight pouring through the cabin windows in a soundless fall of silver radiance. Sad harmonies shivered through the clearing, shadows of despair braiding through the pale brilliance of moonlight.

Slowly, like a sigh, the song changed into silence. The last transparent notes of music were carried away on a cold swirl of wind.

Alana stood at the edge of the clearing, transfixed by music, aching with silence. Only her face was visible, a ghostly oval above the textured darkness of her robe and the sliding black shadows of evergreens flexing beneath the wind.

She hesitated, feeling the wind and tears cold on her cheeks. Then the mournful chords began all over, sorrow coming back again, unchanged.

I heard a lark this morning . . .

Alana couldn't bear to stand alone in the haunted, wind-filled forest and listen to her

yearning song played by the only man she had
ever loved.

Slowly she walked across the clearing, seeing only tears and moonlight, hearing only
song and sorrow. She went up the cabin steps
like a ghost, soundless, wrapped in darkness.
The front door stood open, for there was neither warmth nor light to keep inside.

The cabin had only one room. Rafe was
stretched out on the bed that doubled as a
couch during the day. Only his face and hands
were visible, lighter shades of darkness
against the overwhelming night inside the
cabin.

Silently, without hesitation, Alana crossed
the room. She didn't know if Rafe sensed her
presence. He made no move toward her, neither gesture nor words nor silence. He simply
poured himself into the harmonica, music
twisting through her, chords of desolation
shaking her.

Alana knelt by the bed, trying to see Rafe's
face, his eyes. She could see only the pale
shimmer of moonlight, for the sad strains of
music had blinded her with tears.

I heard a lark this morning
Singing wild.

With each familiar chord, each aching harmony of note with note, Alana felt the past
sliding away, nightmare draining into song
until she knew only music and no fear at all.

Swaying slightly, her body lost to the music,

Alana's mind slowly succumbed to emotions that were as wary and elusive as trout shimmering deep within a river pool. She didn't know how many times the song ended and began, notes curling and curving across her inner darkness, music drifting down, floating, calling her, luring her up from the dark depths of her own mind.

Alana knew only that at some point she began to sing. At first her song was wordless, a supple blending of her voice with the harmonica's smooth chords, clear harmonies woven between instrument and singer. The melody line passed between them, changed by one and then the other, renewed and renewing each other by turns.

And then, like a wild lark, Alana's voice flew free.

It soared and turned on invisible currents, swept up emotions and transmuted them into pouring song, a beauty so transparent, so flawless, that a shiver of awe rippled through Rafe. For an instant the harmonica hesitated. Then he gave himself to the music as completely as Alana had, pursuing the brilliant clarity of her voice, soaring with it, sharing her ecstatic flight out of darkness, touching the sun.

Finally there was nothing left of the song but the last note shimmering in the darkness, sliding into moonlight and the soft whisper of the wind.

Alana put her head in her hands and wept soundlessly. Rafe stroked her hair slowly, gently, until her lips turned into his palm and he felt her tears slide between his fingers. With careful hands, he eased Alana onto the bed beside him, murmuring her name, feeling her shiver as she came close to him. Her hands were cool when she touched his face, and she shivered again.

Rafe shifted until he could free the sleeping bag he had been lying on. He unzipped it and spread smooth folds of warmth over her. When he started to get out of bed, she made a sound of protest and sat up. He kissed her cold hands.

"Lie still," he said. "I'll start a fire."

But first Rafe closed the cabin door, shutting out the wind. He moved swiftly in the darkness, not bothered by the lack of light.

There was a muted rustle of paper and kindling, then the muffled thump of cured wood being stacked in the fireplace. A match flared in the darkness.

Alana blinked and held her breath, shivering again. Rafe's face looked like a primitive mask cast in pure gold, and his eyes were incandescent topaz beneath the dense midnight of his hair. For long moments he and the fire watched one another, two entities made of heat and potent light.

With the silence and grace of a flame, Rafe turned toward Alana, sensing her eyes watching him. He stood and came toward her, his expression concealed by shadow.

The bed shifted beneath his weight as he sat and looked at her face illuminated by the gliding dance of flames. Her eyes were both dark and brilliant, her skin was flushed, and her lips were curved around a smile. Reflected fire turned and ran through her hair in liquid ribbons of light.

"You are even more beautiful than your song," whispered Rafe.

His fingertip traced Alana's mouth and then the slender hand that rested on top of the sleeping bag. He took her hand and rubbed it gently between his palms.

"You're cold," Rafe said. "How long were you outside?"

Alana tried to remember how long she had stood in the clearing, but all that seemed real to her now was Rafe's heat flowing into her as he touched her.

"I don't know," she said.

Silently Rafe rubbed Alana's hand until it no longer felt cool to his touch. When his fingers went up her arm, he encountered the heavy cloth of the robe she wore. He made a startled sound, then laughed softly.

"So that's where it went," said Rafe.

"What?"

"My bathrobe."

"Yours?" asked Alana, surprised. "I thought it was Bob's. The sleeves come down over my knuckles and the hem drags on my toes and—"

"—I'm such a shrimp," finished Rafe, smiling.

"Rafael Winter," Alana said, exasperation and laughter competing in her voice, "you're

more than six feet tall and must weigh at least
a hundred and seventy pounds."

"Closer to one-ninety."

In startled reappraisal, Alana looked at the
width of Rafe's shoulders, outlined by firelight.

"Those are hardly the dimensions of a
shrimp," she pointed out.

"I know. You're the one who keeps thinking
that my clothes belong to Bob."

Rafe's weight shifted, sending a quiver
through the bed. Alana's breath caught as she
sensed him coming closer.

"You're such a tiny thing," he said. "I'll bet
you got the hem all muddy. Unless you're
wearing high-heeled slippers?"

"No. Twice."

Rafe looked at Alana. A smile made firelight
glide and gleam over his mustache.

"Twice?" he asked.

"I'm five feet five. Not a tiny thing at all.
And I'm barefoot."

"Barefoot?"

All amusement was gone from Rafe's voice.
He moved to the end of the bed and pulled
aside the sleeping bag until he could see Alana's feet.

"There's glass on the path from here to the
main cabin," Rafe said. "Not to mention sharp
rocks and roots."

He hissed a curse as he saw thin, dark lines
of blood on Alana's feet.

"You cut yourself," he said flatly.

Alana wiggled her toes. She tucked her feet

up beneath the warm sleeping bag.

"Little scratches, that's all," she said.

Rafe got up, went to the stove, and tested the water in the kettle. He had intended to make coffee, but when he found the harmonica on the kitchen shelf, he had forgotten about everything else.

Although the fire in the stove had long since died, the water was still warm. He poured some into a basin, took a bar of soap from the sink, and searched for a clean cloth. When he found one, he returned to Alana.

"Give me your feet," he said.

"They're fine."

Rafe flipped back a corner of the sleeping bag, captured one of her feet, and began washing the abrasions with warm water. He sat sideways on the end of the bed, resting her ankle on his thigh.

"Rafe," Alana protested, squirming slightly.

"Rafe what? Am I hurting you?"

"No," she said softly.

"Tickling you?"

Alana shook her head, watching Rafe as he washed her feet and rinsed them carefully. Then he examined the cuts with very gentle touches, making sure that all the dirt was out.

"Hurt?" he asked.

"No."

"I don't have any antiseptic in this cabin."

"I don't need it."

"Yes, you do," countered Rafe in a firm voice. "Dr. Gene made a big point about how run-down you were, fair game for any bug that came along."

"Dr. Gene is wrong."

Rafe grunted, then smiled crookedly.

"I take it back," he said. "I do have some antiseptic here, after a fashion."

Alana watched while Rafe took rag, soap, and basin back to the tiny corner kitchen. He opened a cupboard and pulled out a fifth of Scotch. He knelt by the end of the bed, one of her feet in his hand.

"I'll bet it stings," she said.

"Bet you're right. Bet that next time you go walking you'll remember to wear shoes, tenderfoot."

Using the tip of his finger, Rafe applied whiskey to the first cut. Alana's breath came in sharply. He blew across the cut, taking away some of the sting. Then he went to work on the next scrape, applying Scotch, blowing quickly, his eyes and the whiskey glowing gold in the firelight.

When Alana's breath hissed out over the last cut, Rafe's fingers tightened on her foot.

"Why am I always hurting you?" he asked.

Pain turned in his voice, tightening it into a groan. He bent his head until he could kiss the delicate arch of Alana's foot. His lips lingered on her skin in silent apology for having caused her pain, no matter how necessary it might have been.

One hand cradled the arch of her foot, warming her, while the other hand stroked from the smooth skin at the top of her foot to the graceful curve of her ankle. He caressed her warmly, hands and mouth moving over her, savoring the heady mixture of Scotch and her sweet skin.

"Rafael," cried Alana softly.

Her toes flexed and curled against his palm with an involuntary sensual response.

Rafe's whole body tightened as he fought a short, savage battle with himself for control. With an invisible shiver of rebellion, his hands obeyed the commands of his mind.

Swiftly he put Alana's feet under the sleeping bag and tucked it around her.

"Rafe . . . ?"

Without answering, he stood and went to the fire. Using swift, abrupt motions, he added wood to the fireplace until the flames rushed upward into the night with a sound like wind. Only then did he turn from the savage leap of flames to face Alana.

"Warm enough?" he asked neutrally.

"No."

She shivered slightly, watching Rafe with dark eyes, wondering why he looked so hard, so angry.

He crossed the room in three strides, grabbed the daybed, and pulled it closer to the fire with an ease that shocked Alana. Because he was so gentle with her, she kept on forgetting how powerful he really was.

Rafe turned away from Alana and watched the fire with eyes that also burned.

"How's that?" he asked. "Better?"

"Not as warm as your hands felt," Alana

said softly. "Not nearly so warm as your mouth."

Rafe spun toward her as though she had struck him.

"Don't," he said, his voice harsh.

Alana's eyes widened. Then her eyelashes swept down, concealing her confusion and pain. But nothing concealed the change in her mouth from smiling softness to thin line, happiness flattened by a single word.

Rafe saw and knew that he had hurt Alana once again. He swore silently with a savagery that would have shaken her if she had been able to hear him.

"I'm sorry," Alana whispered. "I thought—"

Her voice broke. She made a helpless gesture, then slid out from beneath the sleeping bag and stood up, pulling the robe tightly around her. His robe.

"I thought you wanted me," she said.

"That's the problem. I want you so much I get hard just looking at you. I want you so much that I don't trust myself to be petted and then to let you go. I want you—*too much*."

The gesture Rafe made was as curt as his voice.

"A thousand times I've dreamed of having you in my arms," he said, "of loving you, touching you, tasting you, and then burying myself in your softness, feeling you loving me deep inside your body until nothing is real but the two of us and then there is only one reality. *Us*."

Alana made a breathless sound that could have been Rafe's name. His words had washed over her in a torrent of desire so consuming that she could barely breathe.

Rafe looked away from her to the fire raging in the hearth.

"I've dreamed too often, too much," he said bluntly. "You'd better go, wildflower. Go now."

Instead, Alana sank back onto the bed, for her legs felt too weak to support her. She thought of Rafe holding her, her body helpless beneath his strength as he became a part of her, and then she waited for the fear to come, freezing her.

Fire came instead, freeing her.

Slowly Alana stood. She walked soundlessly across the short distance separating her from Rafe. He stood with his back to her, his neck corded with tension.

When her arms slid around his waist, his whole body stiffened.

"I'm yours, Rafael," she said softly.

16

ALANA FELT THE TREMOR
that went through Rafe at her words. Then she
felt the slide and flex of powerful muscles as
he turned in her arms and looked down into
her eyes. Watching her, waiting for the least
sign of withdrawal, of fear, he closed his arms
gently around her.

Rafe's arms tightened slowly, inevitably,
drawing her against his body. He gathered her
close and held her with the power and hunger
that he had fought so long to conceal from her.

Alana tilted back her head and watched
Rafe through half-closed eyes. Her lips parted,
hungry for his kiss.

With a muffled groan, Rafe bent his head

and took what she offered, searching the softness of her mouth with hard, hungry movements of his tongue. The force of his kiss bent her back over his arm, but she didn't protest.

Instead, she clung to him with fierce joy, giving herself to his strength. She sensed that he was testing her, trying to discover if she would freeze, trying to find out while he could still stop himself and let her go.

Rafe shifted Alana in his embrace, holding her head in the crook of one arm and bringing her hips against him with the other. She answered with a soft moan and a supple movement of her body that sent whips of fire flicking over him.

Despite the passion and power of Rafe's embrace, he was careful not to lift Alana off her feet. He didn't want to test either of them to that extent, for he suddenly knew that he couldn't let her go.

He had dreamed of Alana too long, and this was too much like his dreams, cabin and firelight and her sweet, passionate abandon in his arms.

"You aren't afraid," Rafe murmured against Alana's lips, pleading and urging and asking at the same time.

"I'm not afraid of you."

Slowly Alana turned her head from side to side, rubbing her moist lips over Rafe's, savoring the heat and life of him.

"You were never the one I feared," she whispered.

Alana felt one of Rafe's strong hands slide

up to her neck, felt gentle fingers trace the gold chain he had given to her, felt the slight roughness of his fingertip resting on the rapid pulse beating beneath her soft skin. She sighed and softened against him even more.

His head moved and his lips slid down Alana's neck until his tongue touched her pulse so delicately that he could count her rapid heartbeats. Then his hand shifted, sliding inside her robe until the firm curve of her breast fit into his hand and her heartbeat accelerated wildly.

"Yes," Rafe said hoarsely. "This is my dream. Your response, your hunger, the way your nipple rises against my palm, wanting my touch."

Alana's body curved against Rafe, enjoying the hard muscles of his thighs, the heat of him as he moved against her, the texture of his flannel shirt beneath her palms. With a small sound, she slid her hands up to his head and buried her fingers in his hair.

"Winter mink," she said, sighing. "Thick and soft and silky."

She flexed her fingers sensually, shivering as Rafe arched against the caress, his whole body tightening against her, stroking her.

"I'd like to feel you all over me," Alana said. "All of you. All of me."

"You're going to," Rafe promised.

He bit her neck in a caress that was neither wholly gentle nor wholly wild.

"Every bit of you," he said deeply. "Every bit of me."

Yet even as Rafe spoke, his embrace gentled. The certainty that Alana wasn't going to run away brought a greater measure of control back to him. He no longer felt driven to steal what he could before she became afraid.

Alana wasn't retreating from his strength. She was coming closer to him with every breath, every heartbeat, every touch.

Rafe untied the heavy robe with slow motions. Then he took it from Alana with hands that cherished the pleasure of the moment and the woman who turned to him, smiling.

When Rafe dropped the robe onto the bed, the indigo cloth shimmered invitingly in the firelight. He didn't notice. He saw only Alana and the soft, floor-length nightgown that was the color of a forest at dusk.

Tiny, flat, silver buttons flickered, reflecting the dance of flames. The silver flashes tempted Rafe's finger to trace the shining circles from Alana's throat to her thighs. His hand lingered on the buttons, gently kneading the slight, resilient curve of her stomach before continuing down.

When he stroked the soft mound at the apex of her thighs, her breath rushed out. He stroked more deeply, shaping the thin gown to Alana's hidden curves, cupping her in his palm. She moaned and her fingernails dug into his shoulders.

Rafe laughed softly, triumph and hunger combined. And then he groaned as Alana's satin heat reached out to him, spilling over him like sunrise.

"You tempt me without mercy," he said, his voice deep.

"Look who's talking," Alana said shakily.

Slowly Rafe retreated, tracing once again the line of tiny buttons until it stopped just below the hollow of Alana's throat. His fingers moved over the first button, trying to open it.

But the button was very small, very stubborn, and his hand was less than steady, for every breath he took was infused with the elemental perfume of Alana's desire.

"This nightgown would try the patience of a saint," Rafe muttered, amusement and passion mixed equally in his voice.

Alana bent her head to brush her lips across Rafe's fingers. Her teeth closed delicately on his knuckle. Her tongue slid between his fingers, caressing the sensitive skin.

"You're not helping," he said.

"The neckline is wide enough that I don't bother with the buttons."

"But I've dreamed so many times of undressing you slowly, so slowly . . ."

When Alana looked up, Rafe was smiling and very serious. The heat of his eyes made her feel deliciously weak.

"I'm going to enjoy each button, Alana. Each new bit of you revealed. And when I'm done, I'm going to look at you wearing nothing but firelight."

The shimmering promise in Rafe's eyes sent an answering fire through Alana.

"I won't even touch you at first," he said, brushing the back of his fingers lightly across

Alana's soft lips. "I'll just look at you and remember all the times I could see you only in my dreams. I've dreamed of that, too, a dream within a dream."

Alana trembled, caressed as much by Rafe's words as she was by his hands.

Rafe saw her shiver, felt the warm rush of her breath against his fingers. He moved both hands to the line of buttons, but he became distracted when Alana's breasts brushed against the sensitive skin of his inner wrist.

It felt so good that Rafe couldn't resist moving his wrists lightly against her soft, firm curves. Alana's breasts changed as he stroked her, until her nipples stood boldly against the tantalizing softness of her nightgown.

Rafe bent his head and caressed the tip of one breast with his teeth. The response that shivered through Alana made him want to groan with pleasure and raw need combined. He wanted to part her soft thighs and feel the silky heat of her welcome washing over him. He wanted that until he was shaking with his hunger.

But he wanted the dream, too. He wanted that even more.

Reluctantly Rafe's hands returned to the tiny buttons. One by one he unfastened them until Alana's skin glowed between dark green folds of cloth. She watched with eyes that also glowed, and her breath made soft, tearing sounds in the hushed darkness.

Rafe kissed the satin warmth of Alana's skin, following the yielding line of buttons with his mouth. Slowly, sensuously, his tongue slid down her body, following the buttons that melted away, unveiling her for his caresses. In a silence that shivered with possibilities, he tasted the heat and sweetness of his dream.

He paused to cherish one breast, then the other, caressing her with teeth and tongue until Alana moaned and her fingers tangled helplessly in his hair. Only then did he continue down, his hands less steady, his breathing quicker, the taste and feel of her consuming him while passion pooled heavily, urgently, between his thighs.

With a swift, supple motion Rafe knelt in front of Alana, his fingers moving over the remaining buttons until they were all undone. Gently he tugged at the cloth. Soft folds clung to each feminine curve for breathtaking moments. Finally, reluctantly, the gown slid to the floor, yielding the secrets of Alana's body.

For the space of several breaths, Rafe simply looked at Alana. Her skin was flushed by firelight and passion. Her breasts rose smoothly and their tips glistened from the caresses of his mouth. The rich contrast of her dark nipples against her glowing skin held his eyes for a long moment, and then he looked at the tempting midnight gleam of hair below her narrow waist.

When the tip of Rafe's tongue teased Alana's navel and his hands found the taut swell of her hips, she swayed even closer to him, calling his name. He closed his eyes, letting the sound and scent and feel of Alana sink into him, healing and inflaming him at the same instant.

He had dreamed of this so many times, of touching her until she was too weak to stand and then carrying her to the bed, caressing her softness intimately until she cried aloud her need for him.

But now Rafe was afraid to lift Alana, to carry her. He was afraid he would shatter both dream and reality with a single incautious act.

Rafe brushed his mouth across Alana's stomach, savored again the sweetness of her breasts, taut and flushed with heat, beneath his hands. Dream and reality fused into a passion that raged at the restraint he imposed on himself.

Quickly he came to his feet, ignoring the hammer blows of desire in his blood, the talons of need raking him until he could count his heartbeat in the hardened flesh between his legs. With impatient hands he pulled off his own clothing and threw it aside.

At the sound of Alana's swiftly drawn breath, Rafe turned toward her, suddenly afraid that she would flinch from the blunt, heavy reality of his desire.

And then Rafe stood motionless but for the tremors of hunger ripping through him, a hunger that increased with each instant. Alana was looking at him the same way he had looked at her, raw yearning and hunger and tenderness combined. Her eyes reflected fire as she touched him with hands that shook, want-

ing him with a force that made her whole
body tremble like an aspen in the wind.

Alana's fingers went from Rafe's shoulders
to his thighs in a single, shivering caress that
almost destroyed his control. For an instant he
let her fingertips trace the hard outline of his
desire and count the heavy beats of his blood.
Then he caught her hands between his own.

"No," said Rafe hoarsely.

"But—"

"If you touch me again, I'll lose control. This
time, let me touch you. Next time you can
tease me until I go crazy, but not this time.
This time is too much like my dreams. This
time it's all I can do not to pull you down and
take you right here on the cabin floor."

Alana closed her eyes, knowing if she
looked at Rafe right now she would have to
touch him. With a graceful motion she turned
away and stretched out on the daybed. Only
then did she open her eyes and look at the
man standing beside the bed, Rafe with firelight licking over his powerful body, molten
gold pooling in his eyes, the most beautiful
thing she had ever seen. When she spoke, her
voice was a soft, husky song.

"Then come dream with me, Rafael."

He came down onto the bed and gathered
Alana into his arms in one continuous movement. He held her as though he expected
something to wrench her from his embrace,
ending the dream, leaving him to awaken
hungry and despairing, the past repeating it-

self endlessly, dream sliding into waking nightmare.

Alana felt Rafe's mouth demand hers, felt his arms close powerfully around her, felt the bruising male strength of his body, the hardness and the hunger of him; and she returned the embrace, holding on to him with every bit of her strength.

After a long time, Rafe drew a deep, shuddering breath and released her.

"I'm sorry. I didn't mean to hurt you," he said, kissing Alana gently, repeatedly, tasting her with each word, unable to stay away from her for more than a second at a time.

"You didn't hurt me."

Rafe touched Alana gently. His hand trembled as it moved from her temple to her lips. Eyes closed, she twisted blindly beneath him, seeking to hold him again, to feel the heat and power of his body against hers, sliding within her, moving with her.

With a throttled groan, Rafe trapped Alana's restless hands. He kissed her palms, bit her fingertips and the flesh at the base of her thumb, sucked lightly on her wrist and the inside of her arm. She moved against his loving restraint, wanting more than his inciting, teasing caresses.

Rafe laughed softly and watched Alana with smoky golden eyes. He stroked her body almost soothingly, and when he spoke his voice was deep, husky with memory and desire.

"At first," he said, "after they tortured me, I dreamed only of revenge. Blood and death and the devil's laughter. But later . . ."

Rafe's head bent until he could touch the tip of Alana's breast with his tongue.

"Later, hatred wasn't enough to keep me alive," he said. "It was for some men, but not for me. That's when I began to dream of you, deep dreams, dreaming all the way to the bottom of my mind, dreaming with everything in me."

Rafe's teeth closed lightly, tugged, then he took Alana's nipple into his mouth and cherished her with changing pressures of his tongue until she cried his name and her love again and again.

"Yes," he whispered, smoothing his mustache across her taut nipple until she shivered, "I heard you calling for me when I wanted to die, calling for me and crying . . . and so I lived, and I dreamed."

The words came to Alana like another kind of caress sinking into her soul, Rafe's voice dreaming of her while his hands and mouth moved slowly over her, memorizing her as she burned beneath his touch.

Strong fingers stroked down her stomach, her thighs, sensitizing her skin until her breath came in raggedly. When his cheek slid up from her thigh and ruffled the blackness of her hair, she moaned his name. His hands smoothed the curve of her legs, pressing gently, asking silently. Her legs shifted beneath his touch, giving him another measure of his dream.

When Rafe felt the waiting heat and need of

Alana, his hand shook. She was even softer than his dreams, hotter, more welcoming. His fingers slid over her, cherishing and parting her in the same loving caress.

Alana tried to say Rafe's name, but she could only moan while he caressed her deeply, telling her of his dream and her beauty as she moved sinuously, helplessly, clinging to his touch.

When his mouth brushed over her, tasting and teasing her, she gave up trying to speak, to think. She cried for him with each ragged breath, each melting instant, fire spreading in rhythmic waves through her body.

Rafe moved over Alana slowly, covering her body with his own, sliding into her, filling her, and she came apart beneath him. Motionless, rigid, he listened to the song of her ecstasy, better than his dreams, wilder, hotter, sweeter.

And then Rafe could hold back no longer. He moved within Alana's melting heat, sliding slowly, fiercely, then more quickly. She called his name huskily, tightened around him, holding him with all her strength.

They moved together, wound tightly around one another, sharing each heartbeat, each rhythmic melting of pleasure, until neither one could bear any more. Rafe cried out and gave himself to Alana even as she gave herself to him and to the incandescent ecstasy they had created.

Finally they knew the shimmering silence and peace that followed such a complete sharing.

It was a long time before Alana stirred languidly and looked up at Rafe. He was watching her with smoky amber eyes that remembered every touch, every cry, every moment, everything.

She smiled and smoothed his mustache with fingers that still trembled.

"I love you, Rafael Winter."

Rafe gathered Alana against his body a little fiercely, like a man hardly able to believe that he wasn't dreaming.

"And I love you, Alana. You're a part of me, all the way to my soul."

He kissed her eyelids and her cheeks and the corners of her smiling lips, and he felt the kisses returned as quickly as they were given.

"As soon as we get off the mountain," Rafe said, "we'll be married. On second thought, the hell with waiting. I'll get on the radio and have Mitch fly in a justice of the peace."

Rafe felt the change in Alana, tension replacing the relaxed pressure of her body against his. He lifted his head and looked into her dark, troubled eyes.

"What is it, wildflower? Your singing career? You can live with me and write songs, can't you? And if you want to do concert tours, we'll do concert tours."

Alana opened her mouth. Words didn't come. But tears did, closing her throat.

"I'd like to have kids, though," Rafe added, smiling. "Boys as clumsy as me and girls as graceful as you. But there's no rush. You can do whatever you want, so long as you marry me. I can't let you go again."

"Rafael, my love." Alana's voice broke and tears spilled over her long eyelashes. "I can't marry you yet."

"Why?"

Rafe looked at Alana's dark eyes. Where passion had recently burned, there were only shadows now.

"Because Jack has been dead only a month?" Rafe asked bluntly. "The marriage was a mistake. A pretend mourning period would be a farce."

"Jack has nothing to do with it."

"Then—"

Alana touched Rafe's lips with gentle fingertips, silencing him.

"I want to be the woman who gives you children," she said softly. "I want to live with you and love you all the way to death and beyond, because I can't imagine ever being without you again."

Rafe took Alana's hand and kissed her palm with lips that clung and lingered over her skin. He began to gather her gently into his arms, then stopped.

She was still speaking softly, relentlessly.

"But I can't marry you until I can trust myself not to shatter into a thousand pieces with every thunderstorm," Alana said. "I can't marry you until the sight of a big, blond stranger doesn't send me into a panic. I can't marry you until I can come to you whole, confident of myself, of my sanity."

Alana felt Rafe's retreat in the withdrawal of his hand, saw it in the narrowing of his eyes and the expressionless mask that replaced a face that had been alive with love for her.

"Until you remember what happened on Broken Mountain?" asked Rafe, his voice neutral.

"Yes. Before I marry you, I have to be able to trust myself," she said, pleading with him to understand.

"Trust yourself—or me?" retorted Rafe.

The amber eyes that measured Alana were remote, as cool as his voice, showing nothing of the pain that his words cost him.

"I trust you more than I trust myself," Alana said.

Her voice was urgent, almost ragged, and her eyes searched Rafe's face anxiously.

"Then trust me to know what's best for us," he said. "Marry me."

Alana shook her head helplessly, wondering how she could make Rafe understand.

"So much for trust," said Rafe, his voice clipped.

"I trust you!"

"Yeah. Sure." He said something savage beneath his breath. "Well, at least I know how long you were standing by the cascade today. Long enough to hear Stan. Long enough to believe him. Long enough to kill a dream."

"No!" Alana said quickly. "I don't believe Stan. You aren't like that. You couldn't kill Jack like that!"

Rafe's laugh was a harsh, nearly brutal

sound that tore at Alana almost as much as it tore at him. With a vicious curse, he rolled off the bed and began pulling on his clothes.

When Rafe snatched up his shirt, the harmonica fell out of the pocket onto the floor. Firelight ran over the instrument's polished silver surface, making it shine.

He scooped up the harmonica, looked at it for a long moment, then tossed it casually onto the bed.

"Rafe?"

"Take it. Souvenir of a dream," Rafe said roughly, kicking into his boots. "I won't need it anymore. Any of it."

Alana picked up the harmonica, not understanding, not knowing what to say, afraid to say anything at all.

But when Rafe pulled open the cabin door and started to walk into the night, Alana came off the bed in a rush and threw her arms around him, preventing him from leaving.

"Rafe, *I love you*," she said against the coiled muscles of his back, holding on to him with all her strength.

"Maybe you do. Maybe that's why you forgot."

Rafe started to move away, but Alana's arms tightened, refusing to let him go.

The pain that had come with her refusal to marry him raged against Rafe's control, demanding release. He jerked free of Alana's arms and spun around to face her, his pain naked in his expression—and his anger. Yet when he spoke, his voice was so controlled, it lacked all inflection.

"I tried to be what you wanted, wildflower. I tried everything I could think of to lure you out of your isolation. I reassured you in every way I could. And it wasn't enough."

Rafe's voice roughened with each word, sliding out from his control. To see Alana in front of him right now, so lovely, so unattainable, to lose her all over again . . .

Rafe made a harsh sound and closed his eyes so that he wouldn't touch her, hold her, stir desperately among the ashes of impossible dreams.

"No matter how carefully I constructed my lures, you didn't want them enough to trust me," he said. "Finally, I even tried music. I hadn't played the harmonica since the day I found out you were married. I had played it too often for you, loving you with music the way I never could with words. After you married Jack, even the thought of touching that harmonica made me blind with rage."

"Rafael," Alana began, but he talked over her.

"Music had always been irresistible to you. So I picked up that beautiful, cruel harmonica and I called to you with it."

Tears trembled in Alana's eyelashes. "Yes."

"And you came to me."

"Yes."

"You sang with me."

"It was the first—"

But Rafe was still talking, and his eyes were as haunted by pain as his voice.

"You made love with me more incredibly than in my dreams," he said. "But it wasn't enough to make you trust me. Nothing will be enough for you."

"That's not true!"

"What's true is that you may never remember what happened on Broken Mountain. And even if you do—"

Rafe shrugged and said nothing more.

Tears and firelight washed gold down Alana's cheeks. Her hands reached for him.

"No," Rafe said gently.

He stepped away, out of reach of her slender hands.

"I once said my hooks were barbless, Alana. I meant it. I can't bear hurting you anymore. You're free."

Frozen in disbelief, Alana watched as Rafe turned and walked away from her, Rafe passing from silver moonlight into dense ebony shadows, Rafe moving as powerfully as the wind, leaving her alone with the echoes of her pain.

And his.

"Rafael . . . !"

Nothing answered, not even an echo riding on the wind.

17

FOR A LONG TIME ALANA
stood in the cabin doorway, staring into
moonlight and darkness, unaware of the cold
wind blowing over her naked skin. Finally, the
convulsive shivering of her body brought
Alana out of her daze.

She closed the door and stumbled back into
the cabin. With shaking hands she pulled on
her nightgown, but her fingers were too numb
to cope with all the tiny, mocking buttons. She
kept remembering Rafe's long fingers unfas-
tening the buttons one by one as his mouth
caressed her body with fire and love.

With a choked sound, Alana grabbed Rafe's
heavy robe. The harmonica tumbled free of the

303

indigo folds and fell gleaming to the floor. She hesitated, looking at the firelight caressing the harmonica's chased silver surface.

Then she bent and picked up the instrument and put it deep in the robe's soft pocket. She pulled the robe tightly around her and sat at the edge of the broad granite hearth, staring into the hypnotic dance of flames.

But all her eyes saw was the darkness that came after fire was lost.

Eventually dawn came. Alana realized she was cold. The rock hearth she sat on was cold. She ached from the chill of unforgiving stone.

Cold.

Stone.

Darkness.

Heart hammering, Alana tried to move but could not. She was chained by stiffness and memories summoned by the icy touch of granite.

"Rafe—"

Alana's voice was hoarse, as though she had spent the night calling futilely for help that never came.

But not last night.

She had called all through the darkness nearly four weeks ago, when she had spent the night on the rock ledge by the lake. She hadn't called to Jack that night. She remembered now.

She had called to Rafe, crying his name again and again, cries that had come from deep inside her, from the love for him that was as much a part of her as her own soul.

Jack had laughed.

Cold. Helpless. A prisoner tied to stone.

It was devastating to be so helpless, to know that beyond the tiny, icy circle constricting her, there was a world of heat and sunlight and laughter and love.

And none of those things could reach her.

Cold.

Ice raining down. Darkness and wind lifting her, tearing her from . . .

"No!" said Alana fiercely, denying her nightmare. "There's no ice here. I'm in a cabin. I'm not tied by that lake. I'm not waiting helplessly for Jack to come and either free me or maul me. I'm not a tiny, shivering aspen leaf at the mercy of cold winds. I'm Alana. I'm a human being."

Her body shivered convulsively, repeatedly.

"Get up," Alana whispered hoarsely to herself. "*Get up!*"

Slowly, stiffly, she pulled herself to her feet. She moved awkwardly toward the cabin door. When she finally managed to open it, she saw that a new day was pouring down the stone ramparts in a thick tide of crimson light.

Alana stared up at Broken Mountain's ruined peak, rocks shattered and tumbled, cliffs and miniature cirques sculpted by winters without end.

She climbed down the cabin's steps to the clearing. Her feet were too cold to feel the impact of sharp stones. She hurried to the main lodge, wanting only to get dressed before Bob got up and saw her and asked questions that she had no way to answer and no desire to hear.

Stumbling in her haste, Alana went up the lodge's steps. For an instant she was paralyzed by the thought that Rafe might be inside, that she would run to him and he would turn away from her again, leaving her freezing and alone.

A nightmare.

No, worse than that, for in Alana's nightmares Rafe didn't turn away from her, he came to her and—

Alana froze in the act of opening the door.

Rafe. In her nightmares. Like Jack.

Shaking, suddenly clammy, dizzy, Alana leaned against the closed door, wondering if it was memory or nightmare or a terrible combination of both that was breaking over her, drenching her in cold sweat.

Rafe had been on Broken Mountain.

He had told her as much. He had told her that with the horror she had buried beneath a black pool of amnesia, there was an instant of beauty when she had turned to him.

Did Rafe tell me that only to help me remember? Alana asked silently. *Did he use the promise of beauty like a single, perfect lure drifting down onto the blank surface of my amnesia, luring me beyond its dark, safe depths?*

Alana waited for memory or nightmare to come and answer her questions, freeing her.

Nothing came but the too-fast beating of her heart, blood rushing in her ears like a waterfall . . .

Ice and darkness and falling, she was falling to the death that waited below!

With a hoarse cry, Alana wrenched herself out of nightmare. She opened the lodge door and hurried up the loft's narrow stairway. She pulled on clothes at random, caring only for warmth.

The fiery orange of Alana's sweater heightened the translucent pallor of her face and the darkness below her eyes. She rubbed her cheeks fiercely, trying to bring color to her face.

It didn't help. Her eyes were still too dark, too wide, almost feverish in their intensity. She looked brittle and more than a little wild, as though she would fly apart at a word or a touch.

Abruptly Alana decided that she would find Rafe. She would find him and then she would demand that he tell her what he knew.

"To hell with what Dr. Gene said about what would or would not help me remember," Alana whispered savagely. "To hell with what everyone else thinks is good for me. *I have to know.*"

No matter how horrible the truth, it could be no worse than what Alana was enduring now . . . Rafe turning away from her, sliding

into night, nothing answering her cry, not
even an echo.

Alana heard someone in the kitchen. She
went down the stairs quickly, determination in
every line of her body. She would confront
Rafe now. She was through running, hiding,
feeling screams and memories clawing at her
throat.

But Rafe wasn't in the kitchen.

"Morning, sis," Bob said as she walked in.

His back was to her as he finished filling the
coffeepot with water, but he had recognized
her step.

"You're late, but so are the rest of us," Bob
said. "Poker game didn't break up until after
three."

Still talking, he turned toward her as he set
the coffeepot on the hot stove.

"Janice is the luckiest—my God, Alana!
What's wrong?"

"Nothing that coffee won't cure," she said,
controlling her voice carefully.

Bob crossed the room in two long strides.
He reached for Alana before he remembered
Rafe's very explicit instructions about touch-
ing her.

"I'm going to see if you're running a fever,"
said Bob, slowly raising his hand to her forehead.

"I'm not."

Alana didn't step away from her brother's
touch. Nor did she flinch. Finally she could see
him clearly, no nightmare to cloud her eyes.

Bob's big palm pressed against Alana's fore-head with surprising gentleness.

"You're cold," he said, startled by the coolness of her skin.

"Right. Not a bit of fever." Alana's voice was as clipped as the smile she gave her brother. "Have you seen Rafe?"

Bob's dark eyes narrowed. "He left."

"Left?"

"He told me he'd gotten a holler on the radio from the ranch. Something needed his attention right away. Said he'd radio us as soon as he got home."

"How long?"

"It's a long ride to his ranch house, even on that spotted mountain horse of his. Tonight, probably."

"When did he leave?"

"About an hour ago. Why?"

"No reason," Alana said, her voice as dry and tight as her throat. "Just curious."

"Did something happen between you two? Rafe looked as rocky as you do."

Alana laughed strangely.

"Did you know that Rafe was on the mountain four weeks ago?" she asked.

Bob gave her an odd look.

"Rafe was on Broken Mountain when Jack died," Alana said fiercely.

"Of course he was. How did you think you got off the mountain after you were hurt?"

"What?" whispered Alana.

"C'mon, sis." Bob smiled despite his worry. "Even you can't walk down three miles of icy mountain switchbacks on a badly wrenched ankle. The storm spooked all the horses, so Rafe carried you out on his back. If he hadn't, you'd have died up there, same as Jack did."

"I don't remember," Alana said.

"Of course not. You were out of your head with shock. Hell, I'll bet you don't even remember Sheriff Mitchell landing on the lake and flying you out of here in the middle of a storm. Mitch told me it was the fanciest piece of flying he'd ever done, too."

"I don't remember!"

Bob smiled and patted Alana's shoulder gently.

"Don't fret about it, sis. Nobody expects you to remember anything about the rescue. When I got to the hospital, you didn't even recognize me."

"I—don't—"

"Remember," Bob finished dryly. "Hypothermia does that to you. Turns your brain to suet every time. Remember when we went after that crazy rock climber way up on the mountain? By the time we found him, he had less sense than a chicken. He did fine after we thawed him out, though."

Alana looked at Bob's very dark eyes, eyes like the night, only brighter, warmer.

Eyes like her own before she had forgotten.

But Bob remembered and she didn't. Even when he told her, she could hardly believe what she was hearing. It was like reading about something in the newspaper. Distant. Not quite real.

Rafe had carried her down Broken Mountain.

She didn't remember.

No wonder Rafe hadn't told her what had happened. Telling her would do no good. Being told wasn't the same as remembering, as *knowing*.

Rafe had saved Alana's life, and she didn't even know it. He had carried her down a treacherous trail, ice and darkness all around, risked his own life for her.

And to her it was as though it had never happened.

"Rafe waited for you to remember after you ran out of the hospital," Bob said.

"I didn't. Remember."

She hadn't remembered, hadn't called Rafe, hadn't even known that he was waiting back on Broken Mountain.

Waiting for her.

"Yeah," Bob said. "Rafe figured that out for himself. So he gnawed on me to get you back here."

Numbly Alana nodded. She had come home, and Rafe had treated her with gentleness and understanding, asking nothing of her, giving everything. When being in the mountains frightened her, he apologized as though he were responsible.

Rafe had shared her pain to a degree that she hardly believed even now. He had given her all the reassurance he could. And never once had he shown how much she was hurting him.

He had loved her, cherished her, done everything possible for her, except remember. No one could remember for her.

That she must do for herself.

"Sis?" asked Bob, his voice worried. "You better sit down. You look like death warmed over."

"Thanks a lot, baby brother."

Alana's voice was as thin as the smile she gave Bob. She forced her throat to relax, using the discipline she had learned as a singer.

It was important that Bob not worry about her.

It was important that he not hover or watch over her, preventing her from doing what must be done.

It was important that she act as though there was nothing wrong with her that breakfast and a day lazing around the lake wouldn't cure.

Nothing wrong.

Absolutely normal.

"Check the wood box in the kitchen, okay? I don't want to run out of fire halfway through the eggs."

Alana's voice sounded calm, if a little flat. The smile she gave Bob echoed her voice precisely.

"Why don't you let me do breakfast?" asked Bob, a worried frown creasing his forehead. "You go sit and—"

"I'll sit later," she interrupted, "while you and the dudes are out fishing. I have a place all picked out. Grass and sunshine and a perfect view of aspen leaves."

Alana's throat constricted as she remembered counting aspen leaves with Rafe while he lay quietly with his hands locked behind his head, smiling and aching as she touched him.

Rafe.

She closed her eyes and forced herself to take a breath.

"Get cracking on the wood box, baby brother. I don't want to spend all day in the kitchen."

Bob hesitated, then went out the back door of the cabin. A few minutes later the clear, sharp sound of a ten-pound maul splitting cured wood rang through the dawn.

Carefully thinking of nothing at all, Alana moved through the kitchen, letting the routine of cooking and setting the table focus her mind. Whenever her thoughts veered to Rafe, she dragged them back ruthlessly.

First she had to get through breakfast. When everyone was safely caught up in fishing, when she was alone with only her erratic memory, then she would think of Rafe.

Thinking of him would give her the courage to do what had to be done.

A moment of panic rippled through Alana. A piece of silverware slipped from her hands and landed with a clatter on the table. With fingers that trembled, she retrieved the fork and put it in its proper place. She finished setting the table just as Janice came in.

"Good morning," Janice said cheerfully.

"Morning. Coffee's ready."

"Sounds like heaven. Is Rafe up yet?"

"Yes. I'll get you some coffee."

Quickly Alana turned away, avoiding the scrutiny of the other woman's eyes. The former psychiatrist was entirely too perceptive for Alana's comfort right now.

"Is that Rafe chopping wood?" asked Janice, falling into step beside Alana.

In an instant of memory that almost destroyed her control, Alana's mind gave her a picture of Rafe working by the woodpile four years ago. His long legs had been braced, his shirt off, the powerful muscles of his back coiling and relaxing rhythmically as he worked with the ax beneath the July sun, chopping stove wood. She could see him so clearly, the heat and life of him so vivid, she could almost touch him.

Yearning went through Alana like lightning, hunger and love and loss turning in her, cutting her until she could feel her life bleeding away.

"No," whispered Alana.

Desperately she pushed away the memory. If she thought of Rafe right now, she would go crazy.

Or crazier.

Before Janice could ask any more, Alana said, "Bob drew the short straw this morning."

Despite Alana's efforts to keep her voice normal, Janice looked at her sharply.

"You look a bit feverish," Janice said. "Are you feeling all right?"

"Fine. Just fine."

Alana poured coffee. Her hand shook, but not enough to spill the coffee.

"Tired, that's all," Alana said. "Altitude, you know. I'm not used to it. That and the cold nights. God, but the nights are cold on Broken Mountain."

And I'm babbling, added Alana silently, reining in her thoughts. And her tongue.

She handed Janice her coffee.

"Breakfast will be ready in about twenty minutes," Alana said.

Janice took the cup and sipped thoughtfully, watching Alana's too-quick, almost erratic movements around the kitchen.

"I thought I heard a horse ride by earlier this morning," Janice said. "Before dawn."

"That must have been Rafe," said Alana very casually.

She concentrated on laying thick strips of bacon across the old stove's huge griddle. Fat hissed as it met the searing iron surface.

"Rafe left?" asked Janice, startled.

"He has to check on something at the ranch. He'll be back later."

And pigs will fly, thought Alana, remembering Rafe's pain and anger. He won't come back until I'm gone. I've used up my chances with him. Rafael, I never meant to hurt you. Never . . .

Alana's hand shook, brushing against the griddle. She took a steadying breath and thought only about getting through breakfast.

One thing at a time. Now, this moment, that meant frying bacon without blistering herself through sheer stupidity.

Later she would think about Rafe leaving her, about his pain, about what she must do, about remembering.

Later. Not now.

"I hope everyone likes scrambled eggs," Alana said.

She went to the refrigerator and opened the door. No light came on. Rafe had forgotten to start up the generator. She pulled out a bowl of fresh eggs, then went to the back door and called to Bob.

"Do you know how to start up the generator?"

"Sure thing." Bob gestured toward a pile of split wood with the maul he was holding. "How much do you need?"

Alana remembered the night before, when she had found the living room wood box all but empty.

"Enough for the fireplace, too," she said. "You'll want a nice fire tonight."

"What about you?" asked Bob dryly, looking over his shoulder at Alana. "Don't you want a nice fire tonight, too?"

I won't be here tonight.

But the words were silent, existing only in Alana's mind.

"Does that mean I have to chop it myself?" she retorted, her voice sounding rough.

"Just teasing, sis," answered Bob. "You

never could split wood worth a damn."

He swung the maul again, burying its edge deep in the wood, splitting it easily into two smaller pieces.

Alana turned back to the stove. She was relieved to see that Janice had gone. The woman's eyes were just too intent, too knowing.

Breakfast was an ordeal Alana hoped never to have to repeat. The toast was impossible to chew, much less swallow. She forced herself to eat anyway. If she didn't, Bob would stick to her like a mother hen for the rest of the day, worrying over her.

Alana couldn't allow that to happen. So she ate grimly, washing down eggs and bacon with coffee, eating as little as she thought she could get away with.

As soon as Bob finished, he looked at Alana, then at Stan and Janice.

"I'm going to stay behind and help Alana with the dishes," Bob said. "Rafe thought you should try the water on the north side of the lake, where that little creek comes in. Some real big trout hang around there, feeding on whatever washes down."

"Sounds good to me," Stan said.

"Rafe suggested using dark flies," Bob added, "or the grasshopper imitation he tied for each of you. Me, I'm going to use the Lively Lady."

Alana got up, her plate and silverware in her hands.

"I'll take care of the dishes," she said, grateful that her voice sounded casual rather than desperate, the way she felt. "If you're doing dishes while Stan is fishing, he'll get the prize for the biggest fish."

"What prize?" asked Bob.

"Apple pie," Alana said succinctly. "Winner takes all."

A friendly argument began over big fish and winner taking all of the pie. In the end, everyone stayed and helped Alana with the dishes. When the last lunch had been packed and the last dish was draining on the counter, she turned and smiled rather fiercely at everyone.

"Thank you and good-bye," she said. "The trout are rising. The best fishing time of the day is slipping away. Have fun. I'll see you for dinner."

Stan and Janice exchanged glances, then left the kitchen. Alana looked expectantly at Bob.

"I'll leave in a while," Bob said, smiling genially and reaching for an apron. "Stan needs a handicap in the trout sweepstakes. I'll help you with the pie."

Alana looked at Bob in disbelief. Determination showed in every line of his face. He didn't know what was wrong, but he plainly wasn't going to leave until he did.

"You'll have a long wait," she said finally. "I'm going to take a bath. A very long, very hot bath. And no, baby brother, I don't need you to scrub my back."

Bob had the grace to laugh. But the laugh faded quickly into concern.

"You sure?" he asked softly.

"I've never been more sure of anything in my life." Alana's eyes held her brother's. "It's all right, Bob. Go fishing. Please."

Bob expelled a harsh breath and ran his hand through his black hair.

"I'm worried," he said bluntly. "Rafe looked like hell. You look worse. I feel like the guy who grabbed for the brass ring and came up with a handful of garbage. I want to help you, but I'm damned if I know what to do."

"Go fishing," Alana said.

Her voice was soft and very certain.

"Hell," Bob muttered. Then, "I'll be at the north side of the lake if you need me. Why don't you come over for lunch?"

"I'll probably be asleep."

"Most sensible thing you've said today," retorted Bob.

He looked pointedly at the dark circles beneath his sister's eyes. Then he threw up his hands and walked out of the kitchen.

"We'll be back for dinner about five," he called over his shoulder.

"Good luck," said Alana.

A grunt was Bob's only reply.

She held her breath until she heard the front door of the cabin close. Then she ran to the window and looked out. Bob had picked up his rod, net, and fishing vest. He was stalking over the lake trail with long, powerful strides.

"Take care," whispered Alana. "Don't be too mad at me. You did everything you could. Like Rafe. It's not your fault that it wasn't enough. It's mine."

Alana pulled off her apron with shaking hands and hung it on a nail by the back door. Then she raced upstairs and began stuffing warm clothes into the backpack she had found in her closet.

Broken Mountain could be cold, brutally cold. She of all people knew that.

Alana went back down the stairs, listening to her racing heart and the harsh thump of her hiking boots on the wooden stairs. She ran to the kitchen and began throwing food into the backpack. Cheese, raisins, granola, chocolate. She closed the flap and secured it tightly.

For a moment Alana stood and looked around the kitchen, wondering what she had forgotten.

"A note," she said. "I have to leave a note."

Alana scrambled through kitchen drawers, looking for paper and a pencil. But when she found them, she couldn't think of anything to say.

"How can I explain in words something that I barely understand myself?" Alana asked, staring helplessly at the paper.

Yet she had to write something.

She owed Bob that much. If he came back early and found her gone, he would be frantic.

Alana bent over and wrote quickly:

If Rafe calls, tell him I've gone to find the lark.
This time it will sing for me.

18

ALANA WALKED ALONG THE
trail, grateful for the trees screening her from
the lake. Through the breaks in the forest, she
could see three people spaced out along the
north side of the water. Bob looked no bigger
than her palm. Bits of sound floated across the
lake to her, fragments without meaning.

When she came to a fork in the trail, she
hesitated for a moment. The right-hand path
wound back to the lake, coming out just in
front of the cascade where she had overheard
Stan and Rafe arguing. The left-hand path
skirted the worst of the rock jumble that
caused the cascade.

Alana adjusted the backpack and turned

onto the left fork of the trail. Once past the fork, the trail began the long climb to the top of Broken Mountain.

The first part of the climb consisted of long switchbacks looping through the forest. Before Alana had gone half a mile, she wished she had Sid to do the work for her. But taking the horse would have been too great a risk. Sid would have spent the first mile neighing to the horses hobbled in the meadow behind the main cabin. Short of a siren, nothing carried better in the high mountains than the neigh of a lonely horse.

Sunlight quivered among aspen leaves and fell silently through evergreen boughs. The air was crisp, fragrant with resin, motionless but for the occasional stirring of wind off the lake. The cascade's distant mutter filtered through the forest, telling Alana that she was approaching one of the open, rocky sections of the trail. She would have to be careful not to be spotted by the fishermen below.

The forest dwindled, then vanished as the trail crawled over a steep talus slope. Broken stone of all sizes littered the ridge. The thunder of the cascade came clearly across the rocks. To the right of the trail the land fell away abruptly, ending in the sapphire depths of the lake.

Alana took one look, then did not look again. Fixing her eyes on the rugged ground just in front of her feet, she picked her way across the talus. For the first hundred yards her breath came shallowly, erratically. Then she regained control of her breathing. Slowly her fear of heights diminished, giving strength back to her legs.

Just before Alana dropped out of sight over a fold of Broken Mountain, she turned and looked down at the lake. Wisps of brilliant white cloud trailed iridescent shadows over the water, emphasizing the clarity and depth of both lake and air.

Alana's heart beat faster and her palms felt clammy, but she forced herself to look at the north shore. There were three specks, dark against the gray granite of the shoreline.

Three fishermen.

No one had spotted Alana and run after her to bring her back. With luck, no one would even notice that she was gone until dinnertime. And then it would be too late to come after her.

No one rode or walked high mountain trails at night unless a life was at risk.

Besides, even when Bob discovered that Alana wasn't at the lodge, he wouldn't know where she was. The last place he would expect to find her was farther up Broken Mountain, all the way up to the first and highest lake, up to the lip of the cliff where water leaped into darkness, standing in the exact spot where Jack had died and she had lost her mind.

Surely there, if anywhere, I'll remember, Alana told herself. Surely there, where conditions most exactly match the environment of my nightmare. . . .

There she would rise from the bleak, safe

pool of amnesia into the transparent light of
reality. There, if anywhere on earth.

If Alana didn't remember right away, she
would simply stay until she did, sleeping on
a rock by the lake if she had to. She would do
whatever she must to remember. Then she
would accept whatever came.

In truth, now there was little at stake. That
was why she finally had come to Broken
Mountain.

She had nothing left to lose.

Alana climbed steadily through the morning. Though the second lake was less than two
miles from the cabins, it took Alana three
hours to make the climb. Part of the problem
was the altitude. Another part was the roughness of the trail.

The hardest part was her own fear. Every
step closer to the first lake was like a pebble
added to her backpack, weighing her down.

By the time she scrambled up the saddle of
land that concealed the second lake, Alana
was sweating freely and felt almost dizzy. She
stood and looked down on the tiny, marshy
stretch of water. More pond than true lake,
during the driest years the second lake existed
only on maps. This year, though, the winter
had been thick with snow and the summer
ripe with storms. The water was a rich wealth
of silver against the dense green of meadow
and marsh plants.

The lake had been full the last time Alana
was there. Clouds seething and wind bending
the aspens, wind shaking the elegant spruce

trees, storm winds moaning down the slopes.

It hadn't rained, though. Not then. Just clouds and a few huge water drops hurled from the heights by the wind.

Thunder had been distant, erratic. The peak next to Broken Mountain had been mantled in blue-black mist and lightning. But not Broken Mountain. Not then. Thunder hadn't come to Broken Mountain until the next night.

Seeing nothing but the past, Alana stared blindly at the ribbon of water nestled in a green hollow between folds of granite.

Remembering.

They had rested the horses there. She had gone to the edge of the small meadow and leaned against a tree, listening to the distant song of water over rock.

Jack had come up behind her, and she had wanted to put her hands over her ears, shutting him out. But she hadn't been able to then.

She was remembering now, Jack and the argument and the mountain rising cold and hard . . .

"Jilly, don't be stupid about this. We won't be famous forever. A few more years, that's all I ask."

She wanted to scream with frustration. Jack simply wouldn't accept that she couldn't go on with the farce of Country's Perfect Couple.

She had to be free.

"Jilly, you better listen."

"I'm listening," she said flatly. "I'm just not agreeing."

"Then you don't understand," he said confidently. *"As soon as you understand, you'll agree."*

"You're the one who doesn't understand. You're not getting your way this time, Jack. You shouldn't have demanded that I marry you in the first place. I shouldn't have given in."

Not looking at Jack, she ran her hand down the long black braids that fell between her breasts.

"It was a mistake," she said finally. *"A very bad mistake. It's time we faced it."*

"You're wrong. Think about it, Jilly. You're wrong."

"I've thought of nothing else for several years. I've made up my mind."

"Then you'll just have to change it."

She had turned suddenly, catching the black look he gave her. Then Jack had shrugged and smiled charmingly.

"Aw, c'mon, Jilly. Let's stop arguing and enjoy ourselves for a change. That's why we're here, remember?"

Yes, Alana was remembering.

Too late. Rafe was gone. She was remembering.

And she was afraid.

Alana shuddered and shifted the weight of her backpack, letting echoes and memories of the past gather around her as she climbed.

At first she remembered small things, a little bit at a time, minutes slowly building into whole memories. The closer she came, the higher she climbed on Broken Mountain, the thinner the veil of amnesia became—and the greater her mind's rebellion at what she was demanding of herself.

Alana no longer told herself that her rapid heartbeat and dragging breaths came from altitude or exertion. She was struggling against fear just as she had struggled against Jack's stubborn refusal to face the reality of her decision to leave him.

Suddenly Alana realized that she had stopped walking. She was braced against a rock, shaking, her eyes fixed on the last, steep ascent to the highest lake.

Broken Mountain rose behind the lake, granite thrusting into the sky. It waited for her, the cliff and the talus where wind howled and water fell into blackness and exploded far below on unyielding stone.

It waited for her, and she was terrified.

"Pull up your socks and get going, Alana Jillian," she said between gritted teeth. "Like Dad always said, you can't keep the mountain waiting. Besides, what do you have to lose that you haven't already lost?"

Nothing.

Not one damned thing.

Alana fastened her eyes on the trail just in front of her feet and began walking. She didn't look up, didn't stop, didn't think.

One by one, memories came, wisps of cloud gathering over the blank pool of amnesia, clouds and memories condensing into columns of white seething over the mountain-tops, over her.

She stood at the edge of the tiny, hanging

valley where the first lake lay beneath the sullen sky. Thunder rumbled distantly, forerunner of the storm to come.

But not yet. The clouds hadn't met and wrapped around each other and the peaks. Only then would the storm begin, bringing darkness in the midst of day, black rain and white ice and thunder like mountains torn apart.

But not yet. She had a breathing space in the shelter of the stunted trees that grew in the lee of the mountain looming raggedly against the sky.

Broken Mountain.

At the base of the shattered gray peak lay the lake, mercury-colored water lapping at the very lip of the valley. Alana looked away from the white water leaping over the valley's edge, water falling and bouncing from rock to boulder, water exploding like thunder.

Jack flying out, turning and falling, white water and screams.

Alana slipped out of her backpack and went like a sleepwalker to the end of the trail.

Was it here Jack fell? she asked herself.

She looked over the edge, suffered a wave of dizziness and forced herself to look again.

No, it hadn't happened here.

Where, then? she asked herself impatiently.

The trail turned to the right, keeping to the trees. To the left was the end of the lake and the beginning of the waterfall, lake and rock and land falling away from the lip of the hanging valley.

Nausea turned in Alana, and a fear so great that it hammered her to her knees.

The lake. The lake lapping at the edge of space, water churning, thunder bounding and rebounding, darkness and screams. She was screaming.

No, it was the wind that screamed. The wind had come up at dawn and she shivered until Jack came to her. . . .

"Change your mind yet, Jilly?"

She closed her eyes and said nothing, did nothing, helpless, tied to stone.

"That's okay, babe. We've got all the time in the world."

"Untie m-me." *Her voice came at a distance, a stranger's voice, harsh as stone scraping over stone.*

"You going to listen to me if I do?"

"Y-Yes."

"You going to stop crying for that bastard Winter?"

Silence.

"I heard you, Jilly. Last night. Lots of nights. I'm going to break you of loving Winter, babe. I'm going to break you, period. When we get down off this mountain, you'll come to heel and stay there."

Alana listened, all tears gone.

She listened, and knew that Jack was crazy.

She listened, and knew that she would die on Broken Mountain unless she stopped crying and started using her head.

Her mind worked with eerie speed and clarity, time slowing down as she sorted through probabil-

ities and possibilities, certainties and hopes.

And then came understanding, a single brilliant fact: She must get Jack to untie her. Then the second fact: Jack's only weakness was his career; he needed her.

"If you l-leave me on this rock any longer, I'll be too s-sick to sing."

Jack put his hand on Alana's arm. It was cold enough to shock him. He frowned and fiddled with the zipper on his jacket.

"Are you going to listen to me?" he demanded.

"Y-Yes."

Jack untied her, but Alana was too stiff, too weak to move. He hauled her off the rock and set her on her feet.

She fell and stayed down, helpless, tied by a kind of pain that made her dizzy and nauseated. Finally feeling began to come back to her strained joints and limbs. Then she cried out hoarsely, never having known such agony.

Jack half dragged, half carried Alana to the camp, jerking her along, her braids wound around his hand. He dropped her casually by the fire. She lay there without moving, her mind spinning with pain. Eventually the worst of it passed and she could think.

She concealed the fact of her returning strength, afraid that Jack would tie her up again. When he spoke to her, she tried pretending that she was too dazed to answer. He hit her with the back of his hand, knocking her away from the fire. She lay motionless, cold and aching and afraid.

"You listen to me, Jilly. I need you, but there are other ways, other women who can sing. I've been sleeping with one of them. You can sing circles around her, but she comes to heel a hell of a lot better than you do. Don't be more trouble than you're worth.''

Alana shuddered and said nothing.

It seemed hours before the moment came that she had been waiting for. Jack went to get more wood. She came up off the ground in a stumbling rush, running in the opposite direction, seeking the cover of the forest and the mountainside.

That was the beginning of a deadly game of hide-and-seek. Jack called to her, threats and endearments, both equally obscene to Alana's ears as she dodged from tree to thicket to boulder, her heart as loud as thunder.

Storm clouds opened, drenching the land with icy water mixed with sleet. Weakened by cold, her mind fading in and out of touch with reality, Alana knew she was running out of time and possibilities.

Her only chance was to flee down the mountain. She had begun working toward that from the first moment, leading Jack around the lake until he was no longer between her and escape.

Now only the margin of the lake itself lay between her and the trail down Broken Mountain, the lake where water lapped over boulders and then fell down, down, to the rocks below. There was no shelter there. No place to hide from Jack.

Lightning and thunder shattered the world into black and white shards. Ice sleeted down, freezing her.

And then a rock rattled behind her, Jack coming, reaching for her.

Water rushing down, cold, and darkness wait-ing, lined with rocks, ice and darkness closing around, clouds seething overhead, lightning lanc-ing down, soundless thunder.

Fear.

It was too cold, no warmth anywhere, only fear hammering on her, leaving her weak.

She tried to run, but her feet weighed as much as the mountains and were as deeply rooted in the earth. Each step took an eternity. Try harder, move faster, or get caught.

She must run!

But she could not.

Something had caught her braids, jerking her backward with stunning force.

Jack loomed above her, anger twisting his face, her braids wrapped around his fist. Jack cursing her, grabbing her, hitting her, and the storm break-ing, trees bending and snapping like glass beneath the wind.

Like her. She wasn't strong enough. She would break and the pieces would be scattered over the cold rocks.

Jack slipped on the rocks where white pebbles of sleet gathered and turned beneath his boots. He let go of Alana's braids, breaking his fall with his hands.

Running. Scrambling.

Breath like a knife in her side.

Throat on fire with screams and the storm chas-ing her, catching her, yanking her backward while rocks like fists hit her. She was broken and bleeding, screaming down the night, running.

Caught. Her braids caught again in Jack's fist,

*ice sliding beneath her feet, wind tearing at her,
Jack lifting her as she screamed, lifting her high and
when he let go she would fall as the water fell,
down and down over the lip of the valley, exploding
whitely on rocks far below.*

*Clawing and fighting. But she was swept up,
lifted high, helpless, nothing beneath her feet, earth
falling away and her body twisting, weightless, she
was falling, falling, black rushing up to meet her
and when it did she would be torn from life like an
aspen leaf from its stem, spinning away helplessly
over the void.*

She called to Rafe then.

*Knowing that she was dead, she cried Rafe's
name and her undying love for him into the teeth
of the waiting mountain.*

And Rafe answered.

*He came out of the storm and darkness like an
avenging angel, his hands tearing her from Jack's
deadly grasp.*

*At the last instant Rafe spun aside from the
drop-off, balanced on the brink of falling. With certain death in front of him and Alana at his feet,
Rafe whirled and launched himself in a low tackle
that carried Jack away from Alana, helpless at the
edge of the cliff.*

*The two men grappled in the darkness, pale sleet
rolling beneath their feet, their struggles bringing
them closer to the brink with each second.*

*Rafe kicked away, freeing himself and coming to
his feet in a poised, muscular rush. Jack staggered
upright, his hair shining palely with each flash of
lightning, his face dark with hatred. He leaped
blindly for Rafe.*

But Rafe wasn't there. He slipped the attack with a supple, disciplined movement of his body, leaving nothing but night between Jack and the lip of the cliff.

Jack had an instant of surprise, a scream of fury and disbelief, and then he was falling, turning over slowly, screaming and falling into night.

Silence came, and then the sound of Alana's tearing screams.

"It's all right, wildflower. I've come to take you home."

Alana shuddered, giving her mind and her body to the cold and blackness. . . .

Alana stirred and slowly surfaced from memories. She was surprised to find that it was day rather than evening, fair rather than stormy, and she was huddled on her knees rather than unconscious in Rafe's arms.

She shook her head, hardly able to believe that she wasn't still dreaming. Rafe's words had sounded so real, so close.

She opened her eyes and saw that she had walked to the treacherous margin of rock and water and cliff. With a shudder, she turned away from the edge—and then she saw a man silhouetted against the sun.

She froze, fear squeezing her heart.

Rafe's face tightened into a mask of pain when he saw Alana's fear.

She had remembered and he had lost her.

"Stan was right," Rafe said, pain roughening his voice. "You were running from me,

too. You didn't want to believe that the man
you loved was a killer."

"No!"

Alana's voice shook, making a ragged cry
out of the single word.

"Yes," said Rafe flatly. "I killed Jack Reeves.
And you remembered it."

"It wasn't like that," Alana said quickly.
"Stan was wrong. You didn't come up the
mountain planning to kill Jack and seduce me
and—"

"But Jack's dead," Rafe interrupted. "I
killed him."

"You were saving my life!" Alana said, trying to understand why Rafe's face was so
closed, so remote.

Rafe shrugged.

"So it's manslaughter, not murder one," he
said curtly. "Jack's dead just the same."

"It was an accident!" she cried fiercely. "I
saw it, Rafe! I know!"

"Technically, yes, it was an accident," Rafe
said, his voice as controlled as his expression.
"When I ducked, I didn't know that Jack
would go over the cliff."

Alana let out a ragged breath.

"But there's something about the fight that
you still haven't faced, Alana." Rafe spoke
slowly, clearly, leaving no room for evasion or
misunderstanding. "When I saw Jack trying to
kill you—after that instant, Jack Reeves was a
dead man walking. There was no way I'd let
him leave the mountain alive."

Alana's eyes closed, but it wasn't in horror

at what Rafe was saying. It was the pain in him that made her flinch.

"You knew that," Rafe said. "Yet you couldn't stand knowing that the man you loved was a murderer. So you forgot. But not well enough. Somewhere, deep inside you, you knew. You didn't trust me enough to marry me."

"That's not true!" said Alana desperately. "You saved my life! You—"

"It's all right, wildflower," Rafe said, cutting across Alana's urgent words. "You don't owe me anything. You gave it all back to me that night."

"But—"

"When you were certain you were going to die, you screamed, but not for mercy or revenge. You called to me, telling me that you loved me. *And you didn't even know I was there.* In those few seconds you wiped out all the bitterness that had been destroying me since I found out you were married."

"Rafael," she whispered.

"You don't owe me anything at all. Certainly not trust."

Alana looked at Rafe wildly.

"But I do trust you!" she cried.

Rafe's mouth turned down in a sad travesty of a smile.

"I don't believe you, wildflower."

Before Alana could say anything more, Rafe turned toward the trail where his big spotted stallion stood patiently.

"We'd better go," Rafe said. "Bob has probably found your note by now, and mine. He'll be beside himself with worry."

Rafe began walking toward his horse. After a few steps, he realized that Alana wasn't following. He turned back and saw that she was still sitting on a rock very near the edge of the cliff.

"Alana?"

She sat motionless, watching Rafe, her eyes dark.

"I'll need your help," she said distinctly.

With a few swift strides Rafe was at Alana's side. He knelt in front of her and began running his hands from her knees to her feet.

"Did you wrench your ankle again?" he asked. "Where does it hurt?"

"Everywhere," Alana said softly. "You'll have to carry me."

Rafe's head snapped up.

He searched Alana's eyes and her expression, afraid to breathe, to hope. Even when she had given herself to him in the moonlit cabin, he had not dared to lift her, to hold her helpless above the ground.

And now she was at the edge of the same cliff Jack had held her over, held her high above his head, getting set to throw her out into darkness and death.

Silently Alana held her arms out to Rafe.

He stood and looked down at her for a long moment. Then he bent and caught her beneath her arms.

Slowly Rafe lifted Alana to her feet, waiting for the first sign of fear to tighten her body.

He held her almost level with him, her toes just off the ground.

She smiled and put her hands on his shoulders.

"Higher, Rafael. Lift me higher. Lift me over your head."

"Alana—"

"Lift me," she whispered against his lips. "I know you won't let me fall. I'm safe with you, Rafael. You aren't like Jack. You won't throw my life away. *Lift me*."

Rafe lifted Alana as high as he could, held her, watched her smile, felt her trust in the complete relaxation of her body suspended between his hands.

Then he let her slide slowly down his body until their lips met in a kiss that left both of them shaken, clinging to each other.

They rode the same way down the mountain, clinging to each other, whispering words of love and need. Rafe's arms were wrapped around Alana and her hands were over his as he guided the big stallion along the trail.

Rafe was the first one to spot the plane bobbing quietly on the third lake.

"Sheriff Mitchell," Rafe said. "Bob must have hit the panic button."

Alana shrank against Rafe and went very still.

For the rest of the ride she was silent, her hands clinging to Rafe's wrists, her mind racing as she tried to figure out ways to protect the man she loved.

No matter what Rafe says, he isn't at fault for Jack's death, Alana thought. Jack brought it on himself. Rafe doesn't deserve to be punished for Jack's selfishness, his murderous rage.

Yet Alana was afraid that was exactly what would happen.

Sheriff Mitchell was sitting on the porch of the lodge, his feet propped against the rail. When he heard the big stallion's hoof strike a rock, Mitch looked up.

"I see you found her," Mitch said, satisfaction in his voice. "Just like I told Bob you would."

Alana spoke before Rafe could.

"My memory is back. Jack's death was an accident, just like Rafe said. It was icy and Jack fell and I passed out from shock and cold."

Mitch looked at Alana oddly. His homely face creased into a frown.

"That's not what Rafe told me," the sheriff muttered. "He said that Jack tried to kill you, they fought, and Jack ended up dead. Is that how you remember it?"

Alana made a helpless sound and looked over her shoulder at Rafe. He kissed her lips.

"I told Mitch everything when we rode back in to bring out Jack's body," Rafe said. "When we came off the mountain, you were gone."

"But—but that's not how the newspapers explained Jack's death," said Alana.

Mitch shrugged.

"Well," the sheriff said, "I didn't figure that justice would be any better served if we went to the hassle of arraigning and then acquitting

Rafe on a clear-cut case of justifiable homicide."

Alana's breath caught. She turned and looked at the sheriff with hope in her eyes.

"And then there would have been reporters hounding you for all the bloody details," the sheriff drawled, "what with Jack being such a famous son of a bitch and all. You didn't need that. You were having a hard enough time staying afloat as it was."

Alana let out a long sigh of relief.

"So I told the reporters the only truth that mattered," the sheriff concluded. "In my opinion, Jack's death was legally an accident."

Mitch paused and looked at Alana, his gray eyes intent. "Unless you remember it some other way and want to change the record?"

"No," Alana said quickly. "Not at all. I just didn't want Rafe to be punished for saving my life."

Mitch nodded. "That's how I had it figured."

He pulled out a pipe from his jacket pocket, struck a match, and held it to the bowl. He sucked hard a few times, then looked at the lake.

"Well, now," Mitch said, changing the subject with finality, "what's the fishing been like?"

Rafe tilted his head and kissed the nape of Alana's neck.

"You're too late, Mitch. I just caught the most beautiful trout on the mountain."

Mitch grinned around a cloud of pungent smoke.

"Keeper size?" he asked dryly.

Rafe laughed and slid off the big stallion. When he was on the ground, he held his arms out to Alana.

She smiled and let him lift her out of the saddle. For a few moments he held her off the ground, enjoying the sensation of her body pressed against the length of his own.

"Definitely keeper size," Rafe said.

Mitch laughed.

"Unless," Rafe whispered too softly for Mitch to hear, "the trout doesn't want the fisherman?"

Alana kissed Rafe gently, brushing her lips across his mouth as her fingers slid deeply into his thick hair, dislodging his Stetson.

The front door of the cabin slammed open.

"Mitch, when in hell are you going to— Alana! Are you okay?"

Mitch laughed. "Bob, are you blind? She's never been better."

Reluctantly Rafe released Alana so that she could reassure her brother.

"I've remembered," she said, turning to face Bob. "And I'm fine. I'm sorry I worried you."

"Hell, sis, it was worth it!" Bob turned to yell over his shoulder. "Stan! Janice! Alana's got her memory back!"

There was a triumphant whoop from the cabin. Janice and Stan ran out onto the porch. Stan looked at Alana, wrapped securely in

Rafe's arms, relaxed and smiling, obviously not afraid.

Then Stan turned and gave Janice a thorough, hungry kiss.

Bob looked startled.

Rafe simply smiled.

"I think I'd better make a complete introduction this time," Rafe said. "Bob, meet Mr. and Mrs. Stan Wilson."

When Stan finally let go of Janice, she smiled.

"Now we can wash out the blond highlights and get rid of the blue contacts," she said to Stan. "If I open my eyes, I feel like I'm kissing a stranger."

Alana watched, speechless, as Stan removed his dark blue contacts, revealing eyes that were light green.

"Blond highlights?" asked Alana weakly.

"Yep," said Janice, tugging on a lock of Stan's fair hair. "I'm used to my man being a sun-streaked brown, not a California blond."

"I don't understand," Alana said.

"I'm afraid you've been caught in a conspiracy," said Janice gently. "But it was a conspiracy of love. When Rafe told me what had happened to you, I told him to give you a few weeks to remember on your own. Then he called again and told me you weren't sleeping, weren't eating, were having nightmares—"

"How did you know?" asked Alana, turning to Rafe.

"I told you, wildflower. You're a lot like me."

"In short," summarized Janice, "you were tearing yourself apart. Rafe thought that if you came back here, you would see him and know that you were safe, that it was all right to remember what had happened. I agreed, so long as you came willingly. If you came back it would mean that you wanted to remember. That you wanted to be whole again."

"Some travel agent," Alana said dryly. Then, "Oh. You're still a practicing psychiatrist, aren't you?"

"One of the best," said Rafe, his arms tightening around Alana. "Damn near every word we said in front of you was vetted by Janice first."

"Not every word," Janice said crisply, looking sideways at Stan. "I nearly choked my husband when I found out about the fight by the lake."

Stan almost smiled. "Yeah, I know. I don't take orders worth a damn. We've argued about Rafe a lot," said Stan, flashing Alana a pale green glance. "I thought she was too gentle on Rafe after he got back from Central America. And then, when she couldn't put him back together, it took two years for me to coax her into marriage."

Janice looked surprised. "Two years! You only asked me out two months before we were married!"

"Yeah. So much for being subtle. I wasted twenty-two months tiptoeing around, thinking that you held it against me that I was the one who'd been wounded. If it wasn't for me, Rafe would have flown out of the jungle with the rest of us."

Rafe started to say something, but Stan cut him off.

"No way, buddy. I'm not finished. I thought you were being too gentle with Alana to get any results. Hell, I didn't even know you had that much gentle in you! I'm still having a hard time believing that you're the same man I worked with in Central America."

Stan shook his head. "Anyway, I wanted to stir up Alana, to make her think. I didn't believe you'd snuffed good old Jack to get Alana. If you'd wanted to do that, you wouldn't have waited almost four years, and you sure as hell wouldn't have been caught after you'd done it. You're too smart for that."

"Thanks . . . I think," said Rafe dryly.

Alana looked from Stan to Janice to Rafe. Finally she gave her brother Bob a long, considering look. He flushed slightly.

"You aren't mad, are you, sis?"

"Mad?" Alana shook her head. "I'm . . . stunned. I can't believe that you knew about the whole conspiracy and kept it a secret. Old in-the-ear-and-out-the-mouth Bob. I'm impressed, baby brother."

"It wasn't easy. I thought I'd blown it more than once," admitted Bob.

"We didn't tell him everything," Rafe said dryly. "Oh, he knew that he wasn't trying to start a dude ranch, but that's about it. He didn't know that I'd worked with Stan and Janice before. He didn't know that Stan was camouflaged as carefully as any lure I'd ever made. And he didn't know that Janice was a practicing psychiatrist."

"Well," Mitch said, "I'd better get down the mountain before the light goes."

"Can you fly back tomorrow?" asked Rafe.

"Sure. Need something in particular?"

"Champagne. A justice of the peace."

Mitch smiled. "Somebody getting married?"

Rafe looked at Alana, a question in his amber eyes.

"Damned right," she said, putting her arms tightly around Rafe. "This time, the trout is landing the fisherman."

19

ALANA STOOD BY THE hearth in the small cabin, wearing only Rafe's warm robe. She let the song fade from her lips, watching Rafe as he played soft notes on the silver harmonica.

He was stretched out on the bed, eyes closed, sensitive fingers wrapped around the harmonica as his lips coaxed beautiful music from it. He wore nothing but firelight, which clung and shifted with each breath he took. His hair gleamed like winter mink, alive with the reflected dance of flames.

Rafe looked up, sensing her watching him.

"Happy, Mrs. Winter?" he asked, holding out his hand.

"Very happy."

Alana took Rafe's hand and curled up beside him, enjoying the hard warmth of his flesh beneath her cheek.

"Even though you haven't remembered everything?" he asked quietly.

She looked at Rafe's eyes, gold in the firelight, and wanted nothing more than to be loved by him.

"I don't care anymore," Alana said, "because I'm not afraid anymore."

Rafe let out a long breath. Tenderly he traced the satin darkness of Alana's eyebrow with his fingertip.

"Good," he said softly. "I don't think you'll ever remember coming down the mountain. You were bruised, bloody, out of your mind with cold and shock."

His eyes closed, as though he was afraid she would see too much looking into them.

"Frankly," Rafe said in a low voice, "I'd forget it if I could. I loved you so much and I thought you were dying, that I'd come too late."

" 'Come too late,' " Alana repeated. "You say that as though you knew I needed you."

"I did."

"How?" whispered Alana. "Why did you come to the highest lake when I was there with Jack?"

"I can't explain it. I just . . . knew."

Rafe looked at the harmonica for a moment before he carefully set it aside.

"The night before I rode up Broken Mountain," he said, "I kept thinking I heard you calling me again and again. But that was impossible. I was alone at the ranch. Nothing but the wind. Yet by morning, I was wild, half crazy, certain that *you needed me.*"

Rafe blew out a long breath. "I had no choice but to ride up the mountain and find you, Alana. It was irrational, crazy, but I had to do it."

"You weren't crazy," said Alana, trembling. "When Jack tied me and left me by the lake, I called for you all night long. I couldn't help myself."

Rafe's breath came in sharply. He rolled over and faced Alana, touching her as though she were a dream and he was afraid of awakening.

"If only I hadn't fought against it so hard," he said in a low voice. "I should have come to you sooner."

"It's a miracle that you came at all. You hated me."

"No," he said, kissing Alana's eyebrow, her eyelid, the corner of her mouth. "I never hated you. I wanted to, but I couldn't. We were tied too deeply to each other, no matter how far apart we were."

"Yes," she whispered, returning the tender kisses.

"That's why I couldn't ride away from you after we made love," Rafe said, "even though I thought you didn't trust me. Every time the wind blew down the canyon, I heard you calling me. I had to come back to you."

Rafe's fingertip traced Alana's lips. "I love you more than you know, more than I have words to say."

With slow, caressing movements, Rafe unwrapped the robe until Alana wore only firelight and the fine gold chain he had given to her. The elegant symbol of infinity gleamed in the hollow of her throat, speaking silently of love that knew no boundaries.

He gathered Alana close to his body, kissing her gently at first, then with a passion that was both restrained and deeply wild. She gave herself to the kiss, to him, melting in his hands, wanting him, loving him. He listened to the soft sounds that came from her, and he smiled.

"Yes," Rafe whispered, "sing of your love for me, a lifetime of love. And after that . . ."

His lips touched the golden symbol at Alana's throat, and he knew there would always be a song of love that knew no bounds.

SEEDS OF RACISM

IN THE

SOUL OF AMERICA

Paul R. Griffin

Foreword by Gayraud S. Wilmore

The Pilgrim Press
Cleveland, Ohio

The Pilgrim Press, Cleveland, Ohio 44115
© 1999 by Paul R. Griffin

Printed in the United States of America on acid-free paper

04 03 02 01 00 99   5 4 3 2 1

Library of Congress Cataloging-in-Publication Data

Griffin, Paul R., 1944–
    Seeds of racism in the soul of America / Paul R. Griffin ; Foreword by Gayraud S. Wilmore.
        p. c.m.
    Includes bibliographical references and index.
    ISBN 0-8298-1313-6 (cloth : alk. paper)
    1. United States—Race relations. 2. Racism—Social aspects—United States—History. 3. Racism—Religious aspects—Christianity. 4. Calvinism—United States—History. 5. Liberalism—United States—History—20th century. 6. Feminism—United States—History—20th century. I. Title.
E185.615.G75 1999
305.8'00973—dc21   98-53545
                                                          CIP

To Barbara Diane, my wife
To Jevon and Felicia, my children
To Charlie, Lottie, and Joe, my siblings
And to the memory of my parents, Sarah and Joseph Sr.

CONTENTS

FOREWORD

After my first reading of Professor Paul Griffin's manuscript of this book, having already committed myself to "writing something" for its publication, I leaned back in my desk chair with the uneasy feeling of someone whose old automobile has stalled on a grade crossing and who suddenly becomes aware of the distant sound of an approaching express train. In such a situation the urgent question is whether to continue fooling around with a stuck clutch and an accelerator that is flooding the carburetor, or simply abandon the car and start running up the track, waving a red flag.

After all, for most of my life I have been an ordained minister of the Presbyterian Church, one of the denominations of the Reformed family that traditionally has been identified with the Puritanism this book takes to task for its intrinsic racism. Though I have long since been disenchanted with the legalistic interpretations and ascetic discipline of old-school Presbyterianism, I must confess to having had a more positive experience of the fruits of Reformed theology than my friend Paul Griffin has had.

As one who was involved during the 1960s with one of the predominantly white churches that inherited American Puritanism, I helped craft the surprisingly liberal pronouncements and policies that brought thousands of church dollars to Dr. King's Southern Christian Leadership Conference. I headed the staff of the Commission on Religion and Race of my church that worked for the passage of the 1964 Civil Rights Act and the 1965 Voting Rights Act. Some thirty-five years ago, as field commander for many young white clergy from the North, I saw them risk their careers, and sometimes their lives, by walking picket lines and getting arrested for civil disobedience in Mississippi and Alabama. That's why, when I read the last page of Paul's indictment of New England Puritanism and Reformed theology as the taproot of Christian racism and reflected on the task of writing this foreword, I couldn't help hearing the horn of that diesel locomotive thundering down the track. My first impulse was to save myself and leave what appeared to be an ill-fated vehicle to its own eschatological terminus.

But then, on a second and more careful reading, I decided to stay with the project. Why did I arrive at that second judgment? My decision had to do with reflection on the settling in of my own theological predisposition about the complexity of American racism and its convoluted relationship to the faith I profess. What I mean is that in addition to being a Reformed churchman whose roots are in the Calvinism that this book deplores, I happen also to be an African American Christian who went through a second, adult conversion to Jesus Christ as Liberator during the 1960s. That second conversion was preceded and instigated by the Black Power movement, a new and radical awareness of the theological meaning of what black people in America and South Africa had experienced during the past four centuries at the hands of white Christians.

This second conversion was influenced by the ethnotheological analyses of George Kelsey, James H. Cone, James Deotis Roberts, Jacqueline Grant, Diana Hayes, and other African American theologians—young and old, female and male—whose iconoclastic deconstruction of white Christianity is today all but ignored by both white and black believers. Because of these colleagues and the paths into which my own study has led me, I continue to wrestle with the values and disvalues of Reformed doctrine when we are bold enough to filter it through the four hundred years of black suffering and struggle in Africa and the Americas. To put the matter another way, I am too committed to a black theology of liberation, grounded in some of the basic doctrines of Protestant neoorthodoxy and postmodern liberalism, to accept a blanket condemnation of ideology; but at the same time I am too determined to work my way out of the fatal ideological distortions of white Calvinists who benefited from and tried to vindicate the Euro-American and South African institutions of slavery and racism to run from a fight.

This book, by a church historian who is a member of the African Methodist Episcopal Church and is thus more attuned to John Wesley than to John Calvin, takes a position with which most black theologians are familiar. It is, however, less of an effort to straighten out the distortions of racial theologies (which actually go back as far as the Babylonian Talmud and legends of Judaism and medieval Roman Catholicism) than to trace the development of those distortions from seventeenth-century colonial America to the present in order to show why many white liberals and feminists have succumbed to their influences.

In other words, if I understand the intention of the author, the book has little to do with forging a black theology that African Americans can claim today, after purging and renovating those doctrines from which white Christians received their ideas of race. Rather, it is his purpose to give us a hard, unsparing, and sometimes admittedly uncharitable look at the history of race relations in the United States as shaped by racist strains in Puritanism. Finally, by drawing sometimes admittedly extreme conclusions, the author seeks to expose the betrayals of many so-called white liberals since those heady days when we held one another's hands at civil rights rallies and sang with revivalistic gusto, "Black and white together, black and white together, we shall overcome someday!"

Although most American scholars in recent years have been generous toward Puritanism or have skirted the issue of its ideas about race altogether, there is good reason to suspect that the connection between this dour form that Christianity took in this country and anti-black racism has had both positive and negative consequences in American history. This book focuses relentlessly on the negative consequences and, as a result, reminds us of the irony of a fundamental Calvinistic belief—that even in the highest pretensions of our American covenant with God we are miserable sinners and that Satan sometimes appears as an angel of light!

While there still remain serious questions about saddling New England Puritanism with the total responsibility for the peculiar form into which American racism crystallized, there can be little doubt that one of the tendencies of pious intellectuals in Great Britain and North America was to remove illogical contradictions between Christian doctrines and what honest people perceived to be the commonsense realities and requirements of practical life. What were the commonsense realities of colonial and early eighteenth-century America with respect to the strange black people from Africa?

The color, physiognomy, culture, religion, and intelligence of "Negroes," by English standards, appeared to most white people, whether

Protestant or Roman Catholic, to be incontrovertible realities of the black condition—that is, characteristics which were plainly inferior to those of white people. Given those "facts of life," and given the felt need to bring all earthly phenomena into conformity with biblical revelation and the Reformed and Lutheran confessions, it is no stretch of the imagination that we can believe that the ultimate explanation and justification for the problem of the debasement and inferiority of blacks had to be found in some natural law or divine ordinance. Most historians would have to agree that early American Protestantism, if not New England Puritanism per se, was supremely equipped for such an analysis and resolution. This is what I understand to be the main burden of Professor Griffin's argument in this book, and it is worth serious consideration.

The question of how this plays out in the twentieth century, particularly in the defects of white liberalism after 1965 and the intrigues of white feminism under patriarchal assault, is less certain and ripe for a great deal of controversy. Whatever position one takes, it is not to be doubted that the ideas of race—conscious and unconscious, overt and covert—have had a corrupting influence in American culture, politics, and religion and thus need to be subjected to the most exacting assessment. This is not the first book to attempt to do this, although it breaks important new ground in searching for the provenance of racism in mainline religion. But perhaps even more critical is the question of what to do about such an assessment today when the churches—both white and black—seem unable to speak with a clear and unified voice on such race-tinged issues as affirmative action, welfare reform, poverty, and the deterioration of our central cities.

That is where black theology has its work cut out for it, if indeed it purports not simply to analyze the historical matrix of racism in American Christianity but also to mount the kind of education-and-action campaign at the grassroots level of black and white churches that can more effectively combat racism. But that is not the book that Paul Griffin set out to write. I mention it only because even if his analysis of the power of ideas is 99 percent on target, we are still left with the problem of what kind of new ideas our theologians and public intellectuals can generate that will help us escape the ineluctable fate of our excessive faith in color blindness, traditional family values, pop psychology, and rampant individualism. Here, it seems to me, the greatest resistance to the new world that is coming in with the twenty-first century will be found not in the mainline churches that continue to cling insensibly to the theology of the Continental, English, and American Puritan reformations, but in the postmodern conservative and New Age movements like the apolitical Pentecostalism and Holiness churches that promote ardor over order and promote the Christian Coalition, and the Promise Keepers over the pragmatic spirituality of the left wing of the civil rights movement.

This book will be hotly debated, but we need such debates in order to shake ourselves out of lethargy about who we are as a nation and how we got this way. It will remind us that things, no matter how well-meant, are not usually what they appear to be; just as "race" is an extremely slippery term, racism is one of the most complex, most frustrating, and least understood characteristics of our society and, indeed, of world societies. To the extent that the thesis of this book drives us beyond ideas to action, beyond recrimination to repentance, and beyond the theology of suspicion to the theology of ecumenical action on a broad political and cultural front, it will serve a commendable purpose for difficult days ahead.

GAYRAUD S. WILMORE

PREFACE

S eeds of Racism in the Soul of America is the first book to search
out and examine critically the specific theological ideas that were
used to justify slavery in the past and are still used to support
racism. So many white liberals continue to believe not only that slavery
and racism began in the South in the search for cheap labor, but also
that it has been continued mostly by white southerners as a southern
phenomenon. Here I will show that the distant roots of racism trace
back not to southern plantation owners but to Puritans in the North,
who first used theological ideas to justify slavery and racism.

The book then proceeds to examine critically how liberal whites—
both men and women—are as guilty of perpetuating these theological
ideas as are religious conservatives. Yes, I mean the white liberals who
often marched arm in arm with black activists during the civil rights era.
I also include white people today who caution—as the eight clergy in
1963 cautioned Dr. Martin Luther King Jr.—that aggressive objectives
and tactics are too extreme and untimely. Wait awhile, they say; affirmative action does not seem prudent at a time of unemployment, or of
full employment. I even dare to include white feminists who have rightly
sought to free themselves from centuries of sexism but who often then
seek to move their agenda ahead of blacks and other minorities.

During the more than two decades I spent researching and writing this
book, I had the privilege of meeting a small group of people who shared
their insights and gave me much-needed encouragement to stay the

course, especially during those moments when I was ready to abandon the book. Although I cannot name all of these men and women here, I must mention a few whose input greatly aided me in this journey. Professor James D. Nelson, my mentor when I was a student at United Theological Seminary in Dayton, Ohio, was among the first persons with whom I shared my ideas. Concerned that my book could not help but incite intense debate and possibly some rabid responses from certain quarters, Jim often insisted that I make a documented case. Professor John Kampen, a former academic dean at Payne Theological Seminary, Wilberforce, Ohio, continued this insistence. Many times I would telephone John late in the evening to garner his responses to particular points.

Although they may not have always known it, students at Wright State University in Dayton also were helpful to this book as they tested early drafts of some of the chapters. Their verbal and nonverbal responses, especially when I was lecturing on Calvinist theology and Puritanism, often caused me to go back and do additional research so that I could answer questions I had previously neglected.

I also recognize here the members of the planning committee of the Wright State University National Conference on the Future Shape of Black Religion for inviting me to essay some of my research and thoughts on American racism. Sharing the lecture platform with Professor Derrick Bell at the fifth annual conference in 1995 proved most helpful.

I am especially grateful to Pilgrim Press and editor Timothy Staveteig for seeing in this book one response to President Clinton's June 1997 initiative to open up a national dialogue on race. Howard Ramsby III, summer publishing intern for persons of color, deserves my thanks for reviewing the entire manuscript.

Special gratitude goes to Dean Perry Moore (now provost), Associate Dean Bill Rickert (now associate provost), and the members of the Faculty Development Committee in the College of Liberal Arts at Wright State University for deeming my sabbatical proposal worthy of a year's leave so that I could complete the writing of this book with only small measures of interruption. Here I also thank Dr. Willis Stoesz, former chair of the Department of Religion, for his support and encouragement.

Professor Gayraud Wilmore is one to whom I am most indebted. He not only interrupted the normal routines of his life in retirement to read my manuscript and to offer crucial suggestions, he also on one occasion even took time out from a well-deserved vacation with his wife, Lee, to critique some of my chapters so I could meet a deadline. Professor Wilmore's critical insights and rigor were of the utmost value to me as I labored to produce this study.

I also want to thank my surrogate mother, Yvonne Walker Taylor, one of the first African American women to serve as president of a major university, black or white. Her responses to some of my conclusions were always penetrating and straightforward.

Finally, special thanks go to my wife, Barbara Diane. Without her steadfast encouragement and gracious sacrificing of some of the rest and relaxation time we had set aside for ourselves, this book would not have been possible. I dedicate this book to her and also to the memory of my late mother, Sarah, and my father, Joseph Sr., who was the son of slave parents.

INTRODUCTION

W
hen and where did American racism begin? Why did it begin there and why does it persist in this society? What must be done to bring it to an end? These are not new questions for Americans but the same old questions we have been asking and trying to answer repeatedly for hundreds of years.

To be raising them again at the end of the twentieth century can sound like a huge, insolent joke. Haven't such questions already been answered? And if not, won't our unprecedented scientific and technological progress soon make such questions humorously irrelevant?

The continual raising of these old questions is no joke, for three reasons. First, even though many times solid and insightful answers have been given to questions about racism, much information has received little, if any, detailed examination. Second, racism in America as a social phenomenon eludes our technological radar in part because we have characterized the primary source of the problem as white southern conservatives and rednecks. Third, we continue to hope that blacks in the United States will somehow get over the unfortunate treatment of their previous generations and will behave more like Asians or Hispanics.

PERSONAL ENCOUNTERS WITH RACISM

I wish my interest in this subject were merely a historian's musings over a previous era and the problems that others faced. It is not. Like many millions who have been and still are the objects of racial prejudice, my personal concern with it began shortly after my birth. My first memory of this peculiar American disorder occurred when I was around five or six years old.

My parents were on a shopping tour to the Stone and Thomas department store in downtown Wheeling, West Virginia. My brother and I, like many children in the malls today, were running around the store. Suddenly we came face-to-face with two white women. They were gushing over a black baby in a stroller that a black woman was pushing down an aisle. One woman exclaimed to the mother, "Oh, what a pretty lil' old black bee-bee you have there!" At that moment our parents came hurriedly upon the scene. After they whisked us away, I asked them, "Why did they say it like that—'lil' old black bee-bee'?" I remember that my father, looking disdainfully at the two women, immediately pulled my brother and me aside and mumbled under his breath, "It's just something they can't help."

I did not become fully conscious of racism, however, until late childhood, after we moved to Dayton, Ohio. The second experience occurred one day when some friends and I were coming home from school. We stopped at a downtown restaurant for a soda. Instead of serving us, the waitress called for the manager. He came to our table and told us we would have to leave. When we asked why, his angry retort was, "We don't serve darkies in here."

A third experience happened shortly after I attended my first class at one of the more academically prestigious Dayton public schools, Patterson Co-Op High School. A white girl and I were walking down the hall when the assistant principal grabbed me by my arm and took me into his office. "Paul," he said with a red face contorted with disgust, "we let you come here but this doesn't mean that your kind can date our girls." As I was trying to explain that he was mistaken, because Ronnie and I were simply walking together down the hall, he interrupted me and said in an extremely hostile tone, "You have two choices. You can either leave our girls alone or you can go back to where there are people like you."

When I reported these incidents to my parents, my father repeated what he had said in the department store in West Virginia. I will never forget the awful sound of his voice after the incident with the assistant principal when he said, "I want you to go back to that school tomorrow and clean out your locker. You are going back to Roosevelt High School!" Turning to walk away, he again muttered under his breath what I had heard him say in the Wheeling department store: "It's just something that they can't help." But this time I followed him into another room and pressed him. "Well, why can't they help it, Father?" His response was, "I'll tell you later when I'm not so angry." Because my father became ill and died shortly after that incident, he never answered my question.

Some answers, however, began to emerge as I immersed myself in literature about slavery and other inhumanities against African Americans that have routinely marked our lives. From that time until now, I frequently have pondered why it is that some whites cannot help but be racist. What is it about some white people that makes them unable or unwilling to recognize and affirm African Americans as their fellow human beings?

Because economics, the traditional explanation for white bigotry, was not involved in either of my pre-adult encounters with race prejudice, my questions became even more perplexed over the years. Economics is simply incapable of explaining why white bigotry has continued for more than four hundred years. I began to feel that there was something *more* behind American racism than concrete or material reality. But not until I was studying for a Ph.D. in American religious history did I come across some interesting but unaccountably ignored documents that provide profound and largely neglected answers to why American racism is so persistent.

Researching these sources—at least the particular aspect of them that deals with latent ideas about race—I have found that American racism, whatever else it may also be, is something deeply etched in the American mind. I have been persuaded by this evidence that American racism is what can most aptly be termed a religion. Indeed, the sources demonstrate that it was Christian religionists who first planted the seeds of black people's degradation and inferiority in the soul of America.

MORE THAN ECONOMICS

Over the years the traditional answers to our questions have come from what is commonly called the economic or cheap-labor thesis.[1] According to this theory, racism against black people had its beginning in the sweltering cotton and tobacco fields of the South in the mid-1700s. It was here, so the story goes, that roughneck and uncouth plantation owners became not only the first to legalize slavery but also the first to breathe life into racism as a normative and permanent standard for the United States.

The thesis argues that southern plantation owners invented this way of thinking because of their need for a massive army of free labor to build and sustain their agrarian economy. Supposedly incapable of tilling the soil themselves, and reportedly unable to find a sufficient supply of physically fit white men to do it for them, these southerners quickly looked toward Africa and devolved to its natives the unenviable task of satisfying the economic needs of white America. They not only reduced Africans to the level of brutes but also made racism a permanent part of life on this continent by decreeing that these men and women and all their descendants forever would be subservient to the allegedly superior white Americans.

This economic or cheap-labor thesis casts important light on how material forces of the political economy helped to create and legitimate southern slavery and the deliberate and calculated dehumanization of black people. But there is much more about the origin of American racism than mere economics. Dr. Martin Luther King Jr. affirmed this view two years after he assumed leadership of the civil rights movement. Writing in 1957, King declared that the "problem of race in America is not a political but a moral issue" with roots, fruits, and an enduring legacy that extends far beyond economics.[2]

SEEDS OF NORTHERN PURITAN THEOLOGY

I contend in these pages that this particular "more" than economics in American racism is that its most nourishing roots do not go back to the stifling southern clime and the rough-hewn plantation owners. Rather, its unbending roots are found in the cool, more refined climate and landscape of the colonial North, where they began to shoot out branches—well-developed bodies of ideas—that bore bitter fruit as early as 1634, decades before slavery became a legal institution in Virginia, the state that bears the distinction of being the mother of southern slavery.

I also intend to demonstrate that American racism, as a body of ideas, is a religious confession. Indeed, it is a theological dogma grounded in powerful but distorted Christian understandings of the biblical text. These corrupted biblical and theological ideas did not take shape initially among crude and unlettered southerners. They were first the product of colonial-era northern Christian intellectual ideologues—the

American Puritans. These cultivated Christian ideologues, men and women whom scholars have celebrated for their intense piety and purity of life, were preeminent in planting in the American mind the racist confession that God had created black people to be forever inferior and subject to all other races. Moreover, these devout Christians were the initiators of theories that the Bible, history, and Christian theology together support the plain and obvious truth that white supremacy over blacks is nothing less than a divine decree.

THE ARGUMENT IN OUTLINE

The main challenge is to show the continuity of these supposedly Christian ideas from the Puritan era to our own. Therefore, chapter 1 explores how they originated among Puritan intellectuals and how they became the model for white supremacy all across antebellum America, both South and North. Chapter 2 examines how these theological ideas became hybridized when mixed with racist theories from the fields of science and medicine between 1865 and 1950. Chapter 3 examines the ways that present-day conservative power wielders, fearing that the dramatic and positive shift in race relations that occurred during the late 1960s and early 1970s would equalize the races, cunningly have sought to restore the great white past by resurrecting and refacing the old Puritan ideas of race.

The old seeds of racism have been shown to be sprouting bad fruits all across present-day America. Even so, many will continue to heap the bulk of the blame for the persistence of racist ideas on rednecks (cultural racists), white supremacists (ideological racists), and political conservatives (social racists). While none of these are immune from blame, racism also continues because the taproot of its early seeds has not yet been cut by white liberals. Although they have escaped serious critique, they often have a hidden allegiance to Puritan theological racism. In chapter 4, I argue that even though the actions of these liberals appear egalitarian, they really are in agreement with the racial ideas of white conservatives.

Chapter 5 focuses on radical white feminists, a final segment of white society that reinforces white superiority. To be sure, their cause is just: breaking free from centuries of repressive sexism imposed upon women by their own male colleagues. I examine several representative notions of radical white feminists that emerged in the aftermath of the civil rights movement. And I show that from the late 1960s to the present, an influential group of feminists (but not *all* white feminists) have commonly, if unwittingly, promoted their cause for justice by manipulating old Puritan racial theories so as to claim that they have suffered victimization and oppression in this society equal to, if not more than, blacks.

THE SEEDS OF RACISM AS AN EPIDEMIC

What makes American racism so enduring? Perhaps the metaphor of disease without immediate symptoms and with unsuspected carriers provides the best explanation. Neither scholars nor the general public has attended to how these seeds, as germs or virulent agents, operate.

Racism Is Contagious and Insidious

The antiblack disease is so contagious that it now infects, in varying degrees, almost every person in this society. We readily perceive it whenever we hear innocent white children who have never had any direct contact with blacks speaking about them in the derogatory language with which they have been indoctrinated, often by their parents. We also encounter it when news stories tell how other nonwhite racial and ethnic groups that migrate to the United States with hardly more than the clothes on their backs are able to find an economic and sociopolitical haven—unlike native-born blacks, who, despite continuous racial ostracism, are often viewed as responsible for their own lack of success. Racism as a complex bundle of ideas often can be heard when liberals who swear that they are no longer racists stand at an office's facsimile machine or photocopier and speak of a successful black as an "exceptional black" or "really an intelligent person" who "speaks well" or "is certainly a credit to his [or her] race." No one objects to these comments because they seem so affirming and civil. Yet there is often more behind them—the racial legacy of the distant past.

The reason this white supremacy is so contagious is that it is such a complex body of ideas that its symptoms do not become apparent for a long time. Such racism has a special ability to possess an individual without that individual even knowing that he or she is inflicted. Racism has this uncanny ability because it is an ideational pathology that enters a person's subconscious mind, where it lies inactive until an external stimulus converts it into concrete acts of racial or ethnic antipathy.

Those possessed by this deadly disease are prime candidates for acting out their latent racism in concrete ways.

Racism Is Carried by Intellectuals

A second much-overlooked characteristic of racism as a complex of ideas is evident in the fact that intellectuals are its primary carriers. Their offhand comments and expressions—whether from church pulpits, academic lecterns, scientific laboratories, corporate boardrooms, or the halls of Congress—are rarely challenged. Such intellectuals have always provided the incubative culture for race theories. Working-class whites are then provoked or impelled by these theories toward the concrete expression of what might otherwise remain irrelevant abstractions.

These two characteristics have been and remain the primary reasons for the tenacity of American racism, despite everything we have done in this century to get rid of it. Like many whose lives and experiences were framed between the 1950s and the early 1970s, I once believed that those fateful decades finally signaled an end to our race problem. The past thirty years suggest that I could not have been more mistaken. As we listen to daily reports from every part of this land, we are reminded that racism not only continues to live but does so with an energy and a pervasiveness that we would not have thought possible at the end of the Second World War. We are living in a time not only when many who come under the popular category of "conservative" are renewing their faith in white supremacy, but also when many of those we have called "liberals," who repented of America's racial sins and joined hands with blacks during the 1960s, now seem to be backsliding into various forms of racial bigotry.

RACISM AS A BAD RELIGION OF THE SOUL

To change metaphors, the seeds of racism operate as a bad religion that has been harbored in the American mind and soul for nearly four hundred years. To find a permanent solution, this nation, *person by person*, needs to be converted from the view that white supremacy is a tangible reality of simply a few hate groups. Racism is a bad political and social religion—indeed, the ideational confession—in the soul of this nation.

For this reason, neither the antebellum antislavery crusades nor the Civil War nor the Reconstruction nor the civil rights movement nor the

most recent federal antidiscrimination and affirmative action laws—
none of these has offered a permanent cure for the malady. Each of
these efforts failed because, despite laudable sincerity and powerful
sanctions, it was grounded in the presumption that racism is funda-
mentally an economic, legal, or political issue.

As King warned in his early book *Stride toward Freedom* (1958), if we
are successfully to confront the centuries-old but still prevalent notion
that God created black people to be the footstool of whites, we must first
"get back to the ideational roots of race hate, something that the law
cannot accomplish." Although he pleaded that white Christian churches
should "face their historic obligation" for sowing these ideational seeds,
King did not live long enough to explicate their theological content.[3]

Accepting King's challenge, I have tried to unravel these ideational
roots as the primary task of this book. I invite all who claim to be racial
egalitarians, as well as those who make no such claim, to join me in tra-
versing both the past and the present paths of Christian ideas gone awry.

NOT ALL WHITES AND NOT PURITANISM ALONE

It should be made clear at the outset that I am not contending that
all white men and women have been or are racists. Such oversimplifi-
cation belongs to the realm of cultic fantasy. Historically, many from
the majority culture have been sympathetic to the plight of African
Americans. Some, as we all know, sacrificed their lives in the fight for
black humanity. But this is true not only of those we call white liberals
but also of some who are regarded as the proponents of conservative
political and religious viewpoints. Had it not been for the concern and
egalitarianism of some conservatives in church and state, there would
not have been the antislavery crusades, the Civil War, and the federal
legislation of both the Reconstruction years and the twentieth-century
civil rights period. Let the truth be told.

A few final words to my scholarly friends are in order. First, this
study focuses solely on the theology of American racism that was first
constructed by New England Puritan Christians in the early 1600s.
Although I concentrate on these particular confessors as the first sowers
of racist ideas in this country, this does not ignore the historical fact
that other Christians (Protestants and especially Catholics) and Jews, in
varying ways and degrees, also must bear responsibility for having
employed twisted theological ideas to delineate and justify slavery and

racism against persons of African descent, not only in North America but also throughout the world.

Second, this study uses the methods of traditional intellectual history to recover and interpret the twisted ideas informing and defending American racism. Some might say that concentrating on these ideas as if they were the essence of material events is historical reductionism at its worst. But in view of the almost complete absence of any analysis of the ideas that have historically stood behind American racism, I believe that a work such as this is more than overdue, if not as a final word then at least as a beginning.

Third, I am conscious of the widespread position that passion is a grave error in historical analysis. I can only reply in the words of Professor James H. Cone: "If you have had as much fire put under you as black people, then you also would be emotional."[4] At every turn I attempt to present a credible, reliable historical account. If I appear to be excessively intense here and there, it is only because the fire, as the prophet Jeremiah says, is "shut up in my bones" (Jeremiah 20:9). I invite the scholarly reader not to pardon me but, through his or her teaching and writing, to help stamp out this fire that at one time or another rages in the heart and soul of every person who has experienced oppression.

THE SOWING
OF THE SEEDS

I n 1638 a slaveholder announced that he had been holding blacks
in slavery for some time and would continue that practice "forever
or during his pleasure." One's first impulse might be to assume
that these were the words of some crude, mean-spirited southern plantation owner. They were not. They were the utterance of a prominent
and cultured Puritan Christian, Theophilus Eaton, the first governor of
the Connecticut Colony.[1]

Governor Eaton's proclamation illustrates how slavery and the
racism that helped slavery become an institution in the United States
were not peculiar to unlettered and racist southern slave owners. The
twin evils of slavery and racism were common among learned early-
colonial-era New England Christians. These first-generation New
Englanders (or New Canaan Puritans, as they called themselves) promoted racism and slavery just as aggressively as did their southern
counterparts. In fact, it was they who passed the earliest laws sanction-
ing slavery in this country. In 1641, a mere decade after they began
arriving en masse, Massachusetts Bay Puritans enacted their Code
of Fundamentals, or Body of Liberties of the Massachusetts Colony
of New England. Article 95 states, in part, that "there shall never
be any bond slavery or captive among us unless it be lawful captives
taken in just wars, and such strangers as willingly sell themselves or are
sold to us."[2] This code became formal law two decades before Virginia
(in 1661) and Maryland (in 1663) passed legislation giving legal
sanction to slavery.[3]

The Puritans' southern colleagues justified slavery by claiming that the demands of their agricultural economy necessitated "a cheap labor force." In contrast, the first generation of New England Puritans could not defend northern slavery by appealing to any "compelling economic demand for Negroes."[4] Shipping, manufacturing, and fishing were the economic foundations of colonial New England; these industries did not require any massive labor force.

In fact, New England Puritans relied on the system of indentured servanthood to fill their labor needs. This system was common in colonial North America and enabled thousands of whites, as well as some blacks, to settle in both the northern and southern colonies.[5] Servants would work for benefactors, who paid for their passage to America for a fixed number of years—usually no more than seven—after which they became free citizens. The indentured system was more than adequate to meet the labor needs of the Puritans. As their towns and economic structures developed, former servants fit rather neatly into the expanding economy.

Governor Eaton's announcement would have been surprising, then, because the northern colonies could have continued to draw their workforce from indentured servants, white and black. But several New Englanders decided against that option in favor of holding blacks back from release "forever or during [their] pleasure." They chose to exclude blacks from the system and to condemn them to perpetual servitude.

What prompted the early Puritans to exclude blacks from indentured servitude and to choose instead to engage in slaveholding and slave trading when there was no demand for an abundant supply of cheap labor in New England? And how did these devout Christians manage to legitimize their racism and still maintain their claim to be God's new chosen people?

To answer these questions, American racism can be compared to a mighty oak tree whose branches are not only strong but also far-reaching. Some of the branches can be traced back to southern plantation owners and their appeal to economic necessity. But other limbs and the massive trunk of this oak must be traced to the first generation of northern Puritans. Not only were these pious people the first to promote legal slavery in this land, they also were the first to twist Christian ideas into a theology of racism that gave divine justification to slavery and other acts of violence against African Americans. The construction of such a theology when there was no need for a cheap black labor force shows that American racism through the centuries has not primarily

been the consequence of material realities viewed from the standpoint
of economics. Rather, it has been a consequence of racist minds that
were poisoned by the idea that blacks were innately inferior to whites
and therefore had to be subjugated and degraded. Throughout America's history, intellectual ideologues have been at the forefront in
developing ideas that incite some white people, who are predisposed
out of fear and ignorance, to practice acts that characteristically begin
with bigotry and end with violence.

THE CONTEXT

At first glance no one would have predicted that Puritans would
use theology to justify their racism. They had come to New England
with the certainty that God had made them a chosen people who were
supposed to turn this land into God's "city set upon a hill." Writing
about this conviction during his initial voyage to New England in
1630, John Winthrop, the first governor of the Massachusetts Bay
Colony, proclaimed that

> the work we have in hand . . . is by mutual consent, through a special
> overruling providence and a more than an ordinary approbation of the
> churches of Christ, to seek out a place of cohabitation and consortship.
> . . . Thus stands the cause between God and us; we are entered into a
> covenant with Him for this work. . . . He shall make us a praise and
> glory, [so] that men shall say of succeeding generations: The Lord make
> it like that of New England. For we must consider that we shall be as a
> city upon a hill, the eyes of all people are upon.[6]

A surface reading suggests that the Puritans were committed to
building a heavenly city where all people, regardless of color or nation-
ality, could live together as equals in an inclusive society. Such was not
the case. They almost immediately turned their self-proclaimed New
Canaan into colonies that were anything but heaven for blacks and
Native Americans.

Like most of the other early European settlers, Puritans initially came
without any intention of establishing chattel slavery. They had no plans
to enslave blacks because they did not anticipate encountering or having
to live alongside people whose skin color was darker than their own.[7]
Thus, when they spoke of building a holy city based on cohabitation and

consortship, they envisioned a society comprising only white people.

Not that they were unaware of other racial groups. The first Puritans carried a racial phobia and hostility that had been planted in their minds like bitter seeds by European voyagers who had traveled to Africa during the late fifteenth and early sixteenth centuries. English voyagers, upon returning home, wrote about their perceptions of the curious people they called Africans. Richard Hakluyt was the foremost English chronicler of those impressions. Hakluyt perceived Africans as a "black, beastly, mysterious, heathenish, libidinous, evil, lazy, and smelly people who are strangely different to our superior white race."[8]

Hakluyt's portrayals of Africans became an ideational standard by which the English generally viewed and judged black people. As the historian Winthrop D. Jordan writes, the English people "from the first [began] to set Negroes over against themselves, to stress what they conceived to be radically contrasting qualities of color, religion, and style of life, as well as animality and a peculiarly potent sexuality."[9] Puritan minds latched onto these racist ideas of blacks as innately different from and less than white people. Even though there was neither reason nor opportunity to translate such ideas into concrete practice in England, the ideas were planted as seeds waiting for opportunities to germinate.

And germinate they did. The Puritans quickly removed blacks from the indentured system and enslaved them, because the ideas about black inferiority quickly blossomed into acts of racial hatred and oppression. One of Plato's major premises was that ideas have the ability to lie inactive in the mind until a real-life need provokes them into concrete expression.[10] This is precisely what happened to Christians in the New Haven Colony.

Translating racist ideas into acts of racism should have stood in stark tension with Puritan Christian ideals. After all, the Puritans were a devout people who on occasion acknowledged that slavery stood in gross contradiction to the religion of Jesus, in which the conscience is freed and all thoughts and deeds correspond to God's will. Yet Jordan suggests that they "rather mindlessly accepted slavery for Negroes and Indians but not for white men."[11] Here Jordan seems facile; he parenthetically admits that making knee-jerk decisions simply "was not their way." More likely, the Puritans were acutely aware that reducing black people to slaves stood squarely against both God and their religion.

Such awareness was expressed, for example, by the Reverend Cotton Mather, a slaveholder who has been hailed as one of the great American

Puritan divines. Reflecting on the care Puritans needed to take to ensure that slaveholding did not undermine their special relationship with God, Mather told his slaveholding colleagues, "I would always remember [that my slaves] are in some sense my children."[12]

To single out and consign black people to a life of slavery was not a mindless decision. On the contrary, it was an un-Christian act that required Puritans to engage in a profound and crafty distortion of Christian ideas. Most scholars, in their zest to capture the history and nature of American racism, have either neglected or completely ignored the theological depths to which the Puritans had to go in order to justify slavery. They have also neglected one other crucial aspect of this history. If all that the Puritans needed was an abundant supply of cheap labor, why didn't they employ the huge army of able-bodied white men and women who already resided in their colonies? Literally thousands of white social deviants—child molesters, thieves, murderers, prostitutes, rapists, and vagabonds—were either brought or came voluntarily to the British colonies under the indentured system from England, Germany, and Ireland between 1607 and 1776.[13] Except for initially requiring a few of them to engage in uncompensated manual labor, the Puritans never condemned these deviants to the permanent slavery they imposed on blacks.[14]

Attempting to explain why Puritans reserved slavery only for blacks, Jordan and others have suggested that, in part, the Puritans viewed blacks as heathens who would defile their holy empire.[15] Although Africans were indeed regarded as heathens by the Puritans, this idea does not explain why they refused to enslave the large numbers of ex-felons and other unrepentant whites who were free to roam the colonies. If they viewed blacks as heathens who would corrupt their holy commonwealth, then what did they think these white ne'er-do-wells would do to its sanctity? Indeed, Governor John Winthrop complained in 1645 that the "wars in England kept [white] servants from coming to us, so as those we had could not be hired, when their times were out."[16] The glaring contradiction in this matter is that although they believed that ungodly whites were a threat to the faith, the Puritans accepted them into their commonwealth without dehumanizing them as they did black people.

The refusal to ban white deviants from the indenture system and to commit them to the same perpetual slavery they imposed on Africans clearly exposes the Puritans' prejudice—their unrelenting belief that God had created blacks as innately different from and inferior to whites. That is, even whites who were unregenerate social misfits were held to be of a higher order than blacks, whatever the social potential of the latter. Because blacks were relegated to the bottom tier of human creation, the Puritans denied blacks participation in their holy empire.[17]

To validate this racist decision, the Puritans twisted Christian ideas to prove that white superiority was not their own invention but God's eternal will and purpose for their society. To do this, however, they first had to give racism a theological justification that was consistent with their quest for absolute purity in everything they did. This was not difficult. Their theology was preset for racism, because it was undergirded by a strict biblical literalism that could easily be made to support white supremacy.

The Puritans were heirs of the Calvinist tradition. A hundred years earlier, John Calvin had developed Reformed theology (also called Calvinist theology) in Geneva, Switzerland. His theology was rooted in a literal interpretation of the Bible, especially the Hebrew Scriptures. Let us be clear here. Although Calvin himself did not use his theology to support any notion of white superiority over black people, his theology—especially as developed by his successors—supported at least two historic Christian teachings that could easily accommodate such claims. These two pillars were the doctrines of sin and predestination.

Calvin (following Paul and Augustine) taught that sin is hereditary and that every human being born after Adam and Eve is an absolutely depraved sinner who lacks the capacity of altering that state. Salvation to Calvin, then, was completely the work of an all-sovereign God; no human could claim glory for it, and no signs of it were given. Concerning how evil afflicts some people more than others, Calvin concluded that this is God's sovereign will. Calvin's followers moved predestination (or divine election, as it also is called) to a chief organizing position. Therefore, God predetermined who would be redeemed to eternal life and who would be condemned to eternal damnation.[18]

Puritan theology was an heir to these understandings of sin and predestination; it also espoused distinctive views of covenant and creation. Regarding the doctrine of covenant, the Puritans' biblical literalism led them to argue for a federal or full covenant, modeled after the Mosaic covenant, by which they insisted that God had predestined them to be the new chosen people. They further argued that only those who could give visible proofs of their divine election by living a life of absolute purity could be members of this full covenant.[19]

Regarding the doctrine of creation, their central thesis was that God had not created humanity equal. Human beings had been created hierarchically. This meant that there were levels of humanity ranging from the highest to the lowest. "God Almighty in His most holy and wise providence," they delighted in proclaiming, "hath so disposed of the condition of mankind as in all times some must be rich, some poor; some high and eminent in power and dignity, others mean and in subjection."[20]

It is not necessary to probe deeply into this theology to see how the doctrines of sin, predestination, covenant, and creation, in the hands of bigoted Christians, could readily become powerful instruments of oppression. Each of these theological ideas, wrongly avowed, could enable such religionists to claim divinely imputed superiority not only in religious status but also with respect to racial, gender, social, economic, and political status.

This is precisely what happened. After their emergence from the English Reformation and throughout their struggles to establish their religion over Anglicanism, the Puritans used the doctrines of sin, predestination, covenant, and creation to argue that God had favored them by a special act of grace, redeeming them from original sin and placing them at the top of the hierarchy of humanity. Such claims were not unique in Judeo-Christian history; they go back to the ancient Hebrews. But the Puritans of New England were the first Christians to use them to build a theological argument that God had created black people innately inferior to other human beings.

THE TWISTING OF BIBLICAL THEOLOGY

How precisely could Puritans justify this racial prejudice and still maintain their priority as an elect people? The Puritans manipulated biblical texts and these four cardinal doctrines into a theology that could show racism to be the essence of God's will and design. Governor Theophilus Eaton's early boast that he held slaves and would continue to do so "forever or during his pleasure" provides a good example.

Eaton directly applied the ancient Israelite law codes in the book of Leviticus to his own situation. According to Leviticus 25:45–46, the covenanted Hebrews were under a divine mandate:

You may . . . acquire [slaves] from among the aliens residing with you, and from their families that are with you, who have been born in your

land; and they may be your property. You may keep them as a posses-
sion for your children after you, for them to inherit as property. These
you may treat as slaves.

Note that Eaton corrupted the Leviticus codes, altering the "families
that are with you" to include persons who had been snatched from
another land. On the strength of an otherwise literal reading of this text,
Puritans claimed that they were God's new covenanted people and that
God was speaking directly to them, telling them to organize their "New
Canaan" in the same manner that the ancient Hebrews had organized
their Canaan across the Jordan. It was possible, therefore, to theologize
that slavery was not inconsistent with the claim to be God's favored
people; as Eaton insisted, it was a divine decree "according to Leviticus."[21]
This corruption of the Levitical law codes allowed Eaton to argue that
the Puritans had not only a godly right but also a duty to enslave the
strange people snatched from Africa and brought to their New Canaan.

Around the time that Eaton advanced this racist biblicism in Connecticut, Governor Winthrop was promoting a similar point of view in
Massachusetts. Although Winthrop did not offer a detailed discussion
of all four theological doctrines, his words clearly indicate the particular way in which Puritans would employ the doctrine of predestination.
Writing in 1640 about how Puritans came to be involved in the slave
trade, Winthrop declared that "it pleased the Lord to open to us a trade
with Barbados and other islands in the West Indies."[22] This idea, not
yet fully developed, skillfully contorts the doctrine of predestination
into an argument that makes slavery the result of God's eternal decree,
established since the creation of the world, rather than a product of the
Puritans' own initiative.

The writings of the Reverend Cotton Mather offer an even clearer
example of how creation, predestination, and sin were bent to the purposes of racism. Mather has been portrayed as one of the liberal friends
of black people when such friendship was most dangerous.[23] Yet his
writings call African slaves "the miserable children of Adam and Noah"
who are "the Blackest Instances of Blindness and Baseness" and "the
most Brutish of Creatures upon Earth." Going even further, he argues
that "it is God who has caused black people" to "fall into a dreadful
condition [of slavery] because they were created the vassals of Satan."[24]

In many ways Mather's attitude was a precursor of the attitudes of
some present-day white liberals. On the one hand, he preached that

blacks were no different from whites, because they had souls and, on that account, should at least be treated as human beings. On the other hand, when necessary he could quickly equivocate, if not outrightly disavow equality between blacks and whites.

The most blatant distortion of the doctrines of creation, predestination, and sin appeared in 1701. John Saffin, a Boston Puritan and jurist, published the first systematic defense of slavery in America—a document that historians of Puritanism have all but ignored.[25] His treatise, titled *A Brief and Candid Answer to a Late Printed Sheet, Entitled, The Selling of Joseph,* was a response to the first written opposition to slavery, the famous pamphlet of Samuel Sewall, published in 1700.[26] Sewall, who has received only passing attention, was also a Boston Puritan and jurist and was a staunch opponent of slavery. Saffin's response to Sewall's antislavery stance is filled with distortions of both the Hebrew and Christian Scriptures. For example, responding to Sewall's comparison of American slavery with man-stealing, as in the selling of Joseph in Genesis 37:25–36, Saffin argues that blacks have neither a legal nor a divine "right to liberty and all outward comforts of this life," because this would "invert the order that God hath set in the world." God "hath ordained different degrees and orders of men, some to be High and Honourable, some to be Low and Despicable; . . . others to be Subjects, and to be commanded; . . . yea, some to be born slaves, and so to remain during their lives."[27]

When Saffin speaks about the "High and Honourable," it is clear that he is referring to the white race, which he later says was predestined to be the "monarchs, kings, princes and governors, and masters and commanders." When he speaks about slaves, he claims that they were predestined to be the subjects of the elect white race. This odious white supremacy he defends by recasting the apostle Paul's discussion of the various members of the body in 1 Corinthians 12:12–26. He portrays Paul as having taught that Christians "must dare not to think" God created human beings "equal and of like dignity," lest they nullify "all the sacred rules, precepts and commands [that the] Almighty hath given the sons of men to observe and keep in their respective places, orders, and degrees."[28]

It was Saffin's position, following Eaton, Winthrop, and Mather, that the Puritans were serving God's predetermined plan for a Christianized America, because slavery was a part "of the Divine Wisdom of the most High, who hath made nothing in vain, but hath Holy ends in all his Dispensations to the children of men." Saffin believed that by enslaving "strange" Africans, the Puritans were fulfilling the law of God in Leviticus that no "heathen" should defile the homeland of the chosen. Moreover, it was just as certain that Christians had no responsibility "to tender Pagan Negroes" with any of the "love, kindness, and equal respect [that should be given] to the best of men."[29]

Saffin's corruption of the doctrine of sin comes out at the end of his treatise, where he discusses the psychological "character of the Negro." Contrasting blacks to Joseph, he poetically casts them as "utterly evil and sinful" men and women whose enslavement is in no way comparable to that of the biblical Joseph, because

> Cowardly and cruel are those black innate,
> Prone to Revenge, Imp of inveterate hate.
> He that exasperates them, soon espies
> Mischief and Murder in their very eyes.
> Libidinous, Deceitful, False and Rude,
> The Spume Issue of Ingratitude.
> The premises consider'd all may tell,
> How near good Joseph they are parallel.[30]

The few scholars who have studied racism in American Puritanism have focused on the doctrine of predestination over the other three doctrines.[31] The doctrine of creation, however, was the real centerpiece of racist theology, because the Puritans were obliged to go beyond the contention that God had predetermined blacks for enslavement. They had to link black inferiority to the very act of creation and to the hierarchy of races in which white was at the top and black and red were at the bottom.

When they appropriated this land from the Native Americans, the Puritans dreamed of building a "holy commonwealth," a theocratic state where church membership determined one's status not only in the church but also in the society as a whole. To become a full member of a Puritan church, one had to exhibit visible signs of divine election from the creation of the world. Unregenerate whites were not the only whites who were unable to attest to their election by signs of purity. The offspring of the first generation of Puritans also had difficulty offering such a testimony. Their fathers and mothers argued that they and they alone were the new chosen people. This narrow view failed to make provision for later generations who could not, in good faith, demonstrate an experience of saving grace.

Concerning this problem, Sidney Ahlstrom writes, "The most troublesome problem for the Puritan commonwealths was the decline of experimental piety that was almost inevitable in communities organized at so high a pitch of [religious] fervency." Calling this a problem related to "normal biological processes," Ahlstrom continues, "Though these unconverted [second-generation] persons were usually professing Christians and leading a moral life," they were nevertheless only in "the external covenant and therefore could not present their children for baptism."[32]

In varying ways and degrees, the doctrines of creation, sin, predestination, and covenant became the standard Christian ideas used to justify racism and the enslavement of black people. By the beginning of the eighteenth century, these theories had attracted such widespread acceptance that one historian has called New England "the greatest slave-trading section" of colonial America.[33] While it is painful for many Americans to accept the evidence, racial hatred and the oppression of blacks during the formative years of this country found its greatest expression not among southern plantation owners but among northern white Christians. Although scholars have largely ignored the behavior of these so-called pure Christians, their theology deserves to be repudiated in view of their unrelenting conviction that God, the Bible, and Christian theology irrevocably confirm that black people are a subhuman species that must be subordinated lest they somehow corrupt an immaculately white and godly society.

THE EARLY ABOLITION OF SLAVERY

The year 1790 is particularly noteworthy in the history of American racism. In that year, New England Christians, appearing to be well on the way to freeing themselves of the reputation of fostering human bondage, officially abolished slavery.[34] In the attempt to explain why these Christians finally decided against slavery, scholars such as Winthrop Jordan have invoked an egalitarian ethos that presumably surrounded the colonists' own battle for freedom from England and resulted in the Declaration of Independence in 1776.[35]

It is wise to tread carefully here, because it would be a serious error to suppose that the doctrine of the natural equality of the races was finally an accepted idea or practice in New England after 1776. To be sure, some early antebellum egalitarians, such as the Reverend Samuel Hopkins of Rhode Island, championed abolitionism in New England.

Such forerunners took up the antislavery cause in part because they came to see human bondage as an evil that violated the doctrine of natural rights that they had so aggressively employed in their own struggle for freedom from England. In a dramatic break with their proslavery ancestors, they argued that slavery was a sin diametrically opposed to God and the Christian faith. Hopkins argued that God had created blacks equal to all other people and that slavery was the creation of wicked white people.[36] Despite this nascent abolitionism, the theological ideas of race already planted in the colonial mind continued to control the behavior of antebellum New Englanders.

Plato taught that ideas are the eternal reality and hence cannot be eradicated; they simply take new expression. The racist ideas that New England Puritans planted in the soil of North America have proved tenacious enough to give plausibility to Plato's notion. Although these seeds were sown more than four centuries ago, they have proved to be perennial noxious weeds with deep roots. Despite the sincere efforts of many to uproot them, they continue to regenerate themselves year after year, decade after decade, and century after century.

The eighteenth-century abolition of legal slavery in the North did not end the prejudice against blacks. Indeed, this prejudice not only carried over into the nineteenth century but took on a new intensity in the fierce social, economic, and political segregation of free black people. Like Plato's eternal ideas, racist ones have the uncanny ability to change faces whenever confronted by new circumstances.

Segregation had existed for the free black population in New England almost from the time the Puritans first landed in 1630. Blacks obtained a pseudofree status in the early colonies through one of two ways: indentured servitude, which permitted them to become free after completing a specified indenture; and manumission, by which slaveholders willingly granted them freedom. True, a small number of blacks were free in prerevolutionary New England.[37] Yet even for them, gaining social freedom was rare. Social segregation was their lot, and everywhere they were reminded that they were inferior to whites.

For example, almost from their arrival in 1630, the Puritans instituted laws and practices designed to ensure that blacks would never be a part of their holy cities.[38] These constraints—forerunners of the black codes instituted in the North in the nineteenth century—were a litany of human degradations shocking to find among supposedly saintly men and women. Blacks were denied unrestricted travel and had to have a pass to move from one place to another after 9:00 P.M. They were monitored in order to restrict who could enter their homes. Their homes could not be next door to whites, but only in nonwhite residential areas. They were banned from owning most types of property, including, in many instances, even livestock, such as sheep, swine, and horses. Blacks were excluded from the military, prohibited from serving on juries, and denied full citizenship, thus preventing them from voting (even though they had to pay taxes). Many were barred from jobs because of their color; others were harassed and sometimes beaten by mobs who claimed that blacks' jobs belonged to them. Blacks were even segregated in schools, churches, and cemeteries.[39]

The American patriots fought to overthrow their British oppressors, yet their segregationist practices did not diminish in the post-Revolutionary War decades. Liberated whites continued their social, economic, and political segregation of blacks with even greater vengeance than in the prerevolutionary period. Why? Because antebellum New Englanders feared that the free black population, which included some former slaves, would rise up against them.[40] Segregation persisted also because New Englanders believed that their ancestors had been justified in isolating blacks from God's white kingdom on earth. Thus, they could exclaim as did Patrick Henry, "Give me liberty or give me death," but they would not hear such cries from black people.

SOUTHERN SLAVERY

From 1700 to the Civil War, slavery swept across the South like a wildfire. A plethora of books have made its rapid proliferation quite clear.[41] This story line has been repeated so often that most whites regard it as truth.

Two facts about southern racism and slavery, however, have been all but passed over. First, colonial-era southerners did not initially show the eagerness to establish slavery that the New England Puritans did. This was true even in Virginia, Maryland, and Georgia, which, along with the Carolinas, became known for chattel slavery by the beginning of the nineteenth century.

Africans coming to New England could expect to be immediately reduced to lifelong slaves. Yet their sisters and brothers in Virginia and Maryland, in bondage themselves, were less degraded by the peculiar institution. It is reported that the first twenty Africans brought to

Virginia in 1619 enjoyed the same status as white indentured servants. After completing their periods of service, Anthony Longoe, Isabella (last name unknown), and the rest of those first men and women from Africa became free to move on and to live in the same fashion as free whites. Thus, they owned property, operated businesses, voted, and raised families, unfettered by claims of innate inferiority.[42] Slavery did not become the exclusive status of Virginia blacks until 1661, forty-two years after the first twenty Africans disembarked at Jamestown. In the case of the Maryland Colony, slavery did not become legally sanctioned until 1663.

The relative slowness with which Virginia and Maryland established slavery as compared with Puritan New England provides an important insight into the nature of American racism. It is clear that southern colonists' attitude toward blacks—at least at the beginning—was not driven by previously planted racist ideas. We have no evidence that their basic perceptions and relationships with black people were initially controlled by the reports of sixteenth-century European voyagers. It was not until well into the 1700s, after slavery had taken deep root in Virginia and Maryland, that their literature spoke of black inferiority as a way of justifying black degradation.[43]

Although colonial Georgia would become, along with Virginia, a bastion of slavery by the late eighteenth century, it did not rush to put blacks in chains. From the granting of Georgia's charter in 1732 until slavery was legalized in 1755, "rum, papists and Negroes" were formally banned from Georgia. Blacks were excluded because the charter set up the colony as a refuge for former white convicts, who were expected to sustain themselves by producing silk, oils, dyes, and wines.[44] After decades of intense debate, slavery was finally introduced in 1755.

Only in the Carolinas was there haste to enact slavery. But even there we find no stated presumption of white supremacy. From the beginning, slavery in the Carolinas was directly tied to their colonial charters. The proprietors of the charter were members of the Royal African Company and were controlled by economic motivations. Hence, even before whites settled in the Carolinas, they had decided on the profitability of slave labor. Sir John Yeamans brought Africans with him to the southern portion of the Carolinas in 1671. Yet there is no evidence that he or the other original founders justified holding Africans in bondage on account of their inferiority.[45]

Thus, southern slavery did not, as Jordan alleges, "pop up overnight," as it did in New England.[46] Only after leaders of the southern colonies had been there for some time and realized that their economies required an abundant supply of cheap labor did they legislate black slavery as a way of meeting that need.

The second fact that has been overlooked is that from the time slavery emerged in the mid-1600s until well into the 1700s, southern slaveholders did not attempt to use biblical and theological ideas to buttress the institution. Until the eighteenth century, southern literature was virtually devoid of Christian racism—in sharp contrast to the northern literature. The nearest thing to religious justification is statements by the Virginia Assembly in 1667, such as "Baptisme doth not alter the condition of the person as to his bondage or freedom."[47] Beyond such earnest assertions, southern colonists in the early period simply reduced black people to the level of brutes; the colonists did not attempt to undergird their brutality with a theology of white supremacy.

This attitude, of course, does not merit the southern colonists any special admiration. It simply means that theological racism per se was not part of the baggage that southern colonists brought to the slave mart. Unlike the learned and refined Puritans of New England, these largely unlearned and crude slaveholders lacked the formal biblical and theological expertise that would have enabled them to construct a theology of racism. Thus, from the 1660s to the 1700s, they acted out their racism rather mindlessly, as Jordan mistakenly claims the Puritans did.

WHAT MIGHT SOUTHERNERS HAVE DONE ON THEIR OWN?

At least three important questions now come to mind. First, what might have happened if the southern colonists had immigrated to a geographic area that did not require a massive force of free labor? Second, would southern colonists have resorted on their own to slavery, or would they have built a society in which blacks and whites lived and worked together as equals? Third, would southern Christians have twisted the age-old tenets of classical Christianity to make them serve the same ends that the Puritans pursued in New England?

To speculate about what might have been requires historians to step outside their usual role. Yet these questions call for some kind of response. It seems plausible that in light of what we know about the southern colonies, relations between the races might well have been different. As Kenneth Stampp has noted about early-seventeenth-century

Virginia, "Blacks and whites seemed to be remarkably unconcerned about their visible physical differences. They toiled together in the fields, fraternized during leisure hours, and, in and out of wedlock, collaborated in siring a numerous progeny."[48]

Despite the fact that black and white indentures at first may have been unconcerned about visible physical differences, racism and slavery became the hallmarks of the antebellum South by the late 1700s. Still, it might be asked why these twin evils attained such vigor in the South. Speculation is not necessary here. According to most historians, racism and slavery became normative in the South because of economics. This standard explanation is accurate as far as it goes, but there is more to the story. It was not the largely unlettered white masses who owned the majority of slaves. Typical southerners were small farmers and non-slaveholders. Until the institution became firmly rooted in southern culture after the mid-1700s, they made no invidious distinctions between themselves and black people. They did not even join with the voices that championed slavery.

It was the planter class, the intellectual ideologues and power elites of southern society, that made racism and slavery so violent and widespread in plantation America.[49] This is another critical fact that has been largely neglected. Although history books have quietly passed over the bulk of their brutal misdeeds, the cultured elites have long been the preeminent force behind racial prejudice in North America. The religionist sector of these power elites gave currency to theological ideas of white supremacy. They then stood back to watch lower-class whites, acting largely out of ignorance, put their hands to actual deeds of racial violence.

Southern slaveholders do not show any indication of having initially been influenced by sixteenth-century racist images of Africans. Yet it could have been predicted that they would soon learn the stereotypes and give them a theological foundation. This is because many slave-holders were either members of the clergy or prominent laymen. They came from every Christian group in the colonies, but Anglicans, Methodists, Presbyterians, and Baptists predominated.

One of the earliest examples of how southern Christian ideologues used theological ideas to legitimize racism appeared in 1728. William Byrd, a Virginia planter appointed to help draw the dividing line between Virginia and North Carolina, wrote to John Perceval, earl of Egmont and cofounder, with General James Oglethorpe, of the Georgia Colony. After congratulating Perceval and Oglethorpe for legally excluding Africans from their colony, Byrd lamented their presence in his own:

> They import so many negro's [*sic*] hither, that I fear this Colony will sometime or other be confounded by the name of New Guinea. I am sensible of many bad consequences of multiplying these Ethiopians amongst us. They blow up the pride, & ruin the Industry of our White People, who Seeing a Rank of poor creatures below them, detest work for fear it should make them look like slaves. . . . We already have at least 10,000 men of these descendants of Ham. . . . The farther importation of them, into our Colonys, should be prohibited, lest they prove as troublesome, & dangerous everywhere.[50]

Byrd's rhetoric not only denigrates blacks but also parallels the Puritans' distortion of the doctrines of sin and creation. Just as the Puritans had insisted nearly three-quarters of a century earlier, Byrd was convinced that God created black people to be descendants of Ham and predestined them to such depravity that they were below all the rest of God's creatures (Genesis 9:20–27).

From 1701, when the Church of England created the Society for the Propagation of the Gospel in Foreign Parts (SPG) to oversee the spiritual welfare of the English colonists, Anglicanism was the established religion in the South. From then until the Great Awakening of 1738, when the Anglicans' dominance was supplanted by Methodists, Presbyterians, and Baptists, the SPG was the driving force behind ideas of white supremacy. The ideas were exactly like those the Puritans had contorted earlier. Even before the SPG began its mission to white colonists (Native Americans and enslaved blacks were subsequently included in that enterprise), prominent Anglicans in England were laying the doctrinal groundwork. As early as 1673, Richard Baxter, the celebrated Anglican cleric who held what was considered a moderate view of black people in his day, wrote to slaveholders about their charges: "They are reasonable Creatures, as well as you. . . . If their sins have enslaved them to you, yet Nature makes them your equals."[51] Baxter's moderation notwithstanding, he shared the Puritan understanding of sin and creation and used that theology to support his own claim that slavery was the consequence of black people's sin.

Baxter's moderate view was not shared by one of the leading nineteenth-century southern bishops, William Meade of Virginia. Described as a leader "of proslavery ideology,"[52] Bishop Meade once told a group of slaves that "Almighty God hath been pleased to make you slaves here, and to give you nothing but labor and poverty in this world, which you are obliged to submit to, as it is in His Will that it should be so."[53] Meade had no difficulty in manipulating the doctrine of creation so that it made slavery the consequence of divine providence. In this, he too imitated the old Puritans.

Baxter and Meade represented a long line of eighteenth- and nineteenth-century Anglican theologians who authenticated the racist ideas that the colonial-era Puritans had employed. These clerics were notables among Anglican leaders, including, in varying ways and degrees, such prestigious persons as Morgan Goodwyn, Thomas Bray, Samuel Thomas, and Thomas Hasel.

That Anglicans turned to Calvinist theological ideas shows how far they were willing to go to validate slavery. Since the sixteenth century, Anglican theology had stood in direct opposition to Calvinism, especially as taught by English Puritans. Anglicans did not subscribe to predestination or divine election. Instead, they insisted that salvation came through faith, grace, and good works. Concerning sin, they—at least before coming to America—taught that it was original, but they never identified it with any specific race. The doctrine of covenant was not a part of their theology, nor was the doctrine of hierarchical creation.[54] Anglicans were not Calvinists. They did not split with the Catholic Church because of a desire to endorse the four pillars of Calvinism. Instead they wanted to break from what they believed were ecclesiastical and papal, rather than theological, abuses in Roman Catholicism. During the English Reformation they sided with government officials and often endorsed the use of violence to combat the very Puritan ideas they later embraced. This embracing of Puritan theology reveals how far they strayed from the classical Christian position in order to justify racism.

Anglicans were not the only Christians in the American South whose racism had an affinity with Puritan theology. This was also true of the Methodists, Presbyterians, and Baptists. The wealthy members of these churches held the majority of slaves by the time of the Civil War. The ways in which they justified slavery are exemplified in the thoughts of the Presbyterian minister Frederick A. Ross. In 1859 Ross published a small book titled *Slavery Ordained of God*. According to Ross, slavery was the permanent status for Africans in this life, because of two antediluvian decrees of God. One was "the law of the control of the superior over the inferior." The other was the special curse on Canaan that

God placed against Ham and all his descendants, making them the basest
of sinners who must forever be under white people's control.[55]

It comes as no surprise that Ross would assert the same theological
ideas promulgated by the Puritans. As a Presbyterian, a Calvinism not
unlike Puritanism constituted Ross's roots. It also is not surprising
that Baptists would have no difficulty with Puritan racial theories.
The theological heritage of most American Baptists, like that of the
Presbyterians, went back to forms of Calvinism.

We might have expected otherwise from the Methodists, a reform-
ing movement within the Anglican Church. John Wesley, the founder
of Methodism, stood in the tradition of sixteenth-century Dutch theologian Jacob Arminius and thus was a staunch opponent of Calvinist
teachings—especially those dealing with predestination, sin, covenant,
and creation.[56] Wesley was a vigorous opponent of slavery. He
instructed Francis Asbury, the first bishop of the American Methodists,
to ban all slaveholders from the church.[57]

Despite Wesley's prohibition, racism and slavery dominated American Methodism even before the church was officially organized at the
Christmas Conference of 1784. Racial hatred and slavery were so widespread in antebellum Methodism that one of its historians wrote in
1881, "I have no doubt that had all our ministers done their [Chris-
tian] duty [and released their slaves], there would not have been a slave
left in this country twenty years ago."[58]

Methodist ideologues seemed determined to give racism an irre-
futable theological grounding, publishing numerous writings bearing
the distinctive imprint of the early Puritans' teachings. Among such
publications were Thornton Stringfellow's *Scriptural and Statistical
Views in Favor of Slavery*; William A. Smith's *Lectures on the Philosophy
and Practice of Slavery as Exhibited in the Institution of Domestic Slavery
in the United States*; and Albert T. Bledsoe's *An Essay on Liberty and
Slavery* (all dated 1856). The central thesis of these writings was that,
as Smith proclaimed, "Slavery per se, is right. . . . Domestic slavery, as
an institution, is fully justified by the condition and circumstances
[that God has sanctioned for] the African race in this country."[59] The
way in which these writers defended their thesis is best summed up by
the words of Stringfellow:

> I propose to examine the sacred volume briefly, and if I am not greatly
> mistaken, I shall be able to make it appear that the institution of

slavery has received, in the first place, 1st. The sanction of the Almighty in the patriarchal age. 2d. That it was incorporated into the only National Constitution which ever emanated from God. 3d. That its legality was recognized, and its relative duties regulated, by Jesus Christ in his kingdom.[60]

Although they have received only passing attention, the racist Christian ideas first planted by cultured Puritans during the early decades of the 1600s became the general standard of white Protestantism in the South. Puritans such as Governor Theophilus Eaton, Governor John Winthrop, the Reverend Cotton Mather, and Judge John Saffin created racist dogma that became a blueprint for religious confessors and other ideologues throughout the antebellum era. One has only to look at the titles of a few tomes from the 1700s to the Civil War: Richard Nisbet's *Slavery Not Forbidden by Scripture* . . . (1773); Leander Ker's *Slavery Consistent with Christianity* (1840); *Slavery: A Treatise Showing That Slavery Is neither a Moral, Political, nor Social Evil*, by "A Baptist Minister" (1844); Josiah Priest's *Bible Defense of Slavery; and Origin, Fortunes, and History of the Negro Race* (1852); Samuel B. How's *Slaveholding Not Sinful: Slavery, the Punishment of Man's Sin, Its Remedy, the Gospel of Christ* (1855); and John B. Thrasher's *Slavery a Divine Institution: A Speech Made before the Breckinridge and Lane Club, November 5, 1860*. While economic realities certainly influenced the rise of racism and slavery in the South, theological notions that first raged across New England drifted southward and infected southern white minds in the period just before the Civil War.

AGAINST THE PREVAILING WINDS

Because of the attention given to renowned antislavery men such as William Lloyd Garrison, Theodore Dwight Weld, and Arthur and Lewis Tappan, the roles that the clergy (including Puritan clergy) played in the nineteenth-century abolitionist movements have been slighted.[61] Clerics were active in the antislavery movements that began in the 1830s. Their voices contradicted the biblical and theological propositions of slaveholders and racists during both the colonial and antebellum periods.

According to Ruchames's *Racial Thought in America*, one of the earliest protests came from George Keith, a Quaker. As early as 1693,

Keith, who later became an Anglican, wrote "An Exhortation and Caution to Friends concerning Buying or Keeping of Negroes."[62] Convinced that the best way to rebut the allegation that God had created black people as inferior heathens was to turn to the very Bible that racists used to construct their arguments, Keith drew on both the Hebrew and Christian Testaments. Quoting Deuteronomy 24:14–15, he told his Quaker friends, "You shall not oppress a hired servant who is poor and needy, whether he is one of your brethren or one of the sojourners who are in your land within your towns." Moving to Revelation 18:4–5, 10, and 14, he mixed these passages and posed them as reasons that Quakers should

> Hearken to the Voice of the Lord, who saith, Come out of Babylon, my people, that ye be not partakers of her sins, and that ye receive not her plagues; for her Sins have reached unto Heaven, and God hath remembered her Iniquities; for he that leads into Captivity shall go into Captivity.[63]

The only non-Quaker rebuttal for almost three quarters of a century after Keith's protest in 1693 was Judge Samuel Sewall's *The Selling of Joseph* in 1700, followed by seven other Quaker challenges to white racism. Ruchames identifies these Quakers' refutations as John Hepburn's *Defense of the Golden Rule* (1715); Ralph Sandiford's *A Brief Examination of the Practices of the Times* (1729); Elihu Coleman's *A Testimony against That Antichristian Practice of Making Slaves of Men* (1733), which was immediately followed by his *The Mystery of Iniquity in a Brief Examination of the Practice of the Times* (1773); Benjamin Lay's *All Slavekeepers, That Keep the Innocent in Bondage, Apostates* (1737); John Woolman's *Some Considerations on the Keeping of Negroes: Recommended to the Professors of Christianity of Every Denomination* (1754); and Anthony Benezet's *A Caution and Warning to Great Britain and Her Colonies, in a Short Representation of the Calamitous State of the Enslaved Negroes in the British Dominions* (1766). All of these writings attempted to present a nonracist interpretation of the Bible. God, so they argued, had created Africans equal to all other races and therefore they should not be enslaved or ostracized in any fashion.[64]

The strongest Christian protests against white supremacy, however, did not come until the rise of the antislavery movement popularized by Garrison and others during the 1830s and 1840s. A small but dedicated group of Congregationalist, Methodist, Baptist, Presbyterian evangelical, and radical Unitarian clergy began to counter the biblical and theological ideas that had so long buttressed slavery. These clergy provided the ideational framework that slavery was not merely a sociopolitical problem but also a sin against God.

Inspired in part by the ethos of the second Great Awakening, which had begun to sweep across America a few decades earlier,[65] a number of theologians mounted a systematic theological attack on racism. Their primary weapon was perfectionist theology, one of the ideational props of the second Great Awakening. Perfectionism had been popularized in England by John Wesley and had won assent not only from some nineteenth-century American Methodists but also from some Lutherans, Presbyterians, Baptists, and Unitarians. Perfectionism was the antithesis of Calvinism. As taught by Wesley, it was grounded in the belief that God created all humans equal, endowed them with a free will by which they could choose whether to repent and be converted, and required all to move toward absolute perfection—a perfect love for God and all others.[66]

During the nineteenth century, perfectionism was often tied to another popular antebellum teaching, the notion of moral government and agency. Since the early eighteenth century it had become commonplace for American religious leaders to talk about the moral government of God and to preach that "the death of Christ did not so much satisfy God's wrath as preserve the moral order of the universe."[67] According to these theologians, God created men and women to be moral agents with the specific duty of assisting God in the governance of the world so that it might become more Christlike. Aware of the potential that such a notion held for social change, some abolitionist theologians combined it with perfectionist theology and began preaching about the Christian responsibility to assist God in removing slavery from society in order to restore their vision of the holy city (in contrast to the dominant Puritan vision). Thus, the Reverend Orange Scott, a New England Methodist and abolitionist, could write, "The principle of slavery, which justifies holding and treating the human species as property, is morally wrong; its practice is a sin. . . . It is a reprobate, too bad to be converted, not subject to the law of God." Steeped in the idea that Christians must assist God in perfecting the world, Scott held that slavery's "extirpation [was] a legitimate work for Methodists to do" because an untainted reading of the Bible showed that slavery was never ordained by God.[68]

The Reverend George B. Cheever, a Congregationalist abolitionist, was no less fiery than Scott. Confronting the prevailing interpretation of the law codes in Leviticus 25:45–46, Cheever first challenged slaveholders about their lack of knowledge of the original Hebrew and how it had been corrupted over the years. Pointing specifically to their distortion of Leviticus 25:46, he ridiculed them for not knowing that "the word *bondsman* is inserted in our English version, where there is not only no such word, but nothing answering to it, in the original Hebrew." He then informed them that

> it is from the misinterpretation, misrepresentation, and perversion of those laws, that the advocates of slavery have contrived some shadow of pretense for its existence and divine sanction among the Hebrews; although it was never slavery, but free voluntary service, concerning which the whole system of jurisprudence was established.[69]

Slavery, Cheever contended, was at once a "national and personal sin." This was so because government and the masses had conspired in supporting slavery and the denigration of blacks. He was troubled that so few Christians dared to speak out against this sinful union. To those who argued that Christians had no right to involve themselves in political matters, Cheever responded, "I am more convinced than ever of the right and duty of every preacher of God's word to preach on this subject, as contained in His word." Continuing, he said, "The providence that directs and overrules all things is manifesting more clearly than ever the wickedness of the attempt to shield slavery from the reprobation of God's word, by denouncing every mention of it as political preaching."[70]

Sounding like the prophet Amos (and some modern-day activist clergy, such as Dr. Martin Luther King Jr.), Cheever proceeded to preach that although racists and the antebellum government had formed a powerful union, true Christians were not required to submit to laws that supported slavery. "Wicked laws," he insisted, "are no authentication or excuse for personal wickedness, nor any disobedience to God. *They are not to be obeyed, but on the contrary denounced and rejected.*"[71]

Cheever was convinced that a true Christian should not be a racist because, as the title of his book made clear, God was against slavery. The perfectionist–moral government theory that God had created men and women as moral agents in order to help move the world toward perfection directed Cheever's conviction. Slavery was a sin that enslaved both the slave and the enslaver. Hence, he was certain that men and women could be "faithful to God" and "keep their own freedom" only if they helped root out this evil.[72]

Although not nearly as aggressive as Cheever, the Reverend Amos A. Phelps, pastor of the Pine Street Congregational Church of Boston, was equally straightforward. Like Cheever, Phelps saw slavery as "a great and crying national sin."[73] He wasted no time in cutting to the heart of why slavery had become the bane of the land. Christians, he noted, had helped make it a monster. For him, "the sin of slavery" was in large part owing "to northern ministers as well as southern."[74]

Against Christians who held that clergy should not be involved in efforts to abolish slavery, Phelps posed a rhetorical question: would placing "the work of its reform into the hands of those who are personally interested in its continuance, or who, from fear or something worse, dare not say or do aught decisive on the subject [be] a bluster?"[75] His answer was unequivocal. "The time has now come," he said, "when friends of God and man ought to take a higher stand, and adopt and act on principles which lay the axe directly at the root of the tree." Since that root included Christians who had wantonly twisted biblical and theological ideas to justify slaveholding, Phelps believed that God required the true friends of morality and religion to act as moral agents and use untainted biblical and theological ideas to help bring an immediate end to that evil.[76]

Phelps, Cheever, and Scott were not the only antebellum clerics who believed in a moral obligation to attack slavery as a sin that arose from corrupt biblical and theological ideas. Phelps listed the names of 124 northern clergy who endorsed his "declaration of sentiment" that slavery and racism were sins against God.[77] Among them were such imposing figures such as Beriah Greene, principal of the Oneida Institute, and Asa Mahan, president of Oberlin College. Of these ministers, 112 served Congregational churches, 8 served Methodist churches, and 4 served Baptist churches. Interestingly, most of them, 92 in all, pastored Congregational churches in the New England states.

Despite the attempt of some antislavery clergy to fight against the prevailing winds of slavery and racism, their efforts proved futile. There were at least three reasons why they failed, and these reasons give us further insight into the nature of American racism. First, slaveholding whites from the 1830s to the Civil War began to contend even more desperately that God created blacks as subhuman and fit only for white subjugation. Examples of the extreme virulence of the proslavery position are found in the writings of both southern and northern churchmen. In the South, the Reverend E. D. Sims, professor at the Methodist-operated Randolph-Macon College in Virginia, argued:

> Upon the whole, then, whether we consult the Jewish polity, instituted by God himself; or the uniform opinion and practice of mankind in all ages of the world; or the injunction of the New Testament and the moral law; we are brought to the conclusion, that slavery is not immoral.[78]

In the North, the Reverend Wilbur Fisk, a prominent Methodist clergyman and president of Wesleyan University in Connecticut in the 1830s, defended slavery and white supremacy by drawing on 1 Corinthians 7:20–24, "Let each of you remain in the condition in which you were called. . . ." Said Fisk, "This text seems mainly to enjoin and sanction the fitting continuance" that "the slave, unless emancipation should offer [freedom], was to remain a slave." Further, he declared, "The general rule of Christianity not only permits but enjoins a continuance of the master's authority" to enslave black people forever.[79]

There can be no doubt that interest in maintaining an agrarian economy helped slaveholders and racist whites to be relentless in their defense of black subordination. Yet the historical record clearly demonstrates that they had another reason to fight abolition so tirelessly. Racism had become a Christian article of faith. They believed that God had created black people to be heathen and less than all other human beings. Hence, their white supremacy went beyond mere economics. It involved a religious confession of racism on the basis of perverted biblical and theological ideas. The germs of this bad theology had resided in the subconscious minds of Anglo-American Christians ever since their ancestors first voyaged to Africa and met people of a strange and offensive skin color and culture. Those germs multiplied and eventually infected the whole of the antebellum period with outright hatred and public acts of violence.

Second, the efforts of antislavery clergy failed because their crusade became diluted by other sociopolitical issues, such as the women's rights movement. This movement emerged shortly after the rise of the antislavery movement. Partly because of the obvious political ramifications and partly because of the less obvious social implications of the women's rights movement, historians today have not had the courage to examine the impact that the mid-nineteenth-century effort of white women, trying to be equal in every way to white men, had on the struggle of black people to be recognized even as human beings.

For example, it appears that some of the energy that was developing in the protest of slavery was diverted to white women's agenda for civil rights in the 1830s. Timothy L. Smith remarks that "trouble between the evangelicals and the radical Unitarians began in 1836 and 1837," a mere six years after the antislavery movement had begun.[80] This trouble, as Smith describes it, centered around the rights of white women to join the antislavery movement. (To put the matter squarely, the conflict between evangelicals and Unitarians grew out of Sarah and Angelina Grimké's desire to act as touring agents for the movement.)[81]

Convinced that the antislavery movement should not be tied solely to the eradication of slavery (!) but should also include the abolition of sexism and other "isms," William Lloyd Garrison fought to add women's rights to the agenda of the American Anti-Slavery Society. By 1840 the debate over women's rights had completely divided the white abolitionists and, in effect, helped undermine whatever power their movement may have had in helping to bring a swift end to the centuries-old violation of black humanity. A separate feminist movement was organized by 1848.[82] (I find an interesting parallel between these historical facts and what happened to the black civil rights movement of the 1960s and 1970s when white women clamored to be included equally on the agenda; see chapter 5.)

Third, antislavery clergy bore little fruit because of the lack of resolve among some of the northern clergy themselves. More than a few who entered the fray to abolish slavery at whatever cost soon capitulated to the power of the racists. One does not have to probe deeply into the literature of this era to see the signals of surrender. Anxious about schisms, church publications acquiesced to those who wanted to keep blacks in their current roles.

A pastoral address of the General Conference of the Methodist Episcopal Church, meeting in Baltimore in 1840, illustrates this surrender. In reaction to a memorial calling upon the church to take a definitive stand against slavery, the address thanked the memorialists for their view before rejecting their petition:

> [Because of] the diversity of habits of thoughts, manners, customs, and
> domestic relations among people of this vast republic, [and because of]

the diversity of the institutions of the sovereign States of the confeder-
acy, it is not to be supposed an easy task to suit all the incidental
circumstances of our economy to the views and feelings of the vast mass
of minds interested. . . . We pray therefore, that the [abolitionist]
brethren whose views may have been crossed by the acts of this Conference, will at least give us credit of having acted in good faith, and of not
having regarded private ends or party interests, but the best good of the
whole family of American Methodists.[83]

The antislavery position of the northern Methodists was forsaken at
the General Conference of 1840 because of the fear that it would
either divide the church or go against the political machinations of the
secular society.

One can trace a lineage of Christians who first claimed to be the
friends of black people but then withdrew such friendship under duress.
(These are the forerunners of some modern-day liberals.) As far back as
Cotton Mather, one finds them abandoning the cause of black freedom.
Mather did not write *The Negro Christianized* and *Rules for the Society of
Negroes* because he was dedicated to overthrowing white racism. As the
subtitle of the former book reveals, he wrote simply "to excite and assist
that good work, the instruction of Negro servants in Christianity." His
goal was to proselytize blacks and to show them "that if they serve God
patiently and cheerfully in the condition which he orders for them, their
condition will very quickly be infinitely mended in Eternal Happiness."[84]

The Methodists, who portrayed themselves as antislavery and anti-
racist as early as the 1780s, also quickly retreated under pressure from
their slaveholding members. Shortly after the church emerged in North
America, it passed a law forbidding any Methodist to practice slavery.[85]
But a mere five months after the denomination was officially chartered
at the 1784 Christmas Conference, the conference minutes contained
the following retraction: "We thought it prudent to suspend the minute concerning slavery on account of the great opposition that had been
given it."[86]

Charles Grandison Finney, the renowned New School Presbyterian
revivalist and antislavery crusader, also cowered in the face of proslavery
Christians. Called the high priest of the Great Revival, he was initially a
staunch advocate of perfecting America through the "immediate abolition of slavery." His commitment to this goal faltered miserably when
proslavery southern Christians, responding to the antislavery arguments

that slavery was a sin, threatened to withdraw from the Union. Fearing that the continued denunciation of slavery would lead to armed conflict between North and South, Finney quickly assumed the position that "unless the publik [*sic*] mind can be engrossed with the subject of salvation, and make abolitionism an appendage," then "the church and world, ecclesiastical and state leaders, will become embroiled in one common infernal squabble that will roll a wave of blood over the land."[87]

Finney moved even further from his initial stand on immediate abolition with this statement: "If abolition can be made an appendage of a general revival of religion, all is well."[88] Finney and other backsliding abolitionist friends of the African Americans were willing to make abolition a mere footnote to their perfectionist agenda; they are guilty of the charge that they believed that saving the Union was more of a Christian duty than saving black people from bondage. Confronted with the choice of either maintaining a "perfect" political union, or "perfecting the nation" by rooting out slavery, these abolitionist Christians wasted no time in choosing the former. Thus, they abandoned generations to the theological racism that had dominated the nation since its inception as a colony of England.

It was only by the spilling of blood in the Civil War that one aspect of the Puritans' racism—legalized slavery—came to an end. Nothing more needs to be said here to establish that while the efforts of some Christian allies of African Americans were sincere, they had little influence on slavery's legal abolition. Except for the antislavery work of the American Missionary Association, which comprised both black and white Christians working to free blacks and establish schools (a movement that continues today in the United Church of Christ), by 1845 there were hardly any antislavery Christians left to carry on the religious crusade. Slavery's demise was the result of raw politics and the desire to keep the nation unified, not the consequence of antislavery Christianity.[89]

The Civil War ended legal slavery, but it could not—indeed, it did not even seek to—eradicate Christian-supported ideas of white supremacy. These theological ideas have continued to live in our own time. They have survived because their defenders are cunning enough to weave them into other theories that have become more popular in the public square. The roots of this practice of intermixing old racist ideas with new theories lie deep in the Reconstruction era and the first five decades of the twentieth century. It is to this period, from 1865 to 1950, that we now turn.

THE HYBRIDIZATION
OF THE IDEAS, 1865–1950

The noted American historian Sidney Ahlstrom, speaking of America's transition from a group of thirteen British colonies to an independent nation, has written that the "new nation never for a moment lost the Puritan's sense of America's special destiny [to be God's] 'city set on a hill.'"[1] Ahlstrom's conclusion holds true with regard to racism from Reconstruction through the 1920s: although the Civil War brought legal slavery to an end, the Puritan claim of a God-ordained white supremacy was never given up. Post–Civil War Christian propagandists of black inferiority continued to assert that God had created Africans and African Americans to be heathens who were unfit to sit at the table of brotherhood and sisterhood with the rest of humanity.

How odd, then, that most scholars have neglected this aspect of the legacy of racism. American racism has never rested upon the mere social, economic, and political benefits that whites derived from enslaving Africans and their descendants, or from subjecting them to segregation and discrimination. If these and other acts of racial prejudice depended solely upon personal benefits that whites derived from discrimination and segregation, then the efforts that many have made over the centuries to erase these maladies from our body politic should have succeeded. But none of these efforts—the antebellum antislavery crusades, the Civil War, the radical Reconstruction, the civil rights movements of the 1960s, the federal legislation of the 1960s and 1970s—has been able to consign white racism to a historical woodpile.

The reason is that Christian racists and other intellectual ideologues have always found ways to water racism's root system of anchoring beliefs. For example, within a few months after the Civil War ceased in 1865, the southern Presbyterian Church issued a *Pastoral Letter of the Presbyterian Church, South*, concerning the past relationship between slavery and the churches:

> While the existence of slavery may, in its civil aspect, be regarded as a settled question, an issue now gone, yet the lawfulness of the relation as a question of social morality and Scriptural truth has lost nothing of its importance. When we solemnly declare to you, brethren, that the dogma [of antislavery Christians] which asserts the inherent sinfulness of [slavery] is unscriptural and fanatical . . . we have surely said enough to warn you from this insidious error as from a fatal shore.[2]

That is, although the war had resulted in the demise of legal bondage, some Christians were convinced that they had a divine duty to continue to regard slavery as an acceptable Christian practice.

The Civil War not only struck a fatal blow against legal slavery, it also had two other critical consequences. First, it helped usher in dramatic changes in the social, political, and economic spheres of our national life. The rigid caste system that had existed alongside slavery was dramatically altered. For the first time in more than two hundred years, black people were now legally free and ostensibly on an equal footing with whites.

For at least the first few years after the war, blacks were free to sample aspects of American life that they previously could only dream about: establishing families, owning property, attending schools, operating businesses, voting, and moving about as free citizens. They even obtained a measure of political influence by campaigning for and being elected to federal and state offices. During Reconstruction, hundreds of African Americans in the South were either elected as or received state and federal appointments as U.S. senators and congressional representatives, U.S. chaplains, state governors and lieutenant governors, state superintendents of education, state treasurers, secretaries of state, associate justices of state supreme courts, and local postmasters.[3]

These achievements during Reconstruction in the South, however, were little reflected in the North. During this same period, not one African American held an elective state or federal office anywhere in the

North. The first African American to hold a state office above the Mason-Dixon Line was Benjamin W. Arnett, an African Methodist Episcopal minister and bishop, who was elected Greene County representative to the Ohio legislature in 1885, nearly a quarter of a century after the Civil War. The first northern black to hold a federal office, Oscar DePriest, was not elected an Illinois representative to Congress until 1929, well more than a half century after the war.[4]

Second, the war seriously undercut the ability of Christian racists to continue using theological ideas to support white supremacy. By freeing the slaves and opening the way for them to obtain some measure of political, economic, and social power, the war laid bare the fraudulence of the theory that had been most efficacious for Christian racists: their twisted doctrine of a hierarchical creation. That blacks were now free to participate in social practices and institutions heretofore reserved for whites only complicated the allegation that God had created them lowest on the hierarchical ladder of the races. The victory of Union arms, to which thousands of black soldiers had bravely contributed, demonstrated that God was "on the side of the oppressed" (to borrow the language of the black liberation theologian James H. Cone) and not on the side of the slaveholders and detractors of the race.[5]

Yet Christian racists continued to advance their ideas, for two reasons. First, as has been the case with many whites throughout American history, they simply could not tolerate living side by side with blacks enjoying even the smallest modicum of social and economic equality with whites. Their disaffection was exacerbated by blacks in the South obtaining political offices that gave them some semblance of power over their former oppressors. Second, some Christians were convinced that their own salvation was at stake if they did not continue to promote the doctrine of God-ordained black inferiority. These Christians took the position that their struggle for white supremacy was "not alone for civil rights and property and home, but also for religion, for the church, for the gospel."[6]

This quest for a white supremacy grounded in religion, the church, and the gospel was by no means an exclusively southern phenomenon. Northern Christians were no less aggressive in promoting it. Before the Civil War, for example, the Reverend Nehemiah Adams, a minister of the Congregational Church in Boston, warned of the need to keep blacks subordinated to whites. Returning from a visit to the South in 1854, Adams wrote, "The conviction forced itself upon my mind at the south, that the most disastrous event to the colored people would be their emancipation to live on the same soil with whites." Continuing, he portrayed himself as "a friend of the colored race" who nevertheless felt "compelled to believe that while they remain with us, subordination in some form to a stronger race is absolutely necessary."[7]

Such sentiments also can be found in more coded form. For post–Civil War Christian supremacists, the only way to ensure that blacks would continue to remain subservient was to refurbish old theological concepts of race by tying them to new ideas and ideological constructs in the society at large. Hence began a process of hybridization through which old racist ideas were rendered even more powerful.

The reformulated ideas and presuppositions have been able to accomplish this improbable task because of what seems to be the natural ability of old notions to be hybridized. From 1865 through the 1920s, such conspiratorial crossbreeding occurred on several levels. On one level, for example, theological ideas were mixed with scientific and medical ideas that first began to gain widespread attention in the middle of the nineteenth century. On a second level, these hybridized ideas fused with the inchoate fears and aspirations of populism among the white poor and uneducated small landowners and tenant farmers after Reconstruction.

SCIENCE JOINS THE FRAY

Reconstruction-era and early-twentieth-century supremacists did not have to look far to find suitable ideas and agendas that would blend with and cloak their racist theological ideas. The decades from 1865 through 1920 were pregnant with exciting new scientific theories that could easily be interwoven with older theological ideas of black inferiority. Foremost among these so-called scientific theories was the notion of human evolution. Although evolutionary theories originated in Europe, they attracted a considerable following of American disciples as early as the first decades of the nineteenth century. During the 1840s, for example, southern slaveholders called on these European imports to buttress the theological ideas they were using to justify slavery.[8]

One of the first Americans to use evolutionism in this way was the Swiss-born zoologist and geologist Jean Louis Rodolphe Agassiz. After arriving in North America in 1846, Agassiz soon published an essay entitled "The Diversity of the Origin of the Human Race." In this essay he had two clear purposes in mind. One was to claim that his study in zoology and geology confirmed the multiple creations of human races. The second was to argue that whereas some races had evolved to the highest level of humanity and civilization, others had not. The lesser-evolved, therefore, were suitable only for servile subjection to the master races.

Using ethnological differences to compare and contrast blacks with whites and hence to defend slavery, Agassiz pointed to the Africans as "a most forcible illustration of the fact that the races are essentially distinct" and that some of them had failed to evolve to the top rank of human civilization.[9] To reinforce this charge, Agassiz claimed that zoological and geological records revealed that although Africans had been "in constant intercourse with the white race" and other superior races from the beginning, "there has never been a regulated society of black men developed on [the African] continent." Further, he argued that "history speaks for itself" and thus proves that Africans and their descendants in America "are today what they were in the time of the Pharaohs, what they were at a later period, [and] what they are probably to continue to be," that is, the subjects of white domination.[10]

William Sumner Jenkins, the noted scholar of southern proslavery, concludes that because Agassiz's theories emphasized diverse or multiple creations of human races, Christians—specifically southern Christians—who clung to a literal understanding of a single human creation (as related in the Genesis story) rejected them.[11] While it would be unconscionable not to note that some ardent Christian slaveholders argued against Agassiz's theories, it would be an equally serious misrepresentation to overlook the fact that others openly accepted and rigorously defended them.

Indeed, the writings of a number of late-nineteenth- and early-twentieth-century Christians show that they often relied on the scientific ideas put forth by Agassiz to aid and sustain their old theological arguments against black people. These writings include Buckner H. Payne's *The Negro, what is his ethnological status?* (published under the pseudonym Ariel in 1867); D. G. Phillips's *Nachash: What Is It? or An Answer to the Question, Who and What Is the Negro?* (1868); A. Hoyle Lester's *The Pre-Adamite, or Who Tempted Eve? Scripture and Science in Unison as Respects the Antiquity of Man* (1875); and William Benjamin Smith's *The Color Line: A Brief in Behalf of the Unborn* (1905).

Publications during this period also included one of the most extreme and vicious books ever written about black people, namely, Charles Carroll's *"The Negro a beast"; or, "In the Image of God": The reasoner of the age, the revelator of the century! The Bible as it is! The negro and his relation to the human family! . . . The negro not the son of Ham . . .* (1900). Carroll saw himself as the religious crusader to whom was left the task of "harmonizing the teachings of scripture with those of science" in order to prove once and for all that God had not created black people human beings "but apes."[12] Carroll published another book in 1902, entitled *The Tempter of Eve*. The purpose of this writing was again to use theology as an adjunct to science in portraying black people as so beastly and sinful in their nature that they were the cause of humanity's Fall, since they and not a serpent had been the "tempter of Eve."[13]

We should not be surprised that late-nineteenth- and early-twentieth-century Christians would turn to so-called scientific arguments such as those of Agassiz and Carroll to buttress their theological ideas about race. Since the American Puritan era, the notion of a hierarchical creation had been employed to legitimate a creational distinction between the races. Thus, Judge Saffin's characterization of the innate inferiority of blacks (described in chapter 1), for which he never claimed the support of science, now could be bolstered by the pseudoscientific arguments of biologists and zoologists such as Agassiz. If some notions, such as multiple creations, flew in the face of Christians, then racist thinkers would defend slavery by grasping another set of ideas.

Thus, Agassiz's theories were set aside for those of Charles Darwin. Racist Christians found Darwin's evolutionism most helpful for their reconstructions. As is commonly known, Darwin, between 1859 and 1871, popularized the idea that all human beings had evolved from primates and that, because of natural selection, only the fittest of the human species had survived.[14] It is important to note that Darwin did not construct his theories of evolution to show that only black people had originated from apes and were, on that account, unfit. Rather, his purpose was to demonstrate that the process of evolution is common to all human beings because our humanity is hereditary, indeed biological. It was also his thesis that because some men and women did not evolve fully, only the strongest, most hardy of human beings—regardless of skin color—were able to survive.[15]

Darwin, like Agassiz, spurned the Genesis account of a creation in which God permanently conceived and shaped the intrinsic nature of every plant, lower animal, and human being. Human nature, according to Darwin, was not final or finished but was constantly evolving from lower (or animal) characteristics to higher (or more human) characteristics. Christians of the time, especially biblical literalists, should have rejected Darwinian evolution as blasphemy against God—and more than a few fundamentalist and liberal Christians did. Many others, however, just as readily and vigorously turned his hypotheses into a theological-scientific argument against black humanity.

The latter racist Christians were aided by two highly acclaimed figures in the history of American Christianity. Indeed, the racism of the Reverend Josiah Strong and the Reverend Walter Rauschenbusch has been all but ignored. Yet it is from the writings of these two men that we may see more clearly how intellectuals among the clergy wove Darwin's scientific ideas into their own racist theological bias.

JOSIAH STRONG

Josiah Strong (1846–1916) was preeminent among American clergy in fusing racist and evolutionary ideologies into a pious package. As general secretary of the American branch of the Evangelical Alliance, Strong was one of the most influential religious leaders of the late nineteenth and early twentieth centuries. Although scholars have focused on his racism as it was expressed in his xenophobic nativism,[16] a deeper analysis of his writings will show that he was also an articulate and influential Christian proponent of the idea that God, nature, science, and history all legitimated white supremacy over black people. The apparent innocence of the titles of his writings notwithstanding—*The New Era; or, The Coming Kingdom* (1893), and *Our Country: Its Possible Future and Its Present Crisis* (1885)—these books were two of the most vehement and most cunningly nuanced theological and scientific defenses of white supremacy by any Christian leader of modern times.

Strong's intention was to demonstrate that God had been working throughout human history to prepare the American Anglo-Saxons alone to evolve into the "highest civilized people and nation in the coming kingdom [of God on earth.]"[17] To prove his point, he turned to both world history and Christian history, arguing that God in the beginning created three ancient races—the Hebrews, the Greeks, and the Romans. Exhibiting a robust affinity with Georg Wilhelm Hegel's theory of the dialectical development of human history,[18] Strong asserted that God's sole purpose for these ancient races was that they evolve to a specific point, after which the Anglo-Saxons in Europe were to ascend to a still higher level. Coming still later—after the European race—the American Anglo-Saxons alone would evolve into the chosen people of God, who would finally usher in the long-awaited dominion of God on earth.[19]

Strong added science to his theological defense of white supremacy by pointing to Darwin's theory of the survival of the fittest:

> Mr. Darwin is not only disposed to see, in the superior vigor of our people, an illustration of his favorite theory of natural selection, but even intimates that the world's history thus far has been simply preparatory for our future [as God's elect]. . . . There is apparently much truth in the belief that the wonderful progress of the United States, as well as the character of the people, are the results of natural selection.[20]

In Strong's mind, God had not created blacks to be among the fittest but rather the chief footstool upon which whites would step on their upward way to becoming God's chosen.

Strong mostly omitted any consideration of what roles African Americans could be expected to play as America ascended to God's dominion on earth. The one significant exception is found in his *The New Era*, in this reference: "That part of Africa which lies on the Mediterranean has been in contact with the world and has had at times a high civilization." What he gives with one hand, however, he takes back with the other by continuing thus:

> But the remainder of the continent has been for the most part a *terra incognita*. Her people have looked out not upon the highway of narrow seas or straits, but upon the barriers of boundless oceans. The location of Africa and her coast-line are much less favorable to intercourse than those of Asia, her people have been much more isolated, and there we find a lower barbarism than any in Asia.[21]

Even if we were to assume that Strong used the Latin words "terra incognita" to indicate that Africa was literally an unknown land, his tracing of that continent's alleged lower barbarism and its inhabitants' inability to interact with the supposedly superior peoples of Europe and Asia reeks of a cunning and racist distortion of Darwinian evolutionism.

WALTER RAUSCHENBUSCH

Walter Rauschenbusch (1861–1918) is the well-regarded advocate of the Social Gospel movement. His vision of ministry was formed as the pastor of a struggling Baptist congregation in the Hell's Kitchen area of New York City and carried into his teaching at Rochester Seminary. He advocated that pastors should serve human need as heralds of the coming realm of justice and that the church should always stand against superpersonal forms of evil and corporate forms of injustice.

In his writings, Rauschenbusch sought to mix theological ideas with scientific theories. Even though he did not mention Darwin by name, Rauschenbusch made no attempt to conceal his appreciation of Darwin's evolutionism. "The spread of evolutionary ideas," he proclaimed, "is another mark of modern religious thought. It has opened a vast historical outlook, backward and forward, and trained us in bold conceptions of the upward climb of the race."[22]

The way in which Rauschenbusch tied social Darwinism to his theology is most noticeable in his highly regarded *Christianity and the Social Crisis* (1907). Here he pointed to America's supposed progression toward becoming God's dominion:

> Last May a miracle happened. At the beginning of the week the fruit trees bore brown and greenish buds. At the end of the week they were robed in bridal garments of blossom. . . . This swift unfolding was the culmination of a long process. Perhaps these nineteen centuries of Christian influence have been a preliminary stage of growth, and now the flower and fruit are almost here. . . . The generations yet unborn will mark this as the great day of the Lord for which the ages waited, and count us blessed for sharing in the apostolate that proclaimed it.[23]

Like Josiah Strong, Rauschenbusch did not actually discuss where African Americans stood in relation to America's presumed growth toward the dominion of God on earth. Nevertheless, we can perceive in another of his major works—*Christianizing the Social Order* (1912)—a strong denial that blacks made any noteworthy contribution to that glorious progression. Speaking about why the South lost the Civil War, he said, "One reason why the South broke down in our Civil War was that its slave labor had kept it industrially incompetent."[24] One can suspect where the great theologian, who placed the South's industrial backwardness at the feet of the slaves instead of the slave masters, stood regarding the value of African Americans as a people. Could he have believed, like many other liberals of his time, that African Americans had not grown beyond the level of brutes and therefore were inferior to whites?

Additional suspicion of Rauschenbusch's Christian racism may be aroused by particular statements he made concerning slavery. For example, speaking about why slavery ended, he insisted that "slavery has disappeared, not simply because it contradicted the moral convictions of mankind, but because it was inefficient labor and unable to stand against the competition of the free man working for his own good."[25] Such statements as the inefficiency of slave labor can also be found among explicit racists. I take them as disguised racism.

To speak to the other side, one might certainly applaud Rauschenbusch for the insight that slavery did not end simply because of moral convictions. One can also appreciate his implication that slavery was a senseless, stifling, and criminal use of black people's abilities and energies. Nevertheless, a veiled and perhaps unconscious racism discloses itself when we look carefully at the way in which inefficient labor of the South is juxtaposed with "the free man working for his own good." We have a right to ask to whom Rauschenbusch was referring when he posed inefficient labor over against the efficient labor of the "free man." The black men and women who labored without compensation for two centuries were anything but inefficient in helping, under the threat of whip and gun, to amass the coveted and ill-gotten wealth of the prewar South.

A careful reading of Rauschenbusch's thought leaves no doubt about whom he considered inefficient workers. Reflecting back on slavery, he declared that "the slave could be trusted only with the crudest tools and employed at the coarsest forms of agriculture." Going on to explain this totally unfounded charge, he said that a slave could not be trusted because "the higher motives that give the perpetual spring and keenness of edge to our work—the hope of economic advancement, the desire for honor, the sense of duty, and the love of work for its own sake—scarcely touched him."[26]

Such a statement not only exposes the harshness of Rauschenbusch's thinking about blacks, it also betrays how he linked his racist theological assumptions to Darwin's theory of evolution. His claim that the higher motives of morality, industry, and honesty had scarcely touched black people points to the fact that he believed that African Americans had not evolved to the same high level of civilization as whites. There seems to have been no question but that blacks were innately inferior to the highly civilized white race and therefore that they played no significant role in helping America blossom into God's great dominion on earth.

It is quite understandable that Rauschenbusch would harness his racism to the scientific theory of evolution. He was, after all, a Christian intellectual not only trained in evangelical theology but also well informed of the most highly regarded scientific theories of his age. "Translate the evolutionary theories into religious faith," he said, "and you have the doctrine of the Kingdom of God."[27] As it related to black people, his translation of those theories became nothing less than a theological-scientific apology for white racism.

It is a well-attested conclusion of modern scholarship that Walter Rauschenbusch was sincerely committed to the belief that the dominion of God could not be realized until the downtrodden and disinherited were accepted as equal human beings in society. But despite that conviction, he subscribed to the long-standing belief that black people were necessarily excluded from participating in the manifest destiny of the white race. Hence, like John H. Van Evrie and other ideologues of his age, Walter Rauschenbusch seemingly shared the belief that both religion and science confirmed that "the negro is a different being from the white man, and therefore, of necessity, was designed by the Almighty Creator to live a different life."[28]

MEDICAL SCIENCE ADDS A LOUD VOICE

The role of medical science in defining and defending American racism has been largely unexamined. This oversight has occurred despite the fact that during the decades between the Civil War and the 1920s, many prominent physicians, with obvious force, added their theories to the accumulating body of racist theory.[29]

The tenor of the arguments set forth by these learned medical authorities is most clearly sounded in the thoughts of three American doctors: Josiah Clark Nott, a physician and surgeon; John H. Van Evrie, a physician; and Robert W. Shufeldt, a retiree of the medical corps of the United States Army. Although their medical specialties differed, each of these men shared one common assumption about the question of race. Like their theological compatriots, they were certain that black people were inferior savages who posed a threat to the public health and welfare of the supposedly pure white men and women. In setting forth evidence to support these beliefs, they not only relied on theories from their own particular fields of expertise, but they undergirded them with old theological ideas.

JOSIAH NOTT

One of the earliest physicians to publish an extensive work in defense of white supremacy was Josiah Nott. A renowned southern physician and surgeon in Mobile, Alabama, Nott published a massive volume (more than seven hundred pages) on race in 1854—just eight years before the Civil War. This protracted and cumbersome tome was entitled *Types of Mankind; or, Ethnological Researches, Based upon Monuments, Paintings, Sculptures, and Crania of Races, and upon Natural Geographical, Philological, and Biblical History*. As the lengthy title indicates, Nott exhibited an extreme eclecticism in his zeal to demonstrate the unworthiness of black people. He drew not only on medicine but also on other areas of science, as well as on human artifacts, linguistics, ethnology, world history, and the Bible. Writing before the end of slavery, he attempted to use all of these sources to contend that black people were both physically and mentally deficient and thus suited only for permanent bondage to whites.

To accomplish his purpose, Nott began with a novel theory of creation in which he held that there had been diverse creations of mankind, comprising the Egyptian types, the Asian types, the Caucasian types, and the African types. He based this classification on what he called the ancient Egyptians' division of mankind of the fifteenth century B.C.E.[30] With the exception of Nott's speculation that the Egyptians were a race separate from and superior to the Africans, it would seem at first glance that there is no difference between his theory and the thesis of a hierarchical creation first espoused by the New England Puritans.

The Puritans had sought to explain as God-ordained the then-current difference in status between whites and blacks. Nott, following the lead of Agassiz, who was one of his allies, held that the Genesis account was a sacred story of creation that "chiefly related to the history of the white race."[31] With this interpretation of Genesis, Nott understood blacks as so physically and mentally different from and inferior to whites that God did not create them as a part of the original, general creation. The black race, according to Nott, emerged posterior to the white race through a "special creation of black races [that] took place in Africa." He further theorized that God not only created black people subsequent to white people but also gave them black skins that were "best-suited to hot climates."[32]

Nott's understanding of creation was novel in that only a small group of late-nineteenth- and early-twentieth-century Christian intellectuals and secular ideologues used a polygenistic creation to justify racism. Previous racist Christians had largely followed the Puritans' monogenistic understanding of creation: a single creation in which God ordained blacks to be on the lowest rung of the ladder. In contrast, Nott argued that the orders of creation demarked a hierarchy, with the first being best.

From this foundation, Nott argued that "nations and races, like individuals, have each an especial destiny, with some born to rule, and others to be ruled."[33] According to him, the divine destiny of the black race throughout the world was to be in eternal subservience to the superior Caucasians. For him, this divinely imputed white superiority was not racism. As he used a hodgepodge of methods to rationalize it, white domination was actually a great blessing to black people, because it was God's gracious way of placing the latter race in "ceaseless contact with whites who would instruct and feed them" and thus would enable them to escape their "natural improvidence" in Africa as a "half-developed and half-starved race."[34]

Although he taught that subservience was a part of the divine plan to enable blacks to escape their "natural improvidence" in Africa, Nott did not teach that God or nature would ever permit them to overcome their supposed physical and mental inadequacies. Instead he drew the opposite conclusion. Blacks, he reasoned, were forever condemned to be the subjects of white control and manipulation, because "the races or species of mankind obey the same organic laws which govern other animals" and, in consequence, cannot change their "primitive origination."[35]

How, then, could Nott claim that whites were able to advance from their primitive beginnings while blacks could not? First, he argued that, unlike the Negroid race, which alone comprised only one barbaric species, the Caucasian race was "an amalgamation of a number of primitive stocks" and "is the only one which really can be considered cosmopolitan," a general creation.[36] Second, he held that because God had seen fit to make Caucasians an admixture of all the great races of humankind—"Egyptians, Jews, Romans, Greeks, etc."—there was "an exception to the laws which have been established for the other order of mammifers [*sic*]." This exception, he exulted, came about thus:

> The higher castes of what are termed Caucasian races, are influenced by several causes in a greater degree than other races. To them have been

assigned, in all ages, the largest brains and the most powerful intellect; theirs is the mission of extending and perfecting civilization—they are by nature ambitious, daring, domineering.[37]

Here we see the crux of Nott's racism.

Third, Nott was convinced that blacks were not only below the level of the white race physically but also substandard intellectually. Fourth, likening blacks to the lower animals, he claimed that just as "neither climate nor food can transmute an ass into a horse, or a buffalo into an ox," so nothing could change blacks into intelligent and civilized human beings. It was an unalterable law of nature enacted by God that black people could never hope to rise above the aboriginal state in which they had been created. In Nott's view, Africans and African Americans had no option but to live in permanent subordination to the white race.[38]

JOHN VAN EVRIE

Not only did the scholarly physician John Van Evrie share all of Nott's spurious arguments, he went even further in prosecuting the idea of white supremacy. The goal as announced in the preface of his book was "a plain, simple, and truthful exposition of the natural order and social adaptation of the white and negro races."[39] For him, that order and adaptation was slavery and absolute subordination to the superior white race. Van Evrie felt competent as a physician to carry out his task, because his "many years of patient study and investigation" into the anatomy of black people proved that "the negro, as has been shown by physiological and material fact, from the necessities of his organism," is "an idle, non-advancing, and non-producing savage" who must be forever "subordinate to the elaborately organized and highly endowed white man."[40]

Even more than Nott, Van Evrie focused his attention on the mental incapacity of black people. He was confident that his clinical experiences proved that "the negro brain is ten to fifteen per cent less than that of the Caucasian."[41] This brain deficiency meant to him that "the negro reaches his mental maturity at twelve or fifteen." It also meant that black people were such imbeciles that even when "a negro [is] condemned to die, to be hanged, to be burned even, [he] rarely manifests any of the dread or apprehension" that "the elaborate and exquisitely organized Caucasian suffers under these same circumstances."[42]

Van Evrie's anatomical degradation of Africans and African Americans reflected his concern that any intermingling between the races should be avoided. One of his greatest fears was that black freedom would lead inevitably to miscegenation and ultimately to the annihilation of the white race. Determined to spread that alarm, he taught that race-mixing would lead unavoidably to "both white and negro becoming so debauched, degraded, and sinful" that "their progeny [would] become sterile, diseased, rotten, and within a certain time, utterly perish from the earth."[43] In his view, medical studies proved the identical truth that Christian ideologues had long upheld, that is, that "the normal condition" of the Negro in America must be subordination because, whether Americans liked it or not, that was the state that "Providence has assigned him."[44]

It is with Van Evrie that we find one of the clearest and most detailed responses to the interesting and eminently fair question, What should be done with white people whose deviant social behaviors and pronounced mental deficiencies demonstrate that they are no better suited for society than so-called inferior blacks? Van Evrie did not miss a step in dealing forthrightly with this hypothetical question. Lashing out against the commonsense idea that there was no real difference between educated and morally upright blacks and whites of the same training and background, he protested that "there could never be such a thing as negro equality equaling the standard Caucasian in natural ability." His own position was precisely to the contrary. He claimed that "the same Almighty Creator has also made all white men equal—for idiots, insane people, etc., are not exceptions, they are the results of human vices, crimes, or ignorance, immediate or remote."[45]

Enlarging upon what the Puritans had insisted centuries before him, Van Evrie held that black people, regardless of their backgrounds, could never be equal to even the lowest specimen of the white race. To the Puritans, God had foreordained the disparity of rank. To Evrie, "God has made the negro an inferior being, not in most cases, but in all cases."[46]

By promulgating the theory that black people's "entire structure, mental and physical" was defective in comparison to all other races, Van Evrie felt vindicated in setting forth his grand idea: that "negro subordination" was "the normal condition of this race." In his mind, therefore, there never was and never could be a completely "free negro." Such a possibility was unthinkable because unguided black freedom would be a violation of both physical and divine laws. Unshepherded black liberation would destroy those laws, because, unlike whites, whom God had created with all the "physical and mental elements" necessary for being fully human, blacks had been created without these elements, thus constituting their normal condition in the world. Van Evrie went so far as to argue that without such essential elements, black people were not free human beings. Moreover, what little humanity they had been given was like "a blank, barren waste" that had to be cultivated before they could develop into anything other than a hopelessly savage people.[47]

Van Evrie did not shrink from the extreme callousness of his position. He boldly maintained that there was only one way that black men and women could begin to rise above the normal condition of their existence and begin moving toward becoming fully free and fully human. This was to submit themselves to their created condition of absolute subordination and to "wait for the husbandman or Caucasian teacher to [help them] develop their real worth."[48] (If this idea of blacks having to wait for white benevolence to bring some kind of improvement in their condition strikes a familiar chord, it is because the same theme played loud and clear during the civil rights movement of the 1960s when white ministers and rabbis proposed to Martin Luther King Jr. that he too should wait.)[49]

ROBERT SHUFELDT

As objectionable as it was, Van Evrie's racism was mild in comparison to that of some other physicians, especially Robert Shufeldt. Shufeldt was so determined to establish the rectitude of white domination that he wrote two books on the subject between 1907 and 1915: *The Negro a Menace to American Civilization* and *America's Greatest Problem: The Negro*. Generally speaking, Shufeldt's program was no different from that of any other white supremacist of his age. But his incredible brutishness and overweening confidence in the infallibility of his medical background vis-à-vis the issue of race make him a rather interesting read.

Beginning with an ethnological discussion of the status of black people, Shufeldt cut to the core of his views by opining that any good physician would be compelled to assert that God had created black people's entire anatomy, from the top of their heads to the bottom of their feet, "much closer to the anthropoid apes than any other race of the genus Homo."[50] Having thus identified blacks as akin to apes, he proceeded to argue that the Civil War had unleashed a calamity upon the land that, if left unchecked, would soon bring about the destruction of the nation. The disaster that would befall America was nothing less than the consequence of the Emancipation Proclamation:

> The truth is that the negro today, untrammeled and free from control, is rapidly showing atavistic tendencies. He is returning to a state of savagery, and in his frequent attacks of sexual madness, his religious emotionalism, superstition, and indolence, is himself again—a savage.[51]

Continuing along this line, Shufeldt exclaimed that "this animalism, this innate character of the African, will demonstrate itself more and more as he is allowed the liberty of his sway."[52] Even more strongly than his medical colleagues, Shufeldt was consumed by the idea that black people were anatomically inferior to the white race and thus were a threat to whites' well-being: "I have dissected males, females, and young of both negroes and mulattoes and found every fiber of their created structure beastly and therefore physically, mentally, and moral unfit to be in any contact with 'perfect and unadulterated' white people."[53]

Shufeldt's intense racial hatred was driven by fear. He was especially horrified that the freedom that had been granted to blacks was enabling them to attain sociopolitical equality and that, as a result, miscegenation abounded. In an effort to turn back the few sociopolitical advances that the recently freed people may have achieved during that period and to rally supporters who opposed race intermixing, he pictured blacks as "savage apes." He also charged them with posing a serious medical threat to the health of the country:

> It is senseless to trifle with this matter; and it is a thoroughly proven fact that the negro in the United States is, among other things, a constant menace to the health of the white race by reason of his being a pronounced disseminator of some five or six of the most dreaded diseases known to man.[54]

Besides accusing blacks of spreading diseases such as yellow fever and tuberculosis, which Shufeldt thought were somehow peculiar to black people, he charged them also as being carriers and disseminators of such exotic diseases as "leprosy, hemoglobinuric fever, filariasis, [and] uncinariasis."[55] (To unpack these diseases: leprosy is commonly called elephant disease; hemoglobinuric fever is a rare illness characterized by an abrupt onset and termination during which blood appears in the urine [typically striking young men in their twenties]; filariasis is an infection of the lymph nodes; and uncinariasis is commonly known as hookworm disease, which attacks the intestinal system.) These devastating pathologies, according to Shufeldt, were all traceable only to blacks.[56]

In a brazen distortion of fact, Shufeldt went even further to assail blacks as the source of most contagious diseases. Along with his colleague Dr. Henry P. Deforest, an obstetrician, Shufeldt placed blame for communicable sexual diseases primarily on the shoulders of black people. "We cannot eliminate syphilis if we maintain thousands of blacks among us who are spreading it. What progress can we make with the white plague when a large percent of its propagation is due to the black race?" Shufeldt inquired of an anxious and gullible American public, reinforcing a stereotype of blacks as having large, uncontrollable sexual appetites.[57]

Blacks' kinship with apes, their proclivity for disease, and their overwhelming sexual appetites—these characteristics Shufeldt claimed were the cause of most, if not all, of the criminal activities that marked his age. Citing blacks in Washington, D.C., as his prime example, he charged that, "as they do everywhere else in the country," blacks

> furnish nine-tenths of the petty and major crimes on our court calendar; as an element they are more dangerous than ever in the matter of assaulting the female sex among whites; their notions of national and municipal politics are just as rotten and debased as they always have been; they are just as much given to every species of mendacity; and they pose as a race-object lesson before our growing generation, in all that is lewd, most degrading, most objectionable, most ignorant and superstitious of the bestial side of the character of the genus Homo.[58]

Although Shufeldt did not use theological language as extensively as Nott and Van Evrie did, he was no less convinced than they that freedom for African Americans was contrary to the laws of God, natural science, medicine, and human history, and that blacks despoiled white America as God's "chosen land."[59] His solutions to "America's greatest problem"—the continued existence of black people—reflected his utter hatred for the race. On a few occasions, he took a more moderate approach and appealed that blacks be removed and resettled in Africa. Most of the time, however, his was a violent and genocidal position not ashamed to propose that "it would doubtless be a capital thing, if it could be done, to emasculate the entire negro race and all of its descendants in this country."[60]

ALL SOUTHERN PHYSICIANS? OR, WHAT DID THEY HAVE TO GAIN?

One might be tempted to believe that Nott, Van Evrie, and Shufeldt, because of the breadth and viciousness of their diatribes against African Americans, were disgruntled southern plantation owners whose livelihoods had been destroyed by the emancipation of 1863. That was not the case, however. Of the three physicians cited here, only Nott was a southerner. Both Shufeldt and Van Evrie were New Yorkers. Indeed, they have earned an unenviable position on a long list of late-nineteenth- and early-twentieth-century northern physicians who led the post–Civil War crusade to defend white supremacy.

The same question that arose concerning the nature of American racism and the reasons New England Puritans became involved in the slave trade arises here. What did northern post–Civil War physicians have to gain by so vigorously advocating black inferiority? Unlike the antebellum slaveholders and other beneficiaries of free enterprise capitalism who had long used economics to defend their positions, northern physicians had no blacks competing with them or their children for admission to medical schools, faced no competition with black physicians for patients (only a few black physicians were practicing after the Civil War), and did not need to assuage white clients.

A possible explanation for the alacrity with which some northern physicians became champions of white supremacy needs to be sought elsewhere than in familiar and convenient economic considerations. An unguarded comment by Shufeldt suggests the real source of racial prejudice among persons in the medical profession. Speaking about why he believed blacks were "America's greatest problem," he likened his position to that of a naturalist:

> One might as well charge a naturalist with prejudice against a vulture and with favoring a blackbird. Both are black; but what a vulture stands for in nature, and what a blackbird stands for, are entirely different

things. The habits of the first-named are repulsive, while the charms of such a gentle and refined songster as the blackbird captivate all who come within his influence.[61]

What lay behind Shufeldt's race hatred was a settled, irrational state of mind that was fueled, ironically, by a pseudoscience. That pseudoscience not only rejected the humanity of black people but would have willed them to be expunged from the earth. In his inmost being, Shufeldt was convinced that Africans and African Americans were not of the same kind as the rest of humanity and, therefore, would somehow continue to contaminate the white race. Once again the unmistakable reverberations of the old racist theological ideas of the Puritans can be heard, now revivified and enhanced by the spurious science of the medical profession at the turn of the century.

WHITE WARRANTS FOR LARGE-SCALE WRONGS

African American journalist and historian Lerone Bennett has said about the sort of inveterate racism expressed during this period, "White men . . . are so constituted that they cannot do wrong on a grand scale without believing that God or history is at their back."[62] Truth demands that we enlarge upon Bennett's judgment by adding the phrase "and all the powers of nature and human inquiry."

The bigoted assumptions of physicians such as Nott, Van Evrie, and Shufeldt had at least two important consequences. From a theoretical vantage point, they gave additional strength to the old theological claim that in comparison with all other races, God had made blacks substandard. From a practical side, they provided pretentious Christian preachers with yet another justification for using their pulpits to proclaim that in America, despite the abolition of slavery, God demanded that God's chosen people continue segregating and discriminating against African Americans.

In addition to the prominent religious figures already discussed, Christian supremacists such as the Most Reverend William M. Brown (a native of Ohio who later became an Episcopalian bishop in Arkansas) seized every opportunity to announce that "it is not only right for Anglo-Americans to recognize the Color Line in the social, political, and religious realms, but more than that, it would be a great sin not to do so."[63] In Brown's mind, white supremacy had to be maintained because any semblance of black association and equality with whites would open a wide door to a violation of nature, societal disorganization, and the desecration of "God's plan in the creation of different races."[64]

The Reverend Atticus G. Haygood, although a moderate in comparison to Brown, shared Brown's racist mind-set. Haygood was a former president of Emory University and a bishop in the Methodist Episcopal Church, South. He authored a popular book entitled *Our Brother in Black: His Freedom and His Future* (1891). Although this writing does show him sincerely wrestling with his southern heritage, it discloses that he was unable to overcome his belief that God, science, and history all proved that white people were naturally above their black brothers and sisters. Thus, while the book is filled with pious rhetoric about the "brotherhood" of all human beings, its carefully crafted preachments add up to the conclusion that whatever the future of African Americans in this country might be, it must of necessity be under the "guidance and protection of a stronger people."[65]

When we assess the consequences of the twisted Christian, scientific, and medical theories that emerged between 1865 and 1920 regarding black people, it is evident that these strange ideas accomplished exactly what their authors and disseminators hoped. They not only condemned African Americans to a subordinate status in God's creation but also helped sentence them to a new, postemancipation form of slavery. That is, wherever blacks turned during those decades, they were consigned to a bitter economic, social, and political oppression based on skin color, a system that has come to be known as Jim Crow.

Summing up blacks' plight from 1880 through 1920, one scholar concluded that they were left "virtually friendless."[66] This description is no overstatement. The party of Lincoln completely abandoned black people. Even reputedly liberal church leaders in the North deserted them. For example, in 1916 the liberal element of the American Bible Society gave its support to racial segregation by joining with conservatives in demanding that black Christians hold their own separate pageant celebrating the one hundredth anniversary of the prestigious society.[67]

Not only were blacks friendless during these years, they also found themselves attacked by a new enemy. This new threat was none other than the leadership of a movement of largely uneducated farming and working-class whites, commonly called the Populist movement.

Strangely, up to that time, these men and women had not voiced openly the doctrine of white supremacy. Although the writings of the movement's leaders do not show them relying on scientific and medical ideas to support white supremacy, the publications of some of the more educated among them indicate that they too found a stronghold for their racism in theological ideas.

An example is found in the writings of Tom Watson, the recognized leader of the Populists in Georgia and a one-time state legislator, U.S. senator, and candidate for vice president of the United States. In a rambling, confused way, Watson drew on the idea that God had created black people savages. On those grounds he declared that because they were a "Hideous, Ominous, National Menace" to society, they had to be segregated from white people. Watson was such an extremist that he was able to condone even murder.[68] He held that it was no sin to use violence against blacks inasmuch as that was the only way to keep them from "blaspheming the Almighty by [their] conduct, smell, and color," which were offensive to all upright white people.[69] The lunacy in this reasoning, grounded in the Christian religion, underscores the desperate tactics that many poor whites and their leaders adopted in an effort to harness theological ideas to a most vicious and reprehensible form of race prejudice.

The occasion of the poor white masses bursting forth to carry the torch of a theologically grounded racism marks a pivotal moment in American history. For the first time, power brokers of the society— church leaders, scientists, physicians, politicians, business tycoons—had a huge army of pawns to do their bidding. These patricians believed that the best way to maintain their power was to take the focus off themselves by creating envy, division, and animosity between the white and black have-nots.

Ironically, the cynical strategy of these patricians did not deceive all Populist leaders. Early in Watson's career as the foremost spokesman of the People's Party movement, he became so painfully aware of this manipulation that he formed a coalition of poor blacks and poor whites. His purpose was to lead this biracial alliance to oppose the racism and classism that power elites were imposing on the two groups.[70] He was convinced that the only way the two impoverished populations could overcome their plight was to rise up against their common oppressor— the overlords of the society. Watson warned both whites and blacks in 1892 that it was these upper-class guardians of the status quo who had developed the strategy of dividing and inflaming them against each other in order to "perpetuate a monetary system which beggars you both."[71]

But this clear-sighted analysis of capitalist oppression was short-lived. Watson and his Populists soon abandoned an alliance with blacks that was indispensable for their own struggle against the classism of the privileged rural and urban bosses. C. Vann Woodward, the noted scholar of Populism, sets forth two reasons for this turn of affairs: first, the personal ambitions of white Populist leaders to get themselves elected to political offices; and, second, black venality in dealings with both Republicans and Democrats, especially during and immediately following Reconstruction.[72]

The merit of these explanations notwithstanding, they fail to consider one other critical factor. Gerald Gaither, another scholar of the Populist movement, has written that the Populists were caught between the "Scylla of race and the Charybdis of reform."[73] That is, the Populists were also ensnared between the two unchangeable realities of whiteness and blackness; from the Puritan era to the era of Populism, Christian theologians had taught that whiteness was godly and superior, while blackness was evil and inferior. Although the Populists found unbearable the economic hardships and social alienation imposed on them by the white upper class, they simply could not transcend the "gospel news" preached by their learned peers that God had given whites priority over African Americans. It is most unfortunate that they failed to see that this racist gospel, preached by the privileged oligarchy, harmed not only blacks but also poor whites.

FROM 1920 TO 1955

An unparalleled shift in the promotion of these ideas occurred between 1920 and 1955. The poor white masses became virtually the only exponents of the corrupt gospel of racism. The voices of educated leaders of the church, the academy, and medical science became strangely silent. The unprecedented silence of these public intellectuals did not mean—as one scholar has speculated—that "a marked change was occurring in the attitudes [among the white intelligentsia] toward race."[74] There was, in fact, little real change in the attitudes of the intellectual opinion makers of the society. Rather, the calm seems to have signaled that the ideologues were merely preoccupied with other problems that they considered to be, at least for the time being, greater threats to their vision of America as the most Christian and most civilized nation in the world. Chief among the problems claiming their attention were the Great Depression and the Second World War.

The silence of the white intellectual community also indicated that many saw no need to continue defining and articulating the racial theories of the nation. Argued about for more than two centuries, the racial doctrines I have discussed had by now crystallized into America's most widely accepted creed. Not only were average poor white citizens now preaching this creed with evangelical fervor, they were also making it dangerously concrete in acts of violence, particularly in the case of organized terrorist groups such as the Ku Klux Klan. The stated mission of the Klan—which had been revived in 1915 by William J. Simmons, a sometime camp-meeting preacher—was to "unite native-born Christians for concerted action in the preservation of American institutions and the supremacy of the white race."[75] This terse statement of purpose had been spawned out of the theological, and to a lesser degree scientific, argument that God or nature had ordained blacks "morally unfit" to live and prosper alongside white people in American society.[76]

The hushed voices of Christians and other intellectuals between 1920 and 1955 proved to be nothing more than a nervous, deceptive calm before the storm. Just as the Union victory in the Civil War had brought on a backlash of racist Christian ideas in both the North and the South, the gathering storm over the successes of the civil rights movement of the 1960s would unleash a similar burst of fury against black people. This time the fury would be directed against the liberation movements in the black community that helped finally to secure a modicum of social, economic, and political freedom and equality for African Americans.

Although this second response of white America, like the first, has been ignored in most studies of American racism, it was predictable that participants in the black movements, together with their radical white allies, would incite a new generation of intellectuals, scientists, and assorted ideologues to rise up and resuscitate old theological ideas of race. The one critical difference this time would be that the changing racial ethos of the nation would force these learned gatekeepers of society to reclothe dying theories in cunningly refashioned garb. It is to this second refacing of the old religious ideas about race that we turn in the next chapter.

THE QUEST FOR THE GREAT
WHITE PAST, 1955 TO...

From the early decades of the 1600s, when Puritan Christians first defined black people as inferior and made slavery their "normal condition," until the mid-1950s, blacks used every means available to free themselves from this brutal racism. Some put their trust in prayer, some turned to social protests, others tried reasoning, and still others staked their hopes on open revolt.[1] Nothing they or their sympathetic white allies tried was able to extract and deal a deathblow to the ideas of inferiority rooted in the American mind.

AWAKENING AMERICA TO CIVIL RIGHTS

But a miraculous change in the American mind appeared to be occurring during the early 1960s. The disparate black civil rights movements that began to emerge during the mid-1950s seemed to be the forces that would finally transform this hardened and racially intolerant mind into one that would accept real freedom and equality for African Americans. Collectively, the Southern Christian Leadership Conference (SCLC), led by Martin Luther King Jr., the Congress of Racial Equality (CORE), led by Floyd McKissick, and the more in-your-face movements of Malcolm X, Stokely Carmichael, Angela Davis, and H. Rap Brown at last seemed to be awakening America to rid itself of its old ideas of white supremacy.

Despite their differing strategies for racial uplift, these movements combined to expose the rawness of the acts of race prejudice. Such brutality was notably disclosed in 1963 in Birmingham, Alabama. In the early spring of that year, police unleashed a ferocious attack on a group of demonstrators as they were being led by Dr. King in protest of racial discrimination in the city. Inundated with letters and telegrams from across the world expressing outrage at this inhumanity, President John F. Kennedy went on national television on June 11 to declare that "the events in Birmingham and elsewhere have so increased the cries for equality" that "the time has come for this nation to fulfill its promise" of freedom and equality for all people, regardless of their skin color.[2]

Following Kennedy's assassination in November 1963, President Lyndon B. Johnson sought to complete Kennedy's promise by signing into law the well-known Civil Rights Act of 1964 and the Voting Rights Act of 1965. The goal of these unprecedented secular laws was to help usher in Johnson's vision of a Great Society in which the institutional race hatred that had enslaved, segregated, impoverished, disenfranchised, and killed countless blacks since the Puritan era would finally be abolished.

Aided by continuing pressure from the black civil rights movements and by the actions and voices of sympathetic white allies, this is precisely what the new laws seemed certain to do. For only the second time in their experience in this land, persons of African descent now had a legal right to privileges and opportunities they previously could only long for. No longer could racist practices legally force them to retreat to the rear of society. They now began to become visible and active participants throughout mainstream America. They were free to work, live, study, and move wherever they desired and could afford. From a legal perspective, integration at last had become a reality for this race. At least this was the dream.

But the ink on the civil rights laws had barely dried before the vision of the final demise of racism proved to be yet one more in the long history of broken promises. The reason: the legal and political deposing of racism as a set of concrete institutional practices did not address the need for a moral transformation. African Americans now had a legal right to the freedom and equality that had so long been denied them; but this right, unlike the rights enjoyed by others, did not include any widespread affirmation of a moral and theological presumption that God had created all human beings equal and had endowed all human beings with inalienable rights to liberty and the pursuit of happiness.

On the contrary, the minds of many Americans remained clouded with the Christianized arguments that God had singled out and imposed on black people an inferiority that made them heathens who were eternally unfit to possess the same human rights others enjoyed. Without a conversion from these ill-omened theological confessions, racism would not be ended. These wicked religious ideas needed to be rooted out, because they had been the driving element that defined and legitimized the actual practices of racism, in both the secular and religious realms.

MARTIN LUTHER KING JR. AND MALCOLM X

The two most prominent black civil rights leaders of the 1950s and 1960s, Dr. Martin King and Malcolm X, primarily focused their demonstrations against bigotry as acted out in institutions and everyday practices. Each was well aware that old racial ideas were the heart and soul of American racism. King had been active as a civil rights leader for only three years when, reflecting on race relations, he concluded "that in the final analysis, the problem of race in America is not a political but a moral issue." He warned that if there was any hope of removing race as the number one issue in society, then the nation must first "get to the ideational roots of race hate, something that the law cannot accomplish."[3] As he so rightly pointed out, white churches had a "historic obligation in this crisis," because, although they had been "called to be the moral guardian of the community," they historically had been in the forefront of promoting and preserving "that which is immoral and unethical," including the un-Christian doctrine of black inferiority.[4]

Not only did Malcolm share King's view that the first priority must be to "get to the ideational roots of race hate," but, as one might have expected, he pointed out this need in an even more straightforward manner. "The Holy Bible in the White man's hands and his interpretations of it," Malcolm declared, "have been the greatest ideological weapon for enslaving millions of non-white human beings."[5] Both King and Malcolm were convinced that there could be no end to the actual deeds of racism until there first was an end to the Christian teachings that informed those practices.

THE EARLY 1960S, A TIME OF TRANSITION

If there ever was a moment in American history when it should have been easy to rid America's mind from the age-old racist theological claims, it was during the early 1960s. Just as the Civil War had done a century earlier, the black civil rights movements of these years bared the lie of such notions. But even more so than the Civil War, these movements demonstrated for the nation, as well as the world, that racism was a moral issue and that white churches historically had played a leading role in making it so.

Although leaders of the many movements that sprang up were not the first African Americans to cast race hate in this fashion,[6] they did it at a most propitious time. The early years of the 1960s were ones of widespread dissatisfaction with status quo ways of thinking and acting. Spurred on in large part by the black civil rights movements, calls for revolts against dated standards and customs were everywhere in the air. Most, if not all, of America's established and cherished institutions and philosophies came under this unparalleled scrutiny and assault. Even churches and their theological ideas—heretofore one of America's most protected bastions—now came under serious attack.

THE NATIONAL CONFERENCE OF BLACK CHURCHMEN

Among those questioning and challenging the morality of established white Christian teachings and practices was a small army of African American clergy and academicians who were members of the National Conference of Black Churchmen (NCBC). The NCBC was first organized in 1966 as the National Committee of Negro Churches, a movement dedicated to leading the fight to help bring real economic, social, and political power to black people.[7] The NCBC became quite prominent in the wake of Dr. King's assassination on April 4, 1968.

King and other leaders of the more moderate civil rights movements of the late 1950s and early 1960s had been content with the social integration wrought by the civil rights laws of 1964 and 1965. In contrast, leaders of the NCBC insisted that such laws and integration had not gone far enough in liberating and empowering black people. Gayraud Wilmore, the noted African American historian, theologian, and member of the NCBC, provides a clear assessment: NCBC leaders were convinced that integration in the marketplaces and neighborhoods had not effected any genuine change in the attitudes of traditional power structures "that [had long] molded public opinion regarding race relations."[8]

From the viewpoint of these Black Power advocates, the secular and ecclesiastical religious rulers of this nation not only still clung to the old theological notion of black inferiority but—despite the civil rights laws of 1964 and 1965—also made sure that black people did not share in the real economic, political, and social power that could make a genuine and positive difference in black life in this land. These clergy rightly argued that without such black empowerment there could be no real integration. African Americans would continue to be the oppressed and subordinate race in society.

To make their position clear, in 1966, leaders of the NCBC formulated "Black Power," a statement they addressed to both the secular and the ecclesiastical custodians of racist power structures. Confronting white Christendom for its refusal to affirm the legitimacy of black empowerment, the statement read in part as follows:

> It is not enough to answer that "integration" is the solution [to the race problem]. . . . Without [the] capacity to participate with power—i.e., to have some organized political and economic strength to really influence people with whom one interacts—integration is not meaningful.[9]

Elaborating on what true integration must entail, the statement declared that "a more equal sharing of power is precisely what is required as the precondition of authentic human interaction."[10]

In 1969, three years after the issuance of the NCBC Black Power statement, a black economic development conference was convened on the campus of Wayne State University in Detroit. Participants in this conference included representatives from the NCBC, the Interreligious Foundation for Community Organization (IFCO), and a number of other prominent Black Power advocates.

One of the most significant outcomes of this conference was the famous "Black Manifesto" of 1969. Not only did this document challenge white Christians for their past leadership role in promoting slavery and race subordination, it also demanded that both they and Jews now make amends for their "exploitation and rape of black people since the country was founded."[11] This compensation was to be economic reparations in the amount of $500 million.

Not since Henry Highland Garnet's *Address to Slaves* in 1843 had there been such a powerful appeal for black people to rise up and demand freedom and justice from their oppressors.[12] This appeal was more than just a written document to be mailed to the churches. It took concrete form on Sunday morning, May 4, 1969. On this day,

James Forman, the international affairs director of the Student Non-violent Coordinating Committee, marched down the aisle of one of America's most prestigious churches—Riverside Church in New York City—and delivered the "Black Manifesto" to the pastor and congregation. Over the next few months, Black Power advocates presented the manifesto to other churches across the nation.

The Rise of Black Theology

The next few months also saw the publication of one of the first twentieth-century critiques of the racist theology of white churches: James H. Cone's *Black Theology and Black Power*. Cone wrote this book as a scholar of the history of Christian theology and also as a black man who was angry at the devastation and death of his people. Martin King had just been assassinated; racism was continuing to be heaped upon black people.

Turning to the churches, Cone called their attention to the racism of an integration that "at this stage [in America's history] too easily lends itself to supporting the moral superiority of white society" through its refusal to acknowledge the common humanity of black people and their right to be economically and politically empowered. "If there is any contemporary meaning of the Antichrist," Cone declared, "the white church seems to be a manifestation of it." He castigated the churches for their history of placing "God's approval on slavery" and God's "blessings on the racist structure[s] of American society" today. Going even further, Cone scolded the churches for their theological hypocrisy in condemning the black quest for power while at the same time not "saying a word about white power and its 350 years of constant violence against blacks."[13]

Cone continued his critique of the churches in *A Black Theology of Liberation* (1970). This was the first writing of this era to decry the bankruptcy of a Christian theology that was used to single out and dehumanize a people because of their skin color. Among other points, Cone argued that "in a society where men [and women] are oppressed, [genuine] Christian theology must become *Black Theology* because of its symbolic power to convey both what whites mean by oppression and what blacks mean by liberation."[14] Cone rightly perceived that any theology that championed racism was neither truly Christian nor moral.

Cone was not the only African American theologian to critique American Christianity and find it wanting. Others included Vincent

Harding, J. Deotis Roberts, Preston Williams, and Albert Cleage. Although these scholars took differing angles, they agreed that traditional white Christian theology was an obscenity that continued to support the robbery and degradation of black humanity.

Radical White Critiques

African Americans were not the only ones rising up during the late 1960s to declare the fraudulence of a theology that kept human beings oppressed and dehumanized. Although these groups included a few white male theologians and white feminist theologians and did not focus on racism and the debasement of black people, each of these two groups, in varying ways, raised serious doubts about the morality and utility of conventional Christian ideas.

For example, some white male theologians went so far as to propose that the traditional God was dead and that theological ideas from the distant past were therefore useless. Writings of these theologians included H. Richard Niebuhr's *Radical Monotheism* (1960); Schubert Ogden's *Christ without Myth* (1961); Harvey Cox's *Secularization and Urbanization in Theological Perspective* (1965); Philip Berrigan's *No More Strangers* (1965); and Thomas J. Altizer and William Hamilton's *Radical Theology and the Death of God* (1966).[15]

Seeking to free themselves from the exploitation of theological and sociopolitical sexism, white feminist theologians also began to assail historical Christianity. The writings of feminist theologians such as Rosemary Ruether's *The Church against Itself: An Inquiry into the Conditions of Historical Existence for the Eschatological Community* (1967) and Mary Daly's *Beyond God the Father: Toward a Philosophy of Women's Liberation* (1973) sounded passionate calls for their female peers to confront and "move beyond" the patriarchal theologies that had long kept them outsiders to the faith.[16]

Even some white middle-class college students joined in rebelling against historic Christian teachings. Seeking to transcend the antiquated dogmas of the religious faith of their parents, they turned to "New Age" religions, forming groups such as the Jesus Freaks, Street Christians, the God Squad, and the Children of God. By 1971, this "Jesus movement" had settled on college campuses across the country through more formal organizations, such as Young Life, Navigation for Christ, Campus Crusade for Christ, and Inter-Varsity Christian Fellowship.[17]

The White Churches' Fizzled Response

Several white Christian denominations, faced with these unprecedented diverse and thunderous demands for an end to old racist, sexist, and imperialistic theological ideas and ecclesiastical practices, initially showed some signs of repentance from their past sins. As this apparent atonement bore directly on racism, powerful denominations and religious bodies such as the United Methodist Church, the Episcopal Church, the Presbyterian Church U.S.A., the United Church of Christ, the Lutheran Church in America, the Disciples of Christ, and the Unitarian-Universalists initiated various programs that suggested a rejection of their racist past. Besides issuing official statements denouncing racism in thought or deed, these initiatives included forming caucuses to study and improve race relations, establishing black and white co-pastored churches, ordaining black bishops to oversee integrated episcopal districts and dioceses, providing funding for programs to assist with racial elevation, and recruiting African American students to church-related universities and seminaries.[18] These ecclesiastical-sponsored programs seemed to promise to combine with the civil rights laws of 1964 and 1965 in helping usher in a new day in race relations in America. The churches finally seemed to be discarding the antiquated notions of black inferiority.

But this promise was short-lived. Less than a year after Forman took the "Black Manifesto" into the sanctuary of Riverside Church, mainline churches began to back away from their commitments to the struggle for black liberation and justice and began to reaffirm old theories of race. Using the theological language popular during this time, one interpreter has said of this abrupt falling away of the churches, "By 1970 the *kairos* moment of the 1960s in race relations had disappeared for the National Council of Churches and for the mainline denominations, and *chronos* once again had taken over."[19]

Several explanations have been given for why the churches forsook the opportunity (*kairos*) to break with the status quo (*chronos*) of race relations. These include

- the failure of those at the top of the ecclesiastical hierarchies to communicate their personal change in racial attitudes with their grassroots constituencies, whose voices ultimately would decide whether to abandon racism
- the decline in church membership that resulted from a white backlash against efforts to promote racial equality

- the fatal decision of the Presbyterian Church to help fund the legal defense for Angela Davis, who had been charged with being an accessory to the murder of a trial judge in California[20]

But lurking beneath these and other possible explanations were the twisted theological confessions of white supremacy that the churches had so long preached. Despite whatever sincerity may have been behind their initial efforts to seize the moment and root those ideas out of their being, the churches, like secular institutions, could not expunge and purify their minds and hearts completely of these age-old confessions. Apart from everything else they might attempt, these romanticizers of the past could not bring themselves to view black people as anything but black and certainly less than themselves.

Indeed, fearing the prospect of having at last to affirm the humanity of African Americans and thus to share power with them, the conservative ideological foes of black people wasted no time in searching for new ways to keep America's mind fixated on the racial patterns of thought from the distant past. Their goal of immediately restoring the great white past, however, was not easy to achieve. They were confronted by the same problem that has confronted romantics whenever successful revolts against the status quo have taken place. This problem is how to maintain conventional patterns of thought and social custom in light of dramatic intellectual and sociopolitical changes in society.

Although no one would dare claim that antidiscrimination laws and ideological and cultural revolts had erased racism from this land, these forces did combine to make it difficult for America to continue doing racial business as it had in past eras. Overt acts of discrimination now became subject to legal redress, while overt use of derogatory and racist language became subject to boycotts and economic censorship. In today's vernacular, bad ideas became politically incorrect in the late 1960s and early 1970s.

THE CUNNING NEW FACES OF OLD IDEAS

Here we see still another side of racism as a set of religious ideas. Even when there should be no way to keep such ideas alive, confessors of the notion of black inferiority have always found cunning ways to rescue them from history's dustbin and breathe new life into them. The often overlooked lesson is that racist ideas, like viruses, have not only a long life in the body but also an ability to mutate to look like respectable ideas. Or, to change metaphors, racist ideas have a masterfully cunning ability to change faces, especially when their existence is threatened by unparalleled racial, gender, and sociopolitical revolutions in the society.

Edward C. Banfield

The year 1968 is infamous for two reasons: racism struck down Martin Luther King Jr., and Richard M. Nixon was elected president. In just over six months, the 1960s dream to end racism died. Or, better, it went up in the fiery flames of a counterattack on black progress that was just as cunning as it was blistering.

This white backlash was led by those who have commonly been called right-wing conservatives. These idealizers of the past had lacked the political power necessary to restore white supremacy during the Kennedy and Johnson administrations. But when Nixon was elected president, their fortunes changed. A staunch defender of traditional systems and beliefs—indeed, even racist ones—Nixon announced his fundamental agenda, "to restore law and order in this country" as quickly as possible.[21]

Here is our first glimpse of the cunning track American racism began to take during the late 1960s and early 1970s. According to conservatives, their theme of restoring law and order had to do not with race per se but rather with the violence that often was associated with the various protests and dissenting movements of the era, such as the anti–Vietnam War protest, the abortion conflict, the radical "burn, baby, burn" Black Power movement, the emerging drug culture, and so on. Despite what conservative men and women said publicly, the law-and-order motif was in fact nothing but a craftily disguised strategy for helping reclaim the great white past. Although they were shrewd enough not to declare it openly, Nixon and his right-wing colleagues were convinced that the social, economic, and political gains black people were beginning to obtain through civil rights laws and desegregation and affirmative action programs were a serious threat to America's traditional way of conducting its racial business.[22]

In the minds of Nixon and conservatives all across the country, the tide of black progress had to be stopped. As president, Nixon wasted no time in seeking to achieve this agenda. Shortly after assuming the office, he appointed Edward C. Banfield to chair a task force on the federal Model Cities program that had been initiated under the administration of President Johnson. As is commonly known, Johnson had begun Model Cities as a part of his dream of a Great Society from which the disease of racism would be extirpated.

Before his appointment, Banfield was a renowned professor whose teaching career included tenure at three of the most prestigious universities in the country—Harvard, the University of Chicago, and the University of Pennsylvania. Thus, he enjoyed widespread prestige among elites and politicians alike. The charge to Banfield's task force was to evaluate Model Cities and to recommend whether it was worthy of being continued. Within a short time, the task force recommended overwhelmingly that the program be discontinued with the utmost dispatch.

This recommendation was not simply a pragmatic economic, social, or political policy judgment. It reeked of the racist theological ideas that have been the cornerstone of American polity for nearly four hundred years. Indeed, one could have predicted that the counsel of the task force would be rooted in pseudo-Christian theories of race. The evidence comes from Banfield, who published *The Unheavenly City Revisited* in 1968. His book provides great insight into the historic interconnectedness between American religion and racism.

This book, like few others of the time, captured the changing faces and new directions American racism would begin to take in response to the dramatic changes in race relations of the 1960s. Despite civil rights laws, uncorrupted theological, biblical, and scientific evidence, and other proofs to the contrary, intelligent persons so inclined can still use old racist claims to declare black people inferior to whites and therefore unfit for equality in society.

The Unheavenly City Revisited begins with an epigraph from the most heralded Puritan divine, Cotton Mather: "Come hither and I will show you, an admirable Spectacle! 'Tis an Heavenly City . . . A City to be inhabited by an Innumerable Company of Angels, and by the spirits of Just Men. . . . *Put on thy beautiful Garments, O America, the Holy City [of God]*!"[23]

It is no coincidence that President Nixon chose Banfield to head the Model Cities task force. Aware of Banfield's book, Nixon knew that this intellectual ideologue shared his determination to incite the white masses into reviving and restoring their ancestors' vision of making this nation a city of God where the affirmation of black humanity could be viewed as not only a social error but also a theological sin. (The holy city is peopled with smiling white people clothed in white baptismal garments and backed by angels and their virtuous men.) African Americans were never to ascend beyond the lowest rung of God's alleged hierarchy of humanity. But I am getting ahead of an analysis of Banfield's book.

Banfield skillfully disguised his book as an urban studies analysis, a pragmatic evaluation of Model Cities and the black people whom the program was supposed to be helping. Accordingly, he proposed that the program was proving to be not only ineffective but also threatening to the sacrosanct vision of what America should be, precisely because it encouraged the continuation of the blight and urban decay that, in his view, was defiling this nation as God's New Jerusalem.

Instead of openly using the doctrine of creation to justify his conclusion, Banfield attempted to justify it by employing a new way of arguing black inferiority. He pointed to the psychological and class differences between blacks and whites. Cunningly (or naively?) following in the footsteps of his Puritan ancestors, Banfield began the defense of his position by rejecting the notion that white racism played any role in the persistence of the urban blight and disintegration that he claimed were destroying the land of his forebears.

Instead of directly invoking the Puritan theory that God-ordained black inferiority and black people's alleged proclivity to sin caused them to be outsiders in God's holy land, he recast these old ideas under the rubric of the "imperative of class culture." By "class culture" he meant a state or condition governed by people's innate psychological abilities rather than by external social forces. He then categorized human beings on the basis of their psychological "ability (or willingness) to take account of the future." According to him, upper-class human beings are those born with a native ability to plan for the future, while lower-class human beings are born psychologically unable to plan or even to think beyond the present:

> The lower class individual lives from moment to moment. . . . Impulse governs his behavior either because he cannot discipline himself to sacrifice a present for a future satisfaction or because he has no sense of the future. He is therefore radically improvident: whatever he cannot use immediately he considers valueless. His bodily needs (especially for sex) and his taste for action, take precedence over everything else—and certainly any work routine. He works only as he must to stay alive,

and drifts from one unskilled job to another, taking no [enduring]
interest in his work.[24]

Banfield then drew a distinction between lower-class and working-class
people. In comparison to a working-class person, a lower-class person
"doesn't want much success, knows he couldn't get it even if he wanted
to, and doesn't want what might help him get success." Going even
further, he wrote that lower-class people, "in [their] relations with
others," are "suspicious and hostile, aggressive."[25] Now, who might fit
under his category of lower-class people? Unfortunately, he concluded
with a teary face, the majority of lower-class persons are African
Americans. So what is the news?

Banfield simply camouflaged the racist theological language that
has dominated this land since the Puritans' time. True, now it was
masked in the new garments of psychological and sociological language. But even here there is nothing new. John Saffin, a Puritan, had
used almost the exact same method of psychological, class, and cultural
character assassination of black people (albeit in embryonic form)
nearly three centuries earlier (see chapter 1). Banfield merely—but,
indeed, ever so shrewdly—repackaged old theological theories into the
same three categories.

By skillfully recasting the Puritans' Christian theories into psychological, class, and cultural categories, not only did Banfield help rescue
them from their apparent deathbed, he also provided his fellow conservatives a slick new way of restating and using those age-old theories
against African Americans. The easiest way to reawaken the white
masses against African Americans was to rekindle the hatred that still
dominated the American mind. Here we have come to the ability of
American racism to change faces cunningly when its sacredness is
threatened by powerful transformations in the society.

Charles Murray and Richard Herrnstein

Other social scientists have been prominent among those imitating
Banfield's reclothed theological ideas. The more notable in the field
have been Arthur R. Jensen, William Shockley, Charles Murray, and
Richard Herrnstein. Building on Banfield's theory that black inferiority is a psycho-class-cultural matter, Jensen and Shockley have focused
on intelligence and education among black people. They use these
themes not merely to argue that African Americans have an intelligence

deficit as compared to whites, but also to strike fear in the minds of the masses through their prediction that a "dysgenic trend" among black Americans "threatens to make [them] a race of idiots" who should have no place in America.[26]

The recent (but not new) trend of attacking black people's mental capacities and mental backgrounds has continued in the theories of Murray and Herrnstein. In 1984, just sixteen years after Banfield published his book, Charles Murray published his *Losing Ground: American Social Policy, 1950–1980*. This work echoes many of Banfield's ideas. The affirmative action programs of the Johnson administration, Murray contends, succeeded only in wasting taxpayers' money and encouraging lower-class poor people to continue to prey upon the society.[27] Who are the lower-class poor people? Mostly African Americans.

Murray and Herrnstein collaborated to publish *The Bell Curve: Intelligence and Class Structure in American Life* in 1994 (the year Herrnstein died). The central thrust of this book is that out of all the inhabitants of this world, black people possess the most genetically inferior intelligent quotient (IQ). Thus, black people are the greatest threat to the well-being of any advanced civilization. These men prophesied that the only way to ward off this threat would be for the superior race to create a "custodial state" in which "genetically inferior" black people would be "policed" and governed by "the cognitive elite."[28]

Like both Banfield and the Puritans before them, Herrnstein and Murray were convinced that there is a hierarchy of humanity and that black people—except for a gifted minority, the so-called exceptions— are the lowest in this "great chain of being." Attempting to temper the racism of such a position, they offered the apology that the majority of African Americans have become this way "through no fault of their own but because of inherent shortcomings about which little can be done."[29]

Here again is the fruit of Puritanism's theological seeds of racism. The spirit of these ethnocentric ideas is remarkably similar, whether articulated by Banfield or others before him. In this same vein, Herrnstein and Murray denied that racism or any other external forces have caused these mental and moral aberrations among black people. Such denial could bring only one other conclusion. In their minds, they were certain that persons of African descent are intellectually and morally inferior to all other races (whether God or nature created them that way).

Republican Presidents

In the past thirty years, presidents—for the first time since the antebellum years—have also been at the forefront in using ethnocentric racial theories to legitimize white supremacy. Following the tradition of Richard Nixon, Presidents Ronald Reagan and George Bush called on Banfield's ideas of race to legitimate their positions.

Reagan's entire public career was fraught with the conviction that black people are unfit for full participation in this society. As governor of California, he supported the repeal of the Rumford Act, which made it illegal for a property owner to offer property for sale and then withdraw the offer because of the racial or religious background of a potential buyer. He also fought vigorously against the Civil Rights Act of 1964. During his eight years as president, he did many things within his authority to ensure that this society would not become color-blind. Among his more glaring acts, Reagan appointed William Bradford Reynolds—a staunch enemy of the black civil rights movements and its leaders—as assistant attorney general for civil rights; fought initially, in 1982, to gut the 1965 Voting Rights Act when it came up for renewal; initiated a supply-side economic program that funded the rich but was devastating to all lower- and middle-income people and especially to African Americans; and appointed judges to the Supreme Court who were unsympathetic to black civil rights.[30]

George Bush's record on black civil rights was far more positive than either Nixon's or Reagan's. In part, this may be because he had benefited from the work of his Republican predecessors. Yet Bush was not above using Banfield's reformulation of old racist and ethnocentric ideas for his own political ends. His television campaign commercial depicting a black man, Willie Horton, being freed from prison only to rape a white woman was not subtle. But neither did it need interpretation. The unheavenly city was revisited in a mere sixty seconds.

Republican Politicians

The fact that Patrick Buchanan has never had much hope of being elected president has not stopped him from using cunning racial theories like those of Banfield to undermine black progress. His record, both as a politician and as a host of a television talk show, demonstrates how determined he and his conservative colleagues have been to recover the great white past. As a presidential candidate in 1992, he craftily built his campaign on race:

This election is about more than who gets what. It is about who we are. It is about what we believe and what we stand for as Americans. There is a religious war going on in this country for the soul of America. It is a cultural war as critical to the kind of nation we shall be as the Cold War [was] itself.[31]

Although his words on this occasion did not appear to reflect race, the religious and cultural war that Buchanan has eagerly waged over the past thirty years focuses on whether a traditional (white) America, in its families, can continue to dominate, or whether a modicum of diversity will be enfranchised. Included on the diversity side are women in non-traditional roles, gays and lesbians, and African Americans—all of whom are threats to biological clusters of white fathers, mothers, and children when such diversity is not controlled. Yet I zero in on race because of Buchanan's other remarks. For example, in 1992, contrasting present-day Washington, D.C., with that city in his youth, he lamented that "before all that crowd came rolling in," with "these guys [lobbyists or African Americans?] playing bongo drums," his hometown had been a dignified and respectable place.[32]

To clarify just who might have made Buchanan's Washington undignified and disrespectful, we need only examine his campaign in the Georgia Republican primary. A master of slick innuendo, he played Banfield's view of blacks (now often called "the race card") to an extreme in that primary. For example, he used a television commercial that depicted gay black men dressed in leather harnesses, wearing chains, dancing, and celebrating their homosexuality. The message? The cultural diversity crowd, depicted in black men, is "culturally and morally" bankrupt vis-à-vis righteous white folk.[33]

Rising to the powerful position of Speaker of the House in 1994, Newt Gingrich has been just as aggressive as Buchanan in continuing Banfield's cunning racism. Gingrich, a historian who is familiar with the thoughts and practices of the Puritans, is well aware of the historic racial buttons that can be pushed to perpetuate the myth of black inferiority. Despite his facades to the contrary, he is fervently committed to the idea that African Americans are unworthy participants in the holy land of his forefathers and foremothers.

For example, Gingrich has spoken publicly on many occasions about how urban "welfare Americans" are not only societal piranhas who refuse to work so that they can remain on the good welfare of the state, but also enemies of "traditional family values" who are prone to having illegitimate children and wallowing in the gutters of life.[34] This public servant, who is frequently seen in church praying to God, has combined his understanding of Banfield with his knowledge of Puritanism to foster among traditional whites a perception of African Americans as immoral, uncouth, and indolent threats to the sanctity of this holy empire.

Conservative Religious-Political Organizations

The Reverend Pat Robertson, founder of the powerful and highly influential Christian Coalition, continues to inundate the airwaves and print media with affirmations of the Puritan notion that America can never become the "heavenly city" as long as African Americans are indulged in federal entitlement programs. Robertson employs flaming and tearful emotionalism to convince his television viewers of their sins. Yet he has attempted to mute his own racism by employing the more politically correct language of "traditional family values."

Ralph Reed served as the executive director of Robertson's Christian Coalition from 1989 to 1997. During his last year, Reed founded the Samaritan Project, whose goal was to bring white conservative Christians into an alliance with African American Christians to revitalize inner-city neighborhoods. He said he was determined to form this alliance in part because of the sad history of conservative evangelical Christians relative to slavery and other forms of racism:

> The past complicity of the white church in the mistreatment of African-Americans and Jews is too large a blot on our history to deny. Tragically, white evangelicals did not merely look the other way as African-Americans were denied full equality and participation in American life. They were among the most fiery champions of slavery and later segregation—all the while invoking God's name and quoting the Bible to justify their misdeeds.[35]

Now examine Reed's double-sided actions on race. On the positive side, his Samaritan Project proposed to bring the network of 125,000 Christian Coalition churches and their tremendous economic power into partnership with 1,000 inner-city churches to aid the rebuilding of urban cities and also the black churches that arsonists recently burned across the country. It also proposed to use white money to help fund a May 1997 conference in Baltimore at which black and white Christians would come together to develop an agenda for cooperation across racial and cultural lines.

On the negative side, Reed continued to be a visible, articulate leader in the conservative war against every federal and state program designed to level the playing field between the races. Moreover, his "plan for action" to "make America stronger and better" in the future glaringly omitted any discussion of racism. Instead it listed four priorities that conservative Christians needed to pursue: working to restore prayer in public schools; joining the Christian Coalition's participation in the political process; using persuasion rather than preaching to convince others of the conservative agenda; and never quitting the conservative struggle to effect political and social changes that will help restore America to its golden past.[36]

Reed made it a practice to denounce openly the white churches' role in racism in the past. Although he professed to be an advocate for "a genuinely inclusive movement that embraces the full diversity of America," he persisted in crafty attempts to discredit liberal black civil rights leaders. For example, quoting a survey of the conservative black economist Walter Williams of George Mason University, Reed proudly lifted up Williams's claim that blacks "have more in common with Jerry Falwell than Jesse Jackson [who] has more in common with white hippies than black people" as an accurate view of the entire black community.[37]

Some might argue that it is too early to judge whether there was any sincerity in Reed's effort to form a coalition of blacks and whites. But his racist tactic of using the words of one black to deride and dismiss another smacks of the divide-and-conquer strategy that guardians of the past have long used to control the black community and to keep it second-class. That Reed and his followers are an apparition of the past becomes even more plausible because of his refusal to place racism high on his list of social ills that demand immediate attention.

Moreover, showing the exact same arrogance and contempt for blacks that white supremacists have always shown, Reed never consulted black church and civil rights leaders about his Samaritan Project. Instead, he simply announced it as if it were a foregone conclusion. "We are bringing our money and this is what we think is best for you colored folk." Thus, it appears that Reed and his fellow conservative Christians do not genuinely have the welfare of black people in their hearts but are interested only in securing their votes for the purpose of supporting white political and social agendas. Based on available evidence, they come, not convinced that blacks and whites are all members of the body of Christ, but weighed down with all the racist baggage of those who, over the past four centuries, may have vehemently preached black and white unity as a political ideal but just as fervently have preached black inferiority as the enduring word of God.

Conservative White Religious Leaders

In light of the positive changes in the racial attitudes of many white religionists during the 1960s and 1970s, one would expect that post-1960s white Christian leaders would have led the way in hurling righteous indignation against the racist theories of their secular comrades. Sadly, this has not been the case. Given an unprecedented opportunity to repent of the sins of their mothers and fathers, these confessors have chosen instead to continue to wallow in bad theological ideas. Thus, like their secular counterparts, post-1960s religious leaders have followed Banfield in dressing old Christianized racism in clever new clothing. Outstanding among these clergy are Billy Graham, Bob Jones, and Jerry Falwell.

In differing ways, each of these religionists has reaffirmed and preached the vision that America is rapidly becoming an unheavenly city. For example, the Reverend Billy Graham (who was a personal confidant of President Nixon) used his revival crusades openly to advance the notion that if America was to remain God's land, then it must recover the confessional ideologies of its forebears (that is, the Puritans).

The Reverend Bob Jones Jr. built Bob Jones University in Greenville, South Carolina. He recruited students by assuring white parents that his university would be a refuge for their daughters, secure from African American males, who could not control their irrepressible sexual appetites.

The Reverend Jerry Falwell built his Moral Majority in the 1980s on the proposition that white America needed to redirect itself back toward its roots. Otherwise it would become what he delighted in calling a modern-day Sodom and Gomorrah—familiar code words for cities dominated by uncontrollable black masses.

Some might argue that the conservatives discussed in this chapter are the worst examples of modern-day racist religious, political, and intellectual ideologues. They might argue that these people do not accurately reflect the more liberal attitudes of whites who joined with blacks in the fight for an end to old racist structures and practices during the 1960s. Let us turn to the recent history of these so-called liberal men and women and probe more deeply into whether they stand guilty of many of the same anti-Christian and racist presumptions held by their conservative peers.

THE RELAPSE OF
POSTMODERN WHITE
LIBERALS

By postmodern white liberals, I have in mind the white men and women who became popularly known in our culture as liberals during the civil rights era of the 1960s. The attitudes and actions of this present-day group, more than any other, vividly point out how difficult it is to free one's mind from the old Puritan ideas of race.

During the early 1960s, white liberals viewed their label as an emblem of a great popular approbation for social activism. They proudly wore it as a testimony to their personal conversion from the racism that for so many years had dominated both the private sphere and the public square. Indeed, showing extraordinary sympathy for the black struggle, unprecedented numbers of white people (especially church leaders, artists, and intellectuals) joined the battles of the 1960s with the red, black, and green banner of black liberation held high. During that period, almost everywhere one looked, America was burgeoning with liberal activists and self-styled revolutionaries rushing to demonstrate that they not only had repented of the sin of racism, with its historic assumptions of black inferiority, but had also committed their lives and fortunes to converting the nation as a whole, to bring it into a new era of liberty and justice for all.

All that has changed now. The liberal views of racial tolerance during the 1960s have become all but a memory. Few who once called themselves liberals and rallied so enthusiastically a mere thirty years ago are now willing to march anywhere under any flag of egalitarianism. The last three decades have painfully revealed yet another failure in the long history of backsliding and betrayal that has characterized white America's efforts to overcome its ideational rejection of equal rights, privileges, and responsibilities for its African American citizens.

True, some white liberal theorists and activists have not yet deserted their black brothers and sisters. But the number is alarmingly small. The majority seem to be moving toward the position of their conservative counterparts. During the Kennedy and Johnson years, conservatives held tightly to the belief that God predestined America to be a holy city. Detractors (African Americans and Communist sympathizers) could go back to wherever they came from. "My country, right or wrong" and "My country, love it or leave it" were the slogans. Strangers and interlopers were not merely to stand outside looking in, they were to go away—one of the key signatures of American racism.

Unlike the racism of conservatives, however (who are discussed in chapter 3), that of these former liberal allies of the civil rights movement has not been as clearly discernible. This is because they have learned to be even more cunning than the die-hard conservatives. These liberals rarely put their racial beliefs in writing anymore, and they avoid the kinds of public discussions of the topic that might expose what have become their true feelings. But actions can speak louder than words. Despite their attempt to conceal lingering or newly adopted racist persuasions, scrutiny of their attitudes and actions since the mid-1960s reveals a culpability no less deplorable than that of their conservative peers.

The reason that many liberals put down their placards and joined conservatives on the sidelines is this: liberals were never able to cleanse their minds of the Puritan ideas of earlier centuries. Over the past thirty years, these ideas have been expressed under two guises. First, from the 1960s through the 1970s, liberals stepped back to a position I call "compensating desegregationism." From the 1980s to the present, they have further stepped back to a position I term "hierarchical multiculturalism."

Compensating desegregationists are pseudoliberals who are eager to portray themselves as having once and for all broken with racism. Publicly they desire to find some way to compensate for its injustices, so they will defend vigorously the merits of mandated social, economic, and political desegregation. But, on close examination, such compensation comes mainly through cosmetic and superficial adjustments in the status quo. Compensating desegregationists are opposed to complete and holistic racial integration—understood as the total transformation of the American mind in a way that would change our way of relating to each other in private and public and would move the nation toward racial reconciliation and equality.

Hierarchical multiculturalists are quasiliberals who, determined at least to give the appearance of liberalism, hasten to defend the position that America must become a multicultural society where all racial and ethnic cultures, gender and age cohorts, and sexual preference and ideological groups are to be affirmed as equal in their dignity and humanity. But, on close examination, such multiculturalism means that each group can bring its foods, costumes, and one holiday (say, adding Martin Luther King Jr.'s Birthday and Cinco de Mayo to St. Patrick's Day and Oktoberfest) to the national agenda. When circumstances mean taking bold and uncompromising stances in defense of these divergent and generally unpopular groups, however, then hierarchical multiculturalists retreat.

Two comments are necessary at this point. First, some who have examined the racial attitudes of liberals over the past three decades have distinguished their adherents as progressives, moderates, or left-wingers.[1] I avoid subdividing liberals in this way, because these categories are not particularly useful as a template for the history of ideas about race in the United States.

Second, some insist that the way liberals react to racial inequities depends upon the class status of the blacks with whom they are involved.[2] I do not find that class distinction among blacks has much to do with the racial attitudes of liberals or, for that matter, of any other white group. Racists remain so regardless of the class status of blacks with whom they must deal. I am aware of the popular assumption that middle-class whites and blacks often form a solidarity. But I find that the currents of un-Christian and racist ideologies flow across all kinds of liberals, including those who not so long ago appeared to stand in solidarity with the black community.

THE COMPENSATING DESEGREGATIONISTS

Desegregation was the hallmark of both the black civil rights movement and the white liberals who participated in it. More than a little excitement and anticipation were generated by the involvement of liberals in the civil rights movement. After all, mainstream African American organizations such as the National Association for the Advancement of Colored People, the National Urban League, and the

Southern Christian Leadership Conference, and leaders such as Dr. King had all insisted, in varying degrees, that legal desegregation of public institutions must be the starting point. And there it was, happening.

Yet the record shows that these white liberals rarely shared the same vision of desegregation held by the African American organizations and leaders. Although public and legal desegregation was to be a start, it was not the ultimate goal of their endeavors. Black people knew that daily racist behaviors were only symptoms of deeper anti-black theories and assumptions. Thus, their fundamental, final goal was to integrate society at every level. Indeed, if pushed to make a clear decision, many believed the final solution lay in the amalgamation of the races.

For example, King's "I Have a Dream" speech (1963) argued for this synthesis of the races, because King and other leaders of the movement were convinced that it represented the best and last hope for eradicating skin color as the determinant of one's humanity.[3] In King's view (shared by many blacks), mandated desegregation was only the first and a somewhat superficial step in the difficult struggle to end race prejudice and hatred. He was convinced that neither laws nor the social programs they enacted could ever lead whites to affirm that God had created black people their equals. Most African American leaders believed—although many never voiced it for fear of being considered hopelessly utopian—that only the complete integration of the two races in every sphere of common life held any hope of accomplishing the task of ending racial hostility and engendering a lasting reconciliation.

In contrast, white liberals as compensating desegregationists did not understand desegregation to be only one small step toward the final solution. They saw it as the final corrective in a world where, forever, black must remain black and white must remain white. From their perspective, desegregation was the panacea because, backed by the power of social legislation, black people would be assured of all the rights and privileges that others enjoyed. They envisioned African Americans as having the legal right to work alongside whites in the marketplace, to learn alongside whites in schools and universities, to live alongside whites in previously all-white neighborhoods, and to have legal recourse against anyone who might attempt to withhold such privileges.[4]

On the surface, then, first-step desegregationist blacks and final-step whites would seem to harbor few if any differences. Do they not reflect two similar views of the same social phenomenon? Like the black leaders, the liberals claimed to be working for a fundamental transformation of the nation that would finally do away with the unjust status quo and would bring African Americans into the mainstream.

What is on the surface, especially as it relates to race relations in the United States, is seldom what it appears to be. The past thirty years have shown not only that there was a vast difference between the two views, but that there was also a cunning deception in the compensating desegregationism of most white liberals. Black preachers such as Howard Thurman, Benjamin Mays, Martin Luther King Jr., and Ralph D. Abernathy alluded in their speeches to the integration of the races as the logic of full integration. Yet when liberals spoke of desegregation, they never had integration or synthesis of the races in view. Rather, behind the white language was a narrower limit on integration, namely, that certain boundaries between the races would always exist.

The Example of Martin Luther King Jr.

White liberals claimed that they had broken with the past and could therefore support desegregation for equal access. But full racial integration? Stop the marching, put down the placards, and blend in with the whites on the sidelines. The white racial provincialism of these liberals was rooted in the same anti-black propositions that had dominated this land since the 1600s. They embraced the concept of desegregation as a means to disavow the racist theology of their forebears. But they either refused or were incapable of purging their minds of the fundamental doctrines of black inferiority.

Some will counter that this assessment of liberalism is harsh, even unjust, because it lacks clear evidence. After all, didn't such pragmatic desegregationists rise to the occasion and vote for the Democratic leadership that pushed through the Civil Rights Act of 1964 and the Voting Rights Act of 1965? Didn't these men and women faithfully fight to desegregate the racist systems of their own states, cities, and local communities? Didn't they form or work through countless interracial councils and commissions?

Already in 1963, the moral failure of the compensating desegregationists had become quite evident. Martin Luther King Jr. had been arrested for protesting segregation and discrimination in Birmingham, Alabama. At the time, a group of eight Protestant, Catholic, and Jewish clerics sent him a letter opposing his demonstrations. Critiques of King's "Letter from Birmingham Jail"[5] have generally emphasized the ethical significance of his response. A careful exegesis of King's letter is not often given, especially by some white liberals who want to hide their true racial attitudes.

King's reply contains an important and trenchant witness to the insincerity behind the position of the compensating desegregationist clergy. These eight men did not write to inquire how Dr. King, their ministerial colleague, was holding up in the squalor of a jail cell. They did not write to pray with him. Certainly they did not affirm his denunciation of Birmingham's notorious racism. These liberal religionists wrote to King for two other reasons. First, they wanted to brand him an extremist who had no right to bring national disgrace and condemnation upon their city. Second, they wanted to denounce his mass protests as both unwise and untimely.

Here the chicanery of compensating desegregationism emerges. These liberal churchmen never attacked King until he brought his protest to Birmingham and began to show that its racial injustices were rooted in immoral and un-Christian ideas. Even though it is not certain that any of them had actually marched in the demonstrations, we do know that King praised some white Birmingham clerics and laity for "recognizing the urgency of the moment and . . . the need for powerful action antidotes to control the disease of segregation."[6] Notice that the supportive attitude of these liberal religionists lasted only so long as King kept his demonstrations focused on the desegregation of those public institutions and structures. They quickly withdrew support and began to condemn him when he turned the spotlight on the immoral and un-Christian theological ideas that buttressed Birmingham's deeply entrenched racism.

One should not be surprised at the position of these clergy. Although they had been proponents of desegregation until King marched on Birmingham, their interest in desegregation seems not to have flowed from any deeply held conviction that God had ordained that black people should be equal with whites. King said that they "admonish[ed] their worshipers to comply with a desegregation decision [only] because it is the law." His criticism of their supposed liberalism rested upon his keen disappointment that they had not endorsed the desegregation of the city because of a conviction that the black quest for "integration is morally right and because the Negro is your brother" in Christ.[7]

King's words make it clear why these liberal religionists promoted the formal desegregation of their city rather than a truly integrated community from top to bottom. Compared with complete integration, desegregation was a much easier step for them to take. Although schol-ars and the general public have largely ignored it, the desegregationism of the 1960s provided many white persons with a convenient escape from having to make costly decisions about American race relations. On the one hand, desegregation was predicated upon mere laws, which could just as easily be circumvented as obeyed. On the other hand, it was an expedient retreat from racial warfare. Integration, if honestly practiced, requires a personal disavowal of white superiority. Put boldly, then, desegregationism enables its proponents to insist that they have labored for black equality; but it does not require the conversion of heart and mind—the acceptance of blacks as human beings, as brothers and sisters in the family of God—that true racial integration requires.

Northern Religious Liberals' Responses

Concerning the treatment that King received from the eight white clergy, some would ask, what could one expect? After all, this happened in Birmingham, Alabama, "of which," as the saying goes, "there is no whicher." Moreover, writers of the letter to King were *southern* clergy. How could they possibly be expected to represent northern liberal attitudes on integration?

The assumptions behind such objections are flawed. First, I have argued that the source of American racist theology is the old Puritan racial doctrines. We have already seen that these seeds, once deposited in the soul of America, have never been confined to any specific geographic area.

Second, the history of the northern position on race during the civil rights era is almost identical to that of the South. The same chicanery and limitations marking the views and activities of southern preachers also characterized those of northern clerics. This is evident in the fact that although the liberal wing of northern mainstream white denomi-nations claimed to be the faithful allies and comrades-in-arms of the black civil rights movement, they in fact followed the southern wing of the churches and synagogues in quickly backing away from that stance when black mainstream leadership began to interpret the movement on their own terms, as one committed to individual and collective racial integration rather than to mere structural desegregation.

One classic example of this northern backing away from a more pro-found understanding of the racial crisis can be seen in the history of the National Council of Churches (NCC), the nation's premiere ecumenical organization. Formed in 1950 and headquartered in New York City, the NCC took a "go slow" position on race issues until 1963. Then the atrocities being inflicted on blacks in the South provoked worldwide attention and protest. James F. Findlay Jr. compared the cautious race relations policies of the NCC in the 1950s with the immature but more courageous policies of its predecessor agency, the Federal Council of Churches, in the 1940s. Findlay attributes part of the NCC's caution on the temper of the times:

> [The] debate [over a strong racial policy] occurred just two years after the formation of the council in 1950; cautiousness in leadership probably was affected by that fact as the council sought to move slowly against its southern constituencies, who were always its most hesitant supporters. The council was continuing the social activities of its predecessor, the Federal Council of Churches, but under different circumstances. In addition to the uncertainties inherent in a large, new ecumenical agency . . . between 1946 and 1952 the cold war had emerged and the intense anticommunism that accompanied it was already creating a national climate of opinion that was different and much more cautious, than that of 1946. Indirectly at least the growing conservative temper of the fifties, even as early as the spring of 1952, probably served as a further cautionary note.[8]

By 1963, however, the NCC had no option but to line up on the side of the freedom fighters. Moved by the inhumanities of southern resistance and the pressures being exerted by black church leaders, the NCC finally came out forthrightly against racial discrimination and segregation, abandoning its innocuous rhetoric and creating the Commission on Religion and Race. The task of this commission was to find ways to bring the nation's mainstream Protestant churches together in a united front against racial discrimination.[9]

The test of the council's sincerity on this matter was not long in coming. In 1964 and 1965, two of the most historic and most divisive pieces of legislation to confront the Congress and the nation since radical Reconstruction came to the fore—the Civil Rights Bill of 1964 and the Voting Rights Bill of 1965. It was clear that the South would vote against these measures. It was also clear that unless something dramatic was done, much of the rest of the country, especially the Midwest, would likely vote against them as well.

Challenged by a variety of black churches and activist groups, as well as by many sympathetic whites, to put its power and resources behind these bills, the NCC launched an all-out and unprecedented campaign on behalf of passage, particularly among grassroots midwesterners. Like some antebellum antislavery clergy had done, the NCC built its campaign on the premise that racism was not merely a social issue, it was also a moral sickness that authentic Christians—as God's moral agents—had a responsibility to help eradicate.[10]

Using the moral-government argument of perfectionist theology, the NCC labored to persuade the midwestern electorate that their Christian duty required them not only to personally support civil rights and black enfranchisement, but also, through a letter-writing campaign, to convince their congressional representatives and senators to vote for those measures. Both the House and the Senate passed the two measures. It is safe to say that had it not been for the efforts of the National Council of Churches and the denominations, neither of these bills would have received sufficient votes for passage.[11]

The NCC was not the only northern religious body that upheld black civil rights during the early years of the 1960s. Several predominantly white denominations, most notably the United Methodist Church, the United Presbyterian Church, the Episcopal Church, the United Church of Christ, and the American Baptist Church, in varying ways and degrees, also rose up to denounce racial discrimination and to support the black liberation movement. Besides participating in protests and creating official commissions to work on solutions to the race problem, a small number of denominational leaders went so far as to voice public support for James Forman's "Black Manifesto," which in 1969 demanded millions of dollars in reparations from American churches and synagogues for their three hundred years of complicity in the Atlantic slave trade. (See chapter 3 for more on this speech.) Some of these denominations proved remarkably receptive to the manifesto. One notable example was the Massachusetts Conference of the United Church of Christ, which gave $1 million of its endowment funds to help establish Boston's Black Ecumenical Commission.

Church-related schools, especially theological seminaries, also joined the new war against racism. For example, responding to challenges from the student body, the board of trustees of Union Theological Seminary in New York City (once closely related to the Presbyterian Church) agreed to invest $500,000 of its endowment toward projects of racial elevation and to try to raise an additional $1 million for programs that were to be under the auspices of the seminary but would be located in Harlem. Other seminaries and universities, such as Harvard and Yale, made unprecedented efforts to recruit black students and employed black professors to inaugurate programs of African American studies (see chapter 3).

Most seminaries, however, took more conservative approaches than Union, Harvard, or Yale. These included a few white faculty traveling to the South for brief periods to participate in the black freedom movements, writing books and articles about the theological contradictions of racism, or otherwise voicing their support for desegregation.

The commitment of northern liberal religionists to the black struggle ended almost as abruptly as it began, no less than was true of the religious establishment in the South. By the close of the 1960s, most of them had all but forsaken their black brothers and sisters. Their relapse stemmed from the exact same cause that drove southern liberal religionists to turn their backs on Dr. King at the time he needed them most. They were compensating desegregationists, not integrationists. They had few inhibitions about fighting for the desegregation of religious and secular institutions and lobbying for voting rights and selected government programs, but they simply found it impossible to take the next step, to fight for the kind of racial integration that would have required the transformation of the American mind. That is, the majority of these men and women were unprepared to accept African Americans, regardless of color or class, as human beings in terms of full partnership in the intimate world of hearth and home, the network of communal groups and relationships among which people live apart from their formal associative and institutional ties. Half-stepping marked the compensating desegregationism of religious northern liberals, just as it did their southern clerical peers.

Other Northern Liberal Responses

Nonreligious northern liberals exhibited this same disinclination to be committed to total integration. From the White House to suburbia, secular liberals backed away from the black struggle with deliberate speed. Even such an admired and intellectually informed liberal as President John F. Kennedy could not transform his mind from the influence of the old presuppositions of black inferiority enough to rise above them. Shortly after becoming president in 1961, he promised to sign an executive order that would end discrimination in federally financed housing. Yet it took more than two years and intense pressure for him to sign the order. Kennedy further showed his ambivalence about full integration as he vacillated on sending federal troops into such places as Selma and Birmingham, Alabama, and Meridian, Mississippi, to subdue the defiant southern mayhem against black protesters.[12]

Kennedy was not the only well-informed political figure or elite intellectual who was torn between doing the right thing about race or capitulating to the old ideological past. Erudite politicians such as Daniel Patrick Moynihan, the scholarly Democratic senator and reformer from New York, were ambivalent. As American historian Dan T. Carter has shown, the stamp of Moynihan's racial attitude "shifted from John Kennedy to Lyndon Johnson to Robert Kennedy before settling for an extended rest in the Nixon Administration."[13] That is, Moynihan's position on race relations, especially as reflected in his work on the black family, went from pro-black to pro-desegregation to anti-black. Like Edward C. Banfield, Moynihan found it convenient to blame black people for their hapless condition while at the same time exonerating racism and racists from responsibility for having played the commanding role in the blacks' dire situation.

The Resulting Urban Decline

Since the late 1960s, America's urban areas and public schools in state after state have gone to rubble. Disguised under shallow explanations, such as white flight and the lethargy of inner-city populations, are the contributing inactions of the compensating desegregationism of both secular and religious liberals. Could old ideas about the inequality of the races perhaps have inspired such flight or the blaming of urban blacks?

Two hard, unanswered questions cut through the usual soft explanations. First, how could powerless poor blacks by themselves ruin sprawling urban metropolises and their public school systems? Second, why did the liberals who so recently supported desegregated institutions suddenly bolt, fleeing the houses, schools, and downtown conveniences with which they once had been so satisfied, if not proud of? Answering these questions casts an unflattering searchlight on how liberal compensating desegregationism has become yet another limb on the mighty oak of American racism, arising out of the acorn seed of racial inequality.

The intriguing arguments of scholars such as Banfield and Moynihan notwithstanding, poor blacks were not the direct cause of the decay of urban America. As is true today, poor blacks during the 1960s had neither the income nor the desire to move into formerly all-white neighborhoods. They did not desire a second vehicle, perhaps a minivan or four-wheel drive, for driving to the suburban mall. They would have preferred instead better housing, schools, public transportation, public safety, sanitation services, and other amenities in the locations where they were.

More than a few commentators have painted a fanciful picture of urban blacks rushing to take up residence in formerly all-white neighborhoods. But poor blacks who lived in the cities at this time did what their low economic status had forced them to do since the urban migrations from the South in the 1920s: they crowded into the slums that historically had been cordoned off (usually by rivers, industrial areas, and railroad tracks) from the more affluent urban residential neighborhoods.

Middle-class blacks became increasingly tolerated in the mainstream, meaning the workplace. But the movement of the black middle class into formerly all-white urban areas prompted many whites—self-described liberals—to move out to suburbia "for the sake of our children," "to find better schools," and so forth. They were so many happy white folks bubbling with goodwill, who fell short of promoting integration (except on someone else's job or in someone else's neighborhood).

Many of these fleeing whites were liberal desegregationists. Again, they moved out from the heart of the city because of the influx of the black middle class, not because of an invasion of poor blacks. No logical reason for their mass exodus can be offered other than an implicit racism. After all, they had recently fought, and some had even sacrificed their lives, to help desegregate those places where black people could now be expected to work and play, travel and dine, learn and worship. Many welcomed aspiring blacks to low-level jobs at the office. But blacks in their neighborhood? attending their schools?

Maybe I have jumped too quickly to ideational considerations brought in from the racist past. Some whites have attempted to rationalize their flight from the cities by pointing to the urban rioting and crime that began to increase in the mid-1960s.[14] Others have pointed to various prudent family concerns: "Property values are bound to go down if the blacks move in," or "Crime will skyrocket," or "Our wives and daughters will no longer be safe," or "The neighborhood will become infested with roaches and rats," or "The city won't pick up the trash regularly," or "The quality of education in our schools will inevitably decline." I ask simply, because of what do such prudent concerns arise? Because of the influx of middle-class blacks?

The minds of many liberals were steeped in these stereotypes of the past, which prevented them from making anything more than superficial adjustments (institutional and compensating desegregation) in the systems of racial injustice that had dominated the nation from its beginning. Although they supported the desegregation of the municipal infrastructure, they were convinced that it would be a grave mistake if African Americans—even those who had a college education and economically stable families—should ever cross the boundary line that separated the inner city from "their" (the liberals') better residential areas by moving next door.

The full integration of the races was something these liberals could not countenance, especially if it meant that a black family might be their next-door neighbors. Even to this day, many liberal whites find it impossible to admit that they abandoned the central cities because they were finally unable to empty their minds of their ancestors' religious conviction about God having created black people—regardless of their economic and educational background—unequal to themselves in every respect and, therefore, unworthy of their close and intimate association.

During the late 1960s and throughout the 1970s and 1980s, this truncated vision of human community received even greater affirmation as liberal whites withdrew deeper and deeper into the old and supposedly discarded ways of thinking about and relating to blacks. Even the conditional commitment of liberal white people of "goodwill" to desegregation began to wane during the post–civil rights era as more and more of them adopted the argument of conservatives and hardcore racists that blacks were the cause of every negative development in the city—from the rapid decay of the housing stock to economic recessions and the general decline of morality. As has consistently been the case with liberals since the mid-1960s, they rarely acknowledged this way of thinking. Rather, from the mid-1960s through the early 1980s, they chose to cloak their new convictions in stony silence.

But times have changed. From the mid-1980s to the present, these white Americans have found it less embarrassing to state their objections to blacks, or—and this has become a more attractive option—to disguise their capitulation to racist ideas by adopting the subterfuge of what is called multiculturalism.

THE HIERARCHICAL MULTICULTURALISTS

The new phenomenon of multiculturalism has been much bandied about by liberals these days. Although a few African American scholars, such as Cornel West and Henry Louis Gates Jr., have become prominent spokespersons of the multicultural movement, it did not have its origins in the African American community.[15] Instead, its most recent roots can be traced back to the white friends and allies of the civil rights movement of the late 1960s and early 1970s: the liberal clergy, secular academics, progressive politicians, and denizens of the popular street culture—hippies and beatniks. It was invented partly as a foil against what they considered to be the runaway upward mobility of blacks and the legitimation of their Afrocentric culture.

Before being called multiculturalism, the phenomenon was called pluralism or diversity. Yet this concept has, ostensibly, the same agenda today as it had then: to transform America so that every racial and ethnic culture, every gender and sexual preference group, and every New Age and nonviolent ideological coterie will be accepted, even celebrated, as fully human and thus endowed with the same rights and opportunities as anyone else.

My approach to multiculturalism is somewhat different. I am somewhat less optimistic about the nature and goals of the movement. I celebrate an honest and authentic effort to honor all cultures and styles of life. Here, however, I choose to concentrate on the blandishments of white male multiculturalists, in which I detect not merely insincerity but danger. I detect this peril because they have turned the once noble goals of pure multiculturalism into racist hierarchical ones. (White women multiculturalists are not included in this discussion; I will examine more specifically in chapter 5 how they, in their own way, use the old Puritan ideas of race to advance their own cause—again, often at the strategic disadvantage of blacks.)

By focusing on white male liberals, we will be better able to grasp how their involvement in multiculturalism, despite their good intentions in the beginning, has evolved into yet another way of perpetuating the old Puritan vision of white supremacy. Put in other terms, a certain brand of multiculturalism is rapidly turning into a predominantly white thing. For all its pretensions of enlightened humanism, it bodes ill for black progress because of how these white liberals have refused to sever its roots in a hierarchical mind-set.

A Multiculturalism That Excludes Many Cultures

Multiculturalism, like compensating desegregationism, seems at first glance a promising movement. The liberal sector of the dominant culture is ready to transform the United States into a nation that truly values and honors its diverse cultures. Yet it is important that, chastened by previous promises, we poke around to test its reality. When we do, we again find the reality to be less promising. Indeed, because many white male liberals have failed to purge themselves of their ancestors' superstitions about race, multiculturalism turns out to be yet another ruse for the subterranean racism that has erupted from the liberal wing of the white male community over the past three decades.

For example, recently, liberal white male clergy and religious scholars have responded with unparalleled zeal to the entreaties of white religious feminists that certain historic confessions deny them equality with men and consign them to a second-class status in the household of faith. For the most part, the clergy and scholars have conceded the truth of this criticism and are now trying to cast aside the traditional male designation of God as Father and to change the language so that God becomes either an androgynous Father/Mother or a completely gender-neutral God. But these same fair-minded men of God, with respect to African Americans, still persistently and resolutely refuse to honor petitions for relief from the erroneous biblical and theological notions in the history of Christianity that have undergirded the degraded image of black people and have kept them out of the normal course of advancement in both the church and the society.

A case in point is the highly acclaimed study *Habits of the Heart: Individualism and Commitment in American Life* (1985). In the first edition of the book, the authors stated that their purpose was to speak with their "fellow citizens in many parts of the country" and to "engage them in conversations about their lives and about what matters most to them . . . to [talk with them] about their families and communities, their doubts and uncertainties, and their hopes and fears with respect to the larger society."[16]

The reader might anticipate that this 355-page study of what Americans consider the crucial issues affecting their lives today would have pursued a truly multicultural inquiry. After all, pluralism and multiculturalism have been in vogue in the academy since the 1960s. The book's authors—Robert N. Bellah, Richard Madsen, William Sullivan, Ann Swidler, and Steve M. Tipton—are among the who's who of the academic elite. But the study was decidedly monocultural. It clearly stated that its focus was restricted to only one group, namely, "white, middle-class Americans."[17]

Toward the end of *Habits*, the authors invited readers to "test" what the study reveals "against [their] own experience" and to let the authors know what they found. Accepting this invitation, Professor Vincent Harding of Iliff School of Theology, a noted African American scholar of religion, wrote to report that he found the work to be seriously flawed because of its glaring omission of African Americans and other ethnic groups from what purported to be a national "dialogue."[18] In 1996, a revised edition of *Habits* was published. Harding's criticism was pointedly ignored. Blacks and other minorities continued to be excluded.[19]

This is disappointing, but it is no great surprise. Bellah and company had attempted to cover their exclusion of blacks in their first edition by stating that because they were "a small research team" with a limited budget, they "decided to concentrate [their] research on white, middle-class Americans."[20] While outsiders are not privy to the nature of the authors' expenses, we must nevertheless wonder how a dialogue that included African Americans and other ethnic groups would have so greatly increased their costs.

Could the real reasons for the omission of blacks and others lie elsewhere? I think the writers reveal their true motivation for the exclusion of nonwhites when they write:

> Apart from the fact that we could not cover all of the tremendous diversity of American life, there were several theoretical reasons for our decision. From Aristotle on, republican theorists have stressed the importance of the middle classes for the success of free institutions. *These classes have traditionally provided the active public participation that makes free institutions work.*[21]

Can even the most casual reader miss that the "republican theorists" these authors celebrate (in several places) are the very aristocrats who have long defended the Puritan belief that God ordained America to be a holy land destined exclusively for white people?

These authors, hierarchical multiculturalists all, must certainly know this. They are trained historians and scholars who have written extensively about American history and culture and about the way religion has shaped and nurtured this nation since the Plymouth landing. Bellah, for example, has written a number of books and articles on American civil religion and its continuing impact on this society.[22] Because these authors are trained academics, they cannot have helped being aware of how the decision taken in their work to exclude non-whites plays into this nation's racist theological and biblical ideas. These ideas not only sustained slavery in the distant past but also continue to lurk beneath the surface to justify the policies and practices that keep blacks today at what Professor Derrick Bell aptly calls "the bottom of the well."[23] We can only conclude that, for these writers, a multicultural society means the same multilayered or racially hierarchical society that the New England Puritans posited as an ideal for the nation some four hundred years ago.

A Disregard for Black Students

A similar disregard for black humanity is found among male secular scholars. Many blacks report the contempt that is expressed to them as students, professors, or administrators by liberal-minded faculty. With respect to black students, many multiculturalists have been heard forthrightly, or more often through a slip of the tongue, making such remarks as, "I had a bad day in class today because of my black students," "The blacks always sit together in the back of my classes," "I caught another African American student cheating today," "Their work tells me they're from a poor family and educational background," "They don't have good minds, but they sure know how to dance and be cool," "All these black students know how to do is jive and talk about sex," or "I do have one exceptionally bright black student in one of my classes—I'm sure you know him [or her, because we have so few bright blacks on campus]."

Let me issue a Bellah-like challenge. Check these examples with black professors teaching in predominantly white colleges or universities. Or ask them to sum up how some of their white peers view African American students. How many hierarchical multicultural phrases are mentioned?

If no black professors are conveniently at hand, then an incident involving Dr. Francis Lawrence, president of Rutgers University in New Jersey, might suffice. His record is reputed to "show a commitment to diversity and to minority recruitment and hiring." Yet, in a statement made to his faculty in fall 1994, this liberal white educator expressed the view that "disadvantaged" African American students do not have "that genetic hereditary background to have a higher average" when taking standardized tests.[24]

How far has this modern-day multiculturalist liberal educator come from the old Puritan ideas of God-ordained black inferiority? Much like Bellah et al., I am a small research team and my funds are limited. Therefore, I need to resort to anecdotes rather than sociological studies. But when this claim is tested, I am confident that its results will add only details to the general pattern here noted.

Black Professors and Black Studies

Hierarchical multiculturalists have developed interesting ways to avoid hiring too many African American faculty and administrators. They have also managed to marginalize black courses and programs, particularly those that deal with the significance of race in Western civilization.

For example, the method of appointing black faculty frequently has two stages. First, to satisfy affirmative action requirements, job announcements that encourage blacks to apply are published. Second, reasons are tailored to explain either why black candidates did not make the short list or what rules them out after an interview. Typical reasons for passing over black applicants that have been reported to me by search committee members include, "They were too qualified," "They were not as qualified as other candidates," "They simply don't fit with our program," "Their scholarship does not seem to be mainstream enough for our needs," "There was something in his [or her] body language," "I don't think he [or she] will make our students feel comfortable," or something equally spurious.

At the same time that white administrators and search committees are finding ways to rule out black applicants, they are also inventing stratagems to rule in white women and other nonwhite applicants. According to a 1993 report, "white women comprised 27.5 percent of full-time faculty staffers," while black women and black men combined comprised less than 5 percent.[25] To borrow words from the title of a recent article on the state of African American faculty members in higher education today, the consequence of these quiet and clandestine developments in American higher education is that "the African American professor on the college campus [is rapidly becoming] an endangered species."[26]

White male hierarchical multiculturalists have become adept at subverting black courses and programs. They consider such offerings a distraction from traditional approaches to American studies, a dead end for postgraduation employment, a questionable source of personal value formation, or—my favorite—a way of ghettoizing black students from the mainstream.

A classic example is the conflict at Stanford University over a first-year humanities course entitled "Culture, Ideas, and Values" (CIV) that was instituted in the late 1980s. The stated goal of CIV is to broaden students' knowledge of the heretofore ignored contributions of African Americans, other nonwhite ethnic minorities, and women to the development of Western civilization through the study of "race, ethnic, and gender issues." The proponents of CIV argue that such a course is necessary because the traditional course offerings in the study of Western culture have focused exclusively on white male heroes, such as Aristotle, John Stuart Mill, Edmund Burke, Thomas Paine, and the rest of the so-called royal road in Western culture.

Although there are a number of issues involved in the debate—many known only to the faculty and administrators at Stanford—a central argument of some professors who teach CIV is that its breadth gives the instructors no time to do justice to the traditional canons and heroes of Western civilization. "How," they ask, "can Stanford compress the development of Western and non-Western thought into two quarters?"[27]

While we are not privileged to know all that is involved in the Stanford debacle, it is certainly not far-fetched to imagine that the issue of race figures in it. Stanford's prestige aside, it is no different from other colleges and universities that profess a commitment to multiculturalism. The school is apparently in the throes of the same struggle over black scholarly interests that, in varying forms, is found in almost every educational institution in the country, expressed thus: "We want to include many cultures and values, but . . . ." The questions of time, balance, and coverage raised by the opponents of Stanford's CIV course are familiar ones that echo through the hallways of the American academy.

Male hierarchical multiculturalist educators rarely pose the issue of time when the course or program does not involve material about African Americans. What prompts them to single out black people? Two reasons. First, since the early 1970s, white women, nonblack racial and ethnic minorities, and gay and lesbian groups have been at the forefront of the demand for multiculturalism in the university curriculum. They have repeatedly petitioned that courses and programs dealing with their experiences be added to the curriculum.

Second, in light of the success of these groups, it seems odd to me that resistance remains on campuses for the inclusion of black experience, viewpoints, and contributions. We find a clue to why this is so in the words of a professor at a major university in Ohio, who wrote a letter to his school's newspaper in 1994 titled "Multiculturalism: Let the Debate Begin." This professor painted a provocative picture portraying black faculty, students, and administrators as the only persons in the university who were pleading for courses and programs that would "talk about the rights of racial, religious, and ethnic minorities in America." (This university is located no more than fifteen miles from the home of the internationally famous black poet Paul Laurence Dunbar.)

This professor began his teaching career long before the 1970s. Thus, he should know that the colleges and universities with solid African American studies courses and programs established them long before white women and other nonblack minorities made multiculturalism their battle cry. Despite what hierarchical multiculturalists would lead us to believe, these schools did not include such black courses and programs because the white faculty had a passionate interest in multiculturalism. On the contrary, these emphases were instituted in response to the campus demonstrations and sit-ins of radical black students and a few courageous professors. Well aware of and opposed to the hypocritical white liberalism of the 1960s, members of the radical Black Power movement on the campuses fought for black studies out of the conviction that the African American experience had to become a part of the American educational curriculum. Their argument was that black students needed the same opportunity to learn about their own history and culture that white students had been given for years.[28] But wherever blacks were not forceful and successful years ago, their more recent requests have largely been bypassed.

Why have hierarchical multiculturalist intellectuals avoided acknowledging this embarrassing fact? If they have a thorough knowledge of America's racial history, and if they profess to be committed to a new multiculturalism that breaks with a racist past, and if black scholars are available to teach such courses, then what makes for the delay? I submit that it is because their definition of multiculturalism is still defined by precisely the same vision of white supremacy that has dominated this country since its founding. (As I will discuss in chapter 5, these same white males eagerly promoted the elevation of their white female colleagues and other so-called underrepresented culturalists, as long as they were not black.) Hence, even though their posture of appearing committed to educational equality for all is politically correct, their minds and hearts remain trapped in the distant past, compelling them to turn deaf ears to the black struggle.

The Black Power Movement as a Polarizing Force?

I have noted the early success in establishing black studies majors and courses, as well as integrating Western civilization courses. But the argument is sometimes made that the radical Black Power advocates who promoted economic, social, and political empowerment turned white liberals away from alliances with blacks. To be sure, the rise of the Black Power movement scandalized some liberal multiculturalists. Yet note that this same kind of demand for countervailing power was and still is being made by nonblack ethnic, feminist, sexual preference, and ideological groups—without a similar alienation.

Many liberals today are aware that their failure to hear black pleas for equal empowerment is a major factor in the fact that blacks still reside at the bottom of America's social, economic, and political well. They are aware that the way Andrew Hacker describes the United States—*Two Nations: Black and White, Separate, Hostile, Unequal*—does not have to be our destiny.[29] They are aware that the onus is upon them to face the unpleasant fact that their strange brand of hierarchical multiculturalism has helped shape things as they are. Their policies and actions, especially since the 1960s, truly have served only to help keep this nation unequally divided.

One of the main reasons for the defection of white liberals is that in their innermost minds, they are still shackled to and confused by the racist ideas of their celebrated ancestors, even when their hearts are in the right place. My hope is that they can scrape such mental plaque from their thinking. But this is not their burden alone. In fairness to the retrenchment of male liberals who have become calculating multiculturalists, we must concede that they have by no means been alone in pushing the nation toward the fragmentation and separatism we are witnessing today. Some of the blame for the divisions, hostilities, and inequalities that remain must be laid squarely, though most unfortunately, on the doorstep of the triumphant white women's movement. It is to those sisters that we must now direct our critical, though not irrevocably unfriendly, lens in our examination of American piety and benevolence gone awry.

5

WHITE FEMINISM
AND THE BLACK QUEST
FOR RACIAL JUSTICE

Since the 1960s, the white feminist movement has delivered a powerful blow against inveterate sexism in Western civilization. It has been particularly effective in exposing the male-dominated (white) institutions and structures of American society. Few white or black male historians, for example, have fairly and fully depicted the courageous role that white women played in the struggle for the freedom and equality of blacks before and after the Civil War. Even now, the significant contribution of women, whether white or black, has received little more than shameful silence whenever the histories of secular or religious movements—especially those against racial prejudice and discrimination from the middle of the nineteenth century to the present—are recounted. That white feminists have added this story is an important step forward, and we are the better for their work.

Since the end of the civil rights movement, however, a small but eloquent group of African American women have noted how some white women stand in the way of the social progress of black women and men.[1] Not that these white women have consciously blocked black progress. Instead, they seem to have perhaps unwittingly been complicit with and assisted subterranean racism as they have advanced their own cause. A less subtle analysis is that these white women themselves have tasted of power.

For a relatively narrow circle of feminist academics, artists, and intellectuals, this criticism is not news. Because the views of these black women scholars have not gained a wider notice, I want to devote a chapter to their explication. The growing internecine struggle between them and their white sisters throws important light upon certain similar characteristics of American racists, whether male or female.

It is increasingly difficult for me to maintain a charitable view of the matter. Yet this subject seems taboo for a man, even a black man, to undertake. For a male interloper, any discussion that smacks of criticism of the rectitude of white women seems graceless, if not actually hazardous, especially because of the broader good that white feminism has initiated. Nevertheless, no male scholar (white or black) has yet examined the peculiar realities and contradictions of white women's attitudes about race, especially as these relate to and reflect the influence of Puritan theological ideas.

Therefore, this final chapter opens up that thorny and somewhat embarrassing question with the contention that the ideological foundations of white women's prejudice, particularly as it is found among post–civil rights radical white feminists, need to be uncovered if we are to obtain a fuller picture of the nature and dynamics of contemporary American race relations. Although some white women have succeeded in disguising their bigotry, the sophisticated racism of others has been just as injurious to black civil rights during the past three decades as the frequently more unabashed hatred of hard-core racist white men. This is because white women, no less than their liberal white male counterparts, often continue to practice and defend the old Puritan idea that God created blacks inferior to whites and unworthy of equal participation with them in American society. As painful and unwelcome as such an investigation may be, now is the time for us to take a hard, unsentimental look at this rarely discussed development.

A GROWING GAP SINCE THE 1970S

In 1970, the National Organization for Women (NOW) filed a class action suit in federal district court against every university and college in the country. The suit resulted in the government's ordering most institutions of higher education to develop and submit plans for "hiring and promoting women and blacks." In that same year, NOW, declaring the American Telephone and Telegraph Company to be "the largest oppressor of women in the United States," received an out-of-court class action settlement in behalf of the company's female employees.[2]

These two historic events marked the beginning of a new era for white women in this country. Not only did they begin to dismantle the sexist structures that white men had erected many years earlier to bar them from the mainstream, they also soon found themselves joining white men as the movers of American society. Not since the long struggle for suffrage had white women been so successful in challenging the sexist bias and discriminatory practices of white men. As with that previous success, their goals were uncompromising and their methods focused. Moreover, as with that previous success, they had asked blacks to wait for them to succeed so that they (white women) could help pull other excluded groups into the centers of power and influence. Laid aside was the coalition that women had formed with blacks during the movement for the abolition of slavery and the modern civil rights movement.

The victories of white feminists did not stop during the decade of the 1970s. As several sets of government statistics and findings of Gallup polls have shown, white women have steadily pushed against and at times have broken through the infamous glass ceiling. In this achievement, white women have vaulted far ahead of African Americans of both genders.

Yet blacks, in their efforts to secure social justice and equality in America, have waited for white women's hands to reach down—and have waited in vain. For example, before the 1970s, white women comprised less than 5 percent of the lawyers, physicians, college and university professors, and business managers in the nation. By 1990, their ranks had surged to more than 33 percent in each of these professional categories. Prior to 1970, African Americans constituted less than 1 percent of all attorneys, 2 percent of physicians, and 3 percent of college and university professors. By 1990, they represented only 3 percent of attorneys and physicians and 5 percent of professors.[3] Percentages similar to these are found all across the white-collar employment spectrum. White women are the single greatest beneficiaries of affirmative action programs, contrary to the anti-black propaganda in California and elsewhere.

Feminists' Perception of the Transition

According to some feminists, the sudden and dramatic shift in white women's socioeconomic and political fortunes is the sole consequence of their boldness and ingenuity as social activists in their own behalf during the 1960s. The whole nation, so they say, ought to be grateful for and ought to celebrate white feminists' creative use of grassroots confrontation and the legal challenges that enabled them, at long last, to fell male discrimination. Only occasionally have white women admitted that these strategies and tactics were actually borrowed from the mass movements and civil rights organizations of blacks and other marginalized ethnic groups:

> Throughout the 1960s we were trying to imagine how to live differently, how to change the world. And the women's movement took much from the civil rights movement, from the new left, from the antiwar movement—but we brought it home. We brought it into the kitchen. We brought it into the bedroom. We brought it into the most personal and intimate aspects of people's lives. It was hard to deny there. It was hard to ignore those issues.[4]

Have white women's signal triumphs in recent years simply been the result of feminists' taking their struggle to the streets or into the kitchens, bedrooms, and extradomestic strongholds of husbands, fathers, brothers, and male friends? True, threats of withholding cooked meals, housekeeping, and intimate bedroom activities have been and probably continue to be among the factors in white women's unprecedented triumph over sexism. Yet there is much more to the story than this. A central factor is how white women have quickly latched onto or moved away from the efforts of the black civil rights movement whenever either strategy seemed more beneficial.

What feminists may not have noticed is how such strategies have been used against others. Many blacks have struggled for survival in government, corporate America, predominantly white churches, and the academy. They describe how white men have been able to use white women to block the progress of both black men and black women whenever the white men have felt threatened by the upward mobility of black colleagues. Moreover, some white women have also practiced such bigotry, whether voluntarily or at the encouragement of white men.

FEMINIST ACTIONS DURING CIVIL RIGHTS LEGISLATION

The story of how radical feminists have latched onto or moved away from black progress begins prior to the passage of the Civil Rights Act of 1964. Before that legislation was placed before Congress, the antisexism campaign of radical feminists had become stagnated in a sea of obscurity and male indifference.[5] In contrast, the issue of black civil rights was gaining momentum. An engine seemed at hand, and many white feminists shrewdly linked their legitimate quest for gender parity to it.

One of the earliest linkages was made with the embattled civil rights bill itself. A small group of feminists sought to add the word "sex" to the phrase "race, religion, and national origin" in Title VII of the legislation. With that word, the sexism issue was added to race—an apparent coup. The group that engineered this linkage included not only members of the National Women's Party but also then-prominent congresswomen, such as Martha Griffiths (Democrat, Michigan), Catherine Dean Mays (Republican, Washington State), and Katherine St. George (Republican, New York).[6]

Again, the problem was not so much in what these women tried to do—strategies for removing white male hegemony on any side can be helpful—but in how they went about it. No doubt fearing that a predominantly white male Congress would refuse to add women's rights to Title VII, the feminist congressional representatives and their national coalitions searched for a way to persuade powerful white male representatives to support their cause.

Finding white men to back the feminist cause was not an easy task. Most southern congressmen were bitterly opposed not only to civil rights for blacks but also to new rights legislation for any group. Moreover, traditional supporters of black civil rights were concerned that adding women's rights to Title VII would spell its doom. Some of their more sexist colleagues, who were straddling the fence on the legislation anyway, planned to use the addition of women's rights as an excuse to vote against the entire bill.[7]

To convince this latter congressional group to support women's rights, radical feminists resorted to a strategy that stood in stark antithesis to their putative ideology of equality and fairness. They formed an alliance with known anti-feminist and anti-black southern congressmen. Among the most prominent of these conservatives were Howard Smith (Democrat, Virginia) and James Russell Tuten (Democrat, Georgia). Smith, at the request of the National Women's Party, introduced the amendment to add women's rights to Title VII.[8]

In forging this coalition with southerners who opposed black civil rights in any form, the women's groups fell back upon a time-worn strategy that was at once disingenuous and racist. Title VII was an "all-black thing" unless amended to include the legitimate demands of white women. Otherwise, white women would be the only unprotected minority in the society. Without including women, the gates of prosperity and privilege would be opened wide to blacks. Would that be fair? (To translate: Should the black race rise above white women?) Martha Griffiths gave this self-serving interpretation of Reconstruction history when she warned her male colleagues thus:

> It would be incredible to me that white men would be willing to place white women at such a disadvantage except that white men have done this before. When the 14th Amendment had become the law of the land, a brave woman named Virginia Minor, a native-born, free, white citizen of the United States and the State of Missouri, read the Amendment, and on the fifteenth of October, 1872, appeared to register to vote. The registrar replied that the State of Missouri had a statute which said that only males could register to vote. . . . So Mr. Chairman, your grandfathers were willing, as prisoners of their own prejudice, to permit ex-slaves to vote, but not their own white wives. . . . A vote against this Amendment today by a white man is a vote against his wife, or his widow, or his daughter, or his sister.[9]

The message attracted the sympathy of white men. Congressional feminists such as Griffiths had no compunction about using such a loose reading of history to win the support of both southern and northern white congressmen. Assumed in Griffiths's appeal is the old racist Puritan idea that a divine hierarchy of humanity exists:

> If you don't add sex to this bill, I really don't believe there is a reasonable person sitting here who does not by now understand perfectly that you are going to have white men in one bracket, you are going to try to take colored men and women and give them equal employment rights, and down at the bottom of the list is going to be a white woman with no rights at all.[10]

In the nature of things secular and religious, white women always come before black women and men.

Feminists rightly claimed that white women were an oppressed group alongside nonwhite racial and ethnic groups. They too were seeking relief from the centuries-old sexism that white men had used against white women. Yet Griffiths's argument makes clear that their real intention was not to lose ground in a hierarchy, not to stand in line behind black women and black men, who were marked to stand at the bottom of God's presumed ordering of the groups.

So that the remarks of one white woman do not stand for the whole, other voices can be added. Catherine Dean Mays also demonstrated this unstated objective. Quoting from a letter she reportedly had received from Emma Guffey Miller (president of the National Women's Party), Mays announced that white women were "alarmed" over Title VII. According to her, they feared that without the addition of women's rights, this legislation would allow "some government officials [to inter-pret] race, color, religion, and national origin in a way that [would] discriminate against the white, native-born American woman of Christian religion."[11] Congresswoman Mays made an artful attempt to veil her purpose with code words that most white men almost instinc-tively understand. The implication is that African Americans should be considered neither native-born persons nor adherents of the Christian religion (as the Puritan ancestors had shaped matters in the United States?). "Native-born" and "of Christian religion" are the same phrases that have been used by hard-core racist groups such as the Ku Klux Klan (see chapter 2 for further discussion).

Of the ten women in Congress in 1964, only one—Edith Green (Democrat, Oregon)—objected to adding white women's rights to Title VII. Challenging her peers, she reminded them that "whether we want to admit it or not, the main purpose of this [Title VII] legislation today is to try to help end the discrimination that has been practiced against Negroes."[12] Going further, she cited three reasons that her col-leagues should think carefully about before making the decision to add a women's rights amendment to legislation for civil rights for racial and ethnic minorities.

First, she asked them to consider how the women's amendment had abruptly come before the House from the floor and not through any stated committee:

> To the best of my knowledge, there was not one word of testimony in regard to this amendment given before the Committee on the Judiciary of the House or before the Committee on Education and Labor, where this bill was considered. . . . There was not one single organization in the entire United States that petitioned either one of these committees to

add this amendment to the bill. There was not one single Member of the House who came to the Committee on Education and Labor or who came to the Committee on the Judiciary and offered such an amendment.

Second, Congresswoman Green reminded her colleagues that the civil rights bill was "primarily for the purpose of ending discrimination against Negroes in voting and in public accommodations and in education, and yes, in employment." Third, turning to her female colleagues, Green said that while she supported their right to "object to discrimination against women," an honest reading of America's race history would require them to admit that "discrimination against the [white] female of the species is not really a way of life . . . [as] it is a way of life against Negroes." She then summarized her opposition to the women's amendment by stating that she was certain that "it will clutter up the bill and it may later very well be used to help destroy this section of the bill [Title VII] by some of the very people who today support it."

Effects since the 1964 Civil Rights Act

Although Congresswoman Green stood alone in 1964, the past three decades have proven her to have been a prophetic voice. Interestingly, many of the women and men who either voted for or in other ways lined up to endorse the addition of women's rights to the civil rights bill have reversed themselves on black civil rights over the past thirty years.

It is the old story of disillusioned liberals becoming disaffected and angry conservatives. They have risen up against laws whose original intent was to help secure racial equality, either assuming a stony silence as others attacked black civil rights or seeking systematically to undo the legislation they once worked for. Moreover, many white feminists, who formerly portrayed women's rights as having special import for black women, who historically have suffered the double jeopardy of sexism and racism, are now turning their backs on women of color as black women seek relief from both forms of discrimination.

Statistics show that in comparison with white women, African American women make up only 10 percent of the total workforce, hold only 5 percent of management jobs, and earn less than 58¢ for every dollar earned by white women (who themselves earn only a portion of what white men earn).[13] White feminists, when confronted with such statistics, generally deny that they have had any intention of keeping blacks outside the mainstream of white privilege in the United States.

But this demur is most unconvincing, particularly in the academic arena, where white women have made some of their most impressive employment gains over the past thirty years.

EXAMPLES FROM THE ACADEMY

In the halls of the American academy, as was the case in the halls of Congress during the 1960s, some white women have engaged in subtle efforts to place their interests in direct competition with the broader and more urgent concern for the redress of the historic disablement of both black women and black men. As much as, if not more than, white men, white women have spent a considerable amount of social and political energy crafting what scholar Saliwe M. Kawewe aptly calls "sophisticated internal mechanisms to subvert affirmative action in recruitment, hiring, retention, and promotion to the advantage of the privileged gender."[14]

Although white women have attempted to conceal their competitive activities, one of the places where their basic orientation and goals are given away is in their assaults on African and African American studies in college and secondary education. To understand their strategy in these educational arenas, we need to revisit the late 1970s and early 1980s, when women's studies first came into vogue.

The Rise of Women's Studies

Prior to the mid-1970s, no such field as women's studies existed. American education institutions saw themselves as a microcosm of the larger society. They simply dismissed gender-based studies as gratuitous in the basic curriculum and as marginal in upper-level curricula. White feminists had to find a way to convince the white men who controlled higher education that the study of their particular history and experience was an integral part of the university's mission.

The story line is similar to that of Title VII of the civil rights bill. White women observed that black people were achieving redress for their grievances in the academy. Such redress provided a solution to the problem of white women's subordination to white men. Some of the major universities (such as Boston, Harvard, and Yale Universities, as well as less prestigious ones) had begun to recognize black studies. This recognition, however, was not forward-looking on these universities' part, but in response to the mounting pressure of civil rights organizations and a few perceptive black scholars and their students.

Almost immediately after black studies achieved recognition, white women's studies also began to emerge, and then it developed with greater rapidity. Such a turn of events was part of the rising concern for diversity following the civil rights movement. In itself, the growth of women's studies is to be applauded. Even so, it points to another critical issue in any careful evaluation of the feminist agenda.

NOW, in 1970, protested that misogyny had kept women out of the academy, filed its class action suit against the universities and colleges, and won. The immediate result of its victory was the hiring of a phalanx of women professors—predominantly white. Statistics show that between 1960 and 1970, the ranks of white women increased from approximately 5 percent to more than 33 percent.[15]

Giving birth to women's studies was not a gradual evolutionary process; it can be traced to this influx of women. They arrived to redress the lack of women's history and perspective in the traditional subjects. They arrived somewhat behind the black studies programs. They found it prudent, I maintain, to side with white men in favor of the flourishing of black studies in order to carve out funds and other goodies for their own programs.

As always with the postmodern problem of racial discrimination, it would be difficult to lay out a broad and binding paper trail to prove, without fear of contradiction, that this development actually took place. That is the nature of the scrims and subterfuges that have been thrown up to protect white privilege in the highly contested fields and power structures of the nation at the end of the twentieth century. Nevertheless, a telling statement by Supreme Court justice Ruth Bader Ginsburg, reflecting on the dramatic rise in the presence of women professors on the campuses in the 1970s, gives some reasonable credibility to our suspicion that white women rode into power on the back of the civil rights movement of the 1960s and 1970s: "When I began teaching law in 1963, few women appeared on the roster. . . . The changes we have witnessed since that time are considerable. Women are no longer locked out, they are not curiosities in any part of the profession."[16]

The Attack on Black Studies

While we can celebrate the liberation of women scholars from the shackles of obscurity and male subordination, we cannot escape the fact that a fundamental reason for this rapid ascent from being mere "curiosities" in higher education to becoming permanent fixtures was white women's cries that they were a "left-out minority." This cry convinced their white male colleagues that something had to be done about it, even if this meant assailing black studies.[17] Some white feminists made up their minds that if they were to get to the level of their male colleagues—at the top of the profession—it would be necessary to unseat the blacks who had unworthily made the ascent before them, even if that required tactics that were somewhat less than honorable.

The upshot has been that scholarship on African and African American studies soon began showing evidence of resistance against its subject matter, methods, and prospects. Casual observers might suspect that white male professors have provided the major resistance to racial and ethnic studies programs. But this is not the case. Instead, white feminists have been the primary source of these assaults. Their target has been Afrocentrism, the field of study that investigates the ways in which world history had its starting point in Africa and therefore how traditional European methods are invalid for understanding African and African American history. The favorite gambit is to charge that Afrocentrist historians of antiquity (and white male professors who have also dared to venture into this area) are nothing more than mythologists whose unscholarly ambition is to reconstruct ancient history so as to promote their own racial and nationalist political agendas.[18]

Let me be clear at the outset. Any scholarly endeavor needs to attend to its methods, pursue its data, and distinguish its results from those of cultural prophets and popularizers. Any scholar who fabricates data or falsifies history deserves to have his or her scholarship called into question, examined carefully, and refined or repudiated when warranted. Only through such processes can others have confidence in a discipline's integrity. And no one is more aware than I of the dangers of illustrating a large claim through examples. Yet the claim is that a pinpoint investigation of a particular conclusion will be borne out by the evidence.

So what is the evidence that the attacks on black studies, and particularly Afrocentrism, have come primarily from white feminists? It is important to distinguish broadsides from women and from feminists proper. For example, Mona Charen, a former speechwriter for President Ronald Reagan and a syndicated columnist and CNN panelist, frequently attacks the work of black scholars with virulence. She is particularly suspicious of the creation of Kwanzaa, whose principles she calls "little more than the self-important gaseousness of 1960s radicalism."[19] Her attacks are well publicized and perhaps well known, but are they from a feminist?

The case can be better illustrated from within the academy. Prominent among feminist detractors of African American historical scholarship is the classicist scholar Mary Lefkowitz of Wellesley College (and, to a lesser degree, the multiculturalist Diane Ravitch, an adjunct professor at the Teacher's College of Columbia University).[20] Lefkowitz has been a vociferous critic of Afrocentrism, especially of such accredited black scholars as the late Anta Cheik Diop, Molefi Kete Asante, and Yosef ben-Jochannan. Her main arguments are typical of all such detractors' claims.

Lefkowitz's central argument is the allegation that Afrocentrists have tried at least to circumvent, if not to destroy, traditional Eurocentric history methods by claiming that such historic figures as Socrates and Cleopatra were of African descent, and that the Greeks "stole their philosophy from the Egyptians." In her view, Afrocentrists have waged this war on European methods because "it has become fashionable to assume that history is culturally determined, and that each culture or ethnic group can write its own history differently." This "cultural relativism," she argues, "has offered an intellectual justification for Afrocentric history."[21]

Again, any scholar worthy of the name should join Lefkowitz in calling Afrocentrists to task if it can be proved that they have deliberately falsified history. Every fair-minded person should be no less critical of any individual or group that engages in a deliberate misrepresentation of historical fact in the interest of personal or group aggrandizement. So let us come at Lefkowitz's contentions from the angle of intellectual disciplines and their methods.

Lefkowitz's main charge is that the Afrocentric school of contemporary black philosophy is guilty of misconstruing traditional European methods of writing history. At the same time, she and other white feminist scholars protest that these same traditional European methods have ignored and distorted the truth about women down through the ages.

Can she have it both ways? As a historian she must concede that in the hands of male (and female) white racists, European methods were used systematically to support the institution of chattel slavery. These methods are still used today to define and defend racist policies and practices against persons of color as well as sexist policies and practices against white women. Just as white women have a right to point that out and to rise up in righteous indignation to denounce sexism, so do black women and black men have a right (at least an equal right, if not a greater one) to defend themselves against the traditional Eurocentrism that helped to enslave and murder millions and that continues to dehumanize and subordinate black women and black men alike.

What might prompt Lefkowitz to characterize Afrocentrists as the sole patrons of cultural history methods? Surely she understands that *Kulturgeschichte* ("history of culture," sometimes called "historical relativism") had its origin among nineteenth-century German historians and philosophers.[22] (These scholars were popularized in this country by celebrated white male historians such as H. Richard Niebuhr.) Surely she is aware of the fact that the University of Chicago Divinity School, one of the most prestigious universities and graduate schools of religion in this country, achieved much of its fame on the strength of its devotion to the methods of cultural history, specifically the history of religions. When she shoots at Afrocentrists, she hits the white European establishment.

Usually a careful and diligent scholar, Lefkowitz cannot possibly deny that white feminist revisionism (the rewriting of Eurocentric histories under revised methods and insights) is one of the most important realities of late-twentieth-century scholarship. Redressing women's long-denied worth as equal partners with white men is an important task. The white feminist gendercentric method of producing "herstories" is today among the largest consumers and promoters of cultural history.

Lefkowitz has justified her criticism of Afrocentrism with the explanation that she wants only to rekindle "the kind of debate that has until recently been a central feature of academic life." It is unnecessary to question the integrity of this statement, because Lefkowitz does so herself. Continuing her explanation, she writes:

> There is a need to show why these theories are based on false assumptions and faulty reasoning, and cannot be supported by time-tested methods of intellectual inquiry. . . . Even though I am not the only classicist who could have written a book about the Afrocentric myth of ancient history, I have one special qualification: a long-standing interest in pseudohistory.[23]

This explanation leaves us to ponder why Lefkowitz's qualifications have not provoked her to question whether gendercentric history is "pseudohistory." Gendercentrism surely breaks with the time-tested traditional Eurocentric history methods she so passionately defends. Historical probability, which has been employed by most Eurocentrists, allows us to offer one conclusion as to the reason she fails to critique gender-centrism in the same fashion as she does Afrocentrism. She sits squarely in the camp of radical feminist academicians who, unwilling to relinquish their partisan alliance with the distortions of Euro-American historical scholarship and their membership in the guild of scholars that continues to give comfort to racists, have decided to undermine Afrocentrism in order to advance their own careers and programs.

EXAMPLES FROM AMERICAN CULTURE

I do not mean to single Lefkowitz out. This same kind of subversion of black studies in the academy by white women can be seen across America's public and private employment sectors. It has especially been harmful to African American women.

Discussing what stands behind this subversion, Shelby F. Lewis, an African American female scholar, blames "white female hegemony."[24] As cultural proof for the racial affinity between white women and white men, she cites, among other incidents over the past few years, how mainstream feminists refused to rally behind Shirley Chisholm's historic bid for the presidency in 1972 but subsequently gave overwhelming support to Geraldine Ferraro's campaign for vice president in 1984.[25]

Racial likeness certainly has played and still plays a central part in the attitudes of many feminists. Yet skin color is not the only force driving their racism. The same ideational distortions that have determined the white supremacist assumptions of men also condition and guide the bigotry of some white women. To see how this plays out among radical feminists, we need look no further than three sensational events that occasioned banner headlines and unusually large audiences in the media: the O. J. Simpson murder trial (1995), the Clarence Thomas Supreme Court hearings (1991), and the Robert Kennedy Smith rape trial (1991).

Both the Simpson trial and the Thomas hearings featured black people. Simpson was charged with the brutal murder of his white ex-wife, Nicole Brown Simpson, and Ronald Goldman; Thomas was portrayed as a sexual opportunist by a black former colleague, Anita Hill. In Simpson's case, the credibility of a black man was pitted against the integrity of a white police investigator. In Thomas's case, the credibility of a black man was pitted against the integrity of a sincere, respected black woman—and the political machinations of white men, particularly U.S. senators. Although Thomas has been portrayed as having betrayed his black brothers and sisters because of his stance on affirmative action, the fact remains that it was white feminists who seized the opportunity to make this black issue a white woman's issue. The same was true in the Simpson case—a case that should rightly have caused all to rise up in condemnation of a man's brutal inhumanity to two fellow human beings. (Here I make no judgment on Simpson's guilt or innocence.)

Recall the similar treatment these two stories received. Feminists such as Gloria Allred rushed to turn a tragic murder, which left two innocent children and two sets of parents and families devastated, into a white, gender-specific issue: a white woman had been brutally killed.[26] These feminists also came to Anita Hill's defense, to a limited degree, but her personal agony was a mere footnote to the main text— that (white) women had been left out of positions of power. Perhaps the two scenes made for this difference. On the one hand, Nicole Brown Simpson's blood was on the sidewalk and fence; on the other hand, Anita Hill fielded questions about her painful experiences with Clarence Thomas before unsympathetic white male Senators. Nakedly put, white women simply could not picture themselves married to a black man, but they could readily picture themselves wielding power over a black nominee and his black accuser.

Now recall white feminist reactions to the William Kennedy Smith rape trial. Oh, you don't remember any? Surely this alleged transgression had unmistakable implications for the white feminist national campaign against sexual violence. However, white feminists were all but silent about Smith. Why? Feminists knew precisely which ideational levers to pull in order to turn the Simpson and Thomas events into alleged attacks on white women. Thus, we all should clearly see, they knew how to incite Christian conservatives (among others) to come once again to knee-jerk conclusions about black men—except that in the case of Smith, no black man was there. Only white male liberals could be embarrassed, and where's the power in that?

A HISTORY OF COMPLICITY

Given the racial attitudes of some radical white feminists over the past thirty years, white feminists not only have joined but also have helped to lead the movements against African Americans. Some feminists, of course, have claimed to support the black civil rights movement.[27] Others, when the occasion has served, have drawn a parallel between their own struggles against the denigrating sexism of white men and the black struggles against dehumanizing white racism. But should I be astonished that some white women (feminists or not) are leading the rejuvenation of old ideas of race? As my father used to say about white bigots, "They cannot help it." Like their male peers, these women are ideologues whose minds and hearts are simply giving blossom to the seeds of racism sewn in America's soul during the antebellum decades of the nineteenth century.

Southern Belles and Northern Feminists

From the moment that slavery and racism first became cornerstones of this nation, many white women have been no less guilty than white men in drawing on twisted theological ideas to degrade, enslave, and ostracize black people. Slaves and former slaves gave striking testimony to how anti-blackness was just as much a part of the panoply of southern white women as it was of white men.

For example, the Reverend Absalom Jones, founder of the first black Protestant Episcopal Church in America, remarked about this when he wrote, "Our God has seen masters and mistresses . . . take the instruments of torture into their own hands, and deaf to the cries and shrieks of their agonizing slaves, exceed even their overseers in cruelty" against black people.[28] That slave mistresses engaged in such barbarism as handcuffing and whipping slaves should not astonish us. These southern belles were products of their age and thus were pious adherents of the same distorted Christian doctrines professed by slave-master fathers, brothers, and husbands. Like the men with whom they shared power, however curtailed because of their gender, antebellum women left this legacy of ideas to their present-day descendants.

Mary Boykin Chesnut

We do not need to rely on the testimony of ex-slaves. Let us listen to Mary Boykin Chesnut, the wife of Senator James Chesnut Jr. of South Carolina. Speaking in the aftermath of the Civil War, she proclaimed with pious certainty that black people were "dirty, slatternly, idle, [and] ill-smelling by nature" because God had created them that way. Like her male compatriots, she defended white supremacy by insisting that slavery had been a godsend for black people, because it was the only way they could ever hope to overcome the "curse of inferiority and savagery" that God had placed upon them. For Mary Chesnut—and she was by no means alone among slave mistresses who held such beliefs—slavery was a divine institution that provided the superior white race the opportunity "to help ameliorate the condition of these Africans in every particular" and to "set them the example of a perfect life, a life of self-abnegation."[29]

Early Antislavery Feminists

Postmodern radical feminists continue a long tradition. Some of them inherited a portion of their anti-blackness from southern slave mistresses. But my argument is that they inherited the greater portion from early northern white feminists who joined antislavery movements during the mid-1830s. This story needs to be told.

When the early feminists began joining antislavery societies, they brought with them a considerable agenda. The abolition of the enslavement of African Americans was only one portion; the liberation of white women from the sexism of their male relatives and friends was the other (see chapter 1). The whole agenda proved to be too much. Like some feminists today, white feminists soon turned away from black people and fell back on or found it expedient to take up the deeply rooted ideas of white supremacy.

A classic example is found in the activities of the Fall River Female Anti-Slavery Society, founded in 1835 at Fall River, Massachusetts. This society stated that its goal was to help raise the nation's conscience in favor of the abolition of southern slavery. Shortly after the Fall River Society was founded, black women, yearning to be involved in the struggle for their own liberation, sought to become members of the society. Hostility toward their participation was immediate and became so intense that there was a hurried call to dissolve the society.[30]

Drafting off the Black Struggles

The driving ambition of some radical feminists today, following in the mold of their antebellum forebears, is to advance, by whatever means necessary, their own liberation from sexism. They are not above using the plight of black men and black women to achieve that goal. Drafting off the black struggles, new life has once again been breathed into their own mission of women's rights on the strength of their insistent entreaty to the men in their lives that there is no difference between their oppression and that of African Americans. Indeed, drawing a useful correlation between gender discrimination and racism has a long and impressive history in the United States that has not gone unnoticed by postmodern feminists.

Is it unfair to criticize the contemporary women's movement for drawing a parallel between their struggle and that of African American women and men? After all, many would argue, both groups are fighting for the same social, economic, and political equity and advancement; why should they not piggyback on each other?

Some white feminists insist that their struggle is against the same white male domination that African Americans are trying to throw off. Yet an important difference exists between what the two groups are trying to realize. On the one hand, feminists seek to break through the economic glass ceilings imposed on them by white men. What drives them is the desire to sit beside white men as the dominant personnel in the offices and boardrooms of the American power structure. On the other hand, African Americans seek to overcome hatred that has incited genocide and institutional racism that has denied black-skinned people equal participation in the American dream. Both seek equal opportunity and civil rights. But African Americans first of all seek dignity, humanity.

Some might maintain that these are not contrasting goals but that they merely lie on a continuum. White women are closer to achieving equal rights than blacks are. Indeed, some women may feel dehumanized by sexism, but most would not describe their plight in such dramatic terms. On such a continuum, if full parity were, say, a 1 and dehumanization a 10, then white women would be located at 3 or 4, while blacks would be at 7 or 8. So let's join hands and together sing, "We shall overcome."

My point is that such a smooth continuum is not self-evident. Even though many feminists project their legitimate fight for equality with men as analogous to the black struggle, blacks need to raise questions to express the depths of their dehumanizing treatment. When, we might ask, was the last time that a qualified white woman applied for a house loan and was redlined? or had a salesclerk or waiter snobbishly refuse to serve her until a white person, who was second in line, had been served first? When was the last time (never mind about the first time) that anybody read of a white woman being viciously beaten as was Rodney King by law enforcement officers in Los Angeles? or sodomized as was Abner Louima by uniformed law officers in a New York police station? or choked to death as was Johnny Gammage by police officers in a suburb of Pittsburgh?

Let me put my concern a different way. Feminists contend that white women share a common oppression with black people, yet they have access to and participate in the same white structures of privilege that, by definition, keep blacks degraded and second-class. Feminists cannot have it both ways, because they have yet to address the idea of black inferiority carried in their minds and hearts. On the one hand, they seek equal advantage, but on the other hand, their advantage is already favorable as compared to blacks. Perhaps Vivian Gordon has best captured the difference: white feminists really want to be a more important part of the present system—"They seek power, not change."[31]

A CRITICAL LESSON

There is a critical lesson to be learned from this strange and frustrating situation that blacks have had to deal with over the past thirty years. The clear message is that during these years some white feminists—not all, but *some*, especially some in white-collar jobs and as managers or employees with professional skills and authority—have become proficient in disestablishing white male hegemony and mitigating the power of sexist ideas that had pilfered their dignity and prostituted them from the moment their Puritan ancestors first arrived on the shores of Massachusetts. This is a good first step. But these white women have not yet demonstrated that same proficiency when it comes to abolishing from their own minds and hearts the old twisted theologies of race that were first sown by those pious Protestant Christians.

Thus, their behavior tells us that they are no less like crabs in a barrel, pulling down those who by stress and strain may have made it a little farther toward the top, than the rest of us who have been on the bottom for as long as we can remember. But more than anything else, it teaches us how difficult it is for members of the majority race in America, whether male or female, to repent of and purify their minds of those old racial beliefs and ideational prejudices and practices that have so long been the hallmark of authentic biblical Christianity gone awry.

EPILOGUE

I n this book I have sought to illustrate a single thesis: behind the large and small everyday acts that, over the past four centuries, enslaved, then routinely segregated, and now subtly discriminate against black people lie distorted biblical and theological ideas. These ideas, deeply embedded in the mind and ethos of Americans, did not originate with crude and unlettered plantation owners in the South. These seeds first took root among pious and highly cultured New England Puritan Christians decades before slavery became a foundational economic institution of the new nation. Even though numerous others—Catholics, Protestants, and Jews—were just as guilty of perpetuating such racism, it was first seeded in the Puritan notions of national destiny and black inferiority.

THE SEEDS OF RACISM

Winthrop D. Jordan has pointed out that the Puritans had no real economic need for slaves (see chapter 1). Their economy was built on manufacturing and shipping. They, along with their indentured servants (whose service was ended after their debt was paid), could have provided more than sufficient labor for these enterprises during the early colonial period. Thus, these devout Christians did not rather mindlessly fall into making slavery the permanent status of blacks. A more deliberate process was at work in their minds.

The Puritans had had almost no contact with Africans either in England or during their Netherlands sojourn. Yet the degrading characterizations that European voyagers had already invented about the people encountered in the "dark continent" were in their minds. After King James I had secretly ordered their presses burned in Leiden, the Netherlands, the Puritans set sail for the New World. They employed the characterizations they had picked up when they first had contact with Native Indians and Africans here.

For these devout Christians, every thought and action had to conform with the Bible and with what they believed to be the will and purpose of God. By twisting theological beliefs to make them more coherent with what had become an Anglo-xenophobia (an inbred aversion to the strange and so-called heathen black people from a remote clime), it was easy for them to reason that God had predestined black people to be woebegone outcasts in this land. And because God had ordained it thus, these blacks were forever to be segregated from and subordinated to all whites, even to those who had proved to be unregenerate social and religious misfits in this holy empire. Otherwise, the holiness and purity of the chosen white race might not be preserved. In this way the Puritan founders of the American nation translated their racist ideas into a doctrine of white supremacy. The rest, as is said, was history. It was the duty of whites to enslave black people in order to participate in the divine arrangement or covenant God made with this chosen white race.

FOUR INSIGHTS ON AMERICAN RACISM

The economic or cheap-labor thesis about American slavery is exploded. Puritan notions of perpetual bondage and racial subordination were more powerful than mere economic expediency. These notions spread southward, as I have shown, and they survived the Emancipation Proclamation (1863) and civil rights legislation (1964–1965). Here I want to draw out four other insights on American racism that scholars have generally ignored or have given only passing attention.

First, racism has a powerful suprarational or fideistic character and thus stands in a starkly antithetical position to authentic Christian faith. The work of black scholars George H. Kelsey and Cornel West has helped us see this.[1] But more than either Kelsey or West has argued, I have stressed in this study that racism is itself a religion in the United States and is practically synonymous with American Christianity. From the first moment the Puritans settled in North America, Christian religionists have employed distorted Christian theological ideas to define and justify their bigotry against persons of African descent.

Martin Luther King Jr., although he did not discuss the issue in detail, warned of this religious character of racism three years after he had been thrust into prominence as a civil rights leader. Speaking in 1958 about the history and nature of racism, he proposed that we cannot begin to understand or successfully conquer racial hatred until we first confess that white Christian religion has "a historic obligation in this crisis" (see chapter 3).

Second, in light of the religious nature of racism, all efforts to erase racism have failed, because they have concentrated on its visible manifestations rather than its ideational character. Since Dr. King's assassination in 1968, public confessions have been issued by both the liberal United Methodist and the conservative Southern Baptist denominations. But these much-heralded verbal admissions of guilt and statements of repentance have done little to erase the notions of black inferiority or the complicity of churches in preserving those notions.

More than sackcloth and ashes is needed to abolish the disease of racism. Despite the sincerity and impetus of efforts by many whites— from abolitionism to the radical Reconstruction (1867–1877) to the civil rights movement of the 1960s to church confessions—racism will continue until its ideational character is rooted out. This sickness of the American body politic is frustratingly tenacious because it is lodged in the American body ecclesiastic. The true nature of our race prejudice has as much, if not more, to do with the persistence of false-conscious and unconscious ideas in the mind as it does with the concrete acts of disablement and violence that have been committed against African Americans since the 1600s, as awful as these are.

Since the 1630s, a small but influential group of white intellectuals has been in the forefront of manufacturing and wholesaling an American brand of racial prejudice. Not southern rednecks but learned northern white liberals were usually the first to leap forward to revive or reface and combine old racist patterns of thought with new ideas and language when changes in the sociopolitical milieu made their rationalizations expedient. Not only Christian theologians (who in the beginning were represented by the Puritan divines) but also scientists, physicians, business leaders, politicians and diplomats, and various postmodern academics have joined in this ideological besmirching of the image of African Americans. Indeed, many who were formerly considered liberals in the field of race relations have succumbed since the 1960s to the temptation to fall back upon the old religious allegations about black degradation and inferiority, disguising them in scientific and academic language when their social engineering strategies proved to be fruitless.

Third, some radical white female ideologues have been no less diligent than their male counterparts in perpetuating racist ideas and practices. As we have seen, some white female abolitionists, viewing blacks as inferior to themselves, refused membership in abolition societies to African American women who sought to work alongside them for black liberation. This was a political decision, but it was buttressed and justified by racist ideology. Postmodern and radical white feminists, despite their protests to the contrary, have continued this pattern of prejudice, though clothing it in the garment of expediency when their interests as a so-called oppressed minority have clashed with those of women and men of color—particularly in Congress, corporate America, and academia.

While they were not as direct with their racism, northern white women in antebellum America shared the views of their southern slaveholding peers. As ironic as it might seem, this attitude can be seen even among some of the women who either joined antislavery movements founded by white men or founded their own.

Postmodern white women—especially some radical feminists who have openly declared war on black men—have continued this tradition. The only difference between them and their male peers is that they have been much more Machiavellian in their attempt to ascend the heights of male privilege no matter who gets crushed along the way.

Fourth, American racism has never needed any reason for its existence other than the offensiveness of black skin color. Does noting that the logic of American racism rests only on the offensiveness of black skin color contradict the preceding three theses? No. The role that Christianity has played in maintaining prejudice and discrimination—beginning with the Puritans in the United States but advanced by other Christian groups in Europe—continues to this day. But some whites have never sought to justify their bigotry beyond the idea that black people are black and are therefore outside the pale of natural human evolution.

A classic example of this kind of thinking is found among both liberals and conservatives who supported black civil rights during the

1960s. Many of them participated in the battles for federal laws that would end legal segregation. Yet they were also among the first to flee the central cities, public schools, and downtown institutions like churches, YMCAs and YWCAs, public schools, libraries, and settlement houses.

No doubt their reports are correct that their rush to suburbia had to do with the search for better housing, better schools, and a higher quality of services. But what was cheapening their housing, lowering the educational value of their schools, and degrading the quality of the services they received? After all, these whites held the most privileged employment, sent their children to excellent schools, and lived in urban neighborhoods that most blacks could not have afforded to move into in the early 1960s, even if they desired to do so. The white flight of the post–civil rights years stemmed from fears that *blackness means corruption*.

RISKING DIALOGUE AND SOLUTIONS

Historians rarely risk proposing solutions for contemporary social problems. But I can sit still no longer to let the next generation of historians simply document time and again the legacy of the bad fruits of the seeds of racism. I would much rather have them recount how, at the dawn of a new century, whites and persons of color made a new story, a new beginning in American race relations, through a sincere and permanent, ideational and spiritual conversion from old racist ideas.

Such conversion—this time—will not seek to root out racism as it expresses itself in institutions and concrete practices. This approach, taken over the past four centuries, has been unsuccessful in terminating this disease. We need to go to the root of the problem: the American mind. This is why President Clinton's June 1997 initiative to open up a national dialogue on race is so important. As a first step, the American intelligentsia—specifically theologians, ethicists, preachers, public school teachers, college and university professors, business leaders, and politicians—needs to pursue a dialogue that challenges all of us to face squarely the reality that bad ideas do exist.

By "bad ideas" I mean those theories that vaunt themselves against all logic, history, and science; I mean the twisted form of American Christianity presented in this book. Here African American Christians have much to share with their white Christian peers, because blacks have preserved and taught a biblical faith without hierarchies of humans. Over many generations, they have resisted the demonic falsification of the religion of Jesus of Nazareth. Many white mainline traditions that have suffered slow but steady decline may actually be rejuvenated by this gospel kept safe by blacks.

How ironic that our national leaders and intellectual ideologues have yet to confront the American mind on this problem. I say "ironic" because relations between racial and ethnic groups in the United States are crucial and should be a vital part of leading a nation. Other areas of our national experience have seen some improvement. For example, some outmoded scientific and medical theories, some ideas of past generations about child rearing, some of our worst expressions of sexism, ageism, and attitudes about the physically handicapped, some negative ideas about social security and national health care, and some old protectionist and isolationist ideas vis-à-vis the United Nations and globalism—many of these have been corrected. But when it comes to racism, particularly against African Americans, a few changes have been made, but on a piecemeal and superficial basis.

For each step forward, we have taken two backward with regard to racism. It would appear that this tinkering with the racial and ethnic imbalances and tensions in our society has prevented us from looking beneath the surface and dealing with the deep-seated ideological taproot of our hostilities and alienations. It has been too difficult and too threatening to admit to ourselves that much of the problem of race in our country began with our misinterpretation of the Christian religion and that what we desperately need is a soul-wrenching conversion from the bad ideas to better ideas—ideas of equality in humanity and pursuit of bliss.

We all would do well to recall these words of Proverbs: "For as he thinketh in his heart, so *is* he" (23:7 KJV).[2] Long has dominant white America wrongly clung to the idea that God, history, and all the forces of nature conspire to consign persons of African descent to the status of inferior misfits and strangers in this land. Before we can make real progress toward racial reconciliation, Americans must confess in heart and mind, beginning in both religious sanctuary and academic lecture hall, that this is an ungodly and illogical theory. I propose, then, that each and every white American go to that personal mountain to declare with a clear, resounding voice, "Let freedom ring. Let freedom truly ring for my black brothers and sisters. Their pilgrimage in this country until now has largely been subjection and degradation. But I will work to change this."

NOTES

INTRODUCTION

1. See, for example, John Hope Franklin, *From Slavery to Freedom: A History of Negro Americans* (New York: Knopf, 1967), 72.

2. Martin Luther King Jr., *Stride toward Freedom: The Montgomery Story* (New York: Ballantine Books, 1958), 167.

3. Ibid.

4. James H. Cone, "Martin, Malcolm, and America: A Dream or a Nightmare?" lecture delivered at Corinthian Baptist Church, Dayton, Ohio, February 16, 1996.

1. THE SOWING OF THE SEEDS

1. The quotation was reported by Eaton's daughter, so the precise date when he made his announcement is debatable. See Simeon E. Baldwin, ed., *Papers of the New Haven Colony, Historical Society*, vol. 7 (New Haven: New Haven Historical Society, 1908), 31; Winthrop D. Jordan, *White over Black: American Attitudes toward the Negro, 1550–1812* (Baltimore: Penguin, 1968), 68; and Lorenzo Johnston Greene, *The Negro in Colonial New England, 1620–1776* (1942; reprint, Washington, D.C.: Kennikat Press, 1966), 17, 290.

2. The entire code appears in *The Colonial Laws of Massachusetts*, by William H. Whitmore, record commissioner (Boston: Rockwell and Churchill, 1890).

3. John Hope Franklin, *From Slavery to Freedom: A History of Negro Americans* (New York: Knopf, 1967), 72, 75. Also see Peter M. Bergman, *The Chronological History of the Negro in America* (New York: Harper and Row, 1969), 15.

4. Jordan, *White over Black*, 66.

5. Franklin, *From Slavery to Freedom*, 101. Also see George Clarence Ray, "A Study of the Indentured Servant in the Colonial Era from a Human Capital Viewpoint" (Ph.D. diss., University of South Carolina–Columbia, 1972).

6. John Winthrop, "A Model of Christian Charity," in *Winthrop Papers*, vol. 2, *1623–1630*, ed. Stewart Mitchell (New York: Russell and Russell, 1931), 293.

7. Jordan, *White over Black*, 44. Also see Lester B. Scherer, *Slavery and the Churches in Early America, 1619–1819* (Grand Rapids, Mich.: Eerdmans, 1975), 21–22.

8. Richard Hakluyt, "The Second Voyage of John Hawkins to Guinea" in *The Principal Navigations, Voyages, Traffiques, and Discoveries of the English Nation* (New York: AMS Press, 1965), 9–64 passim.

9. Jordan, *White over Black*, 43.

10. Plato's concept of eternal ideas is found in his *Timaeus, and the Critias, or Atlanticus*, trans. Thomas Taylor (New York: Pantheon, 1945).

11. Jordan, *White over Black*, 66.

12. Cotton Mather, *The Life of the Rev. John Eliot, the First Missionary to the Indians of North America* (reprint, London: 1820), 109.

13. Abbot Emerson Smith, *Colonists in Bondage: White Servitude and Convict Labor in America, 1607–1776* (New York: Norton, 1971), is a thorough account of these deviants, including an appendix that identifies the numbers and European backgrounds of the individuals who came to the various colonies.

14. Some whites were temporarily held as slaves. See Greene, *The Negro in Colonial New England*, 18–20 passim.

15. Jordan, *White over Black*, 71; Scherer, *Slavery and the Churches*, 26–27. Also see Forrest G. Wood, *The Arrogance of Faith: Christianity and Race in America from the Colonial Era to the Twentieth Century* (New York: Knopf, 1990), 237ff.

16. John Winthrop, "History of New England, 1630–1649," in *Winthrop's Journal*, ed. James Kendall Hosmer (New York: Barnes and Noble, 1908), 2:228.

17. This idea runs throughout Cotton Mather, *The Negro Christianized: An Essay to Excite and Assist That Good Work, the Instruction of Negro Servants in Christianity* (Boston: B. Green, 1706).

18. John Calvin's theology is detailed in his *Institutes of the Christian Religion: Instruction in Faith* (Philadelphia: Westminster, 1949). Also see Justo Gonzalez, *A History of Christian Thought: From the Protestant Reformation to the Twentieth Century*, vol. 3 (Nashville: Abingdon, 1975), 158–61.

19. There is a small army of writings that, in varying ways, examine Puritan "federal theology." One of the oldest is William Ames, *Marrow of Sacred Divinity Drawn out of the Holy Scriptures . . .* (London: Griffin, 1642). Also see E. Brooks Holifield, *The Covenant Sealed: The Development of Puritan Sacramental Theology in Old and New England, 1570–1720* (New Haven: Yale University Press, 1974); Norman Petit, *The Heart Prepared: Grace and Conversion in Puritan Spiritual Life* (New Haven: Yale University Press, 1966); and Emerson Everett, *Puritanism in America* (Boston: Twayne, 1979).

20. Winthrop, "A Model of Christian Charity," in Mitchell, *Winthrop Papers*, 282.

21. Theophilus Eaton, in Baldwin, *Papers of the New Haven Colony*, 31.

22. John Winthrop, "History of New England, 1630–1649," in Hosmer, *Winthrop's Journal*, 1:260.

23. See, for example, Louis Ruchames, *Racial Thought in America*, vol. 1, *From the Puritans to Abraham Lincoln* (Amherst: University of Massachusetts Press, 1969), 59.

24. Mather, *The Negro Christianized*, 2–3. Also see Cotton Mather, *Rules for the Society of Negroes*, reprinted in *Cotton Mather: A Bibliography of His Works*, vol. 3, ed. Thomas J. Holmes (Cambridge: Harvard University Press, 1940).

25. Wood, *The Arrogance of Faith*, 254, says that this neglect "has been reflected in the writings of some of the most influential students of New England history."

26. John Saffin, *A Brief and Candid Answer to a Late Printed Sheet, Entitled, The Selling of Joseph*, reprinted in an appendix in George H. Moore, *Notes on the History of Slavery in Massachusetts* (New York: Appleton, 1866), 251–56; Samuel Sewall, *The Selling of Joseph*, 1785, reprinted in Samuel Hopkins, *A Dialogue Concerning the Slavery of the Africans* (New York: Arno Press, 1969).

27. Ibid., 251–52.

28. Ibid., 252.

29. Ibid.

30. Ibid., 256.

31. See, for example, Wood, *The Arrogance of Faith*, especially 264–67.

32. Sidney E. Ahlstrom, *A Religious History of the American People* (New Haven: Yale University Press, 1972), 158.

33. Greene, *The Negro in Colonial New England*, 24.

34. Franklin, *From Slavery to Freedom*, 146; Greene, ibid., 298.

35. See Jordan, *White over Black*, 294ff.

36. Samuel Hopkins, *A Dialogue Concerning the Slavery of the Africans Shewing It to Be the Duty and Interest of the American States to Emancipate All Their African Slaves . . .* (New York: Spooner, 1776), 50.

37. Greene, *The Negro in Colonial New England*, 290ff.

38. See, for example, Moore, *Slavery in Massachusetts*, 191ff.

39. Ibid. Also see Robert A. Warner, *New Haven Negroes: A Social History* (New Haven: Yale University Press, 1940), especially 7, 11; and George L. Clark, *A History Of Connecticut: Its People and Institutions* (New York: Putnam's, 1914), 155ff.

40. Moore, *Slavery in Massachusetts*, 120–30.

41. See, for example, Lewis Paul Todd and Merle Curti, *Rise of the American Nation* (New York: Harcourt, Brace and World, 1961); John Blum, Bruce Catton, Edmund S. Morgan, Arthur Schlesinger Jr., Kenneth Stampp, C. Van Woodward, et al., *The National Experience: A History of the United States* (New York: Harcourt, Brace and World, 1968); and Winthrop D. Jordan, Leon Litwack, Richard Hofstadter, William Miller, and Daniel Aaron, *The United States* (Englewood Cliffs, N.J.: Prentice Hall, 1982).

42. See Franklin, *From Slavery to Freedom*, 71; Lerone Bennett, *Before the Mayflower: A History of the Negro in America, 1619–1964* (New York: Pelican, 1966), 36; and Donald Robinson, *Slavery in the Structure of American Politics* (New York: Norton, 1979), 13. Although he says that the first twenty Africans in Virginia seem not to have been slaves, Jordan (*White over Black*, 74) also says that slavery did exist in the United States as early as 1640.

43. Ruchames, *Racial Thought in America*, 71ff.

44. Thomas R. R. Cobb, *An Inquiry into the Law of Negro Slavery in the United States of America to Which Is Prefixed, An Historical Sketch of Slavery* (n.p.: T. and J. W. Johnson, 1858), 60–61. Also see Franklin, *From Slavery to Freedom*, 83.

45. Cobb, *Law of Negro Slavery*, 60; Franklin, *From Slavery to Freedom*, 78–82.

46. Jordan, *White over Black*, 72.

47. Statement of the Virginia Assembly, quoted in James Curtis Ballagh, *A History of Slavery in Virginia* (Baltimore: Johns Hopkins Press, 1902), 34.

48. Kenneth Stampp, *The Peculiar Institution: Slavery in the Antebellum South* (New York: Vintage, 1964), 21–22.

49. Ibid., 30.

50. William Byrd, "On Negro Slavery," *Virginia Magazine of History and Biography* 36 (1928): 219–22.

51. Richard Baxter, *A Christian Directory; or, A Summ of Practical Theologie and Cases of Conscience: Directing Christians How to Use Their Knowledge and Faith . . .* (London: Robert White, 1673), 557.

52. See Larry E. Tise, *Proslavery: A History of the Defense of Slavery in America, 1701–1840* (Athens: University of Georgia Press, 1987), 365.

53. William Meade, *Sermons, Dialogues, and Narrative for Servants* (n.p., 1836), 1.

54. Gonzalez, *A History of Christian Thought,* 162–77.

55. Frederick A. Ross, *Slavery Ordained of God* (New York: Lippincott, 1859), 46–50 passim.

56. An early account of Arminius is found in Petrus Bertius, *The Life and Death of James (Jacob) Arminius and Simon Episcopius: Professors of Divinity in the University of Leydon in Holland . . .* (London: Francis Smith, 1672). For an excellent analysis of Arminius's opposition to predestination, see Reinhold Seeburg, *The History of Doctrines,* vol. 1 (Grand Rapids, Mich.: Baker, 1977), 421ff.

57. For Wesley's attitude toward slavery, see John Wesley, *Thoughts on Slavery* (New York: American Anti-Slavery Society, 1839).

58. Lucius Matlack, *The Antislavery Struggle and Triumph in the Methodist Episcopal Church* (New York: Phillips and Hunt, 1881), 60.

59. William A. Smith, *Lectures on the Philosophy and Practice of Slavery as Exhibited in the Institution of Domestic Slavery in the United States* (1856), quoted in Harmon Smith, "William Capers and William A. Smith," *Methodist History* 3 (1964): 25.

60. Thornton Stringfellow, *Scriptural and Statistical Views in Favor of Slavery* (Richmond: J. W. Randolph, 1856), 6–54 passim.

61. A classic history of the antislavery movement is Gilbert H. Barnes, *The Antislavery Impulse, 1830–1844* (New York: Harcourt, Brace and World, 1933).

62. George Keith, "An Exhortation and Caution to Friends concerning Buying or Keeping of Negroes," in Ruchames, *Racial Thought in America,* 41–45. In 1688, five years before Keith's protest, the commissioners of Providence and Warwick, Rhode Island, passed a proclamation denouncing slavery. See "Rhode Island Records, I" in Moore, *Slavery in Massachusetts,* 73–74.

63. Keith, "An Exhortation and Caution," 45.

64. Ruchames, *Racial Thought in America,* 77–132.

65. William G. McLoughlin, *Revivals, Awakenings, and Reform* (Chicago: University of Chicago Press, 1978), 98ff., identifies this revival as having begun in 1800.

66. See John Wesley, *A Plain Account of Christian Perfection* (reprint, London: Epworth, 1975). Also see John L. Peters, *Christian Perfection and American Methodism* (reprint, Grand Rapids, Mich.: Zondervan, 1985).

67. See my discussion of moral government in Paul R. Griffin, *The Struggle for a Black Theology of Education: Pioneering Efforts of Post Civil War Clergy* (Atlanta: Interdenominational Theological Center Press, 1993), 56ff.

68. "Speech of Orange Scott against Slavery," in Matlack, *The Antislavery Struggle and Triumph*, 96–97.

69. George B. Cheever, *God against Slavery* (Cincinnati: American Reform Tract and Book Society, 1857), 148–49.

70. Ibid., v–vi.

71. Ibid., 24.

72. Ibid.

73. Amos A. Phelps, *Lectures on Slavery and Its Remedy* (Boston: New England Anti-Slavery Society, 1834), v–vi.

74. Ibid., 18.

75. Ibid., 19.

76. Ibid., 148–64 passim.

77. Ibid., vii–x.

78. E. D. Sims, quoted in Albert Barnes, *An Inquiry into the Scriptural Views of Slavery* (Philadelphia: Parry and McMillan, 1855), 29.

79. Wilbur Fisk, quoted in ibid.

80. Timothy L. Smith, *Revivalism and Social Reform* (Nashville: Abingdon Press, 1957), 182.

81. Ibid. Also see Ahlstrom, *A Religious History*, 644.

82. Ahlstrom, *A Religious History*, 644.

83. "Pastoral Address of the General Conference of 1840," in Matlack, *The Antislavery Struggle and Triumph*, 137.

84. Mather, *The Negro Christianized*, 12.

85. See "Minutes of the Methodist Conferences Annually Held in America, from 1773 to 1794, Inclusive," in *Journal of the Reverend Francis Asbury*, vol. 2 (New York: N. Bangs and T. Mason, 1821), 151.

86. *Extracts of the Journals of the Late Rev. Thomas Coke* (Dublin: Methodist Book Room, 1816), 74.

87. G. Barnes, *The Antislavery Impulse*, 162.

88. Ibid.

89. See, for example, Jordan et al., *The United States*, 375.

2. THE HYBRIDIZATION OF THE IDEAS, 1865–1950

1. Sidney E. Ahlstrom, *A Religious History of the American People* (New Haven: Yale University Press, 1972), 264.

2. *Pastoral Letter of the Presbyterian Church, South,* in Gross Alexander, James B. Scouller, R. V. Foster, and Thomas C. Johnson, *A History of the Methodist Church, South; the United Presbyterian Church; the Cumberland Presbyterian Church; and the Presbyterian Church, South, in the United States* (New York: Christian Literature, 1894), 426.

3. See Bruce A. Ragsdale and Joel D. Treese, *Black Americans in Congress, 1870–1989* (Washington, D.C.: GPO, 1990). Statistics of the number of African Americans holding elected or appointed state and federal offices also can be found in Lerone Bennett, *Before the Mayflower: A History of the Negro in America, 1619–1964* (New York: Pelican, 1966), 199–200.

4. See William J. Simmons, *Men of Mark: Eminent, Progressive, and Rising* (reprint, New York: Arno Press, 1968), 886–87; and Peter M. Bergman, *The Chronological History of the Negro in America* (New York: Harper and Row, 1969), 441.

5. See James Cone, *A Black Theology of Liberation* (reprint, Maryknoll, N.Y.: Orbis, 1990).

6. Alexander et al., *A History of the Methodist Church, South,* 427.

7. Nehemiah Adams, *A South-Side View of Slavery; or, Three Months at the South, in 1854* (Boston: T. R. Marvin and B. B. Mussey, n.d.), 23.

8. See, for example, William Sumner Jenkins, *Pro-slavery Thought in the Old South* (Gloucester, Mass.: Peter Smith, 1960), 90. Also see I. A. Newby, *Jim Crow's Defense: Anti-Negro Thought in America, 1900–1930* (Baton Rouge: Louisiana State University Press, 1965), 19ff.

9. Jean Louis Rodolphe Agassiz, "The Diversity of the Origin of the Human Race," *Christian Examiner and Religious Miscellany* 49 (1850): 142–43.

10. Ibid., 144.

11. For a discussion of this problem especially among southerners, see Jenkins, *Pro-slavery Thought in the Old South,* 260–70.

12. Charles Carroll, *"The Negro a beast"; or, "In the Image of God": The reasoner of the age, the revelator of the century! The Bible as it is! The negro and his relation to the human family! . . . The negro not the son of Ham* . . . (Salem, N.H.: Ayer, 1900), 87.

13. Charles Carroll, *The Tempter of Eve* (St. Louis: Adamic Publishing, 1902).

14. Charles Darwin, *The Origin of Species by Means of Natural Selection; or, The Preservation of Favored Races in the Struggle for Life* (New York: D. Appleton, 1859); Charles Darwin, *The Descent of Man and Selection in Relation to Sex* (London: J. Murray, 1871).

15. See, for example, Carl Degler, *In Search of Human Nature: The Decline and Revival of Darwinism in American Social Thought* (New York: Oxford University Press, 1991), 14.

16. See, for example, Ahlstrom, *A Religious History,* 849–50.

17. Josiah Strong, *The New Era; or, The Coming Kingdom* (New York: Baker and Taylor, 1893), 79–80.

18. Hegel's dialectic centered around what he called a "philosophy of history." This history of human beings held that God had been moving races through three stages—thesis, antithesis, and synthesis—that ultimately resulted in God revealing God's self fully only to the German people. See Georg W. Hegel, *The Philosophy of History,* trans. J. Sibrel (New York: Dover, 1956).

19. Ibid., 354.

20. Josiah Strong, *Our Country,* ed. Jurgen Herbst (Cambridge: Harvard University Press, Belknap Press, 1963), 210.

21. Strong, *The New Era,* 3–4.

22. Walter Rauschenbusch, *Christianizing the Social Order* (New York: Macmillan, 1912), 90.

23. Walter Rauschenbusch, *Christianity and the Social Crisis* (New York: Macmillan, 1907), 422.

24. Rauschenbusch, *Christianizing the Social Order,* 196.

25. Ibid., 195.

26. Ibid., 195–96.

27. Ibid., 90.

28. John H. Van Evrie, *White Supremacy and Negro Subordination; or, Negroes a Subordinate Race, and (So-Called) Slavery Its Normal Condition* (New York: Van Evrie, Horton, 1868), 312.

29. One of the physicians lists hundreds of names of individuals, including physicians and social scientists, who subscribed to his study: Josiah Nott, *Types of Mankind; or, Ethnological Researches, Based upon Monuments, Paintings, Sculptures, and Crania of Races, and upon Natural Geographical, Philological, and Biblical History* (Philadelphia: Lippincott, Grambo, 1854), 733–38.

30. Ibid., 85.

31. Ibid., 79.

32. Ibid., 63, 85.

33. Ibid., 79.

34. Ibid., 260.

35. Ibid., 79.

36. Ibid., 67.

37. Ibid.

38. Ibid., 265–66.

39. Van Evrie, *White Supremacy and Negro Subordination*, i.

40. Ibid., 141, 169.

41. Ibid., 128.

42. Ibid., 165, 220.

43. Ibid., vi.

44. Ibid., 219.

45. Ibid., 221.

46. Ibid.

47. Ibid., 218.

48. Ibid.

49. Martin Luther King Jr., *Why We Can't Wait* (New York: Mentor, 1964).

50. Robert W. Shufeldt, *The Negro a Menace to American Civilization* (Boston: Gorman Press, 1907), 36.

51. Ibid., 115.

52. Ibid.

53. Robert W. Shufeldt, *America's Greatest Problem: The Negro* (Philadelphia: F. A. Davis, 1915), 1–3.

54. Ibid., 249.

55. Ibid., 240.

56. More extensive definitions of these diseases and their origins can be found in Joan Luckmann and Karen Creason Sorensen, *Medical-Surgical Nursing: A Psychophysiologic Approach* (Philadelphia: Saunders, 1974).

57. Shufeldt, *America's Greatest Problem*, 250.

58. Shufeldt, *The Negro a Menace*, 111.

59. Shufeldt, *America's Greatest Problem*, 80–96 passim.

60. Shufeldt, *The Negro a Menace*, 145.

61. Shufeldt, *America's Greatest Problem*, 2.

62. Bennett, *Before the Mayflower*, 225.

63. William Montgomery Brown, *The Crucial Race Question; or, Where and How Shall the Color Line Be Drawn* (Little Rock: Arkansas Churchman's Publishing, 1907), 125.

64. Ibid., 135.

65. Atticus G. Haygood, *Our Brother in Black: His Freedom and His Future* (New York: Phillips and Hunt, 1891), 34, 188–89 especially. Compare with Newby, *Jim Crow's Defense*, 85.

66. Newby, *Jim Crow's Defense*, 109.

67. See Francis J. Grimke, *The American Bible Society and Colorphobia* (Washington, D.C.: n.p., April 13, 1916), 1.

68. Tom Watson, *Tom Watson's Jeffersonian Magazine*, May 15, 1913.

69. Tom Watson, *Tom Watson's Jeffersonian Magazine* 3 (1909): 97.

70. Scholars of populism are divided over whether Watson was really an egalitarian or a covert racist. See, for example, Gerald H. Gaither, *Blacks and the Populist Revolt: Ballots and Bigotry in the "New South"* (n.p.: University of Alabama Press, 1977), 71ff.

71. Tom Watson, "The Negro Question in the South," *Arena* 6 (1892): 540–50.

72. See C. Vann Woodward, *Tom Watson: Agrarian Rebel* (reprint, London: Oxford University Press, 1963); and C. Vann Woodward, *Origins of the New South, 1877–1913* (Baton Rouge: Louisiana State University Press, 1951).

73. Gaither, *Blacks and the Populist Revolt*, 68.

74. Newby, *Jim Crow's Defense*, 50. Newby's interpretation is not shared by John Higham, *Strangers in the Land: Patterns of American Nativism, 1860–1925* (reprint, New Brunswick, N.J.: Rutgers University Press, 1988), 273.

75. John Moffatt Mecklin, *The Ku Klux Klan: A Study of the American Mind* (New York: Harcourt, Brace, 1924), 35.

76. William J. Simmons, *The Klan Unmasked* (Atlanta: n.p., 1924), 149.

3. THE QUEST FOR THE GREAT WHITE PAST, 1955 TO . . .

1. There are a number of excellent analyses of the black struggle for liberation and justice: Gayraud Wilmore, *Black Religion and Black Radicalism: An Interpretation of the Religious History of Afro-American People* (reprint, Maryknoll, N.Y.: Orbis, 1986); James Cone, *A Black Theology of Liberation* (reprint, Maryknoll, N.Y.: Orbis, 1990); Vincent Harding, *There Is a River: The Black Struggle for Freedom in America* (New York: Harcourt and Brace, 1981); and James M. Washington, *Frustrated Fellowship: The Black Baptist Quest for Social Power* (Macon, Ga.: Mercer University Press, 1986). For a more general study, see John Hope Franklin, *From Slavery to Freedom: A History of Negro Americans* (New York: Knopf, 1967).

2. John F. Kennedy, "Address on Civil Rights" (1963), in *One Hundred Key Documents in American Democracy*, ed. Peter B. Levy (Westport, Conn.: Greenwood, 1994), 401.

3. Martin Luther King Jr., *Stride toward Freedom* (New York: Ballantine, 1958), 167.

4. Ibid., 68.

5. Malcolm X, with Alex Haley, *The Autobiography of Malcolm X* (reprint, New York: Ballantine, 1973), 241–42.

6. A number of nineteenth-century black leaders and white abolitionists had also depicted slavery and racism in this fashion. See especially Daniel Alexander

Payne, "Protestation of American Slavery," *Journal of Negro History* 52 (1967); Henry Highland Garnet, *A Memorial Discourse by the Rev. Henry Highland Garnet, Delivered in the Hall of the House of Representatives* (Philadelphia: Joseph M. Wilson, 1865); and Joseph C. Price, *The Race Problem in America* (pamphlet of speech delivered at Episcopal Church Congress, Buffalo, New York, November 28, 1888). An excellent collection of the writings of white abolitionists is Louis Ruchames, *The Abolitionists: A Collection of Their Writings* (New York: Capricorn, 1964). Also see Milton Sernett, *Abolition's Axe: Beriah Green, Oneida Institute, and the Black Freedom Struggle* (Syracuse: Syracuse University Press, 1986).

7. An excellent analysis of this movement is Wilmore, *Black Religion and Black Radicalism*, especially chapter 6. Also see Gayraud S. Wilmore and James H. Cone, eds., *Black Theology: A Documentary History*, vol. 1, *1966–1979*, 2d ed. (Maryknoll, N.Y.: Orbis, 1993).

8. Wilmore, *Black Religion and Black Radicalism*, 196.

9. Wilmore and Cone, *Black Theology*, 21.

10. Ibid.

11. Ibid., 30.

12. Henry Highland Garnet, *Address to Slaves*, reprinted in *A Memorial Discourse by the Rev. Henry Highland Garnet, Delivered in the Hall of the House of Representatives* (Philadelphia: Joseph M. Wilson, 1865), 44–51.

13. Cone, *Black Theology and Black Power* (New York: Seabury Press, 1969), 19, 73, 75.

14. Ibid., 11–12.

15. H. Richard Niebuhr, *Radical Monotheism* (Lincoln: University of Nebraska Press, 1960); Schubert Ogden, *Christ without Myth* (New York: Harper, 1961); Harvey Cox, *Secularization and Urbanization in Theological Perspective* (New York: Macmillan, 1965); Philip Berrigan, *No More Strangers* (New York: Macmillan, 1965); and Thomas J. Altizer and William Hamilton, *Radical Theology and the Death of God* (Indianapolis: Bobbs-Merrill, 1966).

16. Rosemary Ruether, *The Church against Itself: An Inquiry into the Conditions of Historical Existence for the Eschatological Community* (New York: Herder and Herder, 1967); and Mary Daly, *Beyond God the Father: Toward a Philosophy of Women's Liberation* (Boston: Beacon, 1973).

17. See Terry H. Anderson, *The Movement and the 1960s* (New York: Oxford University Press, 1995).

18. James F. Findlay Jr., *Church People in the Struggle: The National Council of Churches and the Black Freedom Movement, 1950–1970* (New York: Oxford University Press, 1993), is a detailed analysis of the churches' participation in programs of racial elevation during this period, especially in light of the Black Power movement.

19. Ibid., 222.

20. Ibid., 220.

21. For a discussion of Nixon and law and order, see John Ehrlichman, *Witness to Power: The Nixon Years* (New York: Simon and Schuster, 1982).

22. Nixon's efforts to conceal this belief slipped on at least two occasions when he was campaigning for the presidency. One occurred after he had completed taping a television ad about "law and order"; he announced to his supporters that his commercial

had hit it "right on the nose. . . . It's all about law and order and the damn Negro-Puerto Rican groups out there [in the streets]." Another slip took place when he denounced the court-ordered desegregation of schools and declared to a southern audience that integrated education was dangerous, because it would place "mentally inferior" blacks alongside "intellectually superior whites." See ibid., 223; and Joe McGinniss, *The Selling of the President, 1968* (New York: Trident Press, 1969), 23.

23. Edward C. Banfield, *The Unheavenly City Revisited* (Boston: Little, Brown, 1968), epigraph page.

24. Ibid., 52, 57, 61.

25. Ibid., 62.

26. Robert L. Williams, "The Silent Mugging of the Black Community: Scientific Racism and IQ," *Psychology Today*, May 1974, 32–41.

27. Charles Murray, *Losing Ground: American Social Policy, 1950–1980* (New York: Basic Books, 1984), 216–18.

28. Richard Herrnstein and Charles Murray, *The Bell Curve: Intelligence and Class Structure in American Life* (New York: Free Press, 1994), 523.

29. Ibid.

30. An excellent discussion of Reagan appears in Dan T. Carter, *From George Wallace to Newt Gingrich* (Baton Rouge: Louisiana State University Press, 1996), especially 55–67.

31. Patrick Buchanan, quoted in Jack Germond and Jules Witcover, *Mad as Hell: Revolt at the Ballot Box* (New York: Warner, 1992), 410.

32. Ibid., 236. Germond and Witcover suggest that Buchanan's comment referred to white liberal bureaucrats and not to black people. Their position seems unlikely, because of the fact that Buchanan was campaigning at this time against George Bush and Ross Perot—not against Bill Clinton—for the Republican nomination. Moreover, liberals had not been in control of the White House since Jimmy Carter. Their position is further weakened by the fact that bongo drums are usually associated not with whites but with blacks.

33. Ibid., 233.

34. Newt Gingrich, quoted in Carter, *From George Wallace to Newt Gingrich*, 106ff.

35. Ralph Reed, *Mainstream Values Are No Longer Politically Incorrect: The Emerging Faith Factor in American Politics* (Dallas: Word, 1994), 236.

36. Ibid., 251–53.

37. Ibid., 242.

4. THE RELAPSE OF POSTMODERN WHITE LIBERALS

1. See, for example, Gordon MacInnes, *Wrong for All the Right Reasons: How White Liberals Have Been Undone by Race* (New York: New York University Press, 1996).

2. See, for example, Aaron Wildavsky, "The Empty-Head Blues: Black Rebellion and White Reaction," *Public Interest*, nos. 10–13 (spring 1968): 5 especially.

3. See Martin Luther King Jr., "I Have a Dream" (1963), in *One Hundred Key Documents in American Democracy*, ed. Peter B. Levy (Westport, Conn.: Greenwood, 1994), 392–95.

4. See, for example, MacInnes, *Wrong for All the Right Reasons*, 50–51.

5. Martin Luther King Jr., "Letter from Birmingham Jail," in *Why We Can't Wait* (New York: Mentor, 1964), 76–95.

6. Ibid., 89.

7. Ibid., 90.

8. James F. Findlay Jr., *Church People in the Struggle: The National Council of Churches and the Black Freedom Movement, 1950–1970* (New York: Oxford University Press, 1993), 15.

9. See ibid., 3.

10. Ibid., 58ff.

11. My position here differs from Findlay's in ibid., 62ff.

12. See Robert Griffith, ed., *Major Problems in American History since 1945* (Lexington, Mass.: Heath, 1992), 35.

13. See Dan T. Carter, *From George Wallace to Newt Gingrich* (Baton Rouge: Louisiana State University Press, 1996), 36.

14. See Terry H. Anderson, *The Movement and the 1960s* (New York: Oxford University Press, 1995), 132ff.; Findlay, *Church People in the Struggle*, 64–65; and MacInnes, *Wrong for All the Right Reasons*, 63ff.

15. See Greg Thomas, "The Black Studies War," *Village Voice*, January 17, 1995.

16. Robert N. Bellah, Richard Madsen, William Sullivan, Ann Swidler, and Steve M. Tipton, *Habits of the Heart: Individualism and Commitment in American Life*, 1st ed. (Berkeley: University of California Press, 1985), vii.

17. Ibid., ix.

18. See Harding's critique of *Habits of the Heart* in Vincent Harding, "Toward a Darkly Radiant Vision of America's Truth," *Cross Currents* 37, no. 1 (1987–1988).

19. See Robert N. Bellah, Richard Madsen, William Sullivan, Ann Swidler, and Steve M. Tipton, *Habits of the Heart*, updated ed. (Berkeley: University of California Press, 1996).

20. Bellah et al., *Habits of the Heart*, 1st ed., ix.

21. Ibid.; emphasis added.

22. See, for example, Robert N. Bellah, *Beyond Belief: Essays on Religion in a Post-traditional World* (Berkeley: University of California Press, 1970); and Robert N. Bellah, *The Broken Covenant: American Civil Religion in Time of Trial* (New York: Seabury, 1975).

23. Derrick Bell, *Faces at the Bottom of the Well: The Permanence of Racism* (New York: Basic Books, 1992).

24. A report of this incident was carried in local and national newspapers and electronic media across the country. Donna De La Cruz wrote the Associated Press coverage, which appeared in the *Dayton Daily News* on February 9, 1995.

25. Mary-Christine Phillip, "Feminism in Black and White," *Black Issues in Higher Education* 10, no. 1 (1993): 12.

26. Irvin D. Reid, "The African American Professor on the College Campus: An Endangered Species," *Black Issues in Higher Education* 10, no. 1 (1993): 80.

27. See Alison Schneider, "Stanford Revisits the Course That Set Off the Culture Wars," *Chronicle of Higher Education* 43, no. 35 (1997): A11.

28. For a concise view of where radical Black Power advocates stood on multiculturalism and integration, see Stokely Carmichael, "What We Want," *New York Review of Books*, September 22, 1966, 5–6, 8.

29. Andrew Hacker, *Two Nations: Black and White, Separate, Hostile, Unequal* (New York: Scribner's, 1992).

5. WHITE FEMINISM AND THE BLACK QUEST FOR RACIAL JUSTICE

1. See, for example, Vivian Gordon, *Black Women, Feminism, and Black Liberation: Which Way?* (Chicago: Third World Press, 1987); Sharon Harley and Rosalyn Terborg-Penn, eds., *The Afro-American Woman: Struggles and Images* (Port Washington, N.Y.: National University Publications, 1978); Jacquelyn Grant, *White Women's Christ and Black Women's Jesus: Feminist Christology and Womanist Response* (Atlanta: Scholars Press, 1989); Patricia Hill Collins, *Black Feminist Thought: Knowledge, Consciousness, and the Politics of Empowerment* (New York: Routledge, 1991); Darlene Clark Hine, Wilma King, and Linda Reed, eds., *"We Specialize in the Wholly Impossible": A Reader in Black Women's History* (Brooklyn: Carlson, 1995); and Lois Benjamin, ed., *Black Women in the Academy: Promises and Perils* (Gainesville: University of Florida Press, 1997).

2. Robert Griffith, ed., *Major Problems in American History since 1945* (Lexington, Mass.: Heath, 1992), 41.

3. *Minority and Women Doctoral Directory* (Berkeley: MWDD, 1990); *United States Bureau of Census, 1990* (Washington, D.C.: GPO, 1990); Terry Anderson, *The Movement and the 1960s* (New York: Oxford University Press, 1995), 361, 420.

4. Ruth Rosen, quoted in Anderson, *The Movement and the 1960s*, 405.

5. Griffith, *Major Problems in American History*, 39.

6. *Congressional Record*, 110, pt. 2, 88th Cong., 2d sess. (January 30–February 10, 1964): 2578, 2581.

7. Ibid., 2577.

8. Ibid.

9. Ibid., 2580.

10. Ibid., 2579.

11. Ibid., 2582.

12. This and subsequent quotations from Green are in ibid., 2581–82 passim.

13. Charity Anne Dorgan, ed., *Statistical Handbook of Working America: Statistics on Occupations, Careers, Employment, and the Work Environment* (New York: Gale Research, 1996), 567.

14. Saliwe M. Kawewe, "Black Women in Diverse Academic Settings: Gender and Racial Crimes of Commission and Omission in Academia," in Benjamin, *Black Women in the Academy*, 264.

15. *United States Bureau of Census, 1960, 1970* (Washington, D.C.: GPO).

16. Ruth Bader Ginsburg, quoted in Anderson, *The Movement and the 1960s*, 420.

17. For discussions of how white feminists have benefited from black studies and how they strive to marginalize the study of African Americans, see Nellie Y. McKay, "A Troubled Peace: Black Women in the Halls of the White Academy," in Benjamin, *Black Women in the Academy*, especially 19ff.; and Shelby F. Lewis, "Africana Feminism: An Alternative Paradigm for Black Women in the Academy," in Benjamin, *Black Women in the Academy*, 41–52.

18. See Mary Lefkowitz, *Not Out of Africa: How Afrocentrism Became an Excuse to Teach Myth as History* (New York: Basic Books, 1996).

19. Mona Charen, "Don't Look Below Surface," *Dayton Daily News*, January 2, 1998, 13A.

20. The debate over Afrocentrism between Molefi Asante and Diane Ravitch appears in Francis J. Beckwith and Michael Bauman, *Are You Politically Correct? Debating America's Cultural Standards* (Buffalo: Prometheus, 1993), 165–203.

21. Lefkowitz, *Not Out of Africa*, 158.

22. An excellent discussion of the rise of this method, although studied from the perspective of religious history, is found in James C. Livingston, *Modern Christian Thought from the Enlightenment to Vatican II* (New York: Macmillan, 1971).

23. Lefkowitz, *Not Out of Africa*, xiii, xv.

24. Lewis, "Africana Feminism," 45.

25. Ibid. Also see the *New York Times*, November 3, 1988.

26. During both the Simpson trial and the Clarence Thomas hearings, Allred became almost a permanent fixture on television talk shows such as *Rivera Live* and *Nightline* with Ted Koppel. See, for example, the *New Republic* 28, no. 4 (Jan. 26, 1998): 12.

27. For discussion of white women in the black civil rights movements, see, for example, Vicki L. Crawford, ed., *Women in the Civil Rights Movement: Trailblazers and Torchbearers, 1914–1965* (Bloomington: Indiana University Press, 1993); Alexander Bloom and Wini Breines, *Takin' It to the Streets* (New York: Oxford University Press, 1995); and Linda K. Herber, Alice Kesler-Harris, and Kathryn Kish Sklar, *U.S. History as Women's History: New Feminist Essays* (Chapel Hill: University of North Carolina Press, 1995).

28. Absalom Jones, *Thanksgiving Sermon, Preached January 1, 1808, in St. Thomas', or the African Episcopal, Church, Philadelphia: On Account of the Abolition of the Slave Trade on That Day, by the Congress of the United States* (Philadelphia: Fry and Kammerer, 1808), reprinted in Dorothy Porter, *Early Negro Writings: A Bibliographic Study* (New York: Bibliographic Society of America, 1945), 336.

29. Mary Boykin Chesnut, *A Diary from Dixie*, ed. Ben Ames Williams (Cambridge: Harvard University Press, 1980), 163.

30. See Benjamin Quarles, *Black Abolitionists* (New York: Oxford University Press, 1969), 48. Also see Harley and Terborg-Penn, *The Afro-American Woman*, 17ff.; and Robert Allen, *Reluctant Reformers: Racism and Social Reform Movements in the United States* (Washington, D.C.: Howard University Press, 1983).

31. Gordon, *Black Women, Feminism, and Black Liberation*, 47.

EPILOGUE

1. See George H. Kelsey, *Racism and the Christian Understanding of Man* (New York: Scribner's, 1965); and Cornel West, *Prophesy Deliverance! An Afro-American Revolutionary Christianity* (Philadelphia: Westminster, 1982).

2. I have intentionally used the King James Version because of its direct language. Obviously, it refers to women as well as men.

INDEX

Praise for *Seeds of Racism in the Soul of America*

"In 1955, C. Vann Woodward's book *The Strange Career of Jim Crow* exploded the belief that racial segregation was rooted in 'time immemorial,' proving instead that it was a social phenomenon with recent origins. Now, Paul Griffin in *Seeds of Racism in the Soul of America* challenges Christian theologians with impressive evidence that it was their seventeenth-century predecessors who helped lay the intellectual foundations for concepts of white supremacy that neither time nor anti-racist activists have been able to eliminate."

—Derrick Bell, author of *Faces at the Bottom of the Well: The Permanence of Racism*

"Paul Griffin's book is a masterpiece, one of the most important books on religion and race ever published. It is insightful and cogently argued, analyzing the link between religion and racism—and even the nature of racism itself. Yet I do not say this because I agree with all parts of the book. Some, males and females, whites and blacks, might venture to disagree with Dr. Griffin's analysis, but they will have a daunting challenge in amassing evidence to discard it."

—Sandy Dwayne Martin, author of *Black Baptists and African Missions* and *For God and Race: The Religious and Political Leadership of AME Zion Bishop James Walker Hood*

"Paul Griffin's book is a prophetic challenge to those who insist on trivializing the problem of racism in America. The misinformed will be uncomfortable with its honesty and forthrightness, but the sensitive and thoughtful reader will find in it lessons for avoiding a possible racial nightmare in this country."

—Lewis V. Baldwin, author of *Toward the Beloved Community: Martin Luther King Jr. and South Africa*

"I applaud Paul Griffin for having the courage to expose the germ that has fed and continues to feed the disease of American racism, even though that germ is found to be imbedded and festering in our most elevated and cherished institution—the Christian religion itself. He reminds us with almost brutal honesty that there is a sickness of racism in the Christian church that from the beginning of this nation's history has spread through society, and he assures us that only facing it squarely and attacking and destroying it at the core will save the church and all the institutions which it undergirds."

—Mozella G. Mitchell, author of *New Africa in America:
The Blending of African and American Religious
and Social Traditions among Black People in
Meridian, Mississippi, and Surrounding Counties*

"*Seeds of Racism in the Soul of America* is the most thorough and insightful analysis of American racism, especially among present-day white liberals and radical white feminists, that I have ever read. This book is a must-read for everyone who is interested in why race prejudice first began and continues to persist today."

—Jessie O. Gooding, President, Dayton,
Ohio, Chapter of the NAACP

"Paul Griffin's extensive research and analysis on the origins of racism in America and the many faces of modern racism is a must-read, particularly for white liberals and feminists. It cannot help but cause the reader to search his/her own soul. It is a most timely and important book as we approach the twenty-first century."

—James S. Burton, Executive Director,
Greater Dayton Christian Connections

"W. E. B. DuBois said in the early 1900s that the problem of the twentieth century would be along the color line. It looks like we will be entering the twenty-first century with the same challenge unless we convince our white Christian and liberal friends to re-examine their hearts and souls, and rid themselves of this superiority complex nurtured by a flawed Puritan ethic of the past. Reading Paul Griffin's book will be a critical first step in this re-examination and purging."

—Dean Lovelace, Dayton City Commissioner, Dayton, Ohio